Lady Wallflower

Notorious Ladies of London Book Two

BY
SCARLETT SCOTT

Lady Wallflower
Notorious Ladies of London Book 2

ISBN: 979-8-664125-46-7

Edited by Grace Bradley
Cover Design by Wicked Smart Designs

For more information, contact author Scarlett Scott.
www.scarlettscottauthor.com

Lady Jo Danvers has declared war on her humdrum life. Armed with a list of ways to be wicked, she will step out of her role as never-been-kissed wallflower and experience passion. With the right gentleman, of course. She just has to find him.

Mr. Elijah Decker, the handsome businessman she cannot stop thinking about, is definitely no gentleman. And he is decidedly all wrong. Unfortunately for Jo, she has unwittingly given him her list.

When Decker discovers Jo's list mistakenly tucked between the pages of a pamphlet for the Lady's Suffrage Society, he is intrigued. And after she realizes her error and storms his office demanding he return it, Decker agrees on one condition: that she accept his aid in crossing off each scandalous act.

What begins as a lark quickly sizzles into something deeper and unexpected. But Decker's dark side may tear them apart before Jo's sinful quest is complete…

Dedication

For all the strong women in my life.
I'm proud to call you mom, sister, friend.

Chapter One

London, 1885

DECKER STARED AT the list on the desk before him. He had read the flowery script at least half a dozen times since finding it tucked between the pages of a pamphlet he had been tasked with printing for the Lady's Suffrage Society.

The words taunted him.

Tempted him.

Reading them made his cock hard, partly because he had never been meant to see them. Partly because of the woman who had written them. Quiet, shy Lady Jo Danvers, who loved to frown at him. Who looked at him as if he were a footpad about to filch her reticule. Who had delivered her pamphlet to his offices buttoned to the throat, not a hair out of place, looking very much like a governess he longed to defile.

Damn it, he had to stop thinking about her. Had to stop perusing the list. And he would, Decker promised himself. Soon. But first, he was going to read it again.

Ways to be Wicked

1. *Kiss a man until you are breathless.*

2. *Arrange for an assignation. Perhaps with Lord Q?*

3. *Get caught in the rain with a gentleman. (This will*

*necessitate the removal of wet garments. Choose said
gentleman wisely.)*
4. *Sneak into a gentleman's bedchamber in the midst of
the night.*
5. *Go to a gentleman's private apartments.*
6. *Spend a night in a gentleman's bed.*
7. *Make love in the outdoors.*
8. *Ask*

Bloody hell. The items on her list were delicious enough to incite his lust and his interest in equal, ballocks-tightening measure. But that incomplete number eight—only just begun, as if she had stopped in *medias res*, as if she had *more* wonderfully sinful items to add to her list—made his prick twitch every time. He had tortured himself with it. So many possibilities.

What did she want to ask? And who did she want to pose the question to? Was there a number nine? What else would she add to her list?

Most importantly, who the devil was Lord Q?

That question bothered him more than it ought to. Decker told himself it hardly mattered. Lady Jo was not the sort of woman with whom he dallied. First, she was a lady. Second, she was an innocent.

Or *was* she?

The list before him mocked.

It hardly seemed the composition of a virginal miss. But then, how the devil would Decker know what a virginal miss would write? He had not been a virgin in years, and he had never been a damned miss. Moreover, he had not bedded an innocent in…well, *ever*. His predilections tended to be far more depraved than a virginal miss could satisfy.

But oh, how delightful it would be to debauch Lady Jo.

Curse it, his trousers were too tight, drawing against his erection each time he shifted in his chair to ease his discomfort. The spell of yearning Lady Jo's list cast upon him was heavy and thick, unbreakable. He was going to have to take himself in hand if he was going to get anything accomplished today.

There was only one answer to his current predicament.

He had to rid himself of the list.

Remove the temptation.

Return it to its rightful owner, and then forget he had ever seen it.

Right. That last part was never bloody well happening, was it?

On a sigh, he composed a terse note to Lady Jo Danvers.

I believe I have something of yours.

D.

The note was in Jo's reticule as she waited for the hulking Scotsman who served as Mr. Elijah Decker's *aide-de-camp* to announce her. Seven words. Signed with his initial. She had instantly known who had sent her the message. And she had also known what he had in his possession. What she had inadvertently given him.

Her cheeks were hot.

Misery churned in her stomach.

Her list had been missing for three days. She had searched for it everywhere. Initially, she had believed she had somehow misplaced it, shuffling it with some of her correspondence. But when a thorough investigation had failed to produce the list, she feared her older brother Julian, the Earl of Ra-venscroft, had taken it. However, after his protective, brotherly wrath had not been unleashed upon her, she had reached another, far more troubling conclusion.

She had unintentionally mixed her list into the pages of her pamphlet for the Lady's Suffrage Society. And she had given it to the odious, sinfully handsome, utterly self-absorbed rake who owned the publisher that was now printing all the society's pamphlets.

Those seven words written in his arrogant hand, burning a veritable hole of shame through her reticule, confirmed it. Of all the people to whom she could have unintentionally given her list, why, oh why did it have to be *him*?

She detested him and men of his ilk.

Mr. Elijah Decker was rather like a whore. A *gentleman* whore.

Only, he was no gentleman.

"What is it, Macfie?" growled Mr. Decker from some-where within his office, sounding irritated. "I thought I told you not to interrupt me for the next hour."

"Forgive me, sir, but ye have a visitor," Mr. Macfie of-fered. "Lady Josephine Danvers."

Jo clutched her reticule so tightly her knuckles ached. Less than a minute to attempt to compose herself before she had to face him. She inhaled. Told herself she would be firm. That she would not show him a modicum of embarrassment. She would demand he return the list. She would require his silence.

Mr. Macfie turned to her. "He is ready for ye now, mila-dy."

She thanked him and reluctantly moved into Mr. Deck-er's lair. Mr. Macfie snapped the door closed with more force than necessary, making Jo jump.

Mr. Decker rose to his full, imposing height, his impossibly blue stare upon her. "Forgive Macfie. He does not know his own strength."

She stared at Mr. Decker, trying to make sense of what he had just said. She blinked. No words were forthcoming. Her heart was pounding so loudly, she was certain Mr. Decker could hear it.

"The slamming of the door, my lady," Mr. Decker elaborated, raising a knowing brow.

Her ears felt as if they were on fire. "Of course. Mr. Macfie is forgiven. You, however, are not. Where is my list?"

Clasping his hands behind his back, Mr. Decker sauntered toward her. "I do not recall asking for your forgiveness, my dear."

She stiffened. "I am not your dear, and you failed to answer my question. Where is my list?"

He stopped before her, insufferably handsome. "Which list are you referring to, Lady Jo?"

The blighter.

He was toying with her. She would wager her dowry upon it.

"You know very well," she charged.

"Hmm." He tapped the fullness of his lower lip with his forefinger, as if he were thinking. "I believe you may have to give me a hint. What did it say, this list of yours?"

Her cheeks were scalding. "You know what it says."

"Do I?" He grinned, like the devil he was.

She had no doubt he had read every word she had written. Every shocking thing she had drafted thus far after seizing upon her plan to live her life and experience true passion the way everyone else around her was. Her sister was blissfully married. Her dearest friend was happily wed and wildly in love.

And yet, Jo had never been kissed.

"Yes," she hissed. "You do."

"I am afraid my memory is dreadfully faulty. Remind me, my lady." His voice was low. Teasing. Taunting.

Daring.

He did not think she had the audacity to say it, she realized.

Jo kept her gaze trained unwaveringly upon him. "Ways…"

She faltered.

"Ways," he prompted, his stare dipping to her lips.

"Ways to be wicked," she blurted.

"Oh, yes. *That* list. Now I recall." The grin he gave her was sin in its purest, most tempting form.

Curse him.

And curse the curious flutter that started in her belly and slid lower, pooling between her thighs.

Jo was doomed.

"*That* list," she agreed. "You sent me a note saying you have it. I would like it returned to me, if you please."

There. If he were a gentleman, he would spare her additional humiliation and surrender the list without another word.

"What do you plan to do with this list of yours?" he asked, offering further evidence he was no gentleman as he strolled closer.

"That is hardly your concern." She told herself she would not budge an inch. No step in retreat. But he was near enough to touch now.

Near enough his scent wafted over her, a cologne unlike any she had ever smelled before, musky and rich with a hint of bay. Near enough that she detected striations of gray and green lingering in the bright-blue depths of his eyes.

He reached for her, and she found herself swaying toward him. Anticipating a kiss. An embrace. The heat smoldering within her—part embarrassment, part longing—burst into a flame.

He plucked her hat from her head, still grinning that roguish grin. "I am afraid you made it my concern when you entrusted your list to me, *bijou*."

Bijou? Was that what he called all his fallen women?

Jo reached for her hat, irritated with herself for thinking he would kiss her. Worse, for wanting it, even if for the span of a few seconds. What was wrong with her?

"Do not call me that, and give me my hat, you scoundrel!" She lunged for it, but Mr. Decker was too quick.

He held it in the air, high above Jo's head, using his massive height to his advantage. It was hardly the first time in her life she had been dismayed by her petite stature, but the humiliation of the moment rendered this particular scene worse.

"I will return your hat if you answer my question." He raised a dark brow. "I could not see your eyes with this blasted contraption on your head."

"My hat is the height of fashion." Jo lost her composure and jumped, trying to rescue it from his grasp.

But her attempt failed.

And Mr. Decker *laughed* at her efforts, blast him.

"Does it truly require this much plumage?" He shook the hat, dangling it over her head, taunting. "Or a brim so pronounced in the front? It shades half your face, darling."

First *bijou*, now *darling*. She hated him. Well, she *wanted* to hate him. And she also wanted him to return her hat *and* her list. But in truth, the way he uttered terms of endearment in his low, inviting baritone had an effect upon her despite her every inclination to remain as impervious to this man as possible.

And judging from the smile on his lips, he knew it, the rogue.

"The next time I choose a hat, I will endeavor to ask your opinion, Mr. Decker, and do not, I pray, call me your darling." She attempted to inflect acid into her voice and was nettled to realize she sounded breathless.

Affected.

Because she was. Because being in such proximity to Mr. Elijah Decker made her feel things she had no wish to feel. He was entirely unsuitable in every way. From the moment she had first met him—Mr. Decker was a close acquaintance of her friend Callie's husband, the Earl of Sinclair—she had been drawn to him. But his reputation as a lothario and his cocky, handsome mien had made her dislike him instantly.

And distrust him.

"You are a feisty little thing when you are riled, Lady Jo." His grin deepened, revealing more of his teeth. "I like it."

She wished his words did not make her heart pound or a strange glide of need slide through her insides like honey. But it did.

She gritted her teeth. "How nice for you. Please return my hat and my list to me, Mr. Decker."

"I have given you my terms. Answer my question, and you shall have back your hat."

His stare was intense, burning into hers. She could not look away. It was as if he had stripped her of every defense. Oh, she had spoken to Mr. Decker on several occasions. She had hand-delivered the pamphlet to him. She had seen him at Callie's dinner parties and balls. Still, she had never been close enough to notice how long his lashes were. Close enough to experience the full effect of his raw, sensual magnetism.

"I was going to attempt to accomplish the items on my

list," she blurted. "That is what I was going to do with it."

"Hmm," he hummed. "Accomplish them, you say. How?"

She flushed all over once more. "In the ordinary way. By acting upon them."

"I see." Without relinquishing her hat, he spun on his heel and abruptly strode back to his desk, dropping her hat upon it as if it were a dead bird. "With the same gentleman, or with different gentlemen?"

She had not anticipated more questions. Jo blinked. The moment between them had been intense. But if she had expected her heart to slow and the strange heaviness in her belly to dissipate now that he was no longer near, she was wrong. The heaviness remained.

Her gaze lowered to her hat, lying on its side in forlorn fashion. Mayhap if she were fast enough…

"You can try, *bijou*, but I will be faster."

Mr. Decker's mocking voice had Jo's eyes snapping back to his arresting face. "I told you not to call me that."

He gave an indolent shrug. "Make me stop."

Make him stop? She had never heard the like. Elijah Decker was maddening. Infuriating. Rude.

Irresistible.

She frowned. "You are being quite unfair, Mr. Decker. I gave you the list in err, and now I would like it back. If you have any honor at all, you will give me both it and my hat and let me go without further quarrel."

His grin returned. "Fortunately, I have precious little honor."

She already suspected that. "What do you want?"

"Where shall I begin?" His eyes swept over her form in a visual caress that made liquid heat rush to her core.

Jo wished she had a fan to cool herself. Rather, she wished

she had never come to Mr. Decker's offices. She wished she had stayed where she was safe from his insinuations and his smoldering gaze.

"Mr. Decker, my lady's maid is awaiting me in the carriage," she snapped. "I do not have all day."

"Pity."

There was such carnal promise layered in that lone word that Jo's mouth went dry. Elijah Decker was dangerous. But she would not succumb to his lethal charms and become one more of his conquests.

Never.

Her chin went up. "Cease playing games with me, Mr. Decker."

"Who is Lord Q?"

His question startled her. Sent another wave of heat to her cheeks. "Lord Quenington."

"He is a notorious rotter," Mr. Decker said, his tone dismissive.

"The same could be said of you," she shot back.

Perhaps unwisely. After all, he *was* still in possession of both her list and hat.

"Yes," he agreed. "I am. But Quenington cannot possibly compete with me. If you want to do something wicked, you ought to be doing it with the best candidate."

"Who said I want to do something wicked?"

"You and your list." He plucked it from atop his desk and held it aloft. "Shall I read the items aloud and remind you? Mayhap you have forgotten."

She had not forgotten. Of course she had not.

Jo's gaze flicked from her list back to the impossibly alluring man holding it captive. "I know what it says. Do not read it aloud."

"Right, then." He laid the list back down upon his desk.

"We both know what it says. However, you did not finish number eight. What did you want to ask? I have been teeming with curiosity for the last three days."

Ask a gentleman to help you disrobe.

She was not about to reveal that to him, so Jo ignored that part of his request.

"You have been withholding my list for three days?" She ought to be outraged.

And part of her was. She had assumed he had only just discovered her list today. However, if he had known it was in his possession three days ago, that meant there was a reason he had been keeping it. Did it not?

"I have. But I will return it to you in exchange for a promise."

His casual pronouncement took her by surprise and raised her guard all at once. "What manner of promise, Mr. Decker?"

"Just Decker, if you please," he said smoothly in that butter-rich voice. "I find the mister far too formal. If we are going to be friends, you may as well call me what all my other friends do."

"I have no wish to be your friend," she countered, although the notion of being informal with him and being his friend both sounded deliciously intriguing.

And thoroughly wrong and impossible, of course.

She could never, ever be this rakish man's friend.

"You may change your mind about that, *bijou*, when you hear what I propose." His lips twitched, as if he wanted to smile but fought it.

She did not want to like the way he called her that—*bijou*—and yet, she did. All the more reason to frown at him. "I cannot fathom finding interest in anything you propose, Mr. Decker."

"You have a list of objectives to achieve," he pointed out carefully. "And yet, forgive me for the observation, you are an unwed lady of excellent standing. One with an unimpeachable reputation. What do you know about arranging assignations or finding someone who will kiss you until you are breathless?"

Nothing, she longed to say. Hence the creation of the dratted list.

"I fail to see what this has to do with you," she told him curtly. "You are overstepping your bounds, sir. If you will not return my list or my hat, I will simply go without them."

"I will return them both as long as you promise to let me aid you in achieving every item on your list," he said smoothly, surprising her once more. "Including number eight, should you wish to confide in me what it is."

"Let you aid me," she repeated. "How? Why?"

"Because you are a dear friend of the Countess of Sinclair," he said. "And because this list of yours is dangerous business. It would be remiss of me not to offer you guidance. *Assistance.* Whatever you wish to call it. It is my duty to make certain you do not attempt to accomplish any of your objectives with the wrong gentleman."

Her eyes narrowed as she studied him, trying to make sense of the man and failing miserably. "I still do not understand your motive, Mr. Decker."

He shrugged again. "Perhaps I am adhering to the remaining shreds of honor I possess."

Jo did not believe that explanation. Not for a moment. She wondered how he could be so handsome and careless at the same time. How he could make a noncommittal gesture seem sensual and suggestive.

Regardless, the man was continuing to hold her list and her hat captive. She had to end this stalemate.

"Suppose I accept your assistance with my list," she allowed. "What does that entail?"

"Lord and Lady Sinclair are hosting a ball tomorrow night. I trust you will be attending?"

Of course she would be there. The ball was Callie's way of easing her once-ostracized husband back into society's good graces. "Yes."

"Excellent. So shall I. Save me a dance. We will discuss it further then."

He wanted to make her wait an entire day? And why did the promise of a dance with him tomorrow make her heart beat faster than it already was?

"Fine," she agreed grimly. "Now my hat and list, if you please."

He retrieved her hat and skirted his desk, coming to stand before her once more. Again, she fought the urge to retreat. He startled her by running his fingers over her cheek, then tucking an errant tendril of hair she had not noticed behind her ear.

Just one swift graze of his bare skin upon hers.

And yet, she felt that touch.

Everywhere.

"A stray curl," he explained, lest, Jo supposed, she think there was any other reason for that fleeting caress. "In your dudgeon, it came free of your coiffure." Then he placed her hat neatly upon her head. "There you are, darling. The list, I am afraid, will have to wait."

He turned away from her and strode back toward the other side of his desk.

She glared at his broad, undeniably masculine form and long legs as he went. Wishing the back of him was not also beautifully formed, and every bit as compelling as the front of him. He was all tall, sensual elegance. He moved with a careless grace that bespoke a man who knew the effect he had upon every lady in his presence.

Jo included, no matter how much she wished it were the opposite.

"You told me if I accepted your aid, you would give me the list," she pointed out, flustered and irritated.

"I did indeed," he agreed with effortless sangfroid as he faced her from behind his desk. "However, I am a businessman, you understand. I do not surrender all my power for bargaining until I am satisfied the exchange shall be mutual, not reneged upon."

"You scoundrel!" she exploded, as furious with herself as she was with him. "You could have told me that from the beginning."

"I could have." The roguish grin was back. "But it would not have been nearly as amusing. Now, if you will excuse me, I do have a great many concerns requiring my attention today. Macfie will escort you to your carriage. Until tomorrow."

With that, he seated himself and began sifting through the papers atop his desk, as if she had already gone. As if it were entirely acceptable for a gentleman to seat himself in the presence of a standing lady. And one who outranked him, at that. She was the sister of an earl, and he was the bastard son of one.

Jo entertained a brief, wild fantasy of throwing herself across his desk and rescuing her list. But in the end, she gathered the tattered remnants of her pride and left the office of Mr. Elijah Decker, cunning rakehell extraordinaire, just as empty-handed as when she had arrived.

Chapter Two

*I*T WAS NOT yet time for Decker to collect his dance. But one of the excellent advantages of being friends with the host and hostess of the ball meant that he was more than familiar with the layout of the Earl of Sinclair's newly refurbished townhome. It also meant he could avoid being announced. In the interim, he could indulge in one of his favorite vices.

Watching.

Only, this form of watching was not nearly as piquant as the variety he had previously indulged in on the rare occasion. However, since Lady Jo Danvers was present, occupying a place on the periphery of the gathering and looking deliciously innocent in her pink silk gown adorned with white roses, it would suffice.

For now.

Observing the gathering of lords and ladies from a private balcony no one else knew was open had its merits. He had been ensconced here since just after the ball's commencement, having reached the balcony with the ladder his friend—known to all simply as Sin—had made certain was left for him.

Decker wished he had a whisky to keep him company. If Sin had been a truly accommodating friend, he would have seen to it that a decanter and glass had been left tidily in a corner for him. However, Decker could not complain, he supposed. Eventually, he would slither from his hiding place, rather like a lethal snake poised to strike, and he would take Lady Jo by surprise.

He had found great pleasure in their clash yesterday. More than he had taken from any act in as long as he could recall.

Whilst he was fully clothed, anyway. *Hell.* Who was he fooling? Even when he had been naked and ballocks deep in quim, he had not been as stirred as he had been when he had traded wits with Lady Jo the day before.

His cock was hard, just thinking about how deliciously outraged she had been. He had seen Lady Jo Danvers on numerous occasions. But never had she spoken so many words to him. Never had he known the daring lurking just beneath her prudish exterior.

But he knew it now.

And, truth be told, he wanted it for himself.

Just a taste. If she was set upon the path of ruination, what would be the harm in being the man who aided her in accomplishing one of the items on her list? Or two, or three? Or all of them, for that matter? He had always been drawn to the forbidden, to the prurient. Why not Lady Josephine Danvers?

Fucking hell.

He had to temper his thoughts. For the notion of ful-filling every one of Lady Jo's fantasies—and surely her list could not be titled anything but a series of them—*well*, it was too much to contemplate when he was about to enter a ballroom teeming with condescending lords and ladies who loved to scorn him. He had been born on the wrong side of the blanket, after all. He did not belong amongst their vaunted ranks.

A sudden movement caught his eye, then. Recognition

seared Decker. Made his guts churn.

Bloody Quenington.

The same lord Lady Jo had been considering for an assignation.

A pompous arse, if you asked Decker. Not that Lady Jo had.

Either way, he was heading straight for Lady Jo.

Possessiveness blossomed within Decker, unfurling like the petals of a summer blossom beneath a heated sun. He could not bear to watch her dancing with the viscount. And as for an assignation?

Impossible.

Ludicrous.

Unacceptable.

Decker's hand found the cool bronze of the balcony door handle, and he opened it. The raucous din of the ball reached him in full measure, no longer muted, but Decker stepped over the threshold just the same. He left behind him the calm darkness where he so often dwelled in favor of the bold, garish display of the social whirl.

He told himself he was doing this for Lady Jo. To make certain she did not entrust her innocence to the wrong gentleman. Indeed, he was a regular Galahad in his own mind. Except that he did not want to maintain her innocence. Nor did he want to save her from anything, let alone ruin.

Because he wanted to ruin Lady Jo Danvers himself.

There it was, the shameful truth.

If he had an iota of honor, he would leave her to her fate. Allow her to carry on with her list, uninterrupted. Allow Quenington to swoop in and claim his dance or whatever the devil it was he wanted with Lady Jo.

Decker hastened his strides and managed to weave in and out of the gathered throng, ultimately appearing before Lady

Jo just before the viscount arrived. Her honey-brown eyes widened.

He bowed, doing the pretty although part of him railed against succumbing to expected societal interactions. "Lady Jo."

"Mr. Decker." She dipped into a passable curtsy. It was a hasty one.

Quite charming. She was so bloody short and small. He fancied he could tuck her into the pocket of his waistcoat and spirit her away without anyone the wiser.

"I am claiming my dance," he told her.

Her brows rose. "Now? But I am promised to Lord Quenington for this dance."

The blighter in question was approaching them. Decker pinned him with a deadly glare. The sort that promised retribution in slow and painful manner should his warning go unheeded. Quenington's lip curled into a sneer.

Predictable, that.

However, Decker was more than accustomed to the scorn of most lordlings such as the viscount—the sort who suckled on their papa's teat whilst they waited for their courtesy titles to be exchanged for the coronets that would be theirs upon dear old papa's demise.

Decker had the means to see Quenington's long, perfectly straight nose rendered forever crooked—whether by his own brawn or that of hired strength. He also knew the viscount's predilections. Moreover, it was an unspoken rule that all members of the Black Souls club would remain in Decker's good graces if they wished to maintain their membership. If the viscount wanted to remain a part of the club, he would forego his dance with Lady Jo.

Decker and Quenington locked eyes in a silent battle for less than a minute before the viscount inclined his head and sauntered off in a different direction.

Immensely satisfied, he returned his attention to Lady Jo. "No longer."

She began to protest. "But Lord Quenington—"

"Has wisely changed his mind," Decker finished, interrupting her without qualm. "I will be your partner."

"You threatened him," Lady Jo accused quietly, her high cheekbones going pink.

Fuck, she was glorious when she was nettled.

"Do not be ridiculous," he answered without a modicum of compunction. "He realized he could not possibly match me in looks and charm and wisely decided to retreat."

He had not threatened the viscount *with words*. There was a difference. And Quenington was bloody well undeserving of anything to do with Lady Jo Danvers, whether it be an innocent dance or an assignation.

Especially an assignation.

Decker was never going to allow that to happen. Not the chance of a flower blossom in a hail storm.

Lady Jo was still eying him suspiciously. The orchestra struck up the next song, which happened to be a waltz. *Excellent.*

He offered her his arm. "My lady?"

Her nostrils flared, the only indication of her pique. She placed her hand on his proffered arm. "Very well."

"Do not sound so disappointed," he told her, *sotto voce*, as he led her to the gleaming, freshly repaired parquet where their fellow dancers had assembled. "I am a deuced talented dancer. Quenington cannot possibly compete."

He slanted a glance in her direction in time to catch her lips twitch.

"And so very *humble*, Mr. Decker" she added mockingly.

"I know my strengths." He gave her a subtle wink.

The flush in her cheeks deepened.

"Why so embarrassed, *cherie*?" he could not resist asking. "If you were aware of *all* my strengths, that would put you to the blush for certain."

"Mr. Decker," she chastised in disapproving governess fashion, her voice outrage personified.

He barely stifled his grin—it would not do for her to realize how much he was enjoying himself. Or for the rest of the ballroom. Not that he gave a damn about what society thought of him, but he did have a certain reputation to uphold amongst the ladies of London.

Decker assumed his position on the floor opposite her. He placed one hand upon the middle of her back, whilst the other linked with her gloved hand. Her left hand settled upon his shoulder.

"Yes, Lady Josephine?"

She treated him to a ferocious frown. "All my friends call me Jo."

He wanted to be far more than her friend. He wanted to whisk her into a darkened chamber and…*hell*. Best to banish that thought.

For now.

"Am I to be counted amongst your friends, then?" he queried lightly.

"No," she said. "Of course not, but I strongly dislike being called Josephine. The name is better suited to a bitter dowager who takes great pride in mowing down everyone around her with vicious insults."

He did his best to dismiss the disappointment accompanying her rapid assertion she did not count him amongst her friends. What would it require, he wondered, to earn the trust of the woman in his arms?

Why did he care, anyway? He told himself he did not as

the music began. A Viennese waltz. And then they were moving. Whirling. Although he was quite a bit taller than she was, they fit together in a disturbingly natural way. In a way that made him ponder how else they might fit together.

In the bedchamber.

Not the time to entertain notions that may give him a cockstand in the midst of a waltz, he reminded himself.

But something was nettling him. "Why not?"

He spun her.

"Why not what, Mr. Decker?" she asked as they whirled back down the line.

They moved with a mutual grace he could not help but to admire. They danced well together.

"Why do you not count me amongst your friends?" he elaborated, guiding them through the steps.

He had not danced in as long as he could recall, but some things were like riding a horse. One never forgot how to do it properly, after having learned the skill. It shocked him to realize he was *enjoying* this dance.

"I scarcely know you at all," she said. "And need I remind you that you are holding my list hostage?"

"I prefer to think of it as keeping it *safe*." He grinned, then twirled her again.

There was something rivetingly sensual about not just the waltz but *her*. They went down the line, facing each other, then turning away, then facing each other once more, in an echo of their verbal parries and thrusts.

Color rose to her cheeks as they whirled together some more. "Safe is the last word that would ever come to mind in conjunction with you, Mr. Decker."

"Oh?" He guided them through another series of steps. "And what words, pray tell, would come to that sharp mind of yours in conjunction with me, *bijou*?"

He spun her, enjoying the flounces of her gown and the silhouette she presented far more than he ought. She faced him, eyes bright. "Irritating." They began making their way down the line yet again, turning away, and then back to each other. "Meddlesome." More steps until she faced him once more. "Dangerous."

Decker could not contain a bark of laughter as she ended back in his arms and they started another circuit of the floor. "I will take the last, but I contest the first and the second."

"You have better suggestions?" Her gaze was fastened upon his as they moved together.

"Handsome," he tried.

"Vain," she said.

"Excessively witty," Decker continued as if she had not spoken.

"Extraordinarily arrogant," she returned.

"Capable of kissing a lady until she is breathless," he countered before twirling her once more.

Her eyes locked upon his, and for a moment, she was speechless.

"Not this lady," she snapped at last.

They turned away from each other, proceeding with the steps of the dance as if they had not just veered into momentous territory.

"How do you know unless you try?" he pressed.

They faced each other again, her color heightened. "I beg your pardon? What was your question, Mr. Decker? I am sure I misheard."

"And I am equally certain you did not. What I asked was how do you know, unless you give me the same chance you would give a rotter like Quenington?" he repeated, as he inwardly kicked himself in the arse.

What was he doing? What was he thinking? Of all the bad

ideas he had ever entertained, surely proposing to kiss the innocent friend of Sin's countess was the worst.

And yet, as he gazed down upon Lady Jo Danvers now, he could not deny it also was the most intriguing. The most tempting, too.

Just as she was. She truly was a little gem, so much fire hiding beneath her quiet exterior. Before, he had always supposed her prudish. Cold-blooded. Her list had proven otherwise. There was much she hid, simmering beneath her surface. Was it wrong of him to want a taste?

His cock told him no.

His conscience told him yes.

Unfortunately, his cock was winning.

"I would be an utter fool if I did something so reckless," she said, at last finding her tongue as they approached the final steps of the waltz.

He twirled them about fast, faster than necessary. He spun her one final time before the dance ended. He bowed. She curtseyed.

"Meet me in the blue salon in half an hour," he dared, offering her his arm.

"You are wasting your time, sir," she said quietly as he escorted her from the dance floor.

"If you are too frightened, of course, I understand." He led her to the periphery of the *fête*, where he had found her.

"Of course I am not afraid."

"Oh?" He gave her a look that clearly said he did not believe her.

Lady Jo's cheeks were still flushed from a combination of exertion and charming embarrassment. Her honey-brown eyes were glossy, her pink lips parted. He wanted to drag her from the ballroom and kiss her not just breathless but mindless as well.

"I am not afraid," she asserted. "You do not frighten me."

He bloody well ought to frighten her. Indeed, if she had an inkling of the thoughts churning through his mind right now—all the things he could do to her, teach her—she would flee like an outnumbered flank of infantry facing a cavalry charge.

He sketched a bow. "Prove it, then. The blue salon. Half an hour."

Without awaiting her response, Decker walked away from her. He would be lying if he said he did not feel her stare upon him like a caress as he walked away.

JO TOLD HERSELF she was not going to the blue salon.

She was not going to meet Mr. Elijah Decker.

Not in half an hour.

Not ever.

No, indeed. She wanted to be wicked, but not with a man like *him*. In truth, her list had not been drafted completely or with attention to what she was writing down. Compelled by yet another dinner during which she watched the nauseatingly in-love couples around her and had consumed far too many glasses of claret, she had begun her silly catalog before bed one night.

Upon a wine-soaked whim, it was true.

But even a novice like Jo could see that there were gentlemen with whom one could safely dally, and then there was Mr. Elijah Decker. The vexing, maddeningly handsome man was in a class all his own.

"Have you tired of the dancing and the fawning and the nonsense yet?" her sister, Lady Alexandra Marlow, asked abruptly at Jo's side, barely stifling a yawn.

Alexandra was a science-minded lady. She detested balls. But she and her husband, Lord Harry Marlow, had agreed to escort Jo to her friend Callie's ball this evening. Jo did not particularly enjoy balls either, but she would not have missed Callie's first ball as the Countess of Sinclair for anything.

"The ball is scarcely underway," she told Alexandra, frowning. "You cannot mean to flee already?"

"My calculations are awaiting me," Alexandra said. "I am on the cusp of some very important findings concerning rainbands, and my book will not write itself."

Her sister was beloved to Jo, but she would never entirely understand Alexandra's love of the weather. "This is Callie's first ball, and I promised her I would remain until the very end, Alexandra."

Alexandra's nose crinkled in distaste. "I was hoping I could disabuse you of your notion of loyalty, admirable though it is. Good heavens, Jo, neither of us have ever found this sort of spectacle entertaining."

No, Jo had not.

At least, not until a devilishly handsome rake had swept her into a waltz and arranged an assignation. Not that she wanted to meet Mr. Decker, she reminded herself. He was untrustworthy, and entirely too aware of his own masculine beauty. Callie admitted his reputation was dreadful and had warned her to keep her distance on numerous occasions. He was the sort of gentleman one could admire from afar, rather like a lion in a menagerie. She would never dare step inside his cage, trust herself to be alone with him.

At his mercy.

No.

And yet, some part of her remained curious. Some part of her wanted to accept that invitation to the blue salon. To allow him to prove he could kiss her breathless. He was handsome. Tempting.

He was everything she should avoid.

And he was everything she wanted. Jo could admit the horrible truth to herself, if no one else. Mr. Decker intrigued her as no other man ever had.

"Jo?" her sister prodded. "Are you sotted?"

That would be the only proper excuse for the emotions coursing through her. But, alas, Jo had only partaken of the lemonade. "Of course not. I have scarcely had a drop to drink this evening."

Or a bite to eat. Mayhap that was the need, deep within. Hunger, of the ordinary variety and not the carnal.

Mayhap the odd sense of fluttery butterfly wings in her belly had nothing whatsoever to do with Mr. Decker's invitation to sin.

Oh, who was she trying to fool? It had *everything* to do with him. He had planted them there, with his hands upon her and the delicious way he had guided her through the waltz earlier. She had been giddy, in awe of him, longing for...

More.

Whatever that entailed. She was certain a man like Mr. Elijah Decker would have no problem with introducing her to it, whatever *it* was, whatever *it* meant.

"You seem distracted," Alexandra observed, her eyes narrowing as she searched Jo's face.

"I was looking for Callie," she lied. "Have you seen her? This crush is so magnificent, I only had the chance to speak with her once."

"Are you certain I cannot persuade you to see reason, dearest sister?" Alexandra asked, hope tingeing her voice.

"I am not ready to go yet."

How long had it been since he had told her to meet him in the blue salon? Had it been half an hour ago? What if he was waiting for her there, now?

Did she care?

No.

Yes, whispered a wicked voice inside her.

Jo banished the voice. Banished, too, the urge to do his bidding. What would it garner her, after all, save a ruined reputation? Or worse, a broken heart?

"You two look as if you are plotting something diabolical," said her brother-in-law, Lord Harry, as he reached their sides.

"I am not plotting anything," Jo denied. "Your wife is the diabolical sister, of the two of us. Surely you ought to know that by now."

Lord Harry grinned and winked. "I live in fear."

He was lighthearted and easy to converse with and he appreciated Alexandra's peculiarities and her sharp mind in equal measure. He was also madly in love with her. All those qualities made Jo like her brother-in-law quite immensely. He was the perfect foil for Alexandra.

Alexandra swatted his forearm playfully. "Tell your son that, a few months hence."

The smile Lord Harry sent her sister was laden with love. "Or our daughter."

Jo fought off an unwanted pang of envy at the reminder that she was unwed. Unkissed. Untouched. Unhappy. Meanwhile, her sister was wildly in love, carrying her first child with her husband, the roundness of her belly cleverly hidden beneath the fall of her beautiful skirts.

But Jo was a wallflower, unable to free herself from the mold into which she had been poured. She was not intelligent and handsome like Alexandra, with a mind sharp enough to cut anyone else to shreds. Nor was she vivacious and gregarious and beautiful in the way of her friend Callie. She was small and quiet and shy in the presence of others.

She sighed.

"The two of you make me want to retch," she announced without heat.

In truth, she loved them both, and she was pleased they were happy. Was it wrong of her to want that same happiness for herself?

"Or mayhap we make you want to find a love match of your own," Alexandra said, shrewd as ever. "Is there anyone who has struck your fancy?"

An image of Mr. Elijah Decker rose to Jo's mind.

Blast him, he was even beautiful in her thoughts. Every bit as attractive and tempting. Sinfully so.

"No one," she said, perhaps with a touch too much brightness. "I have only just come out. Surely this sort of thing requires time."

Alexandra and Harry shared a telling look.

"Of course it does, my dear," her sister said in a high-pitched voice that Jo instantly recognized.

It meant her sister was lying.

"Just because you and Lord Harry found love instantly does not mean everyone else must," Jo grumbled.

"It was not instant," her sister denied.

"Of course it was, darling," her husband argued back, his tone warm, his gaze radiating with love as it settled upon Alexandra.

Jo sighed. "Have your dance, the two of you. I will find Callie."

Without waiting for their responses, she swept off into the crush. But the amount of people—a staggering number of guests, in truth—meant that covering a small distance required intense effort. She was skirting people, curtseying, engaging in brief conversation, and being so polite, it made her teeth ache.

By the time she found Callie, Jo was grinding her molars.

But her friend's smile chased all the irritation away.

"I was about to find you," Callie told her. "Sin told me I ought to allow you time to mingle before stealing you away from the crush."

Sin was the Earl of Sinclair, Callie's husband.

"Sinclair is consideration personified," Jo returned. "However, I have no wish to be a part of the crush, as you well know. Rescue me from it whenever you wish."

"That is what I told him," her friend agreed, linking her arm in Jo's. "Now come with me, do. There are some ladies I want you to meet whom I think would make excellent additions to the Lady's Suffrage Society…"

Jo allowed Callie to lead her away.

She never made it to the blue salon or Mr. Decker after all.

And she told herself it was for the best.

Chapter Three

*L*ADY JO HAD not come to the salon.

Decker still could not believe it, two days later. He had never, for as long as he had been chasing skirts, been *refused*. Never. Not once.

Not. Ever.

And yet, innocent, proper, prim, wallflower Lady Jo, who had been flushed and breathless following their waltz the evening before, had failed to accept his invitation. It boggled the mind.

He had waited, pacing the newly decorated salon, glaring at the blue damask wall coverings dotted with paintings by Moreau. His strides had all but worn holes in the plush Axminster—a damned improvement upon its threadbare predecessor, Decker could not deny.

He was embarrassed to admit he had arrived ten minutes early and had remained ten minutes after the appointed time. Twenty minutes lost, spent upon a woman who had never had any intention of accepting his offer.

Had she been too afraid?

Did he care?

What he ought to do was discreetly send the list back to her and forget he had ever seen it.

Not bloody likely. It was secreted inside a pocket in his jacket even now.

"Brandy?"

Sin interrupted Decker's tumultuous thoughts, bringing him back to the present where he belonged. He had decided to pay a call on his old friend today, needing some distraction. Not because of *her*, naturally. He was merely restless.

Lady Jo had nothing to do with his affliction.

He blinked, focusing upon the earl. "No brandy today, old chap. I have a manuscript to read this afternoon for the press."

Sin poured a brandy for himself from the sideboard in his study. "Deadly dull these days, Decker."

"I am a man of business," he pointed out *sans* heat. "I must earn my keep. And I may as well say the same of you, now that you are a happily domesticated beast."

Sin grinned. "Domesticity is bliss. Perhaps you ought to try it yourself."

Decker shuddered. "Blasphemy."

He was pleased to see Sin in a marriage that—in spite of its dubious beginnings—contented him. But marriage was not for everyone. And it most certainly was not for Decker. After Nora, the notion of cleaving to one woman made him bilious. He would sooner dip his prick in a pot of hot tar.

Since he was deuced fond of his prick, that was not about to happen.

"Marriage with the wrong woman is hell on earth," Sin agreed, taking a sip of his brandy. "But marriage with the right woman is—"

"Spare me the gory details, will you?" he interrupted.

Little wonder he had drifted into his own musings. What was it about a happily married man that made him think all his friends needed to shackle themselves as well? Thank God Nora had revealed herself for what and who she truly was and jilted him. She had done him a favor.

"I was going to say paradise," Sin groused. "Mark my words, Decker. The day will come for you."

Decker grimaced. "When I allow a woman to lead me around by the ballocks? No bloody thank you."

"Here now." Sin frowned. "My wife does not lead me around by the ballocks."

"You hosted a ball," he pointed out.

"I wanted an excuse to dance with my beautiful countess," Sin countered.

"You have only been to the club once since you married," Decker added.

He owned the Black Souls Club, but it had long been one of their mutual haunts.

His friend shrugged. "I have no need for diversion any longer, now that my wife keeps me otherwise distracted. Besides, I was scarcely there before, whilst I was attempting to court Miss Vandenberg."

True, but Decker had still rather had enough of this blasted conversation. He did have a manuscript to read—that much had not been a lie. To say nothing of countless other tasks awaiting him. Being a man with diverse business interests meant he was also often a man with too little time.

"Damn it, I told you to spare me the gory details, not expound upon them," he grumbled at his friend. "That will be my cue to flee, before you start waxing poetic over the color of Lady Sinclair's hair or the shape of her eyebrows."

"She *does* have beautiful eyebrows." Sin grinned, unrepentant. "And the color of her hair is—"

"Enough," Decker bit out on a strangled laugh. "Thank you for the company, but I must leave you to your sonnets and lovesick whatnots."

"Not very sporting of you, old chap," his friend complained. "Lady Sinclair is occupied with a meeting of the

Lady's Suffrage Society in the library, and I expect her to be similarly engaged for at least the next hour or so. Who will keep me entertained until I can once more have her all to myself?"

"Get a dog," Decker suggested nicely.

Secretly, he was no better than a hound himself, his proverbial ears perking at the mentioning of the Lady's Suffrage Society. There was a certain member who was not far from his mind. Whose list was burning in his pocket.

Lady Jo was here.

Beneath the same roof.

All he had to do was find her.

"Lady Sinclair has requested the addition of a household cat," Sin was saying, stroking his jaw. "Mayhap we should find a feline. I rather fancy the idea of a soft little beast curled up on my lap."

"You see?" Decker raised a brow. "Thoroughly domesticated and utterly ruined. I despair of you, my friend. But as much as I would like to linger and give you the opportunity to provide me with further proof of the fact you've lost your bloody mind, I truly must go."

Sin's expression had turned maudlin. "A cat could be just the thing. You are brilliant, Decker."

"I suggested a dog," he muttered, bemused.

What the devil had happened to his friend?

Love was a horrid thing.

Best to stay his course—wickedness.

Now, Decker just had to find his quarry.

FOR THE FIRST time, the weekly meeting of the Lady's Suffrage Society had convened at the townhome of the Earl and Countess of Sinclair. The gathering was being held in the library, and Jo was listening to Lady Helena Davenport discussing suggestions for hosting a charity bazaar to encourage new society members to join.

And that was when she saw *him* standing at the threshold of the open library door.

Mr. Elijah Decker.

Their gazes connected.

He beckoned her. She glanced wildly about to see if anyone else had noticed him. Everyone's attention was directed toward Lady Helena, however. Her gaze flicked back to him. He was still there.

He motioned again.

She shook her head, mouthed a frantic denial. *No.*

He flashed her the grin that made heat pool between her thighs. His lips moved in a soundless response. *Yes.*

For a frantic moment, she remained where she was, frozen. Wondering if she ought to go, just so that he would cease hovering at the threshold, trying to lure her nearer to danger, or if she ought to stay put and ignore him. He crooked a finger.

She swallowed. Looked away. But Lady Helena's dulcet voice was not sufficient distraction. She could not concentrate upon a single word Lady Helena uttered. When she glanced toward the door once more, he was gone. She could not deny the swift rush of disappointment lancing her.

Had he truly left? Was he so certain she would do his bidding that he was awaiting her now? Moreover, what did he *want*?

She was curious. And foolish.

Jo quietly excused herself and left the library. The hallway was empty. She had a choice. She could return to the safety of the gathering. Or she could try to find Mr. Decker.

Her feet made the decision for her, guiding her down the hall, one tentative step at a time.

"Psssst."

The hushed sound had come from behind her. Jo spun about, heart pounding.

A sliver of Mr. Decker's handsome face emerged from the music room. The corner of his sensual mouth was kicked up in a tempting grin. Then, he disappeared within.

Another decision faced her. Flee or join him.

Taking care to make sure none of her fellow ladies had emerged from the library to see where she had gone, she hastened into the music room. Mr. Decker was nowhere to be found. The new piano Callie had recently purchased to replace the previous old monstrosity, which had never been tuned to suit her, gleamed, the bench empty. So, too, the overstuffed chaise longue and the matching chairs.

The door slid closed at her back.

Jo whirled, finding Mr. Decker at last, leaning indolently against the wall, still grinning as if he had not a care. He was as insufferably attractive as ever this afternoon. His mouth looked like the sort that knew how to kiss. His wavy dark hair was tousled, a lock falling over his brow in rakish fashion, and the most ridiculous urge to run her fingers through those inky strands hit her.

He had been hiding behind the door, the rotter.

Jo clung to her irritation, which seemed the wisest course. "What are you doing here, Mr. Decker?"

"Visiting my friend, Lord Sinclair." His blue gaze swept down Jo's form, assessing.

Bringing heat to her cheeks and elsewhere, too. She fought the urge to smooth an imaginary wrinkle from her skirts. What gown had she chosen? Amethyst satin, trimmed with lace. Not her favorite, but passable, she supposed. Oh, why did she care?

She frowned at him. "You know very well what I meant, sir. What are you doing here, in the music room?"

"I could ask the same of you," he pointed out.

Even his voice was beautiful. Deep and decadent, sending a trill down her spine. It washed over her like silk.

She tamped down the strange, unwanted sensations flitting through her. "I should go. The other ladies will wonder where I am."

He shrugged and pushed away from the wall at last, sauntering slowly toward her. "Let them wonder."

The risk of being caught here, alone with him, was great. Still, she told herself they had unfinished business. He was yet in possession of her list. She wanted it back. Yes, that was the sole reason she remained. Why she held her ground even when he stopped close to her.

So close.

Too close.

"What of Lord Sinclair?" Her eyes narrowed on him. "Where does he suppose *you* have gone? I cannot believe he would approve of you waylaying his guests in his own home for nefarious purposes."

"I am insulted you instantly assumed my purposes would be nefarious." Mr. Decker raised a lone, dark brow, looking sullen and seductive all at once. "Just what is it you think I intend to do to you?"

"I cannot bear to contemplate it." The suggestion in his voice and the intimacy in his searching stare made heat flare in her cheeks. "Whatever it is, you will not be doing it. I can assure you of that, Mr. Decker."

His scent was delightfully masculine. She liked it far too much, the way it inhabited her senses. Lord Quenington was handsome, but he could not compare to a boldly sensual man like Mr. Decker.

His lips quirked, as if he were amused. "Do not be so hasty with your assurances, my dear."

But then, instead of pressing his advantage as she had supposed he might—as she had secretly longed for him to do, much to her shame—he turned away from her. Clasped his hands behind his back and strolled to the piano.

"When do you mean to return my list to me?" she asked, giving in and following him.

Flame, moth, etcetera.

He unclasped his hands and trailed a lone, long finger lightly over the ivory keys. Not enough to make a sound. But there was something about that slow caress of the instrument that felt as if it were meant to be upon Jo's skin instead.

"Mayhap I meant to return your list to you in the blue salon."

The low rasp of his voice, after a lengthy pause during which she was horrified to realize she had been riveted upon the sight of his hand, startled her.

"You never said so when we danced," she pointed out.

"Would you have turned up if I had?" He cast a searching glance in her direction.

And all the air seemed to flee her lungs. Being alone with him was like consuming too much wine, heady and dizzying all at once. If she had a modicum of sense, she would retreat.

Naturally, she stayed where she was. "Surely you did not expect me to meet you alone, in the midst of a ball, Mr. Decker? It would have been most unwise."

"Unwise is drafting a list of ways to be wicked and then delivering it to a gentleman with whom you are scarcely acquainted," he countered, reaching the end of the piano at last and pressing gently on the last key.

A light, haunting sound filled the air for a second, resonating.

"What are you doing? Someone will hear you!" Without thought, she grasped his hand in hers, keeping him from playing another note.

A mistake, as it turned out.

His fingers locked on hers. The jolt skipping up her arm, past her elbow, sending with it a frisson that landed low in her belly, could not be denied. He used their joined hands to pull her nearer.

So near, she was flush against him, her skirts flattened into his trousers, her breasts grazing his chest. Through her many layers, through the thick barrier of her corset, the connection brought her to life. Her nipples hardened, her breasts tingling.

"You worry too much, *bijou*. There is so much nattering going on in that library, they would not hear an entire phalanx of soldiers marching down the hall."

Her free hand settled upon his chest, to push him away. But the fabric of his coat was soft and fine, and the hardness of the muscle hidden beneath it felt even better. Her questing fingertips moved, gliding over his warm strength. All the way to his broad shoulder. She ought to stop touching him. And she ought to sever this moment, end their connection, return to the library.

But she was in a fog which was impenetrable at the moment. Not common sense or the fear of being caught alone with a notorious rakehell like Mr. Elijah Decker could pierce it.

"I want my list," she managed to say, amazed her tongue could still function properly.

"What if I want to keep it?" he asked, his other hand settling upon her waist with a familiarity she could not help but to like.

"You promised you would return it to me," she reminded him.

"I do not make promises." He was suddenly serious. Almost grim.

"Why not?" she wondered aloud before she could think better of issuing the question.

She told herself she should not care. That his answer did not matter.

"Promises are meant to be broken."

His matter-of-fact response took her by surprise.

She wondered what had happened to him in his past, to make him so cynical and jaded. Who was responsible for the hardness in his jaw now, the firm set of his lips? The answer was apparent—a woman. And the jealousy that accompanied her realization was unwanted. Thoroughly so.

"I have always kept my promises," she said, though she did not know why she uttered something so foolhardy.

Or why she sounded shaken.

Or why her heart was beating so fast, as fast as the wings of a hummingbird.

"And what promises have you made in your life, *bijou*?" he asked, sounding intrigued, some of the harshness fleeing his countenance.

"Stop calling me that." She frowned at him again.

But although she remonstrated him, there was no steel in her voice. No biting edge. Because she liked his pet name for her. Jewel, it meant. Jewels were shiny and faceted and coveted and beautiful. Everything Jo was not. Men did not fawn over her. They did not mow each other down in an effort to gain her next dance.

Likely, the diminutive meant nothing. Mr. Decker probably used it upon all the women in his vast sea of acquaintances. The thought left a sour taste in her mouth.

Made her stomach tangle into knots.

"Answer my question," he insisted. "What promises have you made?"

She thought about it.

"None," she admitted.

"None." He laughed, the sound tinged with a hint of bitterness. "You prove my point. You could not uphold your end of the bargain and meet me in the blue salon."

Again with the blue salon. He seemed rather peeved with her failure to materialize. Surely a man such as Mr. Elijah Decker, who had scores of women falling into his bed, would not care that a wallflower such as herself had failed to meet him clandestinely at a ball. Unless…

"Have I wounded your pride, Mr. Decker?" she asked, sensing the true reason for his pique. "Tell me, has no woman ever denied you before?"

He clenched his jaw, the expression on his face saying more than words ever could. "My reputation speaks for itself."

"Am I the only woman, then?"

"Not the only one," he allowed, his hand traveling from her waist, flattening over the small of her back, caressing slowly up her spine. "But a wiser woman would have seen reason and met me in the blue salon."

That lone touch made her want to melt into a puddle.

"You have it all bollixed up, Mr. Decker," she dared to say, as if she did not relish his touch, his nearness—as if she had not taken note of the manner in which his head had dipped toward hers. "A wise woman would not meet a man of your reputation alone at a ball, surrounded by hundreds of lords and ladies eager to spread vicious gossip. Only a weak-willed fool would have done your bidding."

His hand coasted between her shoulder blades, then reached the neck of her gown. When his touch played over the bare skin of her throat, caressing her nape, it was all she could do to keep her knees from turning into pudding.

"Is that so?" he asked, his gaze searing her the way his touch did.

He was holding her, barely. His touch was gentle. She could shake him in an instant. But she had no wish to.

How alarming.

Mr. Elijah Decker was touching her in the way a lover would. And she liked it.

She did not want him to stop, in fact. The slow stroke of his fingertips over her flesh lit her up from the inside. She was incandescent.

"Yes," Jo forced herself to say, though at this point, she was scarcely certain what she was agreeing to.

"Those are hardly the words of a lady who wants to be wicked," he observed calmly.

"All I want is my list back." That was a horrid prevarication. All Jo truly wanted in this moment was Mr. Elijah Decker's lips on hers.

And for him to never cease touching her—for this connection between them to go on forever. *Yes, that, too.*

"I have reconsidered my leniency in returning it to you."

The rotter.

She ran her tongue over her suddenly dry lips. "What do you mean you have reconsidered?"

His fingers sank into her hair now, cradling her skull in the tenderest of touches. He had seduced her, utterly, and he had not given her a single kiss. Their lips were close enough. If she rose on her toes, if he lowered his head, they would meet. As it was, their breaths mingled, heat and temptation combining.

"Simple." His impossibly blue stare seared hers. "The terms of our agreement are no longer acceptable to me."

Without thought, her hand moved as well, navigating the strong ridge of his shoulder. "Why?"

"I will tell you later." Abruptly, he released her, removing his touch, his warmth.

"How?" she demanded, frustrated with herself for her reaction. Irritated by the disappointment surging inside her at his withdrawal.

She felt bereft. For a moment, she felt as if she were about to topple over. As if he had been all that was holding her upright. His presence and intensity overwhelmed, just as his touch had. It was ridiculous, her reaction to this man. It was futile, too.

Men like Elijah Decker broke hearts. Men like him did not marry ladies like Jo. For eventually, it was a marriage she must seek or suffer her brother's wrath.

"I will send a carriage for you tonight," he told her, holding up one of her hair pins. "Eight o'clock. The carriage will be unmarked, waiting in the mews."

She had not felt him pluck that pin from her hair. "I have a social obligation this evening."

He tucked her hair pin into the pocket of his waistcoat. "Feign a headache. Is that not what all ladies intent upon making mischief do?"

"If my brother discovers I have snuck out of the house alone, to meet a gentleman, he will send me to a convent," she protested.

Julian had certainly threatened as much in the past, though she was certain it was bluster. Her brother was all bark and no bite.

Mr. Decker watched her, his expression impassive. "Scared, *bijou*?"

Her chin went up in defiance. "Never. If I agree to this, will you promise to return my list?"

"I will consider it." He grinned, looking very much like a man who knew he held all the power.

Because he did.

Chapter Four

DECKER WAS COMPLETELY and utterly mad.

One moment, he had been determined to return the list to Lady Jo, and the next, he had been arranging an assignation with her. All because he had touched the silken patch of skin at her nape. All because he had settled his hand upon her waist. Just a few minutes alone with her, when they could have been caught at any second, had been the sole requirement for him to commit his current, crushing act of stupidity.

He still had the list in his pocket now, as he awaited her in the carriage he had told her he would send for her use. He had never dallied with innocents. Ladies of experience were his preference. The sort who did not have angry papas or brothers demanding a betrothal. The sort who were happy with one night of passion and nothing more. What had he been thinking, sending for her, spiriting her away, taking such witless risks?

The answer to that question was painfully obvious, and painfully hard, right now. He had been thinking with his prick. Because the potent allure of her innocence was too rich. He had looked down at her lush, pink lips and those glistening eyes fringed with long lashes, and he had been struck by longing so fierce and deep, he had been forced to take a step away from her.

The distance had not cured his need. He had known he could not possibly aid her with this list in any way save one. And he was going to begin tonight, despite the risks of debauching an unwed lady.

The door to his carriage opened. She had come, after all.

"Mr. Decker." Surprise tinged her voice as she accepted a hand up.

"You were expecting someone else?" he teased.

She settled on the bench alongside him, fussing with her skirts. Her scent drifted over him, orange blossom with a hint of jasmine. His cock stirred to life.

"I was not expecting you in the carriage," she said. "You said you would send a carriage. Not a carriage with yourself in it."

A servant closed the door at his nod.

Decker whisked the hat from her head so he had an unobstructed view of her face. "Next time, I will elaborate so there is no room for confusion."

Her lush lips pursed. "There will be no next time, Mr. Decker."

"Yes," he told her confidently, "there will. Just Decker will do for what I have in mind this evening. No mister."

Her eyes widened. "And what is it that you have in mind, sir?"

Sir. He was not certain he liked that either, but mayhap in the proper circumstances…

"Patience, my dear, is an under-appreciated virtue."

She gave a little huff of irritation he found ridiculously charming. It made him want to haul her into his lap and claim her mouth with his.

"I am merely expected to be delivered to my fate, without an inkling as to where I am going or why?" she asked.

"Yes," he said simply.

"When are you going to give me the list?"

He raised a brow. "Is this an inquisition?"

She huffed again, her eyes narrowing. "You expect me to trust you, a man who has been blackmailing me? A man with a reputation for iniquity? A man who has lured me into breaking all the rules I am meant to uphold?"

He could not argue with Lady Jo, not when she phrased it thus, could he?

Decker grinned. "I am deuced trustworthy. I cannot deny my reputation, but I can assure you rules are all quite boring and deserve to be broken thoroughly and often."

"Only a man would say so. Women who break rules suffer the consequences," she pointed out.

"Then one cannot help but to wonder why a lady such as yourself would wish to accomplish all the naughty items on your list," he countered.

He could not deny he was curious.

Decker did not miss the flush that rose to her cheeks. Lady Jo was damned pretty, but when she was embarrassed, she was downright delectable. And he wanted to consume her.

"That is hardly any of your concern, Mr. Decker." She flicked her gaze to the window of the carriage and fiddled with her skirts.

"It became my concern when you gave me your list," he prodded, taking the opportunity to study her without her regard upon him.

Her nose was regal, slightly retroussé, her forehead proud and high. Her tongue ran over her lower lip as he watched, fascinated. Her mouth was so full. He could not help but to wonder what it would feel like upon him.

He shifted in his seat, attempting to ease the sudden discomfort of his trousers.

"I did not give you my list intentionally," she snapped.

He admired her fire. When she was prickly, it made him want to kiss her into softness. To soothe her sharp edges. To quench some of that fire with passion.

But that was not his intention this evening.

"Of course, but are you not glad you did?" he could not resist teasing her. "Admit it."

She cast a nettled glare in his direction. "Why should I be glad you have been withholding it from me and using it as a means of luring me into ruin?"

Lady Jo did not fool him. Despite her quiet exterior, there were untold, hidden depths of passion burning beneath the surface. And neither was she immune to the attraction flaring between them.

The attraction which was blossoming and burning now, in the confines of his carriage.

Decker could not allow her to deny it.

He lowered his head toward hers, bringing their lips perilously near. "If I truly wished to ruin you, I have already had every opportunity. If I had kissed you this afternoon in the music room, you would have kissed me back."

Her eyes had gone wide again. They were luminous. Glittering.

Beckoning.

Kiss me now, those eyes said.

"I have no wish to kiss you," those lips said.

Those lips were lying.

He smiled. "Have you ever been kissed before, *bijou*?"

The flush returned to her cheeks. "Of course! Dozens of times."

"What were their names?" Decker asked.

Her frown returned. "I beg your pardon?"

"The names of the men who kissed you dozens of times," he elaborated. "Tell me them."

So I can plant them facers.

He struck the possessive notion from his mind. He had never been a jealous man. And indeed, he preferred his women to be experienced. To know how to give and receive pleasure without inhibition. Coaching a lover, instructing her…it held little appeal.

Or, at least, it had. Until Lady Jo Danvers and her damned list.

Her mouth tightened. "I will do nothing of the sort."

"Because there are not any," he guessed, hoping he was right for reasons he would ponder later.

Or, better yet, never.

"How should you know?" she demanded.

His lips twitched. "Prove me wrong."

She sighed. "Very well, you beast. I have not yet kissed a gentleman."

Excellent, said the demon that dwelled within his soul.

"As I thought," he said aloud.

But before he could pursue the matter any further, the carriage came to a halt. They had arrived at their destination. Lady Jo's countenance suddenly took on the look of a startled bird. He half-expected her to sprout wings and take flight.

"Where are we?" she asked.

"We are at my home," he revealed. "We are crossing off item number five on your list this evening: *go to a gentleman's private apartments.* You may thank me later, my dear."

JO WAS INSIDE Mr. Decker's townhome at half past eight in the evening. Alone.

Specifically, she was standing within his library, with its walls of books and array of pictures and sculptures. The art seemed innocent enough, at first glance. It was only when Jo studied it in greater details that she realized the pictures and sculptures all shared a commonality. They were erotic in nature.

The picture before her, for instance, appeared to be an innocent enough image of a gentleman and lady standing before a bookshelf in a library or book store. Upon closer inspection, she realized the gentleman had his hand up the lady's skirts, and that her intimate flesh was exposed for his touch.

She could not stifle her startled gasp.

"Do you like what you see?"

The dark, low voice at her back had her spinning around to find him offering her a glass of wine.

She swallowed, eying him and the goblet, his long, elegant fingers. His handsome face. "It is vulgar."

He smiled. "So is your list, my dear."

True.

She accepted the glass from him. "Yes, but you have this on display in your library."

"And?" He raised his glass to her in mock salute. "I am accustomed to born-in-the-purple aristocrats imagining me a philistine. Besides, it is *my* library."

That was logic, she supposed. It was indeed his library. However, it was simply not done to have art of this nature on display. Goodness, what must his servants think? Or any of his guests, for that matter?

"This is what you enjoy gazing at when you are in search of a book?" She took a sip of her wine, thinking it may relieve the sharp edge of nervousness which had been haunting her from the moment she had been handed up into his carriage earlier. "What must your visitors suppose when they see what you have chosen to grace your walls?"

He gave her an indolent shrug—a gesture she was coming to recognize as his signature. "Who gives a damn what they think? I did not ask to hang it on *their* walls, now did I?"

What an odd manner of thinking about things he possessed.

It was eerily refreshing. But subversive, also. Many of the men and women in her social circle flouted convention in one way or another, it was true. But none of them—not the most daring of the lot—would proudly display the sorts of pictures Mr. Elijah Decker had upon his library walls.

"Your female acquaintances," she found the courage to press, "they do not object to the depictions?"

His gaze was inscrutable as it tangled with hers. He was still near enough in proximity that he could devastate her ability to resist him, and she knew it. She treaded on dangerous ground indeed.

"I do not bring female acquaintances here," he admitted in a low rasp, before taking a long sip of his wine.

She was briefly fascinated by his Adam's apple moving as he swallowed. Then by his tongue, licking a droplet of claret from his lips.

"You brought *me* here," she could not resist saying.

"As promised, I am aiding you with accomplishing each item upon your list." He took another sip of wine, watching her.

Fire seemed to lick her, from the inside out. She liked his predatory stare upon her, heaven help her. She liked being here, alone with him. It filled her with a wild rush, with a vast sense of possibility. In this moment, suspended from her ordinary life, she was not Lady Jo Danvers, expected to make a proper match and not embarrass her family by causing a scandal. In this moment, she could be as wicked as she wished.

"Thank you," she said at last, when she could not fathom

what else was expected of her.

He shook his head, a smile playing with the corners of his mouth. "Too easy, *bijou*."

Jo did not bother to protest the use of the diminutive he had bestowed upon her. "What do you mean, too easy?"

"I told you to thank me later, but I did not say how," he elaborated, his gaze sweeping over her. "The uttering of two simple words will not be sufficient, I fear."

Oh.

Surely he did not mean to cross off one of the other items on her list this evening?

A flush crept back to her cheeks. And why did the idea fill her with an incipient yearning instead of the trepidation she ought to feel?

She drank her wine, swallowing hard. "What *will* be sufficient, Mr. Decker?"

The ghost of a smile returned once more. "I shall let you know when the time comes, my dear."

She could not shake the notion that this was all a game to him, and that he was toying with her. Enjoying it. But why? What could she possibly have to offer a man of his reputation and experience?

She gritted her teeth. "I do not want to wait. I want to know now. What is the debt I owe you?"

"What did I tell you about patience earlier in the carriage?" He drained the rest of his wine before sauntering to a sideboard and refreshing his glass.

"That it is an under-appreciated virtue." She raised a brow. "I would argue otherwise."

"Because you like to argue." He treated her to a full, roguish grin now. "I do not mind. Your hidden fire amuses me. I must admit, before I discovered your list, I supposed you a boring, cold little fish."

Jo told herself his words ought not to hurt her. However, those barbs—intended or not—nevertheless found their mark. She was two different versions of herself. With her family and closest friends, she was garrulous and witty. But when she ventured amongst others, she was cool and quiet and shy. A wallflower, forever on the periphery.

"I am shy until I truly come to know someone," she said, unable to strip the defensiveness from her tone.

It was an old wound.

"I have begun to see there is far more hiding beneath your façade." His voice hummed with frank approval. "Tell me, what spurred you to make your list?"

Embarrassment surged once more. "I do not want to speak of it."

But he was moving back toward her with long, purposeful strides. Trapping her in that bright-blue gaze that rivaled a cloudless summer sky. "But I *do* want to speak of it. Tell me."

"Mr. Decker—"

"Banish the bloody *mister*, if you please," he interrupted. "As I have told you, it is merely, plainly, Decker."

She sighed. Somehow, the wine in her glass was nearly gone. A pleasant glow infused her. Surely it was the fault of the claret that she was tempted to give in and refer to him as Decker.

They were locked in a battle. Their gazes met and held. It was as if they were both attempting to see who would flinch first, which of them would blink.

"Why do you wish to be called by your surname, *sans* mister?" she asked.

"Because I loathe titles of all forms," he answered with surprising honesty. "My mother bartered herself to a titled man who thought nothing of abandoning her and her children until it suited him."

Jo was more than familiar with his background. His mother had been the daughter of a country squire, the mistress of the Earl of Graham. Graham had bequeathed everything but his title to his illegitimate son upon his death, and Decker had used those funds to build himself a business empire.

Decker.

Yes, she was thinking of him as he wished her to refer to him. But how could she not, after learning the reason why?

"You did not have a good relationship with your father?" she asked, curious to know more about him.

Mr. Elijah Decker was very much an enigma, and she was beginning to suspect he possessed untold complexities she had never imagined. He intrigued her. Everything about him was impossibly fascinating.

Especially his lips. And his hands. And those stirring eyes. Also, his broad chest and shoulders. To say nothing of his commanding height or his dark, tousled hair…

Cease this nonsense at once, Josephine. No more claret for you.

"I love my mother," he told her, just when Jo had begun to despair he would answer her query at all. "We may disagree, but though we have been estranged for the last few years, I would do anything for her. My father was a selfish man. He took the love of a good woman, one who would be better suited to make some country gentleman an excellent wife. Instead, he stole her chance of respectability."

She drained the remnants of her glass. "And yet, you are a man who cares nothing for respectability, for the opinions of others."

"I began without it. She did not." He took her glass. "More claret, *bijou?*"

She ought to tell him no. The glass she had consumed was

already going to her head, making her feel as if she were someone else. Making her feel more open. Less constrained. Freer, wilder. The danger was there, sparkling all around her. Calling her to be bold and brave.

Jo relinquished her glass. "Was Lord Graham kind to you?"

She did not know where the question emerged from. It was horribly rude, and she knew it. But she could not seem to stop herself.

Decker did not answer, merely snagged her glass and moved to the sideboard with his effortless grace. His broad back was on display, and she could not help but to admire the sharp lines that proclaimed his strength and masculinity. Even from the rear, he was arresting. His dark coat was fitted perfectly to his form, his trousers worn in the ordinary style and yet seeming to somehow render him taller, more imposing. More compelling, too.

"Decker," she tried, using his name. *Er*, his surname. *Sans mister*, just as he had asked.

He tensed but finished refilling her goblet before turning back to her. "At last, she deigns to use my name."

"Will you answer my question if I do so from now on?" she countered, inwardly applauding herself for her bravery.

In truth, she was out of her depths, and she knew it. But everything about this evening was extraordinary. She was alone with a notoriously sinful man. And he had read her most private thoughts. Words she had never intended for anyone else to see or read. Words she was not entirely sure she meant.

He was before her once again, holding out her glass. There was too much claret in it, but she did not protest. Instead, she accepted the goblet from him, their fingers brushing over the crystal stem. The same awareness that infected her whenever he was near returned.

"I will answer your question if you answer mine," he said, his gaze steady upon hers. "I asked you what prompted you to make your list, and you refused to answer. I will respond to your query after you respond. Fair is fair, after all."

Of course he would want something in return for his answer. He was a businessman, was he not? Her every dealing with him had been firmly grounded in bargaining.

Jo took a deep breath and plunged onward. In for a penny, in for a pound.

"I made the list because I want passion in my life," she admitted. "Everyone around me is finding happiness and love. Meanwhile, I remain firmly on the periphery. It was a lark, in truth. I never intended to cross off each item on my list. I never intended to finish the list itself. And yet…"

"And yet," he prompted when she trailed off.

"And yet," she continued, "part of me very much wants to complete it. Part of me wants to be wicked and reckless and bold. To ignore all the rules. To be unlike myself. To be daring. To throw caution to the wind and see where it leads me."

His gaze was intent upon hers.

"It led you here. To me."

There was a gruffness in his voice that sent a frisson down her spine. Not of fear but anticipation.

"Yes," she agreed, doing her best to hide her breathlessness. "It did. However, as you said, fair is fair. I answered your question and now you owe me a response in kind. What was your relationship like with Lord Graham?"

Decker inclined his head, then took a sip of his wine before speaking at last. "He wished I were legitimate. His wife bore him seven daughters. My mother gave him a son. Graham loathed his heir, a wastrel country cousin he feared would leach the earldom dry in the outside of a year. He gave me everything he could, but not because he loved me. Because he could not bear for the next earl to waste it."

She did not think she mistook the harshness in his voice, the bitterness in his expression. "Forgive me for asking. I had no wish to bring back painful memories."

"It is the truth. I cannot change it." Decker finished his claret and placed his empty glass upon a low table before snagging her hand. "Enough of this grim talk. Come with me."

He laced his fingers through hers, and the gesture, while casual, filled her with a profound sense of rightness. She clasped his hand, savoring the way it engulfed hers, so much larger. So different from hers. So capable.

"Where are you taking me now?" she asked as he led her from the library.

"Suspense is half the fun, my dear."

She still held her claret in her left hand. His long-legged strides ate up the distance far quicker than her petite limbs could travel. She had to move at twice the pace to keep up with him, meaning she had to engage in a delicate balancing act to avoid spilling her wine all over his carpets as they traveled.

There was the possibility he was taking her to his bed-chamber. Jo was already in treacherous territory indeed. She should stop him. Demand he take her back home. But whether it was the connection they had made in their conversation, or whether it was the claret she had consumed—mayhap both—she did not want to go.

She was enjoying this clandestine meeting with Decker far too much.

As it turned out, her fears were unfounded. The chamber they entered next was a dining room. He gave a discreet order to a servant, and then seated her at the table. Jo placed her goblet before her and watched as he folded his lean form into the chair opposite her.

"What are we doing here?" she asked.

"What does it look like?" He raised a brow, giving her a look that made her think of bedchambers once more. "I am feeding you."

That was not the response she had expected. What manner of rakehell brought a lady to his home and then led her to the dining room so he could feed her? A contradictory one, she was certain. There were layers to Elijah Decker. And Jo wanted to get to know them all, to peel them away, one by one.

Along with his clothes.

Where had that thought emerged from? Her ears went hot and she forced herself to think of something—*anything*—else. Definitely not the way his chest would look, bereft of his shirtsleeves, waistcoat, and jacket. Absolutely not the muscles she had felt, the barely leashed strength simmering beneath his surface.

"I dined earlier this evening," she told him, finding her voice.

"We are not having an elaborate multi-course meal. We are having dessert."

As if on cue, the servants returned, bringing a tray laden with delicate crystal bowls. She counted almost a dozen, each filled with molds of cream ices in varying colors and design.

"Thank you," Decker said. "That will be all."

When the footmen had gone, his gaze settled back upon her.

"I love cream ices," she blurted.

Her lack of composure she blamed upon the claret, too. She was altogether unsettled.

"I guessed as much," he said, his voice low. "I noted how much you enjoyed it at Sin's dinner party."

The dinner party Callie and her husband had held the previous week had been rather large. Jo had not supposed Decker had taken notice of her at all. They had not been seated near to each other. The knowledge he had been watching her filled Jo with warmth.

And with something else, too…

She cleared her throat. "The pineapple cream ice was splendid."

He gave her a slow, deliberate grin that turned her insides into mush. "Take your pick, my dear. Or try them all."

Each bowl was neatly labeled with the flavor it contained. She read them: cucumber, almond, cherry, orange flower water, and pineapple. Each one sounded equally delicious. In truth, cream ices were one of Jo's weaknesses. She had yet to discover a flavor she did not enjoy.

"Which do you recommend?" she asked, that troubling heat inside her continuing to glow.

She was beginning to fear Mr. Elijah Decker was one of her weaknesses as well. He was certainly every bit as tempting as cream ice.

"I like the orange flower water myself," he said.

"I shall try that one first, then," she decided, selecting a bowl containing cream ice molded into miniature blossoms.

The first cold, creamy spoonful on her tongue was decadent and delicious. Floral with a hint of rich citrus, ending on a note of bitterness that seemed somehow perfect.

"What do you reckon?" he queried, selecting a bowl for himself as well.

She swallowed the tart confection. "It is every bit as splendid as pineapple."

If being alone with Elijah Decker at his home had seemed

surreal, eating cream ices with him in his dining room felt like the sort of silly dream she would have in the morning, when she was half-asleep and half-awake. The sort that made no sense and brought together the most ludicrous combinations. Once, she had dreamt she had commissioned a wardrobe made entirely of crustaceans.

Jo could not stifle her chuckle at the memory.

"Share the joke if you please," he ordered.

"It is far too ridiculous to share," she denied.

"Nonsense." He pinned her with that bright stare, his eyes narrowing. "You cannot laugh and then refuse to tell me the reason why. It is against the rules."

"I thought you said rules were are all quite boring and deserve to be broken thoroughly and often," she could not resist pointing out.

"Saucy minx. My rules are not boring at all." He winked. "Go on, then. Tell me or I shall have the servants come and whisk away the rest of the cream ices before you can sample them."

"Villainy!" she exclaimed in mock horror.

He laughed, that wonderful mouth of his dipping into a smile that hit her in the heart. Sinfully handsome when he was serious, a laughing Decker was *irresistible*. For a moment, she laughed along with him, enjoying their lighthearted banter.

He waggled his eyebrows at her. "I am deadly serious about the cream ices. Tell me or they shall be banished."

He was impossible.

Her heart gave a pang.

The laughter fled her. "Very well. I shall tell you, but you must promise me you will not share it with another soul."

He pressed a hand over his heart. "I vow to take it to my grave. Now, do tell me what it is that makes Lady Jo Danvers smile."

Cream ice, baby animals, good books, comfortable shoes, handsome hats, her family and friends, and now one more to add to the list: *him*. But if Jo had learned anything in the last few days, it was that creating lists of any sort was an endeavor she ought to avoid in the future.

"I was thinking of a nonsensical dream I had, if you must know," she began, feeling foolish but carrying on anyway. "I dreamt I had commissioned an entire wardrobe made of crustaceans. The worst of it was they were all living, and there was a lobster that was pinching me in the side. When I woke up, I realized I had fallen asleep with a book in my bed, and the corner of it had been digging into me in my slumber."

He chuckled. "I see the levity. You, my dear, have an utterly ridiculous imagination. I shan't ask you why you were thinking of such a dream in the midst of sampling cream ices."

Her lips twitched. "Thank you. A lady cannot reveal all her secrets in one night, you know."

His gaze dipped to her lips. "Oh, I am aware of that. Trust me, I am more than aware."

Her cheeks flushed once more. They finished their cream ices in companionable silence.

Chapter Five

*T*HE FIRST NOTE arrived the next morning, just after breakfast. Jo had taken her repast in her chamber, in keeping with her claims of having been ill the previous evening so her brother Julian and sister-in-law Clara would not find her actions suspicious. Miraculously, she had made her way back through the house just after midnight, drunk on claret and Elijah Decker, belly filled with cream ice, and had not been caught.

Jo was still in her dressing gown, taking her tea, reading her correspondence, and trying to distract herself from the nagging regret she had not been able to banish since she had risen that morning. Just after dawn, she had been up with a headache and a churning stomach.

One item crossed off her list, and yet, it had all been— aside from the erotic art on display in Decker's library— shockingly innocent. It had not progressed as she had fancied a few hours alone with him, at his mercy, might.

For one thing, he had not attempted to kiss her.

For another, he had behaved as quite the gentleman, accompanying her on the carriage ride back to her brother's townhome, not complaining when she had leaned against his shoulder and promptly fallen asleep as the carriage and his nearness had lulled her into the arms of Queen Mab.

But she had been beset by nothing but questions for all

the hours since she had left her bed.

Heavens, had she snored? Should she have thrown herself into his arms? Kissed him? Was there a reason why he had not kissed her? Why the devil had she told him about her crustacean dream?

Her lady's maid returned then, distracting Jo from her musings. And she brought with her another note aside from the correspondence she had delivered earlier, which she handed over immediately.

"This just came for you, my lady. I am told there will be a reply."

The moment Jo saw the note, she knew instinctively it was from Decker. But the familiar handwriting confirmed her suspicions. She accepted it with far too much haste.

"Thank you, Burford," Jo said, attempting to remain calm as she took the note to her writing desk and frantically devoured its contents.

I promised you the return of your list if you would allow me to help you in achieving its completion. You have been true to your word. Therefore, I am playing the gentleman and will return your list to you on one condition.

Cross off each item on your list with me.

D.

Her heart was pounding faster than the hooves of a galloping horse determined to win a race at Ascot.

Her hands shook.

She had to read the note twice, certain she had misread it. Then thrice.

"Shall I wait for your answer then, my lady?" asked Burford, interrupting Jo's whirling thoughts.

"Yes," she said too quickly. Too loudly

How was it possible for one word to sound so thrilled?

She snatched up her pen and paper and wrote out her response.

I fail to see how further blackmail is playing the gentleman. However, you did feed me cream ice. I shall consider your request. Lord Q remains a tempting option, however.

Yours truly,

J.

Jo stared at the words she had written, wondering if she dared send such a taunting reply before ultimately deciding that yes, she did. She handed off her note and waited, aquiver, for the response.

It arrived in under half an hour, stark and direct and thrilling.

To the devil with Lord Q.

Choose me, or forfeit all future cream ice.

D.

Jo was smiling at she read those two lines. She dashed off her response.

Why should I choose you?

J.

Her lady's maid was looking rather harried when she returned with yet another note, this time twenty minutes later.

Because no one else will be able to complete the items on your list as well as I can.

*You know it, **bijou**.*
Make the right decision, and I will send you the list.
D.

His words sent a trill straight through her. She felt it in her core. Did she dare give herself over to such a sinful rake? Did she dare trust a man like him? *Yes*, said her heart. *No*, said her mind.

Jo took a deep breath and wrote her answer.

I agree. But only on account of future cream ice.
Now, give me my list, you wretch.
J.

Burford returned in five minutes, and Jo was dumbfounded by the rapidity of his response. How in heaven's name had he responded so quickly? She opened the note, but not before telling Burford that there would be no response. Jo wanted to be alone when she read his answer.

Here you are, my dear, though I do take exception to
being called a wretch. Might I suggest something more
suiting? Such as: oh handsome one, glorious wicked
seducer of innocents, most tempting man in England…I
could go on, but I haven't all day to draft a list. Take
your pick. I shall leave all list making in your capable
hands.

Await me tomorrow at the same time. We shall
commence with Number One.
D.
P.S. Look out your window.

He had her chuckling by the time she finished reading.

He *was* a wretch. But also ludicrously charming. She had not expected him to be the sort of man who would make her laugh, or who would feed her cream ice. There was a softness to him, a warm heart beating beneath his debonair exterior.

And she liked it.

Butterflies had taken up residence in her stomach. She walked to the window and drew back the dressings. There, in the street below, was a gleaming black carriage. The same one he had used to sweep her away the night before. The door opened, and he poked his handsome, hat-covered head out into the world for a moment.

Their gazes met through the distance, his burning into hers even from so far away. Then, he inclined his head to her and disappeared. His carriage lurched into motion. That quickly, he was gone, leaving in his wake a flurry of emotion. Longing, yearning, excitement, trepidation, fear—everything.

How had he known which chamber was hers, where to park his carriage? She was sure she did not want to find out the answer.

They were taking a great deal of risks. More risks than they had taken last night. If her lady's maid were to tell her brother that Jo was receiving so many notes, and if Julian but looked out the window to find Mr. Elijah Decker parked there, she would be in a world of trouble.

And yet, she could not summon a modicum of outrage. All she felt was excitement, bold and true. He had come to her, and there was something so very powerful about the realization he wanted her. He wanted to complete her list.

With *her*, Lady Jo Danvers. The wallflower. The lady who forever seemed to be left behind or overlooked. The lady who was last.

Turning away from the window, she glanced down at her list, back in her possession at last.

Ways to be Wicked

1. *Kiss a man until you are breathless.*

2. *Arrange for an assignation. Perhaps with Lord Q?*

3. *Get caught in the rain with a gentleman. (This will necessitate the removal of wet garments. Choose said gentleman wisely.)*

4. *Sneak into a gentleman's bedchamber in the midst of the night.*

5. ~~*Go to a gentleman's private apartments.*~~

6. *Spend a night in a gentleman's bed.*

7. *Make love in the outdoors.*

8. *Ask*

Dear heavens. He had crossed out number five for her. And he meant to kiss her breathless.

She ought to be horrified at the prospect of completing her list with a man like Elijah Decker.

Jo could scarcely wait.

LADY JO DANVERS had fallen asleep on him in his carriage. She had snuggled up to him like a bloody kitten and then closed her eyes. And he, Elijah Decker, purveyor and collector of erotic art and literature, acknowledged rakehell and heartless voluptuary, had slid his arm around her, holding her close. He had buried his nose in her sweetly scented hair before waking her when they arrived back at the Earl of Ravenscroft's townhome and settling her hat and veil into place.

And before that, he had plied her with wine and cream ice.

The wine had been to soothe any ragged nerves she would have at being alone with him. The cream ice had been purely because it pleased him to give her something she liked, to watch her savor it.

He may as well lie down in the nearest graveyard and call himself finished.

But no.

For reasons beyond his ken, he had asked her to allow him to be the man—the only man—with whom she completed her wicked list. And she had agreed.

Which was why, for the second time, he was awaiting her in the mews in his carriage.

If he had any sense, he would have returned Lady Jo's list and forgotten all about her. He did not have any sense, as evidenced by his current predicament. He felt like a criminal, hovering here in the shadows. Or a lover who was waiting for his mistress's husband to leave so he could sneak inside and make the man a cuckold. There was something so very comical about this scenario…

And yet, he was here.

He was waiting for her.

That knot in his stomach? It was anxiousness. That ache in his ballocks? It was desire. That knife blade of guilt which had been stabbing him ever since he had reached the decision to bed her? Still present.

He tamped it down.

Easily ignored.

Unlike the woman herself.

As on the previous occasion, the carriage door opened, and suddenly, she was invading his territory. In a swish of silken skirts, she settled on the squabs at his side, bringing with her the scent of impending rain and exotic flowers and something else, some other note that was simply, deliciously, *her.*

He waited until the carriage door snapped closed to re-move her hat and veil and drink in the sight of her. *Damn*, she was beautiful. He wanted to kiss her sweet little upturned nose.

When had he ever been so affected by the mere sight of a woman?

This had to end.

He had no earthly idea how it would.

Perhaps after he had bedded her? Yes, that was the key. Of course it was. It had always been thus in the past, with the women who had come before her. Why should this one be any different?

This one is very, very different, whispered a cautioning voice from within.

"Were you seen?" he asked, telling the voice to go to the devil, along with all good intentions.

"No," she responded as the carriage lurched into motion.

Excellent. No irate brothers giving chase this evening. Nothing to distract them from their course.

It occurred to him that unlike the first night, she had no questions.

"You are surprisingly quiet," he observed. "Tell me, what is that sharp mind of yours thinking?"

"I suppose I was wondering," she said softly.

He took a moment to study her loveliness more complete-ly, hoping he would find some flaw. All he saw was the tiniest beauty mark on her jaw, near her ear, and far from being an imperfection, the deuced little mark entranced him.

"What were you wondering?" he forced himself to ask, before he went entirely maudlin.

She lowered her head, breaking the connection with his gaze. "Why you want to be the one who completes the list with me. Surely there are any number of ladies in your acquaintance with whom you could…dally. Ladies who are beautiful and experienced. Ladies who do not have to sneak into the mews and lie to their brothers."

Yes, but none of those ladies would be *her*.

Decker blinked, wondering where the devil that thought had emerged from. "I already told you, my dear, that I feel responsible for you. You are like a sister to the wife of the man I consider a brother. And I cannot very well throw you to a dog like Quenington and continue living with myself."

That sounded rather callous, even to his own ears, and he knew a sharp sting of regret, wishing he could call them back. She stiffened, her full lips going taut, and her head shot up. He called himself every sort of cad for the hurt he saw reflected in those honey-brown eyes.

"You need not feel obligated to assist me, Mr. Decker," she said coolly. "I have been living my life quite well without your intervention."

She was bold, but he knew he must not forget she was all but a chit fresh from the schoolroom although there was something about her which seemed older than her years. And he was almost ten years her senior and a hundred years more jaded, weathered, and weighed down by sins.

"It is not obligation I feel for you, *bijou*," he told her grimly.

Let it be a warning to her. She would not escape this agreement of theirs unscathed or with her maidenhead intact. He meant to make her his in every way. To show her all the myriad facets of pleasure. He meant to ruin her for every damn man who would come after him.

What if she ruined him, too? Decker struck down the notion before it could take root.

"You just said it is. I would sooner be relieved of my

promise to you and complete the list as I choose than accept your sympathy," she said, regal as any queen. "I do not require you, Mr. Decker. I never have."

Damn it. He had not missed her return to the use of *mister* in his name, and he knew what that signified. He had upset her.

There was only one means by which he could fathom proving to her that what he felt was decidedly not obligation. Only one means by which he could undo the damage he had so foolishly done with his half-arsed response.

He reached for her, settling his hands on her cinched waist and then hauled her into his lap. She was petite, and even with all her luscious curves and the endless trappings a lady hid beneath her gown, she was light. She fit in his lap perfectly.

Her hands went to his chest, as if to push herself away.

"You will complete the list with someone other than me over my cold, dead body, Josephine. Do you understand me?" he demanded, utterly serious.

He had never been more serious about anything in his life. In fact, the urge to beat Quenington and any other man who would dare to touch her rose, uncontainable, within him. He had never felt so possessive about a female before. It was bloody disconcerting, was what it was.

And troubling.

But he was not about to let her go, now that he had her where he wanted her.

"You have no right to order me about," she argued, squirming suddenly in his lap. "And no one calls me Josephine."

"*I* do," he said, his hand going to the back of her neck whilst the other remained on her waist. The sensation of her silken skin on his bare hand stirred him. "I call you whatever I wish to call you, because until we complete your list, you are mine. Do you understand? The reason I want to complete your list with you is because I want you. I want to taste you, kiss you, be inside you. I want you in my bed. I want to take your innocence. I want to kiss you breathless. But make no mistake, darling. You are here for the same reasons. You want me every bit as much as I want you."

She swallowed, her lips parting. "I do not want to be a mercy bedding."

He almost laughed aloud at her peculiar phrasing. "Believe me, you would not be anyone's *mercy bedding*. Any man who takes you to his bed will do so because you are desirable and beautiful and because he cannot stop thinking about how soft your lips will be beneath his, or how your nipples will feel in his mouth. He will do so because he will look at you and think about lifting your skirts, trailing his hand from your ankle, up your calf, all the way to your thighs. He will lay awake at night, taking himself in hand as he imagines what you taste like, what you feel like, how deliciously tight your cunny will be as you take his cock."

He stopped when he realized just how much he had revealed.

Too much.

Far, far too much.

Jo's eyes were wide. Her cheeks were flaming.

She looked so gorgeous, his chest constricted, tightening. His cock was already erect beneath her, from the combined product of her nearness, her squirming in his lap, and the trip his imagination had just taken—not for the first time, it was true. He had been thoroughly abusing himself to thoughts of Lady Jo Danvers before he discovered her list. His hunger for her had only grown after the list she had drafted appeared in the midst of the Lady's Suffrage Society pamphlet manuscript.

Her lips moved soundlessly, as if she tried to form words but could not find her voice. And then, in the next instant, she shocked him thoroughly by slamming her mouth into his.

Her movement was so forceful, so sudden and without a hint of finesse, that the result was a violent mashing of lips and teeth. For a fleeting moment, he expected to taste the copper tang of blood. It was, undoubtedly, the worst kiss he had ever received.

And yet, it inflamed him more than any of the kisses which had preceded it. Because the raw, unadulterated desire in that kiss, in that action, was the most potent, heady thing he had ever experienced.

He lost himself as well. To the devil with kissing her the way a seasoned lover ought. He was desperate for her. Provoked to the point of madness. Her innocent kiss made him ravenous. It fashioned him into a beast who could only be sated in one manner: claiming and possession.

His hands were both in her hair now, fingers sliding into the silken mass. He angled her head and took control of the kiss, slanting his lips over hers. Decker kissed her tenderly and yet with all the savagery within, fierce but controlled. He fitted his mouth against hers and sucked her lower lip.

She made a soft, kittenish sound that landed somewhere in the vicinities of his cock and his heart both. And then she opened for him. His tongue dipped inside the velvety recesses of her mouth, tasting her, finding her.

Her arms twined around his neck, and then her nails were tunneling through his hair, raking his scalp as she kissed him back. She sucked his tongue. Her movements were choppy, inexperienced. But her enthusiasm—*bloody hell*, it was the stuff of fantasies. He never wanted to end this kiss. Never wanted to exit the carriage. He could happily remain here, her in his lap, her mouth on his, for all eternity.

Decker found hair pins—prim, cool opposition. He narrowly resisted the urge to pluck them from her coiffure one by one. *Later*, he promised himself. He did not give a damn if she returned home with her hair cascading down her back. Anything keeping him from reveling in her long, brunette locks was going to be savaged and removed when the time was right.

He did not stop kissing her. Could not stop. The carriage rocked over London roads. Her hair unraveled down her back. Her lips firmed over his. Her aggression receded, replaced by gentleness. She moved her mouth in a mimicry of his, learning, teasing, testing.

The irony was not lost upon Decker that he had bedded more women than he could count, and yet this simple kiss— begun in such inexperienced, awkward fashion—was the most erotic, compelling kiss he had ever experienced. He wanted her so much more now. More than he could put into words. His hunger for her was like an entity all its own, festering and rising inside him, demanding to be answered.

He kissed her harder, exploring what she liked. Decker kissed the corners of her lips, then the tempting bow. He sank his tongue deep again, plumbing the depths of her mouth. And she moaned. She moaned into his kiss, her tongue moving against his.

So much for the notion of him kissing her breathless. He was quite sure she had accomplished the feat in the opposite. Sweet, innocent, quiet, secretly wicked Lady Jo Danvers had taken command of his mouth and kissed the hell out of him.

And he had relished every second of it.

So much that he had lost control.

Now? He could not stop kissing her. Not if his life depended upon it. Already, he had forgotten his every carefully laid strategy for the evening. All thought had vanished into the ether, replaced by the yearning and all-encompassing desire he felt for the woman on his lap.

But then, reality intruded, as it was so oft wont to do, in the form of a rap on the carriage door.

"Mr. Decker?" asked his man from the other side of the closed carriage door. "We have been parked for a quarter hour. Do you wish to proceed, or has there been a change of plans?"

Right. Damn it all. His stupid plans.

Decker tore his lips from Jo's, exercising every shred of control he possessed to manage the feat. He sucked on his lower lip and gazed into her face. Her mouth was swollen from his kisses, her expression dazed.

Good.

Pleased at how affected she had been by their interlude, he removed her from his lap, settling her alongside him once more with the greatest reluctance. He found her hat and returned it to her head, flipping down her veil before inspecting his handiwork, making sure she was impossible to recognize.

"No change," he called to his driver. "We shall commence with the evening as planned."

Chapter Six

*J*O HAD KISSED Mr. Elijah Decker.

Shamelessly.

Awkwardly.

Roughly.

Her first kiss, and she had slammed her lips into Decker's with so much force, hers still ached with remembrance as they settled in the sumptuous chamber he had escorted her to. Though they had entered from the rear, even in the low light of the street lamps, she had seen enough of the exterior of the building to know at once that he had brought her to a new location. This was not his townhome.

An acute, intoxicating tangle of trepidation and excitement washed over her as she sat at the intimate, exquisitely carved dining table. Just as he had two evenings before, he sat opposite her, folding his commanding height into the chair with an elegant grace she could not help but to admire.

This time, there were no servants hovering about. Not yet, anyway.

"I am sorry," she blurted, and then cursed herself when her cheeks turned to flame.

His intense stare was upon her, inscrutable. "What are you sorry for, *bijou?*"

Though she had been bold in the low light of the carriage, she felt the opposite now. Her courage deserted her. "You know."

Sky-blue eyes seared her. "No, I am afraid I do not. Else, why would I have asked?"

To torment her, of course. The man seemed to glory in making her weak.

"The kiss," she forced herself to say. "I am sorry for kissing you so…hard."

He bestowed one of his rare, gorgeous grins upon her. "Why should you be sorry? I found your enthusiasm quite infectious. However, since you have yet to reach the point of breathlessness, I consider myself firmly on duty this evening."

Had she not been breathless? She was certain she had. What else could explain the manner in which her heart had raced, the tingly feeling that refused to be banished even now, the shimmering sensation deep within her, as if she had just walked into summer after a lifetime of cold winter wind?

She blinked. What had he said?

Ah, yes.

Jo frowned at him. "I am a duty to you, then?"

"Not a duty," he said softly, "but a pleasure. Everything about you is the height of pleasure. Never doubt it."

She thought then, of his words in the carriage. Wicked words, sinful words, those had been. No one had ever spoken to her thus. She ought to have been horrified. Instead, she was intrigued and gratified.

"Where have you brought me?" she asked, desperate to change the subject.

The impulse to kiss him earlier after his carnal declaration had been undeniable. But now, she was out of her depths. Adrift once more. She scarcely knew what to expect from him.

"To my club," he answered easily, as if it were an ordinary occurrence for an unwed lady to be present at the Black Souls—a club notorious for its secrecy and whispered predilection for vices.

Her heart beat faster. And between her thighs, that same insistent heat blossomed into an ache. How wrong it was for her to be here. How thrillingly delicious.

Before she could utter a word, a subtle rap sounded on the closed door.

"You may enter," Decker called, his eyes never leaving hers.

Liveried servants bustled forth, bringing with them silver trays lined with delicacies. Desserts of every sort—cakes, marzipans, creams, tortes, a raspberry fool. Jo had not been particularly hungry, but the moment the sweet-scented arrival appeared, she could not deny the urge to try them. A crystal wine glass appeared before her and was instantly filled.

Jo lowered her head, attempting to avert her gaze. She had removed her hat and veil, not anticipating she would be seen by anyone else in the privacy of this lush room with its bold red wall coverings and sumptuous furnishings. She very much regretted that haste now.

One nod from Decker, and the servants disappeared as quietly and hastily as they had arrived, closing the door at their backs.

"You need not fear," he said the instant they were alone. "My staff is exceedingly well paid, and each of them is aware that discretion is the most important virtue to possess when in my employ. Even if any of them had recognized you—which I highly doubt—they would not utter a word against you. That is my promise to you."

Jo believed him. "Thank you. I know it is not your intention to put me in danger, but I did not craft the list to ruin my reputation. I have no wish to bring scandal upon my family. I merely wished to live a bit. To be free to experience life."

He inclined his head. "A worthy desire. I cannot fault you for it. What is a life which cannot be freely lived and enjoyed? I applaud your bravery for both the list and the kiss. Especially the kiss."

His words had her cheeks feeling scorched yet again. She had to turn her mind to something else. Something safer. Her gaze dipped to the delicacies laid before them.

"You are forever feeding me desserts," she said, her eye upon a particularly sinful-looking chocolate torte. "No cream ice this evening?"

Her gaze slipped back to him—of course it did—to find him eying her as if she were the only dessert he wanted to consume. She barely suppressed a shiver.

"No cream ice," he agreed calmly. "I want to see what other sweets please you."

All of them, she wanted to say, *but none as much as your mouth on mine.*

Oh dear. Best to turn her mind to other matters. She was curious, of course.

"Why have you brought me to your club this evening?" she asked next.

A smile flirted with his lips. "Because there is something I intend to show you here. Now choose your first dessert, *bijou*. My time with you is sadly limited, and I have a great deal more planned for us."

Us.

Why did she like the way that lone word sounded in his deep, delicious voice so much?

Jo selected the torte that had been beckoning her ever since it had appeared on the table between them. "What more do you have planned?"

Kissing, she hoped.

Breathlessness, naturally.

"Patience." He winked.

"Is an under-appreciated virtue," Jo added.

"The lady is learning." His smile deepened, revealing two grooves.

Dimples.

To accompany the charming little dent that hid in the middle of his proud chin.

Why had she failed to note them before now? Was it that he had not given her a true smile until this moment? She wanted to kiss each one of those dips. To travel the small divots with her tongue. To taste his skin the same way she had tasted his mouth earlier, in the carriage.

Instead, she shoveled a forkful of decadent chocolate torte into her mouth. In ladylike fashion, of course. Sort of.

The moan of bliss that fled her was decidedly not ladylike.

Her gaze flitted back to his, finding him watching her with that same inscrutable expression. Or mayhap not entirely inscrutable. He was looking at her as if *she* were the dessert laid before him. No man had ever stared at her with such frankness before.

She swallowed the bite of decadent cake. "Forgive me for my lapse of manners."

"You need not apologize for enjoying something, Jo," he said, the intimacy in his tone intoxicating. "Not with anything that happens between us. Do you understand?"

She understood he was speaking of something beyond her ken. Jo was a novice. Mr. Decker was decidedly not. But he wanted her to comprehend what he was saying, and in that moment, all she wanted was to please him.

What a strange realization. She had thought her list was about herself, and yet, she cared more about the man seated opposite her than she did about any of the items she had written.

"I understand," she said, her mouth suddenly dry, her heart fluttering.

DECKER KNEW FRIGHTFULLY little of what made Lady Jo Danvers happy.

What a disconcerting discovery it was to realize he wanted to know *more*. Hell, who was he fooling? He wanted to know *everything* that made her happy. He wanted to be the reason for her smiles and her every exquisite moan. More of those throaty moans, *please*, the sort that had rumbled from her when she had taken her first bite of the chocolate torte earlier. He could have kissed his bloody chef for that sound alone.

Yes, she fancied sweets, but he could not very well spend the next few days plying her with cream ices and cakes. The inevitable finite limitation of their interactions settled in his gut like a stone as he led her from the private dining chamber at his club to another chamber entirely. This room, like the last, was also devoted to sating appetites. Unlike the other room, however, this chamber had nothing to do with sating the hungers of the stomach.

Rather, it was a celebration of the most erotic items in his possession, and along with it, his most depraved proclivities. The walls were covered in rich, scarlet damask and hung with treasures he had accumulated over the last few years with the wealth his sainted papa had bestowed upon him after cocking up his toes.

That had been intentional, of course. After all these years, Decker preferred to use the Earl of Graham's funds to carry on with businesses, charitable endeavors, and purchases the man would have considered immoral. Such a patented, born-in-the-purple, sanctimonious hypocrite the man who'd sired him had been.

"What is this room?" Lady Jo asked quietly as she began a circumnavigation of the long, rectangular chamber.

"The wickedest room in my club," he answered honestly.

If she wanted to test the bounds of her virtue, there was no place better suited for the task. Nor was there any better man. The mere thought of her alone with anyone else, attempting to complete her list, still filled him with protective fury.

Lady Jo Danvers was his.

For tonight, he reminded himself.

For this moment.

And why the devil should he care, anyway? He always grew tired of his playthings. The novelty dimmed. The most beguiling beauties and skilled, experienced lovers had not been enough to hold his interest for more than a night after he had bedded them.

He would grow tired of Lady Jo soon. After the completion of the list, mayhap before it. This maddening obsession he had for her would fade.

She trailed her hand over the massive piano dominating part of the chamber, running a finger over the keys. "The mark on this piano—it is the same as the mark on the piano in Lord and Lady Sinclair's music room."

Clever darling. She missed nothing—not a spare detail. She reminded him of a kitten whose eyes had been newly opened, eager to look at all the world around her, to drink it in.

He nodded. "It is. I own a piano factory in Islington. This is one of mine, as is the piano purchased by Sin and his countess. Superior models, if I am not being too proud of my own product."

The hedonist in him appreciated beauty in all forms,

including music. He often sat alone in his own music room, playing until the early hours of the morning. There was nothing quite as satisfying as the haunting strains of an excellent piano in the stillness of the night. Well, perhaps a woman's moans of pleasure, but that was another instrument entirely.

Also one which deserved worship, as it happened.

"You own a piano factory," she repeated, as if she found the notion impossible to believe. Her delicate finger traced over the mark on the polished rosewood case, trailing the gilded design he had added to the pianos after purchasing the factory, which had been declining after a century of excellent business. "Nothing but a stylized letter D, just as you sign your notes."

He nodded. "Not terribly original of me, I am afraid. The company was formerly known as Smithton and Sons. They produced some of the finest pianos in all the world in their day. However, since I am neither a Smithton, nor one of the fellow sons, I deemed it wise to change the name, along with restructuring some of the piano designs. This piano is our newest, one of only a few of its kind—Lord and Lady Sinclair are in possession of one, and there is another as well, aside from this."

She ran a reverent finger over the keys. "It is beautiful, Decker."

"You may play, if you like." He hoped she would, though he had certainly not brought her here to listen to her on the piano.

She shook her head slowly, giving him a measuring look he was not sure if he liked. "Not now, I do not think. I should like to see the rest of this wickedest room in your club first."

Of course she would.

Decker suppressed a grin. "Go on, then, minx. Have a

look."

She did not waste any time in making her way to the framed pictures hanging upon the walls. Her gasp told him she had taken a closer look at what appeared to be tasteful, elaborate lithographs of the alphabet. Twenty-six of them in all, one for each letter, individually framed and on prominent display. Except, upon inspection, hidden within the fancy motif of each letter was an erotic image. Worked into the A, for instance, was a gentleman stroking his cock as he watched a woman lifting her skirts.

"That is positively indecent," she said, and she was flushing once more.

Damn, she was delicious. He could not keep himself from wondering just how far that pretty pink extended on her creamy flesh. Down her throat, for certain. Where did it end? The tops of her breasts?

Think of something else, you bloody scoundrel.

His cockstand was rising and ready.

But there would be no slaking of his needs in this chamber tonight, and he knew it. Tonight was about Lady Jo. About making her breathless. Shocking her, too. If she truly wanted to be wicked, she had come to the right source.

No one had perfected the art better than Decker.

He followed her in silence, prowling like a caged tiger who had been starved, it was true, and had been taunted with the promise of succor. She was moving, taking a stroll of the perimeter, stopping by each letter. Some caused a swift inhalation—such as the G, which depicted a man and woman sucking each other whilst a bare-breasted woman loomed over them and watched. Others made her eyes go wide, her lips part. The gymnastic determination evidenced by the couple curved around the O—whilst the woman tongued the man's cock—made her speak.

"Oh my!" She pressed her hands to her cheeks, which had flushed darker the farther she traveled.

"Do you like it?" he asked, curious if the erotic art appalled her, intrigued her, or excited her.

Perhaps a commingling of all three?

"It is…" Her words trailed off as she looked to him, wetting her lips. "It is shocking. I have never seen the like. And the acts—some of them—are they truly possible?"

"Quite possible," he assured her, his prick pulsing in his trousers. "And intensely pleasurable."

"*All* of them?" she asked, her brows raised.

She was talking about the R, he supposed. That letter involved two gentlemen and one woman.

He held her gaze. "All of them."

"Have you…" She faltered, her question tapering off.

He smiled. "I have not attempted every position in the alphabet, if that is what you are asking. Pleasure is not the same for everyone, but that is part of what makes it such a wondrous gift."

Decker himself did not find pleasure with men, but he had friends and club members who did so, discreetly.

"You are a conundrum," she said softly, then blushed more furiously.

He grinned—she was so damned fetching, without trying. How had no man before him seized her up, made her his?

Ah, yes. She was young. Not yet twenty.

So dreadfully young.

Too young for a man of his jaded experience, it was certain.

For the moment, Decker thrust that reminder aside. "I could say the same of you, my dear. Tell me more about Lady Jo Danvers whilst you familiarize yourself with my wicked chamber, if you please."

Her expression changed—she looked almost surprised. "What do you want to know?"

Everything.

What a clumsy oaf he was. It occurred to him that he did not know how to woo a woman of her ilk—not just aristocratic, because he had known countless ladies—but delicate, on the cusp of realizing her own sensuality. *Innocent.* Desire was a pounding beast lurking within him, and he was drawn in two separate directions, one urge to preserve her naïveté and the other to ruthlessly, savagely debauch her.

"Tell me about your family," he said, wondering where the devil that particular request had emerged from.

Clearly, the former urge rather than the latter.

It was as if a cloud passed over her countenance. "I have a sister, a brother, and a sister-in-law."

He sensed a story there, and he recalled there was another brother who had died in the not-so-distant past. Decker did not make a habit of following societal gossip, but as many of his businesses were tied to the quality, he did take care in making certain he knew as much of their daily dealings and interconnections as possible.

"You are close to them?" he prodded, giving her room to reveal what she wished to him, but not forcing her into any which would make her uncomfortable.

"I am closest to my sister Alexandra," she said, turning away and continuing her slow perusal of his naughty alphabet series. "We are near in age, and we remained together, under the care of our aunt Lydia for many years. My brother Ravenscroft was saddled with our father's debt and pockets to let until he met my sister-in-law, an American heiress. That was when he brought us to live in London. I do wish he had not left us for so long in the care of our aunt after our parents' deaths. However, I understand the life he was living at the time was ill-suited to young, impressionable ladies being beneath the same roof."

Decker moved with her, keeping a safe distance to prevent himself from snatching Jo up and kissing her senseless then and there. Sadness gave her voice a throaty edge. He detected a note of resentment. For her brother the earl, perhaps. But Decker was more than familiar with Ravenscroft's reputation. For years, he had essentially kept himself from utter penury by selling himself to society women who wanted him in their beds.

"You are displeased with your brother for not looking after you and your sister himself," he observed mildly, forcing himself to remain focused upon their conversation instead of the need for her burning within him.

"It felt as if he had abandoned us," Jo said, casting him a glance over her shoulder that made his gut clench again. "He is a good man, in spite of his reputation. He would do anything for those he loves. My other brother was nothing like him. He was a selfish, greedy, heartless bastard."

The vehemence in Jo's tone took Decker by surprise. Unlike some ladies of his acquaintance, Jo did not relish speaking poorly of others. He had never once heard her issue a cutting remark about another.

"This *other* brother you speak of, he is dead?" Decker asked solemnly, trying not to pry too much, and yet curious.

To be sure, it was an odd conversation to engage in when he had been intending to seduce her—with kisses, at least— this evening. And yet, he could not deny he was intrigued. He wanted to know what made her who she was.

Jo nodded. "He died after attacking Ravenscroft and his countess. His jealousy made him mad. He believed he was the only rightful heir of our father. Perhaps that is true, and perhaps not. Our mother took many lovers. None of us shall ever know the truth."

Here was something interesting indeed, the notion that he and Jo had something deeply in common. That both their births were shadowed with scandal. However, where her mother had been properly wed to the former earl, Jo had been shielded from the brunt of scrutiny and scandal.

But Decker was also quite taken aback by the other half of her revelation—that her dead brother had attacked the earl and countess. One could only surmise it had been with the intent to murder them both.

He found himself moving nearer to her, taking her hands in his. "Damnation, Jo, that is a wretched weight to live with."

Her smile was tremulous. "Life is a wretched weight itself sometimes, is it not? We are given struggles and anguish, and yet there always remains that promise of goodness, looming on the horizon, that rainbow after a punishing rain, that keeps us going on. We have had the promise before, and we know it will come again, even if we are not certain of when or why. I cannot change the past, and therefore, I look to the future."

And what manner of future? He could not help but to wonder as he studied her stunning face. He had thought her lovely at the onset of this arrangement of theirs. But now… Now, he could see, quite plainly, that she was utterly glorious, in the rarest sense. She was strong and brave, with a wisdom beyond her tender years. Like an orchid in the wild, fragile, stunning, resilient.

Decker swallowed hard against a rush of pure longing. "You are far too young to be so world-weary, *bijou*."

She gave him a sad smile. "The same could be said of you, I think."

How sweet she was.

Too sweet for the likes of him.

He would have her anyway. Take some of that sweetness

for his own.

"I am not young at all, darling." Indeed, he felt as if he were positively ancient.

He felt as if he were a lecherous satyr presiding over a fairy queen.

"How old are you, Decker?" she asked then, startling him once more with the use of his preferred name.

"Eight-and-twenty in years," he said softly. "Easily twice that in experience."

"I like that about you." Her smile faded, her gold-chocolate eyes searching his with an intensity that scorched him. "Your eyes are very expressive. You are not the man you would have the world believe you to be, are you? You are so much more."

Bloody hell.

She had robbed him of the ability to speak.

He would show her how much more of him there was. And he would give her all of himself. Decker knew it with a certainty that shook him, despite the hardness of his heart. This slip of a woman, so young and untouched and yet, just as she had said about him, so much *more*.

He tugged her into him, forgetting his plans. Forgetting everything but the need to cover her mouth with his. And she was every bit as frantic. She felt it too, this precious connection, this melding of their very souls. It was as if he had waited all his life for it, so rare and deep and real.

Ridiculous, scoffed the remaining shreds of his rational mind.

Complete rot. You are thinking with your cock. You want her cunny, and all the blood in your body has gone to your prick, leaving your pitiful brain unable to function properly.

Fuck that voice. He forgot all about it as her arms wound around his neck. As her fingers sank into his hair. As she rose on her toes in the same instant he lowered his head.

Their lips collided.

This was different from the kiss in the carriage. It was more powerful, one part communion of bitter and jagged and disappointing pasts, one part acknowledgment of the fierce desire burning between them. Her teeth rasped against his lower lip. Her unbridled hunger was the most potent aphrodisiac he had ever known. He kissed her harder, slanting his mouth over hers.

He knew he ought to take his time, break her in, initiate her. Show her what he wanted and how he wanted it. Learn what she liked. But he could not control himself any more than he could tear his lips from hers. His tongue sank inside, plundering. He kissed her brutally, licking the satin heat of her mouth, her tongue, plunging deep the way he wanted to do with his cock inside her cunny.

She whimpered, but not from shock, and not in protest. Instead, she clutched him harder. She stepped into him, fitting their bodies together more fully. They were well-matched, her shorter, petite curves melting into him. There was raw need in her voice, in the way her tongue moved against his.

It became a battle for power, her thrusting her tongue into his mouth, and him retaliating in kind. They went on, kissing and kissing. One of his hands had found purchase on the nip of her waist and the other cupped the base of her skull, his fingers skewering the dark, silky strands of her simple chignon.

Hair pins were falling at last. Locks unraveled. He kissed her harder, tasting Jo and chocolate. Sweetness and mystery, that was what she tasted like. He sucked on her tongue, then bit her lower lip. He wanted to devour her the way she had eaten up her dessert earlier.

And then, a most unwanted intrusion: a barrage of louder-than-necessary raps on the door. Decker knew what the knocks meant and who was dealing the blows. Macfie. He had asked his man to provide him with a subtle reminder when the time had come to put an end to his clandestine evening with Lady Jo and return her to her home.

Of course the brute would pound on the bloody door loud enough to wake the dead.

Reluctantly, Decker tore his mouth from Jo's. What a beautiful sight she was, all flushed, her lips dark and ripe as a cherry. He had conducted a ruinous assault upon her coiffure. She looked as if she had been properly ravished. A fresh bolt of lust pounded through him in time to Macfie's second round of knocking.

Jo blinked, as if trying to collect herself.

He knew the feeling.

"Who is banging on the door?" she asked, breathless just as he had planned all along.

"Macfie," he growled, every bit as affected as she was.

Decidedly *not* part of the plan, that. When the devil had a woman ever affected him the way Lady Jo Danvers did?

Never, that was when.

"Macfie?" she repeated, in question form.

"Giant redheaded Scotsman," he reminded her. "You have met him on several occasions, I believe?"

"Yes. Of course." She blinked again, before lifting a hand to inspect the damage he had inflicted upon her hair. "Oh dear. My hair pins."

Macfie knocked again. "Sir? Have ye fallen asleep?"

Decker cleared his throat. "No, Macfie. See the carriage readied, if you please."

"Aye, sir!" Macfie hollered from the other side of the door.

Decker winced. Yes, every part of the fellow was brash. But he was deuced loyal and intelligent, and Decker trusted him implicitly in all his business affairs. And now, his personal matters as well.

"Must we go already?" Jo asked, frowning.

He echoed the sentiment. It was as if they had only just begun, and now, he would have to leave her once more when leaving her was the last thing he wanted to do. He had not had the opportunity to show her the rest of the peculiarities— and pleasures—this chamber contained.

He would have to save it for another day, supposing they would have another. The notion struck him like a blow. He was unaccustomed to being with a woman who was not free to accompany him, a woman who could not spend the night with him.

This was different, perilous terrain between them indeed, and not just because of her unwed status as a lady. Also because of the way she made him feel. The things she did to him.

He inhaled slowly, trying to gain some semblance of control over his wildly rampaging thoughts. "Yes, I am afraid we must, if we wish to make certain your return is undetected. I dare not keep you here much longer, no matter how much I would like to."

"Yes, you are right, of course. I cannot afford to be seen returning in such a state. Or at all, for that matter."

She touched her lips then, and though he supposed the gesture was instinctive, he had to stifle a groan at the erotic picture she presented. He wanted to finish what he had begun, to take down the rest of her hair until it was wild down her back, cascading over her shoulders. He wanted to kiss her until their lips ached.

But Macfie's timely rapping would not allow any of that,

regardless of how much he yearned for it. Decker bent to retrieve the hair pins he had scattered from the carpet, making short work of them, before rising.

"Your hair pins, my dear." He offered them to her.

She took them, her fingers grazing his palm as she gathered them up. "Thank you."

Such a small touch, and yet he felt it as thoroughly as a caress on his cock. "I am a decent hand with a lady's hair, if you would like me to attempt to restore the damage."

"I suppose I should not be surprised by that," she said softly. "You are an established rogue, after all."

Damn it, that statement stung more than it ought to have done. He had never been ashamed of his past before. And he was not ashamed by it now, not precisely. Still, there was something about the way she called him a rogue that made him wish he were not.

Bloody odd.

"There are many benefits to being an established rogue," he told her, summoning up a cheeky grin.

But for the life of him, he could not summon up a single one as she turned her back and allowed him to settle her hair into place once more.

Chapter Seven

Ways to be Wicked

1. ~~*Kiss a man until you are breathless.*~~

2. *Arrange for an assignation. Perhaps with Lord Q?*

3. *Get caught in the rain with a gentleman. (This will necessitate the removal of wet garments. Choose said gentleman wisely.)*

4. *Sneak into a gentleman's bedchamber in the midst of the night.*

5. ~~*Go to a gentleman's private apartments.*~~

6. *Spend a night in a gentleman's bed.*

7. *Make love in the outdoors.*

8. *Ask*

Jo could not manage to stifle her yawn.

After two delicious nights of sneaking out of her brother's townhome and flitting about London with Decker, she was tired. Tired and excited and filled with a tangled mess of yearning and newfound desire.

Mr. Elijah Decker was many things. Scoundrel. Rakehell. Skilled kisser. Strike that—*exceedingly* skilled kisser. Handsome rogue. Sinfully charming. Observant. Peculiar. Witty.

Tempting. So very, very tempting.

Sigh. What was it about him that was turning her into a ninny? Mere days ago, she had considered him the enemy.

And now? Now, he was decidedly something else. Something she would not contemplate.

"Is something amiss, dearest Jo?" Her friend Callie's voice interrupted her musings. "You look as if you are about to fall asleep into your tea."

Jo was sure she was flushing. Again. Ever since a certain man had entered her life, she had been doing a more than reasonable amount of that.

Lady Helena Davenport, who had joined them for tea at Callie's townhome this afternoon, chimed in before Jo could answer. "Please tell us it is something exciting that has you nodding off at your cup and not that we are boring you dreadfully."

Golden-haired and statuesque, Lady Helena was a welcome addition to their coterie of friends. She was outspoken and had an excellent sense of humor.

"Of course you are not boring me dreadfully," Jo denied. "I have spent a few nights staying up late reading. That is all."

"What book is it?" Callie asked. "I have been looking for something to keep me occupied while Sinclair is busy arranging improvements upon Helston Hall."

Drat. Perhaps she ought to have crafted a better excuse. Jo had not read a book in ages.

"It is the most entertaining book," she hedged, her voice sounding weak, even to her own ears. "Filled with inappropriate humor and…desserts."

That was a rather pathetic attempt, Josephine.

Moreover, it sounded as if she had just described her evening with Decker, *sans* kisses of course.

"What is the title?" Lady Helena asked. "I am in desperate need of an escape from the tragedy otherwise known as my life."

Unfortunately for Lady Helena, her father was pressuring

her to marry one of his political cronies, the odious Lord Hamish White. Lord Hamish was an unforgiving, cold stickler for propriety who promised to make a lively young woman like Lady Helena utterly miserable. A marriage between them would end in one of two ways: she would make him mad with her refusal to bend to his dictates, or he would crush her spirits.

Jo cleared her throat, searching her mind for the title of the last book she had read. When nothing came to mind, she decided to do what she must—invent one. "*The Devil of London*, I believe it is called."

There. One could only hope Callie and Lady Helena would forget all about the book's title before going off in search of it. Moreover, it was a fitting way to describe the man who was haunting her thoughts and keeping her up so late at night. Not just with their illicit jaunts. After she returned home, she would lay awake in her lonely bed for hours, staring at the ceiling, thinking of *him*, and tossing and turning and burning alive.

"Sounds thrilling," Callie said, taking a sip of tea. "I shall borrow your copy when you are finished reading it."

"And I will borrow it from you afterward," Lady Helena decided.

Wonderful. Now her friends were expecting to borrow a book that did not exist. She ought to have known better than to offer a prevarication instead of the truth.

"Er, it is a very long book," she said. "Long and exceedingly complicated. I have many, many pages awaiting me. Indeed, I will probably be reading it for several more weeks, at least."

Lady Helena frowned. "Complicated? I thought you said it was entertaining and filled with inappropriate humor."

"And desserts," Callie added, grinning. "I have been

ravenous for desserts recently. All I want is sugar and kedgeree, all day long. It is the strangest thing, I vow. Poor Sinclair has been suffering through breakfasts and dinners of kedgeree each night for the last week alone on my behalf."

Callie was expecting her first child with her husband, and though her delicate condition was cleverly hidden beneath the fabric of her handsome gown, she would soon begin to show. Although she had been ill at the onset of her pregnancy, recently, she had been spending her days looking like a glowing goddess.

"That is because Lord Sinclair is a wonderful husband," Lady Helena said with a wistful smile. "I am happy for you, that you have been fortunate to marry a man who adores and worships you. When I think of spending the rest of my life tied to Lord Hamish, I want to retch."

Thank heavens they seemed to have fled the topic of the nonexistent book which was decidedly not the reason for her recent lack of sleep. While Lady Helena was a newer acquaintance, Callie knew Jo far too well, and Jo was more than aware her story would collapse like a house of sticks with too much prodding from her friend.

She was not ready to reveal the nature of her agreement with Decker to Callie yet. Not to anyone. Keeping it a secret between herself and Decker made it seem somehow more intimate and potent, all at once. Besides, she was certain Callie would deliver a stern sermon on all the reasons why Jo should not trust Decker. Jo had already told herself as much too many times to count. The man's charm had blasted right through any impediment, including Jo's good sense.

"Surely your father will see to reason and not force you into marrying Lord Hamish," Callie was saying to Lady Helena now, frowning mightily. "Can he not see you would be miserable with the man? You deserve to find a husband who will appreciate your wit, a husband who will not dull your shine but will seek to enhance it. Lord Hamish deserves a bride who is as salty, crusty, and sleep-inducing as he is."

"That is rather harsh of you, Callie," Jo interjected dryly. "I think Lord Hamish deserves to marry one of his own kind. An eel."

Lady Helena laughed wryly. "I do wish Papa shared your opinion of the man. But I am afraid my father is more concerned with his political connections and the state of his coffers than he has ever been about his daughter. I am nothing but an impediment to him, unless I can prove myself useful. As he has told me on numerous occasions, a daughter's worth is in the credit she does her father."

"Forgive me for being blunt, but your father ought to be tossed out a window," Callie said. "You are not a cow to be sold at the market. You are your own person, and your worth is immeasurable."

"There must be some way to ruin your father's plans," Jo suggested, grateful to have something to think about *other* than Decker for the time being.

"I have begged and pleaded, and so have my brother and mother." Lady Helena rolled her lips inward, as if suppressing her emotions.

"You need to ruin your reputation," Callie said. "Lord Hamish detests impropriety. His reputation is spotless. If you cause as many scandals as possible, he will no longer want you as his wife."

"That is the perfect plan," Jo agreed. "You need someone who is wicked. A rogue of the worst order who will agree to be caught in a compromising position with you."

"That could work," Lady Helena said slowly, seemingly turning the notion over in her mind. "It is something I have considered, but I have never had the daring to try it. Nor had

I an inkling of who I ought to enlist for the task. My social circle is frightfully small."

"I have just the man in mind." Callie grinned, her voice triumphant. "Mr. Elijah Decker, Lord Sinclair's good friend."

"No!" Jo blurted with more vehemence than necessary.

Two pairs of eyes shot to her.

Drat. You are not acting suspiciously at all, Josephine.

"Why not?" Callie continued. "He is the perfect gentleman for such a job. He would not think twice about ruining a lady at her request if it is for the noble good. His reputation is already quite dark and I—"

"No," Jo repeated, interrupting though she knew she should hold her tongue. But the thought of beautiful, golden-haired Lady Helena and Decker together was enough to split her in two. "That would never do. Mr. Decker is…his reputation is too outré, certainly. He is too much of a rogue. Lady Helena needs someone else."

Someone who was *not* Decker.

Both Callie and Lady Helena were eying her strangely.

"You only need to ruin your reputation enough so that Lord Hamish will not want to marry you," she added for good measure. "You do not want to damage yourself for any future prospects. What if you wish to marry someone else someday, have children of your own?"

"Improper behavior with Mr. Decker would not necessarily ruin Lady Helena for all others," Callie countered. "Besides, what if she and Mr. Decker like each other? What if they fall in love and wish to marry? I do adore matchmaking. You know, I hold myself responsible for my brother marrying his wife. If I had not thrown them together as often as possible, they would have both been too stubborn to see they belonged together."

What if Decker and Lady Helena fell in love?

Now it was Jo who wanted to retch at a notion.

"That would be horrible, Callie," she snapped. "Why should Lady Helena wish to marry a man who keeps erotic pictures on the walls of his library?"

"What manner of erotic pictures?" Lady Helena asked, sounding intrigued.

"Yes, what manner of erotic pictures?" Callie probed. "And how would you know what is hanging in his library?"

Blast. Collect yourself, Josephine. First, you invented a book, then you interrupted your dearest friend, and now you are treading dangerously near to revealing you were in Decker's library, of all things.

She cleared her throat. "That was the rumor I heard, I believe. And also in his club, the Black Souls."

"I wonder what is depicted in them," Lady Helena said, then flushed prettily. "Oh dear, I do hope the two of you will not think me shockingly forward and vulgar. My poor mother would be horrified."

Callie laughed. "If you have not noticed by now, my dear, we are hardly cut from the same cloth as the paragons of society. And truthfully, I wonder what is depicted in them as well. I do not recall ever having been inside Mr. Decker's library as yet, and of course, I have never gone to the Black Souls. Perhaps I will have Sinclair take me one of these days…"

But Jo did not miss the speculative look her friend sent in her direction. And nor did she fool herself that she was not flushing. She was dreadful at keeping secrets, and Callie knew it.

Jo busied herself with taking a sip from her tea, which was growing cool, studiously avoiding her friend's gaze lest she read too much in Jo's eyes. Namely, the scorching kisses she had shared with Decker the night before, in his carriage and at his club. She had gone home and immediately crossed item number one off her list.

"I have an excellent idea!" Callie exclaimed, grinning like the cat who had gotten into the proverbial cream. "Sinclair and I shall host a dinner party. I will see that Mr. Decker is included. That way, you can see if the two of you suit. And if you do, my brother and his duchess are hosting a country house party in a few weeks' time. I will make certain you are all included in the guest list."

Jo liked the idea of more opportunities to see Decker. Perhaps the potential to find him alone and cross off more items on her list. However, the aim of throwing him together with Lady Helena aggrieved her mightily. How to suggest as much without garnering further suspicions from her friend, however?

"Do you have anyone else in mind?" Jo asked Lady Helena. "Another man who might aid you in your quest to make yourself decidedly *de trop* to the officious Lord Hamish?"

Lady Helena's gaze lowered to her teacup, her lashes sweeping over her eyes. "There is one, but I fear he would not enlist himself in helping me to accomplish such a feat. He is close friends with my brother and I have known him since I was a girl. The Earl of Huntingdon, but he is nearly betrothed to another."

Jo's hopes flagged. Huntingdon was notoriously proper and cold. He seemed a lost cause.

"I shall invite him as well," Callie decided. "The worst he can do is refuse. I do, however, believe him to be friends with Westmorland. Surely we can use the connection in our favor."

"Thank you for wanting to aid me," Lady Helena said with a tremulous smile. "I am not certain anything can save me from the wretched future awaiting me."

Jo knew a stinging rush of shame. She was being selfish.

After all, she was not being forced into an unwanted marriage. Her brother Julian would never do such a thing, as much as he blustered and threatened. He was merely overly protective of his sisters.

And it was not as if Decker was *hers*, was it?

No matter how much something deep inside her suddenly wished he were.

DECKER DETESTED DINNER parties.

He found them appallingly boring and a tedious waste of otherwise useful time.

Unless he was the one hosting, that was. But he had made an art of offering his guests an experience unlike any they would have elsewhere. There had been the time his chef had shaped all the desserts into miniature bubbies. The evening when the famous American actress Eva Silver had dined completely in the nude alongside his guests could not be forgotten. Occasionally, his guests could select their desserts from the body of a naked woman. It made for an excellent table scape. Besides, how many stuffy lords could honestly say they had plucked a berry tartlet from a beautiful woman's rouged nipple?

But the table before him, carefully decorated with flowers and whatnots and sparkling silver and candles and a bloody floating miniature boat in the center, was decidedly not as interesting. To be fair, the Countess of Sinclair was remarkably adept as a hostess. She possessed a natural charm that made every gathering she helmed smoother than the ordinary dull societal events he had occasionally attended in the past because some lord or other wished to solicit advice or to sell him something.

Even so, there was one reason he had decided to attend his second dinner party hosted by Sin and his countess in as many weeks. For as much as Decker loved Sin like a brother, that love had a limit, and engaging in societal nonsense more than once a month was it.

However, Sin had let it slip that Lady Jo Danvers would be in attendance.

What Decker had not anticipated was that Jo would be seated far enough away from him to render conversing with her nearly impossible without hollering over the bouquets of roses and the flickering candles and the damned soup tureen. In keeping with Lady Sinclair's standard flouting of convention, the guests were seated in order of precedence, but rather injudiciously—at least, to Decker's mind—sprinkled about the table. That was why, he told himself, he remained so damned nettled as he watched Jo engaging in conversation with the Earl of Huntingdon, who he could have sworn was either already or nearly betrothed.

At least she had taken a break from speaking to Quenington, who was somehow present as well.

No assignation attempts with Lord Q in your future, my girl, he thought grimly as he forked up a bite of rice and smoked fish. Kedgeree, he realized belatedly, having paid absolutely no attention to most of the courses thus far. For dinner? Another one of Lady Sinclair's idiosyncrasies, he supposed, as it was ordinarily a breakfast dish.

Anyway, he cared naught for the food gracing his plate. All he cared about was *her*. As soon as he got away from the damned table, and as soon as he could find his way to the drawing room, or the music room, or wherever the hell he could find a moment to speak with her, Lady Jo was his.

Yes, the lady is mine.

That sounded right. It *felt* right, to his very core, straight to the marrow of him. Even if she was smiling at Huntingdon in a way that made Decker long to smash his fist into the sanctimonious bastard's teeth. Decker had been waiting to arrange their next meeting because he had wanted to put some much-needed time and distance between that last, incendiary encounter and their next.

But seeing her again this evening proved to him that he could not wait. His hunger for her had only grown in the hours since they had parted ways after he had escorted her into the shadows of Ravenscroft's townhome.

"Mr. Decker?"

The soft voice at his side tore him, at last, from his frenzied musings. Frenzied? Hell—more like jealous, possessive, mad. Yes, those descriptors were far more apt. He was clearly in need of distraction.

He turned to Lady Helena Davenport, who was tall, blonde, and garrulous—quite the opposite of the pocket-sized, dark-haired, quiet Lady Jo. "Forgive me my deplorable manners, my lady. I am doing my utmost to improve them, but I am afraid it may be a hopeless cause."

Her lips twitched with amusement, her lively emerald eyes dancing. "Surely not hopeless, Mr. Decker? However, I must confess I am rather dismayed you did not hear my discussion of the latest bonnets from Paris."

The latest bonnets from Paris?

He could not contain his grimace. "Truly?"

She chuckled, the sound low and throaty. If he were not so thoroughly besotted with Jo, he would have been attracted to Lady Helena. She was an incredibly lovely woman. But she was not the woman who had been driving him to distraction for the last few days. Or, if he were brutally honest with himself, ever since he had first met her.

"I was teasing, Mr. Decker," Lady Helena said. "You do

not look like the sort of gentleman who would appreciate discussing the vagaries of millinery."

He grinned back at her. There was something delightful about her, and he wished he could find distraction in her charms for the rest of the dinner, but he did not fool himself. "Quite discerning of you, Lady Helena."

"Tell me more about yourself, if you please, Mr. Decker," Lady Helena invited. "I find myself curious about your businesses."

What an odd bird. Ladies did not ordinarily trouble themselves to worry about something so common as business.

"I own a club, of course," he began mildly. Everyone knew he owned the Black Souls, after all. "I also own a publisher and a shipping venture, along with various factories."

That was not the extent of his empire, of course. He also owned orphanages, tenements, and two hospitals, including one dedicated to children which had yet to open its doors. But those were hardly paying propositions. The tenements had required vast improvements to make them livable, and he only charged the residents what they could afford, which was a pittance. The orphanages and hospital brought in no revenue at all.

But it would hardly do for anyone to find out about those. He had a reputation to uphold, after all.

"Oh yes," Lady Helena was saying. "You are the new publisher for the Lady's Suffrage Society."

"You are a member of the society as well, I take it?" he asked politely.

"I am." Lady Helena smiled broadly, revealing the tiniest space between her two front teeth. Far from being an imperfection, this flaw somehow rendered her more charming. "Lady Sinclair persuaded me to join, and I am so pleased to be a part of such a worthy cause."

It *was* indeed a worthy cause, and it was one of the many things about Jo that appealed to Decker. She was not an empty-headed society miss, more concerned with the next ball and the newest gown she had commissioned than the world around her.

Blast. He hazarded a glance in Jo's direction to find her gazing back at him. Their stares clashed with the same charge that happened whenever they touched. The intensity awed and shook him, as always. Her lips were pinched, he realized, a slight frown marring her otherwise smooth brow.

Had she taken note of him chatting with Lady Helena? Did she disapprove? Was it too much to hope she was stewing in the same jealousy which had been afflicting him for the duration of this bloody dinner?

Decker inclined his head to her in a mocking salute, and then he turned his attention back to Lady Helena. "Tell me more about the Lady's Suffrage Society, my lady."

The rest of the dinner passed slowly, but at least with the accompaniment of Lady Helena's lively conversation. If Decker continued to steal glances at Jo, it could hardly be helped. And if his blood boiled each time he caught her speaking with Hungtingdon, it could hardly be helped either.

There was the very real, decidedly unwanted, possibility that his wallflower had found her wings and was about to fly far from him.

Decker did not like it. Not one whit.

BECAUSE HE WAS a complete lunatic, Decker was lurking in a darkened chamber, awaiting his prey. The ladies had withdrawn, leaving the gentlemen to their port at the conclusion of dinner. But he had no wish to exchange words with a passel of lords, especially not lords who were as insufferably self-righteous as the Earl of Huntingdon. It was a miracle the prick had even condescended to attend a dinner party being hosted by Sin, a man who had been a societal outcast until recently.

Besides, Decker could not be certain he would be able to avoid planting a fist in the bastard's mouth. To say nothing of Quenington, who had been eying Jo like a pie he longed to devour every time Decker had glanced in his direction.

He had taken a gamble in excusing himself from the gentlemen after he had spied Jo heading to the lady's withdrawing room. Alone. Still, it was a gamble he was willing to make.

Especially when the reward came back into view.

He was probably watching her with the same ravenous hunger Quenington had exhibited earlier, and though he hated himself, it did not stop Decker from striking when she neared his hiding place. He stepped out of the chamber, slid his arm around her waist, clamped one hand over her mouth to stifle any cry of surprise she might make, and yanked her into the room with him.

He closed the door quietly behind them, and then spun them as one, not stopping until her back was against the door.

"No hollering," he warned her, *sotto voce*. "It is me."

Her lips were deuced soft beneath his bare palm. Her breath was hot and moist. Grounding his molars, he removed his hand.

"Decker!" she gasped his name, outrage seething in her voice. "What in heaven's name are you doing?"

Excellent question. Making a fool of himself? Possibly. But when had that ever stopped him before when it came to this woman? The answer was simple, pitiful.

Never.

"Garnering a moment alone with you after suffering through three hours of dinner party hell. What does it look like?" he grumbled.

Had she truly believed he would pass at the opportunity to have her within his grasp after having watched her all evening from afar?

"I have no idea what anything looks like," she shot back. "You hauled me into an unlit chamber. It is darker than ink in here."

Admittedly, his choice of location had not been ideal. However, there was something about having Jo in his arms in the black-as-pitch darkness that honed all his senses to a heightened state of awareness and had his cock twitching to life.

Right. Who was he fooling? His cock was always hard when he was in her presence, and it had nothing to do with the darkness. It had everything to do with her, and this damned obsession of his.

Decker was no stranger to obsessions; however, in the past, his compulsions had always been limited to pictures, paintings, works of art. He had to have them, and then he hung them on his wall, and the fierce need was gone. Because they had been claimed. They were his.

"I wanted to speak to you," he told her then, unable to keep his hands from traveling from her waist, up the small of her back. "You were too busy having your little tête-à-tête with Huntingdon for me to get in a word at dinner."

"You were too far away from me," she protested coolly. "If I had wanted to speak to you, I would have been required to holler."

She was not wrong.

But he was still frustrated at having been seated so

damned far away from her, and neither did he like the stiffness in her form, the ice in her voice. "You would not have had to pay the blighter so much attention, however."

Her hands settled upon his chest, neither pushing him away nor drawing him nearer. "Do you mean in the same fashion you were hanging upon Lady Helena's every word?"

Hmm. How intriguing.

He found the silken skin of her nape, caressing her there. "Were you envying Lady Helena?"

"No," she snapped quietly. "I was enjoying my conversation with Lord Huntingdon."

Stubborn creature.

"He was looking at you as if you were dessert," he groused before he could think better of the words. "I thought he was already betrothed to someone…a Lady Melissa…or was it Amelia?"

Blast, but those words revealed too much. He knew it the moment they left his tongue. They seemed to hang there, between them, alive with meaning.

"Decker," she said, a smile in her voice. "Never tell me you were jealous tonight of the Earl of Huntingdon."

Jealous? Decker?

Fuck. Yes, he was jealous.

"You scarcely glanced in my direction," he said, fully aware he sounded like a petulant child, and damn well feeling like one too.

He was not accustomed to being ignored.

"I did enough to take note of all the smiles you were sending Lady Helena," she countered, her fingers gliding over his chest in slow, maddening strokes.

"I was distracting myself from the torture of being seated so far away from you," he admitted like a complete fool.

"Did you miss me?" she whispered.

"Every bloody second since I saw you last," he breathed.

He had to kiss her. Now.

One dip of his head, unerringly, even in the darkness, and he sealed his mouth over hers. Her fingers tightened on his waistcoat, drawing him nearer. Orange blossom and the seductive scent of woman filled his nostrils. He told himself to go slowly, tenderly.

But the moment her lips parted, the already-frayed reins of his control snapped. He sucked her lower lip into his mouth, then nipped. She moaned. Everything else faded away—the dinner party, their fellow guests nearby, the real possibility of discovery at any moment.

All that remained was desire and the woman in his arms. Each time he held her, she felt more like home than the last. Stupid, this affinity he shared with her. Reckless. Savage and wild, too. Impossible to stop.

Runaway locomotive, barreling down the line—that was what Decker became as he sank his tongue into her mouth. Her tongue rubbed against his in sinuous seduction. She tasted of chocolate and raspberries from the dessert course. He pinned her to the door, without thought, without compunction, and ravaged her mouth with kisses.

She clawed at him like a ferocious wild cat. His hands were all over her, memorizing the curve of her breast, the softness of her throat, her waist, her silken hair. This time, he restrained himself and just narrowly avoided plucking at her hair pins. Some faint part of his brain recalled they were at a social function, that this could not go on, and that if she returned to the drawing room looking as if she had been thoroughly ravished, tongues would wag.

But for now, this moment, he had her right where he wanted her. Her gown was crushed between them, and he had never been more tempted to lift a woman's skirts and plunge into her cunny than he was now. His heart pounded and his cock ached with thwarted lust.

You cannot take her against a door.

No, he could not. And so he kissed her instead. He staked his claim upon her. Kissed her until they were both as desperate for more as they had been the night before. And then, a noise in the hall—voices—gradually filtered through the fog of desire hazing his mind.

He forced himself to stop.

To release her.

Decker took a step in retreat, and slammed straight into the punishing edge of a table. He bit his lip to stifle the howl of surprised pain that threatened to be unleashed. *Fucking hell, that hurt!* The next time he hauled Jo into a chamber, he would make certain there was a goddamn lamp lit within it.

The next time?

Your time is limited with her, arsehole.

"Decker?" she whispered hesitantly. "Have you injured yourself?"

"Do not worry, *bijou*," he returned, rubbing his aching rear where the offending table had bit him. "My arse does not hurt nearly as much as my cock does."

Or my ego.

He ought not to have spoken with such vulgar familiarity with her, and he knew it. But she was the one who wanted to be wicked, was she not? Besides, he had already said far worse to her, and he had shown her his collection of erotic art.

"Shall I rub it for you?" she asked.

Decker almost swallowed his tongue. His prick twitched.

"My arse or my cock?" he could not resist querying, his voice hoarse and thick with lust.

Good God, she could rub both for him. Either. And never stop.

The voices grew nearer, reminding him of the necessity that this interlude between them—regardless of how delicious it had been and how much he did not wish for it to end—had to come to a halt.

"Which hurts the most?" his minx dared to ask.

Bloody hell, he had already debauched her.

And his cockstand was like a granite obelisk in his trousers at the moment. He could not step out of the chamber in such a state.

"Damn it, Jo." He stalked back toward her, wishing he could finish what they had begun. Knowing they could not. "You are a vixen, do you know that? But as much as I would like to linger here with you, doing so is unwise. You want to be wicked, not to be thoroughly, ineffably ruined, and even if you are ruined, I am not the man for you. I have no intention of marrying. You should return to the ladies in the drawing room."

"I should," she agreed. But then, she surprised him by rising on her toes and giving him a quick, chaste kiss.

Likely, she had been aiming for his lips, but in the darkness, she only found his chin. He grinned anyway. "Go before we are discovered."

The voices had faded back down the hall.

She spun about, a swirl of silk. "Decker?"

He gritted his teeth. If she remained in this damned room for any longer than the next minute, he would have her on her back on the carpets, her petticoats raised, his tongue on her cunny.

He inhaled slowly. "Yes, Jo?"

"Do you like Lady Helena?" her question was hesitant.

"Not in the way I like you, *bijou*," he told her tenderly, in spite of himself. "Now go, and no more flirting with Huntingdon."

Her hand was on the latch—he heard it turning.

Before she opened the door, she threw one last parting shot that left him reeling. "I like you, too, Decker. Quite a bit more than I ought."

And then, she was gone, leaving him in the murk with nothing but a raging cockstand, a smarting arse, and her words, sinking their talons deep into the recesses of his forgotten heart.

Chapter Eight

"$\mathcal{W}$E HAVE RECENTLY been blessed with many crates of books for the children, my ladies," said Mrs. Chisholm, the proprietress of the orphanage where Jo, her sister Alexandra, and her sister-in-law Clara were paying a visit. "They were donated quite generously by a benefactor who wishes to remain anonymous."

"Books for the children?" Clara asked in her calm, sweet American drawl. "I was under the impression most of the children were incapable of reading."

"Yet another blessed improvement we can thank the Lord for bestowing upon us," Mrs. Chisholm said.

Apple-cheeked and perpetually flushed, she had a kindly smile and compassionate gray eyes she hid behind wire-rimmed spectacles. She made an odd swishing sound as she walked, and Jo could not be certain if it was the result of her shoes or her undergarments, but whatever the case, Mrs. Chisholm seemed to genuinely care for her charges in a way her predecessor decidedly had not.

"The same benefactor has been generous enough to provide the older children with teachers," Mrs. Chisholm added. "He is of the firm belief that orphans should have the means of bettering themselves. He also provided us with a handsome new rosewood piano, the finest model, with the intention that the children should spend some time gaining instruction in music. A most worthy endeavor, indeed, and ever so much better than the workhouse, you understand."

Jo agreed heartily with the benefactor in that orphans ought to have the same opportunity in their lives as other children. Her heart ached each time she visited the orphanage. But whilst they had been visiting the orphanage for a few months now, these sudden gifts were as much of a surprise as it had been when the orphanage had suddenly acquired a new patron who had placed the softhearted Mrs. Chisholm in charge of the entire affair.

And there was something about the proprietress's revelations which brought to mind the last man she would have ever supposed might play secret benefactor to an orphanage. New books and a rosewood piano? Decker owned a publisher and a piano factory.

"This mysterious benefactor sounds like a man with a very good heart indeed," observed Clara as Mrs. Chisholm led them to the large chamber where the older children often gathered.

"Oh yes, Lady Ravenscroft," the proprietress agreed. "The purest heart. So many are willing to forget all about the plight of these poor, beloved children. We are most grateful for the generous hearts of your ladyships and Lord Ravenscroft and our other benefactors. I will go and fetch the children for your ladyships, if you do not mind waiting?"

With a curtsy, Mrs. Chisholm departed the room, leaving Jo, Alexandra, and Clara alone. Jo's mind instantly began to wander.

Ordinarily, Jo took great delight in their weekly visits to this and a handful of other London orphanages. There had been a time, not long ago—before Julian had married Clara and received her massive dowry—when their familial munificence had been an impossibility. They had been dreadfully impoverished, the Ravenscroft estates in ruin. Being in such vastly different circumstances had left Jo feeling not just thankful but as if she ought to help others in some way, now that she could.

But today, she would be the first to admit that her heart was not entirely devoted to the task at hand. It had been two days since she had last seen Decker. Since he had left her stewing in misery whilst he flirted with Lady Helena. Since she had stolen kisses with him in the darkened room at the Sinclair townhome following dinner.

Since he had told her he had no intention of marrying.

That last bit was not meant to bother her.

She ought not to care a fig whether or not he ever intended to wed. She had already decided he was the last sort of man she would ever wish to make her husband. Had she not?

Yes, of course.

The two of them suited in certain ways, but in many other senses, they were quite ill-matched. It would be the mésalliance of the century, an earl's sister and an earl's bastard. A man who was an unrepentant rakehell with a wicked streak the size of England and a woman who was…

Well, that thought rather brought her up short. It occurred to Jo that she had no idea who she was. Not truly.

And why had Decker failed to send any notes in the two days since that reckless encounter in the dark chamber? The way he had pinned her body to the door with his still haunted her. She had lain awake for the past two nights, thinking of nothing else.

But he had been strangely silent.

"Jo?" Alexandra prodded her quietly, tearing her from her troubled thoughts. "Would you like to play the piano, or sing? You know I am wretched at singing, but Clara has volunteered herself to read, which leaves the two of us with the musical bits."

"You *are* a dreadful singer," Jo agreed without bite, for it was an undeniable truth that her science-minded sister was far more at home in her sphere of studying and experimenting than in any of the feminine arts.

Music was not one of Alexandra's gifts. Careful thought, objective thinking, and rigorous scientific study? Yes—those were much more the sorts of things at which Alexandra excelled.

"I attempted to argue with her whilst you were gathering cobwebs in your mind, but she is feeling rather ungainly these days and wishes a more comfortable seat than the piano bench. As I shall be in her place all too soon, I deemed it wise to be sympathetic," her sister explained.

Clara was heavy with child, her first baby with Jo and Alexandra's brother Julian set to arrive soon. However, in true Clara form, she refused to retreat for her lying in until, as she phrased it, *I am half the size of London and am feeling miserably bovine.*

"Soon, the two of you will have to take my place," Clara said with that airy, sugary-sweet accent, the one that never failed to wrap their brother Julian around her little finger.

In all the best ways, of course.

Julian had been an out-and-out rogue. Clara was just what he needed, rather in the way Lord Harry had been just what Alexandra needed.

Also in the way Decker is just what I need.

No. She must not think such perilous, foolish thoughts. Decker did not want to marry. And neither did she wish to wed him. She was too busy attempting to experience her life. To break free from the ties which had always bound her.

"I am afraid we shall have to leave her here and decamp to the music room after the miniature menaces arrive,"

Alexandra added with a frown

"You shall have a miniature menace of your own soon," Jo could not resist reminding her sister, grinning.

Alexandra's smile was satisfied and warm. Her hand settled over the subtle rounding of her belly. "Such a peculiar notion, tiny version of ourselves, is it not? The children are all quite dear, however. The lads are the most exuberant of the lot. I say *menaces* affectionately, of course. But I do hope I have a daughter."

Jo chuckled as the children arrived, Mrs. Chisholm not far behind them. Jo noted that each one appeared to be wearing dresses and short pants and shirts which were not ragged or ill-fitting or stained.

"Our benefactor also has provided each of the children with new clothing," the proprietress said proudly, "as you will no doubt have taken note."

Generous benefactor indeed, Jo thought, her suspicions mounting. What manner of man would have the coin to so thoroughly aid an orphanage thus? As she and her sister, along with their small cadre of children, reached the room housing the rosewood piano, Jo had her answer.

The piano was identical to the new model standing in Decker's club's wicked room.

She trailed her finger over the lone, gilt letter D emblazoned upon the polished case. His words returned to her.

"This piano is our newest, one of only a few of its kind—Lord and Lady Sinclair are in possession of one, and there is another as well, aside from this," he had said.

Just when she had been convinced it was impossible for him to burrow into her heart any deeper, he did.

Oh, Decker. What other secrets do you keep?

THREE INTERMINABLE, PAINFUL, endless days.

That was how much time had passed since Decker had last felt Lady Jo Danvers' lips beneath his. Since he had last held her in his arms. Since she had uttered those terrifying, ruinous words in that darkened chamber. Words which had been echoing in his mind ever since she had first spoken them.

I like you, too, Decker. Quite a bit more than I ought.

She bloody *liked* him. And not just physically. That was what her quiet little confession had meant. She did not just feel desire for him, that aching want he perpetually felt in his cock and ballocks whenever he thought of her or spent a damned second in her intoxicating presence.

He took a sip of his coffee, attempting to concentrate on the papers before him, and grimaced. "Macfie!"

His bellow was loud enough to hurt his own ears, it was true.

The door to his office opened. His stalwart *aide-de-camp* poked his head into the chamber. "Ye hollered, sir?"

"I did not holler, Macfie," he corrected icily, though it was a wretched lie. "I called for you."

"Aye, Mr. Decker." Macfie raised a bushy orange brow. "And if that is what ye're tellin' yerself, go on. What is it that ye need, sir?"

"My coffee is cold," he said, unable to suppress his disgust.

"And well I'm sure 'tis," Macfie dared to tell him. "I brought it tae ye an hour ago or more. Ye dawdle, and yer coffee goes cold, just like my sainted Ma always told all her bairns."

Decker raised a brow. "I thought you had no siblings, Macfie."

Macfie locked him in a death stare. "Aye, and just as I said. 'Tis what she told all her bairns."

Decker huffed out an exasperated sigh whilst extracting his pocket watch to check the time. Surely he had not spent the last hour lost in thoughts of Lady Jo Danvers, ignoring all the papers awaiting him on his desk, consumed by his need for her…

Fucking hell.

He had. Worse, his ears were hot. He refused to believe the warmth on his cheekbones meant he was flushing. He had not blushed since he had been a lad touching his first cunny.

"Did your mother also tell her bairns they ought to be polite to their employers?" he demanded of Macfie.

"Nay, sir." Macfie had the daring to wink. "She told us we should make ourselves indispensable tae the cantankerous sons of bitches. Ma's words, sir. Not mine, ye ken."

Decker's nostrils flared. Macfie was lucky he was so damned valuable. And that Decker liked him and his excessively bushy eyebrows. "Have you considered trimming those monstrosities, Macfie? They bloody well look like a pair of ravenous caterpillars about to make your eyes into their meal. A proper razor ought to settle it, I should think."

"Not with the eyebrows again." Macfie's eyes narrowed to a blue-eyed glare. "I'll be fetching the fresh coffee for ye then, Mr. Decker. I hope ye shan't burn yer lordly tongue upon it."

He was sure Macfie would make certain the coffee was roughly the temperature of lava. The man was deuced protective of his eyebrows.

"We both know there is nothing lordly about me," Decker told him, frowning. Once born on the wrong side of the blanket, forever tarnished. "Go, then. You are aware how much I dislike cold coffee, Macfie."

"About as much as I like threats tae my puir eyebrows." Waggling the facial feature in question, Macfie took his leave.

"And do not slam the damned—"

The calamitously loud closing of the door drowned out the rest of Decker's words.

"—door," he finished, glaring at the offensive portal.

One would think that by the ripe age of thirty, Macfie would have grown accustomed to his own strength. Decker sighed and rose from his desk, needing to pace. He felt restless and nettled and confused.

He also felt as if he needed to bed a woman.

Nights—and mornings and days, too—spent frigging his hand were not enough. Surely that was the problem. Surely his unquenched lust—that natural urge which had raged and plagued him since he was a lad—was the reason his chest was tight, the reason he was on edge, the reason everything irritated, the reason he had snapped at Macfie, the reason he could not concentrate on his business matters.

Any woman would do, would she not?

He paced to the end of his office again, then back up and down thrice more. There were ladies in his acquaintance who would be happy to be called upon for such a favor. Susannah, the blonde actress who had last acted as the serving vessel at one of his dinner parties, for instance. Her bubbies were the size of melons, and she knew how to suck his cock straight down her throat.

Strangely, the thought of her deflated his cockstand.

What in the hell was *this*?

He stopped in his tracks, staring down at his trousers, bemused. Perhaps he had merely needed to work off some of his steam by striding up and down the length of the chamber several dozen times, barreling locomotive style. Yes, that had clearly been the solution.

Decker sighed with relief. And as soon as he had his warm coffee in hand, he could proceed with his day. The ledgers would not balance themselves, and neither would the stack of expenditures which needed to be reviewed and settled. He stalked back toward his desk.

Lady Jo Danvers had nothing to do with the incessantly rigid state of his prick. He was not wallowing in lust that was for her and her alone. It was merely natural. Scientific. His body needed to empty itself of the poison, and now that he had expended some of his energy in pacing, he could happily think about Jo without…

He stilled. His cock had twitched back to life. Merely at the thought of the woman. And he had not allowed himself to think about her kisses or the silken heat of her mouth, the way her tongue had writhed against his, and those delicious sounds she made.

Shite.

He was completely erect again, pulsing with the need for release.

"No, no, no," he snapped down at his offending cock, which had never been this difficult to control. "What the hell is wrong with you?"

"Sir?"

Decker jumped and bit out another curse as his gaze landed on Macfie. The hulking Scotsman stood on the threshold, bearing a cup of coffee, looking as if he had just realized he had swallowed arsenic and the knowledge of his certain death had walloped him.

Bloody, bloody, fucking, damned, soul-rotting damnation.

His man of affairs had just caught him *yelling* at his own prick.

Beelzebub on a biscuit.

Decker cleared his throat and straightened. At least the sight of Macfie's effusive eyebrows was enough to wilt his cock once more. "For once, you have opened the door soundlessly, Macfie. I applaud you. Now, then. Is my coffee warm?"

"Tell me ye werenae having a talk with yer wee—"

"There is nothing *wee* about it, Macfie," he interrupted grimly. "And if you wish to remain employed—hell, if you wish to live to see another day—you will not complete that query."

Macfie issued a harrumph. "Is it safe for me tae enter, sir? Ye werenae thinking upon my eyebrows, were ye?"

Decker bit out a laugh in spite of himself. "You are indeed fortunate you are invaluable around here, Macfie, or you would find yourself getting the sack for that."

"Eh, ye like my hungry caterpillars far too much." Macfie was halfway across Decker's office with the coffee when he paused, frowning. "Ahem, sir. I didnae mean that in the manner in which it sounded. Ye know I'm not a sod."

Lord help him.

How could this day get any worse?

"That was never in question, Macfie," he said on a sigh. "Although, if you were, it would not be any of my concern."

"Ye're a fair man, ye are, Mr. Decker," Macfie praised, settling the fresh coffee upon Decker's desk at last. "I suppose now would be as good a time as any tae tell ye Lady Josephine Danvers is here, wanting an audience with ye again."

She was *here.*

Decker wished he could say that knowledge did not echo inside him with all the distinction of a chorus of angels singing, but that would be a miserable lie. She was beneath the same roof, after three days. Close enough to touch, if he wished.

He *very* much wished.

Just like that, his cock had twitched back to life. Smothering a curse, he stalked the rest of the way to his desk, hiding himself behind the carved, polished monstrosity topped with all its awaiting work it seemed he would never complete. How to attend to tasks when there was so much delicious distraction determined to ruin all his good intentions?

He sat.

"Send her in, Macfie," he said, congratulating himself on the remarkable calm in his voice.

"She's the one, then?" Macfie asked knowingly. "The set of skirts who has ye all sorts of bothered, like a stag in rut?"

Fucking hell.

"Macfie," he ground out. "You are treading dangerously close to peril at the moment."

"I am not judging ye, sir." Macfie's bushy red brows moved up and down. "She is verra lovely. Excellent set of—"

"Macfie!" he repeated. "*Enough.* Bring her to me, if you please."

"I was going tae say matched horses on her carriage, sir." Macfie's brows raised. "Where *is* yer mind, Mr. Decker?"

Decker clenched his jaw. "Macfie, if you value your position at all…"

"Fetching her ladyship," the devil said, an impish light in his blue eyes. "But if ye dinnae mind me saying so, Lady Josephine would make a lovely Mrs.—"

"I. Will. Sack. You." He glared at his rogue employee. "And then I will throttle you. And then I will shave off your eyebrows myself."

"Anything but the eyebrows, sir," Macfie said, giving him a wink that said he did not fear his position at all.

He was right, of course. Decker would sooner saw off his own arm than sack Macfie. The man was too capable. Too comfortable as well, and aware of his own value. But vital, nonetheless. Loyal, intelligent men were not easily acquired in Decker's experience. Or loyal women, for that matter.

He had certainly never known one.

Quite a thought to have as Macfie took his leave of the

office. Loyalty had never mattered before when it came to the woman—or women—sharing Decker's bed. Did it matter now? Not that Jo was sharing his bed. Not yet, anyway.

Soon.

Hell, not soon enough.

Before he could further contemplate the possibility, Macfie returned with Jo, who was wearing a pensive expression Decker was not certain he ought to like. Either way, it was damned charming. She was beautiful, even if her countenance boded trouble.

"Lady Josephine Danvers for Mr. Decker," Macfie bellowed, his eyebrows performing gymnastic feats.

Jo winced.

So did Decker as he rose to stand out of deference to Jo.

"Thank you, Macfie," he said pointedly. "That will be all."

Macfie grinned and offered an exaggerated bow before backing over the threshold. Decker knew what was coming next, curse the blighter.

"Do not slam," he began, only to be cut off by the deafening thud of the door slamming closed.

He winced again.

"The damned door," he added lamely, sharing a look of exasperation with Jo.

"He does not know his own strength," Jo said calmly, echoing Decker's words from their last meeting at his offices.

"Amongst other faults," Decker quipped. "Have a seat, my dear."

She neared him with a hesitation that also belonged to that day, which seemed at once a lifetime ago, although it had just been a sennight. "This is a brief visit. Forgive me for the unexpected interruption. I have merely come to deliver a new pamphlet for the Lady's Suffrage Society. We would like to run five hundred copies of this, to begin."

Disappointment blossomed in his chest. She was here on official purposes. Not to see him.

What did you expect, you clod? That an inexperienced young virgin would have come to you because she needs to sate the devils of desire keeping her awake at night?

Right. He was an utter fool, wasn't he?

Belatedly, he realized she carried a sheaf of papers as she held them out to him, across his desk. Across the sea of papers which mocked him now, all the symbols of the manner in which she had set him so thoroughly at sixes and sevens. For the entirety of his adult life, two distractions had carried him through: business and pleasure. And yet, since he had last seen her, he had scarcely been able to focus upon his business concerns at all.

He accepted the papers from her, nettled by the tranquility in her countenance. She seemed so unaffected, and he longed to ruffle her feathers. To bring her down to the mud where he dwelled.

"Are there any lists contained within this draft?" he asked, raising a brow as he met her honey-brown gaze.

It was low of him to tease her in such ruthless fashion, and he knew it. But he was feeling rather low at the moment. Desperate, if he were honest. Despicable, pathetic, and randy as Priapus. He had been ruined by a slip of a girl, and he did not like it.

Her generous lips tightened. Her adorably stubborn chin tilted. "Forgive me, Mr. Decker, but I thought you had forgotten all about such matters."

Ah. The corners of his lips mutinied, wanting to lift into a satisfied smile. He suppressed it.

"What is it you thought I had forgotten?" he asked with a calm he did not feel.

In truth, his heart was racing. Pounding. His restraint had been reduced to gossamer thread at the moment. He wanted to pounce upon her and kiss the pout from her delicious lips, and then strip her out of her smart navy promenade gown and…

Hell.

He viciously cut off any more thoughts in that vein.

Her lips had parted in invitation, and her dark eyes glittered, as if she knew exactly the nature of the filth that was happening in his mind.

"I thought you had forgotten my list," she said, her voice cool. "It is just as well if your enthusiasm has waned, however. I have been thinking a great deal since the dinner at Lord and Lady Sinclair's the other night. Surely completing each item with the same man will hinder my—"

"No," he bit out, dropping the manuscript to the sea of other papers and stalking around his desk without thought. "I will be damned if I allow you to conduct any of the items on your list with Huntingdon or Quenington, or anyone else for that matter."

His feisty Jo returned.

Her eyes glinted. "If you *allow* me?"

Wrong choice of words, old boy.

He grimaced. "You know what I mean to say, Josie."

Her eyes narrowed. "Do not attempt to distract me by using yet another sobriquet for me, Mr. Decker."

He reached her and then clamped his hands on her waist. "And do not call me *mister*, damn it. Call me Decker or call me nothing at all."

Her gaze had dipped to his lips. Something in the air changed around them, becoming heady, thick, poignant. His cock swelled to rigorous attention, lust roaring through him. But it was more than desire. It was…

"You do not have any sovereignty over me," Jo said then, breaking into his musings.

His grip on her tightened. How he envied the layers between them—he was jealous of her corset for the way it wrapped around her, envious of her chemise, nestled next to her skin. He wanted that same connection with her, that intimacy, to absorb her, bask in her heat, in her proximity.

Fuck. What was wrong with him?

"Do you *want* other men to complete your list with you?" he demanded.

Her long, dark lashes swept over her eyes, stealing from him those twin windows into her thoughts for a breath. When her lashes lifted, her countenance was grim. "No, I do not, and that is the trouble."

Relief more profound than he wanted to acknowledge washed over him. "In that case, I fail to see the trouble. You want me to complete your list with you. I am here. You are here. Mayhap we ought to cross off another number right now."

"It is the midst of the day, your Scotsman likely has his ear pressed to the door, and my lady's maid is awaiting me in the carriage," she said, quite dashing his fantasies of fucking her on his desk.

Yes, he knew those fantasies were just that. *Fantasies.* But a man could dream, could he not?

"My enthusiasm has not waned." He lowered his forehead to hers. If she were not enshrouded in so many damned layers, she would know firsthand how hard he was for her, how ready, even now. "I was merely giving you time. You told me you were concerned about feigning another illness so soon, that it would have been suspicious to your brother."

Indeed, she had in the last missive she had sent him. But her admission had not been his sole reason for avoiding her.

Of course not. He had hoped some distance and time would lessen the effect she had upon him. He had hoped he would break free of whatever spell she had cast.

Thus far?

Bloody unsuccessful.

Her face softened, and he noted for the first time that she possessed a smattering of freckles on the dainty bridge of her nose. How had he failed to miss them? Now, they riveted him, fascinated him.

"I have been thinking, Decker," she said.

Grievous words, those, especially coming from a female he wanted to bed. What he wanted usually required more action, less thought.

His hands coasted up her lower back, drawing her more firmly against him. "What are you thinking about, *bijou*?"

"About you," she said.

Excellent.

She was all he had been thinking about as well. Not that he would admit it.

"Not a damned thing wrong with that," he said, pleased.

"Do you know that yesterday, I was visiting an orphanage with my sister and my sister-in-law, and I saw the most interesting thing?" she asked.

Damn.

He suspected he knew what she had seen.

But he feigned ignorance anyway. "An orphanage, you say? Did you see children? Wretched little creatures."

In truth, children both perplexed and terrified him. Thanks to his estrangement with his mother, he had not seen his younger sister, Lila, in years. But he felt quite keenly for the plight of little beggars who, unlike himself, had not the fortune to at least be born the bastard of an inordinately wealthy earl.

"No, Decker," Jo told him, her gaze searching his. "I saw a piano. One of *your* pianos. The newest model, the piano of which there are only a handful in existence. The proprietress of the orphanage said it had been recently donated, along with cases of books for the children and tutors to aide them in learning to read. Do you know which publisher printed those books?"

His.

Caught.

"Before you begin to think me a saint, my dear Josephine, have you ever considered a man may have made those gifts with a wish to make the proprietress sweet so he could seduce her?" he asked, though it was furthest from the truth.

Never mind that Mrs. Chisholm was twice his age and produced a most disconcerting swishing sound when she walked.

But Jo was not fooled.

She raised a brow. "You expect me to believe you want to seduce Mrs. Chisholm?"

He sighed. "No, and you damned well know I do not. The only woman I want to seduce is right here in my arms, and she is talking to me about bloody pianos and orphans. Have you any idea how wilting that is for a man?"

Also a lie. Nothing could tame his raging cockstand now that she was here, close enough to kiss. And he was touching her. And her scent, floral and exotic, was punishing his senses.

"Do you know what I think, Mr. Elijah Decker?" she asked, tilting her head and studying him in a fashion that was far too thorough for his liking. "I think you did not want anyone to discover your secret."

His ears were hot once more. Blast the woman, was she making him flush? He refused to countenance it. Elijah Decker, collector of erotic art and literature that would embarrass the most seasoned bawd, had not been put to the blush in years. And now, twice in one day?

"What secret is that?" he returned, attempting to distract her by dipping his head and bringing their mouths closer to touching. "That I want to kiss you?"

"Yes." She blinked. "*No.* That you are not as coldhearted as you would have the world believe."

"On the contrary, *bijou.* I do not have a heart." He could not wait another second without tasting her lips.

If he did not kiss her, he was reasonably certain he would die. That was what it felt like, this need for her, coursing through his veins, consuming his every thought. She was all he desired. All he needed.

Decker's mouth settled on hers. Each time he kissed her was a revelation, a discovery. He had never so thoroughly enjoyed the mere act of kissing a woman in the way he did with Jo. He could kiss her all day, worship her lips, and never grow weary of it. For her, he possessed endless patience. Endless wanting.

She responded instantly, her lips moving beneath his, opening. His sweet tyro was learning. When his tongue slid into her mouth, she sucked. *Ah, fuck.* His ballocks drew tighter. She was so hot and wet, and he could not keep himself from thinking what it would be like to have her mouth on his cock—to know that slick, demanding heat, to slide past those lush lips and down her throat.

He rewarded her by nipping her lower lip. *By God,* she was more delicious than the finest confection. Decker kissed the corners of her mouth, the delectable Cupid's bow. His fingers slipped into her hair, and if he was plucking pins faster than a Whitechapel pickpocket relieved his victims of their coin, it could hardly be helped. He was insatiable where Lady Jo Danvers was concerned. He wanted to thieve everything she had all of her.

He never wanted to let her go. He wanted to keep her with him, all the time. In his bed. In his house, which had never seemed so empty until the hours following her visit…

What the hell?

He would *have* to let her go, he reminded himself as he kissed her harder, punishing her with his lips, claiming her as his. He would have to let her go sooner than he wanted.

It was the midst of the damned day, he reminded himself. There were witnesses.

Macfie, for instance.

As if on cue, the undeniable sound of the massive Scotsman's knuckles abusing the closed door split the moment in two. Jo pushed away from him, and Decker allowed her to go. Her eyes were wide, wild, her hair in disarray, her mouth swollen and glistening. Anyone would take a look at her and know exactly what had passed between them.

Damn.

"Mr. Decker, Mr. Levi Storm has arrived for his meeting with ye, one quarter hour early," Macfie called.

"Damnation," Decker muttered, raking his fingers through his hair. Of all the times for a business associate to be early…

"I… I must go," Jo said lamely, her eyes still wide, her pupils huge obsidian discs in her honey-brown gaze.

"I will be finished here shortly," he called to Macfie, his eyes never leaving Jo's. To her alone, quietly, he continued. "This is not finished between us, Josie."

"Why are you calling me Josie?" she whispered.

"Because it suits you, and I like it."

He did not know where the diminutive of her name had emerged from earlier, but having spoken it once, he could not deny how right it felt on his tongue. The idea of having another name for her that was his alone appealed. He would fret over that perplexing development later.

Her fingers were flying over her coiffure, assessing the damage. "Oh, heavens. This is dreadful."

"Allow me," he said, spinning her around without awaiting her response.

Mr. Levi Storm was a hideously wealthy, brilliant American businessman and inventor whose forays into electricity held incredible promise. He was not a man one kept waiting. *Bloody hell*, who did Decker think he was fooling? The real reason for hurrying Jo from his office was to save her reputation—and innocence—from a hasty deflowering. The first time he took her, he wanted it to be private, in a bed. He wanted to have all damned night long. No interruptions.

How the hell he was going to manage such a feat when thus far, he had only managed to steal her for too-brief chunks of time, was a puzzle he had yet to decipher.

Decker managed to right her coiffure. At least to a passable state. When he had finished, he could not keep himself from settling his hands back on her waist and leaning into her. The crush of her skirts against his trousers taunted his aching cock. He buried his nose in her hair and inhaled deeply, and then he kissed her ear, the side of her neck.

"I will send a note to you," he muttered against her skin, before sucking.

She was so silken, so divine. Even her throat drove him to the edge of control. It was soft and creamy, smooth as velvet. He did not want to let her go.

But he had to.

Reluctantly, he released her.

She spun around, her expression as dazed as he felt. "I will await your note, but do not think I have forgotten, Decker. This conversation will continue."

Of course she had not forgotten. And of course she wanted to further discuss it. Quite like a female, her persistence, her desire to find the best in him when he knew damn well there was none. Somehow, he found it adorable in this particular woman rather than an irritant.

"There is nothing to continue," he said.

"Oh, yes there is," she returned.

He wanted to kiss her again. He wanted to scoop her up in his arms and carry her away.

"Await my note," he told her tersely instead.

"You are a good man, Mr. Elijah Decker," she shot back. "But never fear, your secret is safe with me."

With those parting words, she turned and swept from his office. The door closed before he could argue or disabuse her of her misguided fancies.

Because he was not a good man, especially not where Jo was concerned. And sooner or later, she would learn that undeniable truth herself.

The hard way.

Chapter Nine

*J*UST WHEN JO had begun to fear she would have to go
another night without seeing Decker, the note arrived.
It was after tea, and the missive was hidden within a letter
from his publishing company concerning the publication of
the last pamphlet she had delivered for the Lady's Suffrage
Society.

> *Tonight.*
> *Half past eight.*
> *D.*

From the moment she had read those scant words and
seen his beautiful, masculine scrawl, her heart had been
pounding with exuberant anticipation. Decker haunted her
every thought. She had spent the entirety of the day preoccupied with thoughts of him. Of his kisses. She had been on
edge, laden with anticipation, wondering when his next note
would arrive. Until, at long last, it had.

And now, she was on her way back to him.

This evening's escape had proven more treacherous than
the previous two occasions upon which she had made her way
out of her brother's townhome in the night. Julian and Clara
were in residence this evening. She had shared dinner with
them and then professed she was tired and in need of some

additional rest.

Although it was perhaps down to her inner anxiety at sneaking out with the two of them at home, Jo had sworn her sister-in-law had frowned and that her gaze had not been merely understanding but searching as well. Julian, who had eyes only for his wife, had scarcely seemed to take note of her premature exit.

As Jo slipped into the mews at the appointed hour, it occurred to her that she may have inadvertently left Decker's note behind, nestled amongst her other correspondence. But his carriage was in sight, awaiting her, and she did not dare take the chance of returning and risk being observed. If someone caught her now, she would lose her chance of spending more time with Decker alone.

What were the odds anyone would enter her chamber whilst she was gone? She had dismissed her lady's maid for the evening. Her lights were lowered. As far as the entire household was concerned, she was abed.

Her heart was already lighter. The pent-up excitement tangled in knots in her belly ever since she had gone to his offices earlier could no longer be contained. Her every sense was heightened. The night smelled like imminent rain and the promise of summer. The air was damp and humid. Darkness had never seemed more inviting. In the distance, a low roll of thunder sounded above the ordinary din of the city.

Jo's heart was aflutter by the time his servant gave her a hand into the vehicle.

She entered to find him awaiting her as usual, his long legs on display in black trousers, his eyes almost cobalt in the low light. Their gazes clashed and held as she entered, and suddenly, everything else fell away. She forgot about the note, about the possibility of detection. She scarcely heard the door close at her back. All Jo could do was drink in the sight of

Decker, so big and powerful and handsome.

"Josie." He grinned.

There was his sobriquet for her. *It suits you, and I like it*, he had said. And she liked it, too. And, as she had told Decker, she liked *him*.

Too much.

Far too much.

Her heart plummeted somewhere into the vicinity of the soles of her handsome boots. All the rage, finest leather, crafted just for her, thanks to her sister-in-law Clara's immeasurable wealth. They pinched Jo's toes, but she had worn them because she wanted to look her best for him.

"Decker," she greeted him in return.

His hands clamped on her waist and he hauled her toward him. She let out an embarrassing squeal of surprise, her hands finding his broad shoulders, as she landed sideways in his lap.

"Finally," he muttered.

She inhaled, worrying her lower lip with her teeth, for she felt the same way, as if an interminable eternity had passed between when she had last seen him in his offices and this moment. "You saw me this afternoon."

"And yet, waiting for this evening was torture." He grimaced, but the action did not abate his allure one bit.

As for torture? Jo knew the feeling. Wrong or not, part of her was pleased to know he had been thinking of her and suffering. Perhaps even longing for her in the way she longed for him.

"I have not forgotten about the piano and the orphanage," she reminded him.

"Of course you have not," he said. "But I have not forgotten about something else. You owe me, and I intend to collect your debt."

And then, his mouth was on hers, ending further discussion. She would think about it later, she told herself. She would question him. Get him to admit that he was the source of the piano, that he had sent those crates of books to the orphans, that he actually possessed a tender heart when it came to those who were not as fortunate as him. She would…

Oh.

She would…

Forget everything but the play of his mouth over hers. It was sinful, forbidden, delicious, knowing. So very knowing. He kissed her as if it were the last kiss he would ever give, the last she would ever receive. As if he were ravenous for her.

And her mind became a blank canvas.

All thought was banished by Decker's kiss. His lips were smooth, soft, yet demanding on hers. She was helpless to resist. Not that she wanted to resist. Because of course, she did not. His tongue slid against hers. His teeth were on her lower lip, biting. Delicious.

She moaned into his mouth.

Her bustle was askew, which meant that beneath her bottom, she felt quite vividly the full, thick length of him. His manhood. How intense. How illicit.

How delightful. How *delicious.*

Jo kissed him harder at the thought. Kissed him back with all the ardor that had been waiting every second since she had seen him last. Since that precipitate knock at his office door from Macfie. Since his business interests had interrupted their interlude.

His hand was on her breast. Separated by layers, so many layers, including the most forbidding of all, her corset. Still, her nipple pebbled. Her body hungered for him. She was alive and so very aware of everything. So very aware of *him.*

Jo sucked on his tongue, kissing him harder, trying to match the way Decker's lips moved over hers with so much expertise. She was melting, she was sure of it. Her insides were liquid. She was nothing but a quivering lump of need in his arms.

Some distant part of her mind warned her against her attachment to the man upon whose lap she sat. Still, nothing could dim the calamitous, exciting sensations he aroused in her.

His lips left hers to coast down her throat. He kissed, nipped, and sucked a delicious path. She tilted her head back to grant him greater access.

"Decker," she whispered, her fingers sinking into the thick, wavy strands of his hair. "What are you doing to me?"

"Showing you how much I missed you," he murmured against her skin.

Innumerable, intelligent, coherent responses rose to her lips. And all she managed was, "*Oh.*"

Perhaps because his mouth was open, his teeth grazing over a particularly responsive cord in her throat. Perhaps because he was sucking on her flesh. Because his tongue was licking her, finding its way to the sensitive hollow behind her ear, then traveling over the shell. Because his teeth caught her earlobe.

"Yes," he said into her ear. "I missed you more than you know. And now I shall have to show you just how much."

He could show her anything as far as Jo was concerned.

"Show me?" she managed.

He sucked her throat again. "How do you feel, darling?"

Darling?

That word alone settled deep inside her, residing in a place she had not previously known existed. Jo swallowed hard.

"I am feeling restless," she whispered, her arms twining around his neck for purchase as the carriage rattled over a bump in the road and nearly sent her sprawling.

His hands tightened on her waist.

"Mmm. Restless?" he asked. "Where?"

That delicious baritone of his made her feel weak. Made more heat pool between her thighs. Which was one of the places where she felt restless.

"Everywhere," she told him, nuzzling his hair.

Those silky strands felt so smooth and good against her cheek. She inhaled deeply the scent of him—the shampoo he had used to wash his hair, the delicious scent that was all him. Cologne, musk, Decker, man.

Delicious man.

How had she ever imagined another could help her to fulfill the items on her list?

"Everywhere?" he repeated, his voice a decadent rumble. His fist snagged her skirts, lifting them. "Show me where."

If she had a modicum of honor, she would leap from his lap and throw herself to the squabs opposite him. But was that not why she was here? Her lack of honor? Her desire to be alone with a man, to be wicked, to complete the items on her fanciful list?

Yes, it was.

But still, Jo found herself opening her legs as Decker's hand slid beneath her skirts. Up her calf, past her knee. He lingered on the hollow there, teasing her until she gasped, wriggling. She wanted that touch on her thighs. Higher, too.

The words, however—shocking, inappropriate words— gave her pause.

"Here?" he whispered, caressing her knee.

"No," she told him.

Their faces were close, so close. The striations in his sky-blue eyes were vivid. This was a new intimacy, the sort she had never imagined. The kind she would never have dared.

His fingers skimmed on, daring to trace circles over her inner thighs. "Here?"

Jo was certain she was going to turn into flame. She was desperate for those knowing fingers to find her most intimate flesh.

"Higher," she dared to say, though she was fairly certain a man as experienced as Decker would know where she wanted his touch and how and why. He was simply toying with her, heightening her need, fanning the flames.

But before he could give her what she wanted, the carriage rocked to a halt.

They had arrived at their destination.

Decker's hand withdrew from beneath her skirts. He pressed a tender kiss to her lips. "We are—"

Before he could finish what he had been about to say, the carriage door was wrenched open. The imminent rain had finally unleashed itself upon the city. The night was dark, a torrent of water lashing the street.

But it wasn't the violence of the storm, thunder and lightning booming and flashing overhead, that stole the breath from Jo's lungs. Rather, it was the figure standing on the street in the midst of the deluge. A figure she recognized all too well.

"Josephine." Her brother Julian's voice was cold as Wenham Lake ice, her name cracking like a whip above the din of the tempest.

They had been caught.

DECKER COULD BLAME his current predicament upon his prick.

He could blame it upon lust.

He could blame it upon that cursed list Jo had unintentionally delivered to him, which had made him randy as a sailor returned from a lonesome tour of the seas.

But in the end, the fault for what had happened between Decker and Lady Jo Danvers fell solely upon his inability to resist the forbidden. He was the experienced seducer. He was the jaded man who sought pleasure at all costs. He was the one who had continually pursued her, unable to put an end to the mad attraction between them despite all the risks.

Only one fate derived from dallying with virginal misses. Decker had known it, and yet he had ignored it for the sake of his raging, unabated desire for her. Now, he was about to pay the price.

With his life.

"I expect you want me to marry her," he told the irate Earl of Ravenscroft as he faced the man in his own study, dripping on the carpets.

He was soaked to his skin from the relentless storm still raging outside. Jo had fared little better, but she had been bundled off by his efficient housekeeper, who had clucked over her like a mother hen and taken her to a chamber for tea and towels. Which meant Decker was alone to face his reckoning.

Ravenscroft's nostrils flared, his jaw tense. "Why the hell would I ever allow my sister to bind herself to the likes of you, Mr. Decker?"

Right. Fair enough question, sir.

He supposed *because I almost touched her cunny earlier* would not prove an appropriate response. So close to paradise. Only to be denied. Decker nearly laughed aloud at the bitter irony. But then, the Earl of Ravenscroft's fist connected with his jaw, obliterating all humor.

Damnation, the blighter had a deuced unforgiving right hook. Decker cradled his aching jaw. That blow was deserved.

If he were to encounter a man dashing about with his own sister in the midst of the night when she was old enough for such nonsense, he would be similarly tempted to do the man grievous bodily harm.

Actually, he would slit the bastard's throat.

Decker opened his mouth, testing his jaw's ability to properly function, staring at the earl. "I have compromised her, have I not? That is the way such matters ordinarily proceed, I gather. The gentleman offers to marry the lady he has compromised to keep her reputation from being sullied."

"Yes, you have, you despicable bastard," the earl growled. "She has only recently come out. She is naïve and innocent, and you managed to corrupt her. I want better for her than a scoundrel who would insult her by luring her around London."

Decker could not argue with Ravenscroft. He *was* despicable. And he *was* a bastard. However, Jo was not as naïve and innocent as the earl believed.

Thanks, in part, to you.

He banished the reminder. The list had come from her saucy mind, had it not?

"If you do not want Lady Josephine to marry me, then what do you intend?" he asked.

"Marriage to someone else." Ravenscroft sneered. "A suitable gentleman. But I demand your silence and discretion, Mr. Decker. And I also command you to stay the hell away from my sister from this moment forward. You will never see her again. You will not send her notes. You will never so much as speak her name."

"Out of the question," he snapped before he could think better of the words.

What are you doing, you fool? You do not have to marry her. Carry on with your life.

"You dare to defy me?" the earl asked, his fist clenched anew at his side.

Decker stood his ground. "I owed you the first blow, but consider this a warning, Ravenscroft. If you throw your fists at me again, I shan't calmly allow you to abuse me. I will hit you back."

And hard.

He would slam his fist into the earl's pretty nose.

"You owe me a hell of a lot more than one blow, you cur," the earl ground out. "I caught my sister in your lap in the midst of the night. And this was not the first occasion upon which you spirited her about London to God knows where. I ought to beat you to death for the lack of respect you have shown her."

"She was always safe with me," he told Ravenscroft. "Despite what you think of me, I would never have allowed any harm to come to her."

"*You* were the harm." Ravenscroft took another menacing step toward him once more. "Being in your presence was the harm. You debauched her, you villain. Do not suppose, for one moment, that I do not know all about you and your collections of filth and your Black Souls club. I would sooner hang myself than allow my sister to become poisoned by you any further."

Decker had never gone to any lengths to hide the manner in which he lived his life. He collected erotic art and literature. He ran his club as he saw fit. He indulged in the pleasures of the flesh as he liked, when he liked, and with whom he liked.

But it was not lost upon him that the earl's past was anything but pristine. It had long been rumored that Ravenscroft whored himself out to the ladies of society in exchange for funds. At least, that had been the case until he had married a hideously wealthy American heiress.

"You are shockingly prudish for a man who has bedded half the women of London in exchange for coin," he observed coolly, though he knew he was prodding an angry bear. He could not help himself. Ravenscroft's words stung, as did his outright refusal to consider Decker a worthy candidate for Jo's hand.

He wanted to marry her off to someone else—anyone else—save Decker.

The notion filled him with impotent rage.

"And you are shockingly stupid for a man who was just caught cavorting with my innocent lady sister," Ravenscroft bit out, threat dripping from his voice.

"She is hardly innocent, Ravenscroft," Decker said, giving the earl a smug grin. "Would you truly have her go to another man, possibly carrying my child?"

The earl's face went pale. He snarled. And then he struck again, landing another blow to Decker's jaw. But this time, Decker was not going to stand there and accept a drubbing. He was bloody well going to fight back.

And he was going to fight for Jo, too.

Because as much as he loathed the notion of becoming a husband, he loathed the thought of her becoming some other man's wife a thousand times more.

He swung at the earl, catching him in the jaw.

With a cry of sheer rage, Ravenscroft charged at him in the style of an irate bull. They went crashing together into the bookcase, sending volumes tumbling to the floor.

"I will kill you, you swine," the earl rasped, trying to get in another punch.

Decker deflected his fist and landed a blow of his own in Ravenscroft's midsection. He had only a moment to gloat as the air fled the earl's lungs in one swift rush. In the next second, Ravenscroft's fist connected with his cheekbone.

"Julian! Stop this!"

Jo's outraged cry barely punctured the fog of possessive bloodlust roaring through Decker. He was going to see this through, damn it. And he was going to make her his wife.

"Stay back," he warned her, removing his gaze from the earl long enough to see her bustling toward the melee.

Ravenscroft took advantage of his distraction and landed another blow to his jaw. Decker's head snapped into the bookcase.

"Julian! That is enough!" she hollered, leaping on her brother's back.

Decker would have laughed at the sight if he were not in so damned much pain. Ravenscroft was stronger than he looked.

"Leave this to me, Josephine," her brother snapped at her, attempting to shake her off.

Jo held firm, her arms wrapped around the earl's neck as she held on. "No! Stop hitting Decker! This is my fault, and I will not allow you to hurt him when I am the one who should be punished."

Her defense of him was sweet but unnecessary. He could hold his own with Ravenscroft when she was not there to distract him.

He passed a hand over his throbbing jaw. "I do not need you to defend me, darling."

"I do not want either of you to fight," she said, her countenance stricken. "This is madness."

"Get off me, Josephine, or I will send you to a convent when this is all over," threatened the earl. "He dared to dishonor you, and now he has to pay the price for his sins. I dare say it will be for the first time in his miserable existence."

Hell. Nothing about tonight had proceeded in the way Decker had imagined.

He was supposed to be happily checking off another item on her wicked list. Instead, he was sporting a blackened eye and facing the fact that he had just acquired himself a wife he did not want.

Not as his wife, anyway.

He very much wanted Lady Jo Danvers in other ways—on her back, on her knees, for instance—but that was what had landed him mired in this predicament.

"Ravenscroft is correct," Decker forced himself to admit. "I did dishonor you. The burden to make amends for my actions is now on me, which is why I have offered to marry you."

"Never happening!" the earl roared.

"Marry me?" Jo repeated simultaneously, her eyes going wide. "You cannot possibly mean that."

"It is the right thing to do," he said calmly, holding her stare.

"It is the wrong goddamn thing to do, and as I have already told you, I will never allow you to marry my sister." The earl finally succeeded in dislodging Jo from her tenacious hold upon his person.

Looking angry enough to commit murder, he took another swing at Decker. This time, Decker was prepared. He feinted to his left. The earl's fist connected with a row of book spines, sending more volumes hurtling to the carpet.

"Cease this at once, both of you!" Jo screeched, planting herself between Decker and Ravenscroft.

Damn. He was not going to run the risk of landing a blow upon her, just so he could cause the earl a bit more pain.

Decker glared at Ravenscroft. "The lady is right. Beating each other to a pulp will not solve any problems. The sooner you acquaint yourself with the fact that I will be marrying her to save her from any...*consequences*, the better."

Was he a bastard for emphasizing that word and implying he had taken Jo to bed when he had yet to so much as touch her cunny? Yes. Was he desperate enough to obtain her as his bride rather than see her married to another man? Also yes.

The earl made a guttural sound in his throat.

"Enough," Jo snapped. "I will not have the two of you injuring each other. Julian, please take me home and leave Mr. Decker to his evening."

"I will not go until I have his promise never to so much as speak your name again," the earl said, the proverbial dog with a bone he refused to relinquish.

"And I will not agree to such a ludicrous promise," Decker told him in return. "Since the lady in question is to be my bride, how do you propose I keep from speaking her name?"

Ravenscroft's face went ruddy with rage. "You will never marry her."

"Of course I am not marrying Mr. Decker," Jo agreed quietly. "Please, Julian. Let us return home. Surely Clara will be fretting over you."

What was this? Decker frowned at Jo. "You are marrying me, my dear, and this is final."

Her eyebrows rose. "Am I to have no say in the matter of my future? The two of you are behaving like a pack of wild mongrels!"

She was not wrong, but that did not abate his displeasure over her summarily refusing to marry him. "After the kerfuffle we have created this evening, I am afraid we have no other choice. My servants are discreet, but any one of them could be tempted to speak if given the proper motivation. Moreover, anyone could have seen Ravenscroft here squawking in the streets this evening."

"I do not squawk, you vile hound!" the earl spat.

"Stop it!" Jo hollered. "Stop it, stop it, *stop it*!"

The fury in her voice took Decker by surprise. He blinked. Ravenscroft did as well, looking equally befuddled. Much to Decker's satisfaction, he noted a bruise blossoming on the earl's jaw. His own throbbing cheekbone promised a similar discoloration.

"Julian, I want to go home," she announced into the shocked silence.

"I will call upon you tomorrow," Decker said, "to make a formal offer for your hand."

"And I will be happy to refuse it tomorrow just the same way I did today." Ravenscroft's lip curled.

It occurred to him that Jo's brother intended to oppose him all night long. And Decker was beginning to develop a colossal headache.

"Just go, you stubborn horse's arse," Decker could not resist nettling.

It was wrong of him, especially since he had just been caught with the earl's sister in his lap in the midst of the night, but Decker's rapidly swelling eye demanded vengeance.

Ravenscroft's nostrils flared. "You damned—"

"Enough!" Jo interrupted, her cheeks flushed.

Decker took pity on her. She looked as if she were wallowing in enough misery for all three of them put together. This could hardly be easy for her.

He inclined his head to her. "As you wish. I will see you tomorrow, *bijou*."

"Lady Josephine to you, rotter," the earl said.

Decker bit the inside of his cheek to keep from responding, doing his best to ignore his future brother-in-law.

Good God, he was going to get married.

"HEAVEN HELP ME, where have I gone wrong, Josephine? Two sisters, two forced weddings."

Jo faced her brother Julian's wrath as they journeyed back home, wishing the carriage floor would open and swallow her whole. "Your wedding was forced as well," she dared to remind him.

He pinched the bridge of his nose. "Do not speak unless it is required of you, my lady. My wedding has nothing to do with this."

"You asked me a question," she pointed out, feeling more daring than she probably ought. "I was merely reminding you that you are far from a saint yourself."

"I never should have allowed the two of you to remain with Aunt Lydia as long as I did," he said, disgust lacing his words. "I hold her responsible for the wayward misses she foisted upon me."

"Alexandra is happily married to Lord Harry," she grumbled. "I hardly think her a wayward miss."

"I agree. What you have done is far, far worse than any wrong steps your sister made," he said sternly. "She merely managed to find herself in a deal of trouble in a carriage at a country house party. You, however, have been gallivanting about London in the midst of the night on no less than three occasions with a known rakehell who runs one of the wickedest clubs in London and collects vulgar art and literature."

Jo frowned at her brother. "First, I was not suggesting that what I have done was more egregious than Alexandra. Second, how do you know how many times I met with Decker?"

"A concerned servant spied you going into a strange carriage the evening you claimed to be too sick to attend Lord and Lady Helmhurst's soiree." His countenance was as grim as if he were about to attend a funeral.

"Lord and Lady Helmhurst are terribly boring. She laughs like a braying donkey, she only wants to discuss her various ailments, and all he talks about is hunting," she defended. "Do you know, I once suffered through a dinner engagement during which Lady Helmhurst monopolized the conversation to talk about her gout?"

She was attempting to lighten his dark mood, it was true. Julian was not ordinarily so disapproving. He was a caring, generous brother who she knew loved her as much as she loved him. But the brother before her now little resembled that man, and she did not like it. And if she were completely honest with herself, she would admit that she also felt a great deal of guilt at deceiving him and disappointing him.

To say nothing of the hideous purple bruise marring his jaw.

Poor Decker had hardly been in finer fettle himself, his left eye nearly swelled shut by the time they had taken their leave.

Two good men, sparring like prizefighters. All her fault.

"I do not give a damn if you had to listen to Lady Helmhurst drone on about her gout for an entire year," Julian was bellowing at her now. "There is no excuse for sneaking about with seasoned miscreants such as Elijah Decker. I know his kind. I *was* his kind, once upon a time. Thank the Lord the servant saw you on the second night as well. I began having your correspondence intercepted."

"You had my correspondence intercepted!" The invasion of privacy rankled. Her cheeks went hot as she thought of some of the early missives she had exchanged with Decker. It was personal, all of it. "How dare you, Julian? You had no right to read my private letters!"

"I had every right, as I was attempting to keep you from folly." He passed a hand over his face, looking suddenly, unaccountably weary. "I would have been there to stop you before you rode off with him tonight, but Clara was feeling ill, and with her being so near to her confinement, I hated to leave."

"Is Clara well?" she asked, concern for her sister-in-law taking precedence.

"She seemed so when I left, though I expect my return looking as if I just fought the Battle of Waterloo will hardly be improving upon her delicate constitution," he said pointedly.

Jo knew another stab of remorse for her actions. It was true that she had been selfish when she had begun sneaking away to meet Decker. She had only been thinking of what she wanted, what she desired. She had not had a care for the repercussions to everyone around her.

To Julian and Clara.

To Decker.

To herself.

She winced. "Pray forgive me, Julian. It was not my intention to cause you or Clara further worry, and the last thing I wanted was for you to engage in a bout of fisticuffs with Decker."

"*Mr.* Decker," Julian clipped icily. "Though I suppose the form of address hardly matters any longer since you will never see the blighter again."

The thought of never seeing Decker again filled her with dread.

In such a short amount of time, he had become as essential to her as air. The promise of seeing him again, touching him again, kissing him, striking through the items on her wicked list with him, was the driving force of her days.

Because you are losing your heart to him, you foolish, foolish hen wit.

Dear heavens. It was true.

"I will see him tomorrow," she reminded her brother through suddenly dry lips. "He said he will call upon me then."

Julian raised a dark brow. "And we shall not be at home to him when he does."

"Yes we shall," she countered. "Or at least, I shall."

"Josephine, this is not a small matter," Julian said, sounding quite paternal. Also distinctly unlike a man who had amassed a reputation to rival Decker's before he had wedded Clara. "You were seen by at least one servant. Although I do believe the footman in question is loyal, there is a distinct possibility he has shared his knowledge with others, or that his fellow domestics witnessed you entering Mr. Decker's carriage on subsequent occasions. Furthermore, there remains the matter of the possibility you are carrying Mr. Decker's child."

Jo had not bargained upon the possibility that she had been seen by other servants. The realization gave her pause, but not as much pause as the latter portion of what her brother had just relayed to her did. Jo was not as well-versed on the subject as she would have preferred, it was true, but she knew that kisses did not beget children.

"I can assure you, Julian, your concern is misplaced," she said quietly. She supposed it would only make sense that he would believe the worst, given Decker's reputation.

Would Julian believe the man had done little more than show her lewd art, kiss her senseless, charm her to the verge of distraction, and feed her cream ice? She hardly thought so.

"You can save your assurances, Josephine," he returned, still grim as ever. "Forgive me if I do not trust a single word you utter just now."

That was fair enough. She could hardly argue her actions ought to instill confidence in her honesty. She had deceived him repeatedly. She had also pursued a man she knew he would find unsuitable for her. Whilst it was true that her initial association with Decker had begun because of the list and his taunting blackmail, it had swiftly blossomed into more.

So much more.

"I am sorry, Julian," she apologized quietly.

She was contrite. It had been wrong to lie to her brother. She certainly had no wish to be the cause of any upset in his life. With Clara soon ready to give birth, heaven knew he hardly needed further worries to fret over. However, she was not sorry about the time she had spent with Decker.

Nor was she finished with him.

But did she want to marry him?

Ah, there was the question.

"Apologies do not speak as loudly as actions do, Josephine," her brother reminded her tautly.

"I do wish you would cease calling me Josephine," she said. "You know how much I detest that name. What was mother thinking, burdening me with such a dubious mantle?"

"Mayhap she was thinking you would give your brother gray hair before his time with your antics and I would need a full name to resort to in times of trouble," he said wryly, the first inkling of his sense of humor returning.

She gave him a small smile, relief washing over her. "I promise I will not do anything so reckless again, Julian."

"There will not be further chance to," he said, the hint of a smile on his lips vanishing. "I am going to have to find you a husband now, quickly. Have you any preference? I cannot make any promises, but I will do my best to see you settled with a good man, a man worthy of you."

The only man she wanted to be settled with was calling upon her tomorrow to reluctantly offer to make her his wife. More guilt knifed through her. Of course, she had no wish for

Decker to be forced into an unwanted situation either.

But if Julian was hell-bent upon forcing her into marriage, there was no other man she would prefer.

She cleared her throat. "You cannot force me into marriage, you know."

"Yes I bloody well can force you to do what is right," Julian said, his voice vibrating with fury.

Jo would have offered further argument, but the carriage came to a halt.

"This discussion is not at an end," her brother warned her.

"I dare say it is not," she agreed.

Still, there had to be a better solution.

She just had to find it.

Chapter Ten

*D*ECKER'S HEADACHE DID not show any sign of lessening the next afternoon as he waited in the foyer of the Earl of Ravenscroft's townhome.

"I regret to inform you that his lordship is not at home," the butler announced with staid dignity.

That old bloody trick.

Decker shook his head slowly. "Kindly convey to his lordship that I will not leave without an audience."

Not that he wanted to have this particular audience, mind you.

Not long ago, Decker would have wagered his entire fortune and every last one of his fucking teeth that he would never be in the position where he currently found himself unhappily mired: calling upon a lady's guardian to ask for her hand in marriage.

Until last night, he would have sworn it would never happen. Marriage was not for him, not since his long-ago folly with Nora. He had never wanted a wife since. *By God*, he certainly did not want mutts of his own. The very notion of spawning, furthering the Earl of Graham's detestable bloodline, made him want to retch. He had spent his entire life since reaching manhood doing his utmost to keep such a travesty from occurring.

The butler bowed and disappeared, his expression unreadable.

Part of Decker expected the Earl of Ravenscroft to appear, ready to go another round, fists raised. But part of him was not at all surprised he was on the receiving end of such stinging refusal to gain an audience.

He was a bastard, after all. Everyone knew that. He was a mere mister as well. And wealthy or no, he was an unashamed voluptuary, a man who lived his life as he saw fit and to hell with anyone who did not approve. No man would welcome him as the husband of his young, innocent sister.

Hell, Decker could not blame Ravenscroft.

But that did not mean he was going to allow the earl to marry Jo off to some pale-faced, small-minded lordling who was not fit to lick the soles of her boots. To the devil with born-in-the-purple aristocrats. Jo deserved better.

A sudden flurry of steps and swish of silken skirts heralded the arrival of a female rather than the butler just before Jo rounded the corner and bustled into the entrance hall.

"Decker!" she said, *sotto voce*. "Come with me. We have not long before Osgood returns."

She held out her hand to him.

He had a moment to ponder the wisdom of taking her hand and going wherever she would lead him. But worry was rather a moot point after her irate brother had caught her in his lap the night before, was it not?

Decker went, wishing he was not still wearing his gloves so he could feel her bare skin against his. Also an unwise feeling, he reminded himself. Deuced poor timing. He had arrived here today on a mission.

To obtain her as his wife, not to ruin her.

Even if taking a bride would ruin him in the process.

They disappeared into a library, the door closing behind them.

"You do not have to marry me," she blurted.

He took a moment to drink in the sight of her. She was wearing a lavender-colored day gown trimmed with blonde lace, her dark hair captured in a simple chignon at her crown. *Damn*, but she made his heart pound faster. He could not deny his reaction to her any more than he could deny he was going to have to make her his wife.

Mrs. Elijah Decker.

Those three words made his gut cramp. They hit him in the chest. After Nora, he had vowed he would never marry. And now, before him, stood the deliciously feminine destruction of that vow.

"I *do* have to marry you, Josie," he countered, watching as her golden cat's gaze flitted over his face, lingering on his eye.

Ah, how could he forget his welcome-to-the-family gift from his future brother-in-law?

"I do not care about my reputation," she told him. "The servant who observed me getting into your carriage has been paid handsomely for his silence. No one will ever know what happened except for us. But you must convince my brother there is no need to worry about me carrying your child."

Of course Ravenscroft believed Decker's seed was already planted in Jo's womb. Decker had made certain of it, and he had no intention of disabusing the blighter of that false belief.

He clenched his jaw. "That is the reason you came racing to me just now and pulled me into this library? To tell me I should throw you to the wolves? What manner of man do you think me, to suppose I would do that?"

Her lush lips parted. "You will not be throwing me to the wolves. Julian was angry yesterday, but he is calmer today. He will not force me into a marriage, despite what he said last night. You need not sacrifice yourself for my sake."

How misguided she was. He'd had the night to ruminate

upon his options. And no matter how many times he turned over the facts and possible outcomes in his mind, he could not deny that the mere thought of her marrying another man—ever—filled him with the urge to claim her as his own.

No, the plain truth was that as much as he did not want to marry, as much as he did not want a wife, he could not allow himself to walk away from Lady Josephine Danvers. He wanted her. If she were to become his wife, he could finally have her. And when he tired of her, as he inevitably would, he would not interfere in her life. She would be free to pursue what she wished, and so would he.

The arrangement would not be an entirely unwanted one, aside from the marriage bit. Having her in his bed would sweeten the unexpected bitterness of having to wed. There were only two impediments to achieving his goal at the moment—Jo and her irate brother.

He took her other hand in his, drawing her nearer to him, and studied her beautiful face. "Marriage to me would not be such a horrible fate, I think. I have no need of your dowry; the money will be yours to dispense with as you wish. I have no need for heirs. You would have your independence, and we could cross off the rest of the items on your list."

A frown furrowed her brow. "But you do not want to marry. You are a notorious bachelor."

He dipped his head, bringing their lips nearer. "I do not want to marry, it is true. But neither do I want you to marry another man. That leaves us with only one solution to our current quandary, does it not?"

She blinked. "What if I do not want to marry you, Decker?"

Well, there was always that.

It was his turn to frown. "You do not want to marry me?"

She fretted with her lower lip. "That is not what I said."

"Perhaps you would prefer to wed a lord," he said grimly. "Someone like Hungtingdon or Quenington?"

He would never be able to change who he was. He was the bastard son of the Earl of Graham, and no matter how much he resented his arrogant prick of a sire and the fact that they shared blood, it would forever shape his life.

"No." She shook her head, her gaze searching his. "There is no other man I would want to be my husband, if I must marry."

He snorted. "That is hardly a commendation."

"I—"

"Hush," he interrupted. "Someone is coming."

A flurry of footsteps beyond the library door reached him. Decker had a suspicion they were about to be interrupted once more by the Irate Brother of Doom.

He stole a swift kiss from her lips. Just one, and over far too quickly. "Allow me to handle matters with your brother. I will speak to you afterward, if he permits it."

She looked as if she wanted to argue, but Decker released her hands and took a propriety-observing three steps in retreat. The library door burst open in the next second, revealing the Earl of Ravenscroft.

If glares could kill, Decker would be lying in a pool of his own blood on the Axminster at that very moment.

"Mr. Decker, what the hell are you doing in my library?" he demanded. "And Josephine, if you believe I will not make good on my threat of sending you to a nunnery, you are wrong."

Decker sketched an ironic bow. "I am here to speak with you, just as I promised. However, I was repeatedly informed you were not at home."

"That is true," the earl snapped. "I am not at home to *you*. Now kindly crawl back to whatever rock you emerged from beneath."

"I will not be going anywhere until I have said my piece," he insisted firmly.

"Julian, please listen to what Mr. Decker has to say," Jo pleaded softly. "You promised Clara earlier that you would see reason."

Ravenscroft's glare did not abate at all. "Leave us now, Josephine."

Instead of leaving the chamber and obeying her brother, however, Jo sidled nearer to Decker. That pleased him. A surge of protectiveness blossomed in his chest. Along with that same, troubling feeling that had been haunting him ever since… Well, ever since he had first thought about her conducting any of the items on her list with other men.

Possession.

He felt as if she were already his.

"Perhaps Lady Jo ought to stay as her future is being discussed," he suggested to the earl.

"Mayhap the things I want to say to you should not be spoken before a lady," countered the earl, but there was a grim note of acceptance in his voice.

"I do wish to remain," Jo offered. "Think of Clara, Julian. If we are to settle this matter swiftly, it will ease her stress. She does not need to concern herself with me when she will so soon face her lying in."

"Do not use my beloved wife as a pawn against me," her brother snapped at her. "You owe her a debt of gratitude, you know. If it were not for her, you would be on your way to a convent as we speak."

Decker's lips twitched in wry humor at the notion. Ravenscroft was blustering, of course. Although he was still clearly irate with both Decker and Jo, he did not seem as inclined to begin throwing punches today.

Yet

The afternoon was young.

"Shall we sit?" he suggested to Ravenscroft, gesturing to the divan and chairs artfully placed at one end of the long, bookshelf-lined chamber.

Such an arrangement certainly seemed less conducive to the earl planting him a facer, or vice versa.

"By all means, play the host," the earl said cuttingly.

But he led the way to the seating area. They settled themselves in an awkward horseshoe, Jo and Decker on chairs at one end and Ravenscroft on a divan opposite them. Decker eyed the distance between himself and the earl, judging how much reaction time he would have lest the bloodthirsty bastard decide to pounce once more.

Enough.

"May I begin?" he asked, for he did not have all day to squander upon stroking the Earl of Ravenscroft's abused ego.

This was not his sole call of the day. He also needed to oversee the funds being invested in Mr. Levi Storm's new electricity company. He had a shipment of erotic marbles being delivered. To say nothing of the printing of the latest installment of the erotic serial he was publishing privately for members of the Black Souls club…truly, it was endless. But before him was the most important task of all. He needed to secure Jo's hand, and then he needed to begin making plans.

"By all means, Mr. Decker, carry on with whatever it is you have to say." The earl raised a chastising brow, his voice dripping in icy hauteur as only a nobleman born and bred could truly perfect.

Decker inclined his head. "I will marry Lady Josephine, provided she accepts marriage to me, of course. I have spent the morning having a betrothal contract drawn up, which should be arriving directly from my solicitor's office here within the hour. Within it, you will find ample provisions for your sister's welfare. I do not require her dowry, and all her funds will be entirely within her control to do with as she chooses for the duration of the marriage."

"How magnanimous of you, Mr. Decker," the earl said acidly. "Will that be all?"

"Further," Decker continued pointedly, ignoring Ravenscroft's jibe, "I will settle upon her a stipend of twenty thousand pounds per annum, to disperse as it pleases her. She will, in return, run my household and act as my hostess. I have no objection to her pursuits with the Lady's Suffrage Society—indeed, I deem it a worthy cause. I will require her discretion in the marriage, and I will provide her mine as well. The marriage will occur within one month's time. I propose to bear all expenses for the nuptials. Lady Josephine shall have carte blanche to decide whatever she wishes for flowers, dress, guests, etcetera. *That* will be all, Ravenscroft."

The earl was no longer glaring at him.

Decker knew a moment of triumph. He was reasonably certain he had thought of everything.

"Why would I give my sister to a degenerate voluptuary whose reputation is as black as pitch?" Ravenscroft queried next.

That rather cut to the heart of things, did it not?

"Julian," Jo chastised, interjecting her voice for the first time since their official discussion had begun. "He is none of those things. For all that you think him wicked, Mr. Decker has never truly compromised me."

Blast her innocent tongue and urge to champion him.

"Yes, my darling, I am afraid I have," he told her tenderly, lest Ravenscroft realize he had been lying about the possibility of Jo carrying his child. "The only reasonable course for us to take now is marriage. In time, I will rectify the dishonor I have paid you."

That particular detail was one which could tip the scales in his favor, and he would not discount it. However, he certainly hoped reason would do the work without his having to resort to subterfuge.

"Although Lady Josephine has reached her majority, I am still her brother. I am in control of her dowry. If I do not approve of the match she makes, she will go to her husband with nothing," Ravenscroft told him coolly.

But Decker had accounted for that. He inclined his head. "In the event Lady Josephine has no dowry, there is a provision in the betrothal contract for her to receive thirty thousand pounds per annum."

It was an impressive sum by anyone's account.

Even an earl's.

Especially an earl who had been at penury's gates and had required his marriage to an American heiress to dig him out of the depths of his wastrel sire's financial grave.

"I do not want a dowry," Jo said quietly then. "Nor do I need it if I am to marry Mr. Decker. Julian, please, I beg you to see reason. Mr. Decker is a good man."

The earl's nostrils flared. "If he were a good man, he would not have been squiring an unwed lady about London in the midst of the night, to say nothing of what else occurred. Indeed, I do believe the scene I witnessed yesterday precludes him from being considered a good man. However, I am willing to review the betrothal contract before I make my decision."

"You have three hours from the time the contract arrives until it becomes void," Decker told him, delivering his trump card. "If you do not make your decision in that time, the contract will be revised and amended. The terms will not benefit Lady Josephine nearly as much as the initial contract.

Delay will only have a negative impact upon your sister, which I am sure you do not want."

"What I do not want, Mr. Decker, is for my impressionable sister to make a match with a man who is clearly her inferior in every way," the earl bit out. "That is what I do not want. You do not deserve Lady Josephine as your wife. I will not mince words. Your reputation speaks for itself. I wanted a love match for my sister with a man who cares for her and who can also do her credit."

"We are in perfect accord then, my lord," Decker said with ease. "I agree that I am Lady Jo's inferior. I also agree I do not deserve her. My reputation is dark; I shall not insult your intelligence and suggest otherwise. Nor will this be a love match. But what I can promise you is that, unlike some milksop lord you would select to be her husband, I will appreciate her always. I will also make all the provisions necessary to prove to both yourself and to Lady Jo that her independence and her financial security will remain hers, just as they should be. I may be a sinner, Lord Ravenscroft, but I am also a man of intellect and foresight. I do not seek to dim Lady Jo's shine. Rather, I hope to encourage it."

"You are not my inferior," Jo argued softly, her stare upon him. "You are a good man, Elijah Decker. I have seen the proof for myself on far too many occasions for you to deny it."

The worship in her eyes was misplaced. He was a bastard. A sinner. A jaded, heartless sybarite. She would do well to remember that. But he would not remind her now, because to do so before her brother would only harm his cause.

"You want to marry this man?" Ravenscroft demanded, his attention directed toward Jo, absolving Decker's need to speak.

"I want to marry the man of my choice," she told her brother without hesitation. "If you insist I am to be married, I will choose marriage to Mr. Decker every time.

Decker suppressed his wince. Once again, hardly a commendation, that.

"Of course I insist you are to be married," the earl bellowed, nearly rising to his feet in his vexation. "Have you forgotten the depths of the trouble in which you have embroiled yourself? I will not allow you to be shamed, Josephine. You are my sister, and it is my duty to protect you however I can. However I must."

Ah, they had come full circle. Back to the nonsense about Jo carrying his bastard seed in her womb. Again, Decker would not disabuse Ravenscroft of his assumptions based upon his own suggestions. The possibility of Jo carrying his child was likely the sole commendation for his suit at the moment, and he had no desire to challenge it with honesty. Let the earl think what he would.

"Protect her by seeing her married to the man most suited to the role," Decker said smoothly. "You have my word I will treat her well. Make any changes to the contract you see fit. I am more than willing to offer concessions. However, I am firm in the timing. I want Lady Jo as my wife sooner rather than later."

And in his bed.

Wisely, he refrained from adding that bit. He was a businessman, after all. Decker was more than accustomed to making deals and compromises in the name of his desired outcome. And in this instance, his desired outcome was Lady Josephine Danvers as his wife.

Yes, *wife*.

The one word he had sworn he would never utter—the one institution he had vowed would never claim him—was upon him. And to his shame, he did not dread the outcome. Marriage to Jo would have its benefits, her in his bed amongst them. The rest, he would fret over later. In short, there was no need for his life to change. Nothing would alter.

He would be free to pursue whatever and whomever he wished.

Granted, the thought of pursuing anyone other than Jo was rather murky at the moment. Downright untenable. Unthinkable. Unpalatable to be sure. But still, he had never been so drawn to one woman in his life that he had been able to cease his desires for more. At least, not since Nora.

"I will make my decision after I have the opportunity to peruse the betrothal contract," Ravenscroft said then, his tone undeniably grudging. "I shall send word. For now, Mr. Decker, I do think it best for you to take your leave."

Decker agreed.

His point had been made.

And he had just secured Jo's hand in marriage. He was certain of it.

THE BETROTHAL CONTRACT arrived as Decker promised.

Whilst Julian pored over it, Jo sought out her sister-in-law, Clara, who was much easier to discuss certain matters with than her brother was. Especially since he was still very much wearing the mantle of Furious Protective Brother.

Clara was propped comfortably on a chaise longue in her private apartments, ethereally beautiful with her blonde hair styled *au courant* with a light fringe on her forehead. She was wearing a dressing gown of ivory satin, which did nothing to diminish the size of her belly.

"How are you feeling?" Jo asked, mired in guilt over having caused so much disruption in the household when Clara was about to give birth any day now.

"As If I have been in my delicate condition for the last five years at least," her sister-in-law drawled, a tinge of her American roots softening her words. "Also desperately hungry for kippers and Bayonne ham and chocolate biscuits."

Jo grimaced at the thought of those three disparate foods being consumed. "Separately or all at once?" she ventured, not certain she wanted to hear the response.

"Would it be detestable of me if I said all at once?" Clara asked, grinning. "Do sit, Jo. You know I would stand, but my feet have been replaced by bricks, and I am about as big as a bloody house."

Jo seated herself, smiling back at her brother's wife. "A *bloody* house, is it? I do think my brother's vulgar English vocabulary has infected you as well."

Clara sighed. "I decided if I could not best him, I would join him. What has you looking so Friday-faced, my dear? Do not tell me Julian was being a bear to you again when Mr. Decker came to call."

"He is angry with me," Jo said. "I have disappointed him, and you, and for that I am sorry."

"You took unnecessary risks with your reputation. Julian loves you and is frightfully protective. I think his anger stems more from his own sense of having failed you and Alexandra than your actions." Clara's gaze searched hers. "Do you care for this Mr. Decker of yours?"

Of course she did. Somehow, along the way, he had charmed her. Although, he was far from hers, wasn't he? He had never been hers, and if he married her, part of her very much feared he would remain elusive. An enigma.

Jo fidgeted with her gown, uncertainty assailing her. "How did you know you were in love with Julian? Was it sudden, all at once? Or was it gradual? Was it that one day, he looked at you a certain way, or he smiled at you, and something inside you changed?"

"Oh, Jo." Her sister-in-law's countenance turned sympathetic. "Are you in love with him?"

"I do not know." She bit her lip, searching her mind, struggling with the warring feelings within her, so many of them, so new.

"Perhaps we should begin somewhere else," Clara suggested kindly. "Do you want to marry him?"

Jo's answer arrived without hesitation, unflinching. "Yes."

If she were honest with herself, she would admit that even without her brother's interference and blustering threats, if there was any man she wanted as her husband, it was Decker. He was handsome, charming, and witty. He was protective and considerate. His kisses set her aflame. His sinful side appealed to her in a way she had not imagined possible.

Other men were handsome as well. Lord Quenington, for instance, who was a gentleman who had intrigued her ever since her coming out. But he did not make her feel the way Decker did. She was beginning to suspect no other ever could compare.

"You are certain?" Clara prodded. "Marriage is not the sort of decision one should undertake lightly."

"You and Julian married in haste," Jo could not resist pointing out.

Clara flushed. "Our situation was unusual. We were both seeking freedom, and we hurried into our wedding, it is true. But what we found instead was each other."

Jo knew a pang of envy at her sister-in-law's words. Oh to have that sort of love herself. She had not realized she had wanted it, but she could see now, that what she had been searching for when she had constructed her list had not been wickedness.

Rather, it had been love.

She had tired of watching everyone else around her find their happiness.

She wanted that happiness, too. The question remained whether or not she could find it with Decker. With a man who had never expressed a single tender feeling toward her.

"When did you know, Clara?" she pressed. "When did your heart tell you it was content?"

"It was gradual," Clara told her with a soft smile of re-membrance. "And then, it was also sudden. All at once. Love is almost impossible to explain, Jo. I feel as if my heart has always known his. Does that sound foolish? As if we were always destined to be."

That did not sound foolish at all.

Rather, it explained a great deal about the confusing hodgepodge of emotion tangled up inside her at the moment.

It sounded horribly familiar, in fact.

"It sounds wonderful," Jo said softly. "Thank you for sharing it with me, Clara. I am more convinced than ever that marrying Mr. Decker is the right course of action to take. It was not what I intended when our association began, but…what you just said, about feeling as if your heart has always known Julian's. I feel the same for Mr. Decker. I did not want to feel anything at all for him, but suddenly, no other man will do. There is him, or there is no one."

"Then you know what you must do, my dear." Clara looked as if she were about to say more when suddenly, her expression changed and her hands went to her burgeoning belly. "Oh my. I do think it may be time to send for the doctor."

She did not need to say the words twice. Jo rushed to her feet, excitement replacing the conflicting emotions darkening her heart. She was going to be an aunt.

"I will fetch Julian and tell him," she promised Clara.

In a frantic blur, she made her way to her brother's study, running as quickly as her heavy skirts would allow.

He stood at her entrance, his expression grim. "The betrothal contract appears to be in order, Josephine. I suppose I am left with no recourse other than to allow you to wed Mr. Decker."

Relief washed over her, joining the anticipation.

"I am happy you are finally agreeing to see reason," she told him. "Because Clara's time has come. She says we are to send for the doctor."

"The doctor?" Her brother paled. "Are you certain?"

"Certain."

He collapsed into his chair. "Well bloody hell. I am about to become a father."

Seeing the dazed expression on Julian's face, Jo decided she would have to take action. "I will see that the doctor is sent for myself. Pour yourself a drink, Julian, and then go see to your wife."

She did not wait for his response. A time of change was upon them all. The babe was on his or her way. And she was going to be Mrs. Elijah Decker.

Soon, heaven help her.

Not soon enough.

Chapter Eleven

*T*HE LONGEST THREE bloody weeks of Decker's life had passed with alarming torpidity. He had spent them paying supervised visits upon Jo like a true suitor—*shudder*—and taking himself in hand until his cock was raw.

Finally, Lady Jo Danvers was his wife.

Lady Jo Decker?

Mrs. Decker?

Who the hell cared what she chose to call herself? She was *his*. That was all that mattered now. The ceremony was over. The wedding breakfast was done. He had introduced her to all his servants.

Quite appropriately, it was raining.

Which gave Decker ideas.

The list had not been far from his mind during the interminable weeks of waiting.

He took his wife's hand now and placed it on his arm, guiding her to the glass doors that led to the gardens.

"Where are you taking me?" she asked, laughing.

Damn, he liked the sound of that—her laugh. He wanted more of it. But there was plenty of time for that.

He grasped the cool brass of the handle and opened the door. The weather was warm, summer finally upon them. No thunder or lightning—just an unleashing of the clouds. The fresh scent of rain mingled with the fat blossoms of roses, which were bowing beneath the onslaught of the showers.

"Number three," he told her, grinning. "Get caught in the rain with a gentleman. What was the bit in the parenthesis? I have quite forgotten."

A charming flush stole over her delicate cheekbones. "Choose said gentleman with care."

He *tsked*. "You are missing the bit about the removal of wet garments."

"Decker!" A smile played at her luscious lips as she chastised him. "You want me to drench my beautiful gown?"

"I want to kiss my wife in the rain," he countered, raising a brow. "Unless she is too scared?"

"Of course I am not scared," she denied instantly. "Why should I be scared? It is only water."

"And I only aim to fulfill every one of your fantasies, darling," he told her, his cock twitching to life at the thought.

Down, old chap. It is not your time just yet.

"I want you to dance with me," she said softly. "The way you danced with me at Lord and Lady Sinclair's ball. In the rain."

"There is my girl," he said approvingly, stepping into the rain and tugging her along with him.

The first lash of the rain upon him was a shock to his senses.

She let out a shriek as a fresh torrent of droplets hit them.

He bowed to her as if they were on the dance floor. And then he took her into his arms. They whirled. The showers soaked them within minutes. Through the gravel path, they danced. He twirled her in the shadow of a fountain of Venus holding a bow whilst being serviced by Adonis.

"Oh!" she exclaimed as her curious eyes took in the rather lifelike rendering of Adonis' prick.

He grinned at her, unrepentant. "It *is* rather small, is it not! I can show you something far more impressive later, *bijou*."

The color on her cheeks deepened.

By God, she was lovely. He wondered how many other ways he could make her flush. And how often.

She laughed. "You are a scoundrel."

He was. No point in denying it. "I can do that for you later if you like, darling."

Nothing would please him more than tasting her. Licking her until she came on his tongue. The sensual promise of making her his, which had been haunting him since the day his eye had first fallen upon her naughty list, beckoned. Within reach—tempting. Taunting.

Real.

As real as the water pelting them. Her silken skirts and all her underpinnings were drooping fast as the rains continued to lash them. Another twirl, and her sodden hems tripped her. Decker caught her with ease when she would have pitched into the rosebushes, hauling her into his arms.

She was deuced small, but all her layers were damned heavy when wet.

"You do not need to carry me," she objected. "I am perfectly capable of walking myself."

"Of course you are capable, but what manner of man would I be if I allowed my new wife to go toppling into the daisies on our wedding day?" he asked her, feeling an alarming surge of tenderness rushing inside him.

"They are roses," she corrected, sounding breathless.

Of course he knew what the damned flowers were.

But he liked that she was breathless.

He wanted to make her *more* breathless.

"I stand corrected." He carried her through the rain, making his way back to the doors with as much haste as he could manage. "You have a choice to make, darling. Cream ice or kisses first?"

"Decker!" Her soft exclamation did naughty things to the state of his cock. "Kisses, of course."

So, too, did her response.

Stifling a groan, he managed to elbow and shoulder his way back into the house, where they made a dripping, saturated mess all over the carpets. Perhaps ruining them. He did not give a damn.

"You can put me down now," she said.

"I can," he agreed pleasantly, "but I am not going to."

"But surely I am too heavy! I insist you stop carrying me about as if I am a doll," Jo carried on with her protesting.

He was a man on a mission now. She wanted kisses first, and he intended to give them to her. "I have been waiting three bloody weeks to make you my wife, and now I find myself deuced reluctant to have you anywhere but in my arms."

Which was where she belonged.

There and in his bed, of course.

And anywhere else he could have her. Oh, the delicious possibilities. At long last, he could dispense with fucking his fist.

He told himself that was the reason for the sense of rightness deep within him, that new, unexpected sensation of…what the hell was it? Contentment? *Egad.* That could not be it. He was simply so randy, he could not think straight.

Decker increased his pace. The quicker he could get her to his chamber, the better.

His servants were accustomed to his antics. If dinner parties in which foodstuffs were served upon naked women did not make the footmen blink an eye, their master carrying his new wife—the two of them soaked to the skin—was not cause for a second look. They passed a handful of domestics as he took them up the stairs two at a time. All lowered their gazes and pretended as if they had seen nothing amiss.

"What will the staff think?" she asked, pressing her face into his sodden waistcoat as they passed a chamber maid who busied herself with righting a picture on the wall as they passed.

"Who gives a damn?" he asked as he shouldered his way into his chamber at last and kicked the door closed at his back. "Believe me, they have seen far worse."

Wrong thing to say on your wedding day, you fucking arse.

Jo stiffened in his arms, and as he gently lowered her to the carpets, her gaze was downcast. "Of course. How foolish of me to forget your reputation."

"Josie." He caught her chin in his thumb and forefinger, gently forcing her to meet his eyes. "Look at me. I am far from a saint, as you know. I will not lie about who I am, who I have always been. I have never brought a lover here to my home, however. You need not fear that. This home is yours as much as it is mine, and no other woman has ever belonged here as you do."

He meant those words, to his core.

His parties had been wild, but they had been mere diversion. Something to quell his boredom. His home was his haven, however. He did not bring women here to bed them, because he had no wish for the complication which would inevitably follow suit. Unlike most wealthy gentlemen, he did not seek lasting situations with the women he fucked. His *affaires* had always been discreet and short-lived—one night only had been his codicil ever since Nora.

But Jo appeared unimpressed by his explanation. She remained unsmiling. "You do not have to justify yourself to me, Decker. I am more than aware of who you are."

All the lightness of their dance in the rain had vanished thanks to his cloddish misstep. He would have to revive it. Somehow. Inspiration came swiftly.

There was a raindrop upon the fullness of her lower lip. He lowered his head and pressed his mouth to hers, stealing that drop. He cupped her face in his hands, taking his time, showing her with his lips how he would worship her. Gently at first, then deeper.

She opened to him, their tongues mating. She tasted like the cake they had eaten at the wedding breakfast: orange sweetness. And she smelled like it too, only with familiar, floral notes that made his cock pitch a tent in his trousers. He groaned, angling her head, kissing her harder. He would make her forget all about thoughts of other women or his storied past. Today was not about any of that.

It was about Decker and Jo.

It was about him claiming her at bloody last.

And tomorrow? whispered an insidious voice deep within him.

Would he be tired of her? Would he have her once and never want her again, just as he had all the rest? The thought sent a pang of regret cutting swiftly through him, but he banished it.

No time for worrying about what came after. They were bound to each other now. Nothing and no one—not even the Earl of Ravenscroft—could keep him from making love to her.

Jo's small hands settled on his cheeks, cupping his face, holding him to her. Such a ferocious woman. She had learned how to kiss over the course of their sinful interludes, and he was grateful for it. An apt pupil, his lady wife. He had far more to teach her.

But first, their mouths were uniting. With other lovers, he

had never taken so much time to woo or to savor—not since Nora. One time this evening was quite enough, *thank you very much*. And also, thank Christ Jo was nothing like her.

Jo was…herself.

A revelation.

She was the majestic beauty of late spring's promise realized. She was glorious blossoms and lush verdant grass and golden sun and delicious warmth after the dearth of cold, hideous winter.

He gentled the kiss, reminding himself she was also a novice. His seduction of her had to proceed slowly, and with care. His lady may possess a wicked curiosity and a passionate nature, but she was also inexperienced.

Decker lifted his head at last, dismayed to find his heart pounding.

When was the last time a kiss had left him thus? He could not recall as he took her in a tender grasp and raised her hands to his lips for a reverent kiss on her knuckles. Even this part of her was somehow beautiful. Had he taken note of a woman's knuckles before? Decker thought not.

"I dare say I must get you out of your wet gown before you take a chill, my lady," he said, deciding to test her boundaries. "What manner of lady's maid would I be if I allowed you to remain in these soaked garments a moment longer?"

Her kiss-stung lips were open, and her breaths were as ragged as his. "You are hardly a lady's maid."

He kissed the tops of her hands. "But of course I am. I am a humble servant, here to tend to my mistress." Decker turned her hands over, revealing the pale skin of her wrists, the delicate tracery of blue veins there. "How may I be of service to you, milady?" He kissed the velvet-soft flesh he had exposed. Once, twice. "You must be soaked to the skin."

And, he hoped, elsewhere also.

He swallowed against another rush of lust, meeting her gaze.

The gold in her eyes seemed more vibrant, her lashes thicker, her pupils wide onyx discs that gave her away.

"Yes, I am quite drenched," she said, her voice low and throaty. Sultry.

Ah, hell. He was once more thinking of where else she was drenched. Thinking of at last stroking her slit, parting her folds…

He raised his head, knowing he played a dangerous game. "Turn, my lady. Allow me to make you more comfortable."

She did as he asked, presenting him with the endless line of buttons on her gown. She had looked incredible in it, and when he had spoken his vows to her earlier in the church, he had been blasted with an incredible burst of pride that she was *his.*

Not just a lady, an earl's sister, a woman who had been born with all the legitimacy which had been denied him by his sire, but Lady Jo herself—quiet elegance, humble sophistication. She was not a raucous beauty. She was not the storm; she was the calm that came after it, when the birds sang once more and the rainbow arched over the shattered land.

He swallowed yet another surge of emotion that was entirely unwanted. Hell, *emotions?* He was being disgustingly maudlin and quite unlike himself.

His fingers were on her buttons now, and to his further dismay, he realized his hands were trembling. There was something sacred about this moment. He could not shake the feeling. He wanted to worship her. He was terrified of her. He needed her.

Best to bury himself in pleasure, as he had learned a long time ago.

Decker kissed her crown, inhaling the scent of her luscious, wet locks. Her coiffure was next to be undone. The rains had already done their part at dismantling the perfection she had presented for their wedding. He preferred her this way, however, rain-soaked and wild, rather than the poised lady he had wed.

He kissed her ear next, running his tongue along the whorls there whilst his fingers played over the buttons, freeing them. Ten down and about a hundred of the little stubborn blighters to go.

JO HELD HERSELF stiffly and still as her husband unhooked the buttons on her gown. As his lips caressed her ear, his tongue darting out to lap against her skin and incite those same flames of desire she had come to know all too well ever since she had been summoned to his office that day by his note telling her he had something of hers.

And now she knew he had something else of hers in his possession. Something far more important than the list.

Her heart.

But she would not divulge that secret now. For now, she would live in the moment.

How strange it felt to be a wife. Or, more precisely, to be Decker's wife. To be married to the enigma at her back, the man whose tongue was flicking behind her ear, finding a new way to drive her to distraction.

But even as his mouth and tongue worked over her, his hands never stopped. Those knowing fingers of his were moving, unhooking, sliding the buttons free of their moorings. The stiff silk bodice of her gown, adorned by roses and lace and pounds upon pounds of silver beads, gaped and slid down her arms, weighted by her damp skirts.

They had danced in the rain.

She had fallen beneath his spell even more as he had whirled her through his gardens in the rain. A Viennese waltz, just like the dance they had shared at Callie's ball. He thought of everything. And then, his question—cream ice or kisses. How could she gird her heart against him when he insisted upon being so wonderful, so very much the opposite of every warning she had received from her loved ones?

Decker brought her mind back to the present when his teeth nipped her throat, and then his tongue followed, soothing the sting. Heat unfurled within her, landing between her thighs in a persistent, pulsing ache. She wanted him so much. Too much.

"You are quiet, my lady," he observed against her neck. "Tell me how I may be of service to you. As your humble servant, it is my duty to see you satisfied."

Jo did not mistake his words. Decker was toying with her, playing a role, pretending to be her lady's maid. Did the pretense heighten his pleasure? She could not be certain. She was not even sure if it heightened her own pleasure. All she did know was that she was completely in his thrall. And she was going to play this game with him, see where it led them. For the first time in her life, she was free, truly, unutterably free.

What did she have to lose, when she had already lost everything else of consequence, aside from her maidenhead itself?

"My gown," she said, catching her breath. "It is heavy and soaked. Please help me to take it off."

"With pleasure, my lady," he growled against her skin.

And then his fingers were moving with heightened fury, traveling down her spine. The tapes on her bustle went slack, and the entire dress, along with the wire and linen shaper beneath, fell to the floor in a rush. She was clad in nothing more than her corset, chemise, drawers, and stockings.

But he was already making short work of the knot and lacings on her corset. In the next breath, they were undone. Her undergarments were suddenly loose. His hands clamped on her waist, spinning her around to face him with so much haste, she nearly lost her balance.

Perhaps it was because he was making her knees turn into aspic?

She swayed, her hands planting on his broad shoulders for purchase, holding herself upright. He was so handsome, towering over her with his brooding masculine beauty, his wavy, dark hair falling rakishly over his brow, his bright-blue eyes searing her where she stood.

He was still wearing all his wedding finery. Coat, waist-coat, shirt, neck cloth tied neatly around his throat. He was the picture of a fine English gentleman. So gorgeous, he made her ache.

He grasped her corset then, unhooking her before tossing the undergarment to the floor. Make that only her chemise, drawers, and stockings.

Oh dear.

"Your underpinnings are damp, my lady," he said, his voice low.

Pure, unadulterated seduction.

"Yours are wet as well," she ventured, finding her tongue and her own bravery at last. "Mayhap I should help you to divest yourself of your soaked garments."

He shook his head, his gaze lowering to her lips. "I do not know about that. A lady aiding her servant? It is not done. As your loyal lady's maid, I cannot allow you to assist me. To do so would be wrong."

His words heightened her awareness. Suddenly, the allure of the game he was playing with her became clear. There was something delightfully exciting about pretending, about playing roles. She had already been wild for him, but pretending he was her servant and that what they were doing was wicked and forbidden, made her want him so much more.

Indeed, she was desperate for him.

"I insist," she said. "It is not fair for you to be soaked to the bone. You must remove some of your layers. Let me aid you."

He inclined his head, the look he gave her enough to set her drawers aflame. And herself. And the entire chamber. It would all be engulfed in fire, burning down, all around them, before this was over.

"Assist me as you will, my lady," he told her.

He did not need to offer the invitation twice. Her hands took control of her mind, doing all the work for her, investigating his broad shoulders and hard chest before finding the twain ends of his coat and pushing them down. Next, her fingers discovered the buttons of his waistcoat.

She plucked each one free.

His shirt? Gone.

His trousers were next. But his chest briefly distracted her. Jo had never witnessed a naked masculine chest. And Decker's? It was positively sinful.

"Touch me, Josie," he rasped, his voice low. "I want your hands upon me. I have spent the last weeks dreaming of nothing else."

He had been dreaming of her?

Eagerness made her hands tremble as she did as he asked. His abdomen first. A tentative caress up those ridges of muscle, over the fine trail of dark hair that led to the waistband of his trousers. His skin was warm and damp and softer than she had imagined. He inhaled sharply as she glided her hands higher, to the delineations of his chest.

Curiosity sent her fingertips over the flat discs of his nipples, so unlike her own. A groan rumbled deep in his throat, and she absorbed the vibration. Jo stopped, her hands still on him.

His hands covered hers then, guiding her higher, over the protrusion of his clavicle, to his shoulders. How wonderful he felt, deliciously masculine and all hers. She had dreamt of this too, of being alone with him, of being free to touch and be touched. Of no longer dithering about and observing propriety.

The last three weeks of waiting had been utter torture. Julian had watched her like a thief he suspected planned upon filching the familiar silver. When she had not been within his sight, a servant had attended her. Not even the birth of her nephew had diminished his brotherly determination to make certain she made it to her wedding day without a further hint of scandal.

"If you keep looking at me that way, I am going to ravish you here and now," Decker said suddenly.

Yes, please.

"You do not know what you are asking for, darling," he said, his eyes darkening.

Oh dear. Had she said that aloud? It would seem she had.

"Why do we need to wait?" she dared to ask next.

After all, they were married now. There was no more sneaking about. Nothing that happened between them from this moment forward was wrong.

"I intended to woo you." He lowered his forehead to hers. "I wanted to give you some time to adjust to your new household."

At the moment, she did not give a fig about the household. All she cared about was the man. His lips were near, his breath feathering over her mouth.

"Decker?"

His stare was intent, burning into hers. "Yes, darling?"

"I do not think I require time to adjust."

"Damnation, woman. I am not certain if you are a gift or a curse." His mouth crushed hers in the next second.

His lips worked over hers with voracious precision yet reverent tenderness. That tenderness told her he believed the former rather than the latter. His fingers swept over her, her remaining undergarments falling away until she was clad in nothing but her stockings.

Without ending their kiss, he moved them, backing her across the cavernous chamber. It had not failed to escape her notice that Decker's home was immense and sprawling by London standards, and that the private rooms were every bit as lushly furnished and ornate as the public. He was a gentleman of obscene wealth, as evidenced by their marriage contract.

It felt as if they traveled forever, and yet it must have only been moments. The room was large but not endless. Finally, the massive, carved oak bed she had spied upon their initial entrance loomed behind her. Her bare bottom connected with cool linens, a firm mattress, reminding her she was almost entirely nude. Already, he had made her forget. Of course he had. He was the sun, brightening her world, bringing with him all the light, giving her life. How could she think of anything but him when his lips were upon her?

Strangely, she was not ashamed. Nor was she nervous. Jo knew not a modicum of hesitation. There was only a natural, abiding sense of rightness about the man, the moment, the act they were about to share.

His hands clamped on her waist, lifting her. He deposited

her in the center of the bed as if she were something rare and precious he had only just discovered. When he straightened, their mouths parted, and she mourned the end to their kiss. But her breathlessness only increased when he stood to his full height and, keeping his stare pinned upon hers, began opening the fall of his trousers. She felt like a watch spring, tightly wound as she waited and watched.

Down his hips those trousers went, and with them, his smalls. Although the bed obscured him from mid-thigh down, it could not hide his manhood, thick and long, jutting from his impressively honed body. The lifeless marble of Adonis in the gardens had ill-prepared her for the sight of Decker, in *flagrante delicto*.

"Stunning," she whispered, then flushed furiously at her gauche antics.

What must he think of her? He had known many lovers before her, and surely none of them had ogled him with such naïve astonishment.

"I would have said the same of you, but the word would have never held," he said, his voice husky. "Glorious. Lovely. Breathtaking. Utterly ravishing. All of them pale in comparison to the sight of you, naked."

She pressed her thighs together, feeling at once brazen and…hungry. Yes, that was the word. Starved.

For *him*. For what he would do to her. For what he would show her.

"I am wearing my stockings," she murmured foolishly, her mouth going dry.

"Leave them," he ordered softly as he joined her on the bed, trailing his hand up her calf, past her knee. Beneath the barrier of the fine silk, gooseflesh pebbled her skin. "I like the way you look in nothing but these innocent wisps of silk." He lowered his mouth to her knee, thigh, kissing the bare skin above her garter, where her stockings ended. "I like the way you look in my bed."

"I like the way I feel in your bed," she blurted, continuing her campaign of making herself feel dreadfully inexperienced and the opposite of every woman he must have known before her.

"Good." He gave her a devilish smile as he kissed higher, to her hip bone. "I dreamt of this, too, you know."

"You did?" she breathed as his mouth left a trail of decadence to her breasts.

"More times than I can count." He caressed her breast, cupping it in his palm, flicking his thumb over the peak. "And I thought about this, as well."

Warmth washed over her. She had touched her own breasts before, in the privacy of the bath or late at night, beneath the counterpane when everyone else was abed. She knew how pleasant the sensation was. However, Decker's large hand upon her was nothing at all like touching herself. It was electric. It was... Description failed her. Her nipples were hard, her breasts aching, and the place between her clamped thighs was damp and pulsing.

"Oh," was all she could manage, her hands settling upon him at last. He was within reach, and how could she deny herself the luxury?

"Do you want to know what else I thought about?" he whispered, pressing a kiss to the curve of her breast. "I thought about what color your nipples would be and whether or not your breasts would fill my palms."

She did not have a particularly large bosom. Every part of her was small, and she knew it, from her tiny feet to everywhere else. Whilst some ladies whirled around the ballroom with generous décolletages on full display, hers had been disappointingly as diminutive as the rest of her.

"They hardly fill your palms," she said, feeling once more like the wallflower she was.

"They are perfection," he told her, a reverence in his tone that made her believe him. "And they are the color of summer roses in full bloom." He kissed her other breast, leveraging himself on his elbows as he cupped her in his hands. "And I thought about doing this."

He took a nipple into his mouth and sucked. And she felt that wet suction, the heat of his mouth, followed by the lash of his tongue over the taut bud, everywhere. Once more, he chased the fears. The stagnant voice which had always told her she was not enough—that she would never be enough—vanished.

She arched into his knowing mouth, and his fingers skimmed back down her body, finding the apex of her thighs. Fingers coasted over her mound in a featherlight caress, coaxing her to relax. He made her feel beautiful. Her body was awash in senses: his scent, his touch, his tongue, his mouth, his touch. The heat of him at her side.

He skimmed over her seam, a long finger parting her, finding her throbbing center, the place where all her desire dwelled. The place only she had ever touched before. Decker stroked firmly, with quick pulses that had her gasping with pleasure and made her hips rise from the bed to meet him.

He released her nipple, ran his tongue over the tight bud, and then gave her a sultry look from beneath the sooty fringe of his lowered lashes. "You like this, darling?"

Cruel man. Of course she liked it, as he must know. She loved it, in fact. Everything. All of it. *Him.* Yes, she thought she may love him, too. But she did not dare say that now, and furthermore, she was also not entirely certain her mind and tongue were jointly capable of forming words. *Problem solved.*

"Mmm," she said instead.

A purr.

Goodness, she certainly *felt* feline at the moment. Languorous and ready to be worshiped. Give her a good patch of sun and Decker's hands and lips upon her, and she would want for nothing.

He moved to her other breast as his finger flicked over her with devastating pressure and friction. How quickly he brought her to the edge. Nothing could have prepared her for this, his dark, tousled head bent, his lips drawing on her nipple, sucking. His teeth nipping gently. Tugging. His tongue soothing the sting, running lazy circles around the peak before lapping at the stiff, puckered bud.

So quickly, she turned to flame. Her body was on fire for him. And the fire only increased when he swirled his fingers over her. He released her nipple, his breath hot on her skin. *Kiss, kiss, kiss.*

He raised his head, the astonishing blue of his gaze clashing with hers. "What about this, *bijou*? Slower or faster? Harder or softer? Tell me what you like, what you want."

Good heavens, he wanted her direction? She had never touched herself long enough to know what she liked. She had aspired to being wicked, but she did not fool herself into believing she ever had been.

"Yes," she gasped as he pressed a bit harder, his fingers moving rapidly over her.

"Slower?" he asked, gentling his ministrations.

Not enough.

"Faster," she bit out. "Harder, too."

He grinned. "A lady who knows what she wants. I approve."

Jo was not certain she knew what she wanted, aside from Decker. He was all, it seemed to her now, that she had ever wanted. She thought back on the words her sister-in-law Clara had spoken to her a few weeks and seemingly a lifetime ago. Yes, Jo felt the same way, as if her heart had known Decker's forever.

As if this moment, this closeness, had been destined. Pre-ordained.

It was thrilling and terrifying in equal measures.

He strummed her sex as if he were a musician finely attuned to his instrument. And then he was kissing his way back to her lips. *Kiss, kiss, kiss.* All the way to the hollow at the base of her throat, which he tongued. *Kiss, kiss, kiss.* To her ear. His tongue slid over the outer ridges, then delved inside. He continued playing with her as he went. Tormenting her. Working her into a frenzy with his knowing touch.

And, oh…oh…*oh.*

She was—

The sensation hit her, suddenly, warm and cataclysmic. *Bliss.* She was shaking. Her heart pounded. For a moment, she feared she was dying. Was this the passion she had only ever heard about? Surely not. She could not breathe. Tremors passed through her as she writhed beneath her husband's caresses.

"Are you coming for me, darling?" he asked into her ear.

If that was what this mysterious pleasure was, then the answer was yes. She was. She was caught in the merciless grip of desire so profound she had never imagined it could exist. And yet, it did. But then, his fingers slid down her folds, leaving that tender bud. He prodded her entrance, where she was wet and aching and ready.

"Yes," she gasped as his finger dipped into her channel. Not deep, but a slow, tentative penetration.

Testing her.

It was new and strange and yet also deliciously intriguing.

"You are so wet," he said in that low voice of his, with a

note of praise. "So ready for me, sweet Josie."

Once more, words were beyond her.

But it did not matter then, because his lips were on hers, stealing anything she may have spoken. Drowning her thoughts, her fears. Soothing her with the strong slant of his mouth. He kissed her ferociously. Divinely. She opened for his tongue, tasting him. Wanting him.

And then, a different part of him altogether was prodding her below. The broad head of his manhood. He broke the kiss, his breathing harsh, falling over her lips the same way the tousled waves of his dark hair fell over his brow in rakish abandon. His beautiful face was a study in restraint, his square jaw rigid, his eyes dark, the skin over his slashing cheekbones taut. He was more handsome than any man should be.

He was her husband.

The thought made her weak and wild, all at once.

"I am going to take you now," he warned against her mouth. "From what I understand, it may cause you pain at worst, discomfort at best… I shall try to be gentle."

She could not fathom how he could ever hurt her. Not physically, anyway. Emotionally—she could not bear to contemplate the notion. Jo swallowed, trying to catch her breath, trying to ready herself. To compose herself.

"Take me," she urged him, desperate for the preliminaries to be over. Desperate to feel him inside her. At last.

"Tell me if I should stop," he ground out, sounding as if he were in pain.

His brow was furrowed, his entire countenance rigid. How still he held himself, all to protect her. A new rush of tenderness for him washed over her.

She slid her legs apart, hooking them instinctively around his hips, bringing them together. "Do not. Not now, not ever, I beg you."

"Ah, God, Josie." His forehead dipped to hers, their noses rubbing. His lips were firm, kissing her, his tongue bold as ever, sweeping into her mouth.

And then, in an instant, everything changed. He thrust his hips, and his manhood sank inside her. Lodged deep. One full buck of his hips was all it had taken, and he was there, throbbing and hot and intrusive and wonderful. Painful, but wonderful.

Her breath was gone. Her mind, obliterated.

Instead, she relied upon her body, upon instinct.

She clung to him, kissing him back with all the pent-up fury in her heart. With all the longing, the desire, the confusing, raging, effervescent lust. She moved, discovering he was not seated as fully as he could be. There was more.

He thrust again, a rumble reverberating from his chest, and she swallowed it in their kiss. Decker was all she could think, all she could feel. She wanted everything he would give her. All of him.

And he seemed to understand without her needing to give voice to the innate needs within her. She jerked her body against his, bowing from the bed, her legs wrapped around him. He planted a hand in her unbound hair, clutching a fistful, holding her tight to him as he kissed her.

One more pump of his hips, and he was all the way inside her. Deep. Nothing could have prepared Jo for this moment, this consummation of their relationship, this communion of souls and desires and frantic, all-consuming, pent-up desire. He severed the kiss, raising his head.

"How do you feel, darling?" he asked, holding himself still instead of continuing as her body wanted him to.

"Full," she answered honestly. "And wonderful."

He kissed her on a groan, and then he began moving again. Slowly at first, gliding in and out of her body with a steady pace that threatened to unravel her. She clutched him, instinctively following his motions, her hips undulating in time to his rhythm. As his tongue plundered her mouth, his fingers once more found that slick nub at her center. He played with her. The combination of his shaft inside her, his fingers flying over her flesh, the weight of his body atop hers, and his mouth owning her lips proved too much.

She clenched on him, convulsing as pleasure overwhelmed her. This was more potent than the euphoria which had come before. Different, better, because he was within her, thrusting faster now, less controlled. As the last ripples of desire lingered, his body stiffened. On a low groan, he withdrew from her. Grasping his rigid cock in his hand, he spent into the bedclothes before hurling himself to his back.

Jo lay there, heart thundering, body humming with the aftereffects of lovemaking.

"When do you want the cream ice?" he asked suddenly into the silence, sounding as winded as if he had just run the course of St. James's Square.

"Mmm." She turned to him, smiling shyly, feeling sated, blissful, and wholly unlike herself. "What is cream ice?"

Laughter tore from him. Bold, deep, dark.

Beautiful.

She did not think she had ever heard him laugh before. Or if she had, certainly not with such unrestrained delight. Jo found herself smiling back at him, knowing she was the source of his pleasure, his humor. How intoxicating it was to think that she, a mere wallflower, could so thoroughly please a man like Elijah Decker without trying.

"Vixen." There was no heat in his voice as he made the charge. Indeed, if anything, his voice was laden with undeniable approval.

"You would not have me any other way," she dared to say.

"Come here, minx," he ordered her affectionately.

She scooted nearer, settling against his chest. His arms wrapped around her, mooring her to him. Gently, he brushed a hand over her hair. She inhaled deeply of his scent and returned his embrace.

And as she listened to the steady thump of his heart, that was when she knew for certain what she had been too hesitant to accept until this very moment.

Jo was in love.

Hopelessly, desperately in love with her husband.

I feel as if my heart has always known his.

How terrifying.

Chapter Twelve

Ways to be Wicked

1. ~~Kiss a man until you are breathless.~~

2. *Arrange for an assignation. Perhaps with Lord Q?*

3. ~~Get caught in the rain with a gentleman. (This will necessitate the removal of wet garments. Choose said gentleman wisely.)~~

4. *Sneak into a gentleman's bedchamber in the midst of the night.*

5. ~~Go to a gentleman's private apartments.~~

6. *Spend a night in a gentleman's bed.*

7. *Make love in the outdoors.*

8. *Ask*

Once had not been enough.

A terrifying realization, that.

Decker had woke that morning with an erection to rival Priapus. His new wife had been tucked safely away in her chambers, sleeping soundly, no doubt, leaving him to once more take himself in hand to thoughts of her.

Thoughts which were a thousand times more erotic now that he had actually been inside her tight, wet heat. His cock, however, refused to oblige him. He had been unable to spend.

Frustrated, he had settled himself at the breakfast table where his newspapers awaited him only to discover Jo was already there, looking utterly ravishing and giving him a second go at winning the prize for cockstand of the century. All before half past eight in the morning.

He, who prided himself upon his silver tongue and rakish charm, was unexpectedly speechless. He stopped at the threshold of the dining room, drinking in the sight of her. She was wearing a cobalt-blue silk gown patterned with blushing pink roses. The gown was eye-catching and bright, but it was the loving fit of it, showing off her curved waist, the décolletage trimmed with blonde lace revealing a mouthwatering hint of her bosom, that almost ended him.

She paused in the act of filling her plate from the sideboard, her hair piled high atop her crown, more stunning than he had ever seen her. "Good morning."

Her soft smile and the sudden color in her cheekbones told him she was thinking of all that had passed between them the evening before. So was he. In fact, there was not room for anything else in his mind. Not even words.

And so he bowed to her with something that resembled a grunt rather than a return of her morning salutation. Doing his best to hide his unfortunate condition from the servants overseeing the early morning meal, he strode toward the sideboard.

He was about to snatch up a plate and help himself to his customary bacon, ham, eggs, and fruit when it occurred to him he was a husband now. Eating breakfast was no longer a solitary affair. Perhaps it would now involve manners and communication beyond burying himself in the newspapers.

He was not sure he liked that just yet.

Decker cleared his throat and turned to his still-blushing bride. "May I fill your plate for you?"

Some of the color fled her cheeks at last. "I shall do for myself, thank you. Unless you prefer it?"

It was clear she did not want to displease him. And further that she was as out of her depths as he was. Some part of him—that old, stalwart bachelor—was having difficulty believing this was his new life. That he had a wife.

Nothing has to change, he reminded himself. *My life can be just as it was.*

"Whatever you wish is what I would prefer, my dear," he said.

There. He could be an accommodating husband.

Husband, yes, there was that. He was married. The parson's mousetrap had snapped upon him. The impending horror that ought to have accompanied these thoughts was strangely absent for now. And they did nothing to abate the irritatingly rigid state of his cock.

"Thank you," she returned softly, giving him a smile that also did nothing to quell his rampant erection, for it called attention to the plush invitation of her lips.

He caught a whiff of orange blossom and jasmine as she resumed arranging her selections on her plate with dainty precision. Two things occurred to him then, in rapid succession. One, he was gawking at his wife. Mooning over her as if he had never seen a woman. *Vomitus.* Two, his servants were bearing witness. One of them—a footman named Dawkins—had been smirking until he caught Decker's stare upon him and hastily banished all expression from his countenance.

Wise decision, you smug prick.

Decker turned his attention back to the impressive selection his chef had provided, presumably in an effort to please his new mistress. Without a care for what he was choosing or the quantities, he began to heap foodstuffs upon his plate. His mind was whirling, and his cock was aching, and neither of these two states were conducive to his having a productive day,

Before he knew it, his plate was towering with bacon and sausage and nothing else. There was no space for eggs or the luscious-looking hothouse pineapple and strawberries.

Damnation. He was going to have a gut full of meat.

But there was no help for it. Inwardly stewing at his ridiculous reaction to this morning, he stalked to his customary place. Jo was already there, awaiting him. *Nothing has to change*, he repeated to himself as he settled into his chair. His coffee was prepared just as he liked it, awaiting him. His newspaper was ironed and ready.

He flipped to the State of Trade section, as usual. The price of coal was down. The cotton market was lackluster. His eyes wandered over railroad shares. He felt Jo's stare on him like a touch. He flicked his gaze to her, finding her watching him expectantly.

Well, bloody hell. Did she want to converse?

"I spend my mornings reviewing *The Times*," he explained. "It is imperative, as a businessman, that I keep apprised of all the comings and goings of the world."

Her lush lips compressed. "Of course, Mr. Decker."

Ah, she was nettled. She *did* want to converse.

He lowered the paper to the table. "No *mister*, my dear. Decker will continue to do."

"Hmm," she said, before beginning to methodically cut the wedges of pineapple on her plate into smaller, bite-sized portions.

Each delicate clink of the cutlery on her plate nettled him.

Her silence said more than her words could, and he did not like it. However, he had his morning routine for a reason. It settled him. This was the manner in which he began his day, every day. He would not alter it because he had a wife. Just as he would not alter any part of himself. He was the same man he had always been.

He picked up *The Times* and resumed reviewing the reports. The Exchange on Paris was on the rise. His attention wandered, and he was briefly distracted about an article concerning an explosion on Her Majesty's ship *Inflexible.* Someone was outraged about something Lord Randolph Churchill had said. A case of poisonous cream ices in Lambeth-walk…

He snapped the newspaper closed once more, irritated with himself for his distraction. His wife was calmly consuming her breakfast. She paused when he lowered the paper, her dark eyebrows lifting in question.

"Is something amiss, Mr. Decker?" she asked in her sweet, dulcet voice.

Yes, something is amiss, he wanted to holler. *You are intruding upon my life.*

But of course she was, wasn't she? He had married her. She lived here now. She had every right to have expectations of him. Somehow, in all the fantasies he had entertained during the time he had waited to marry her, he had never envisioned anything other than fucking her until he had effectively excised her from his blood. He had not thought about sharing the breakfast table with her or—*good God*—hosting social events. Would she want to throw balls and dinner parties? Would she expect him to speak to her during breakfast?

"Of course not," he said smoothly, breaking himself free of his thoughts. He cast a glance toward the servants dancing attendance upon them. "That will be all for now, if you please. I will ring when our meal is complete, thank you."

He waited for the footmen to depart before turning his full attention to Jo.

"Why the devil do you keep referring to me as Mr. Decker?" he demanded "Is this some sort of nonsense you insist upon doing before the servants? If so, I can assure you, my domestics are amply recompensed for their service. They do not give a damn if you call me Mr. Decker or Decker or Elijah or Eli or Adam for that matter."

"Mr. Decker seems like the sort of man who would ignore his new wife in favor of burying his face in *The Times*," she returned.

Curse it, he had been correct. She had *expectations* of him. He ought to have warned her not to waste her time.

Instead, he raised a brow. "Have I displeased you already? That was a remarkably short amount of time."

In truth, he was unaccustomed to what followed his liaisons. In the past, he had always made it clear to his lovers what they could expect of him: one night of senseless shagging. That was all. Not since Nora had he been so available to a woman in the way he now was with Jo. He had never broken his fast with lovers.

But Jo was not just any lover, was she?

"I thought we might talk," she said, "that is all. If you are more interested in your newspaper than speaking with me, I shall not force you to suffer."

That was when he heard it—the underlying note of hurt and disappointment in her voice. Something slid through him, clenching his stomach.

Remorse.

Last night had been profound. They had made love and then napped together. Later, he had shared a bath with her and had made her come once more with his fingers on her pearl beneath the warm, soothing water. They dined in his chamber and fed each other cream ice. They had just made love the once, Decker wanting to give her body time to adjust.

And how did he follow up such day?

By being an arse to her, naturally. All because the lifelong bachelor within him was rebelling at the notion of the power she had over him.

"There is nothing more interesting in this newspaper than you," he told her, and that was the truth. "I am simply a man of routine. Forgive me?"

"Of course I forgive you." Her gaze searched his. "This is new for you. It is for me as well. We must grow familiar with our change in circumstances together."

Together.

That was another new word, a new concept.

He wanted to hate it, but he could not muster the sentiment. Instead, all he felt was…hope.

That was it. All the blood had clearly abandoned his brain in favor of rushing to his cock.

He suddenly had an idea of one manner in which they could grow accustomed to their circumstances together. What the devil was he doing, having a civilized breakfast and poring over *The Times* when the woman he could not stop wanting was here, within reach?

Decker rose from his chair, stalked around the corner of the table to her. She watched with wide eyes.

"You are correct, darling." He extended his hand. "I find myself famished, but not for breakfast."

She settled her diminutive hand in his, and even the innocent-enough contact made his prick twitch. "What are you suggesting?"

"That we begin this morning again the proper way, as we should have done from the first." He hauled her to her feet. "With you in my bed."

PERHAPS SHE OUGHT not to have given in with such ease.

But as Decker kissed his way down her naked body, Jo was not sure she cared. Her earlier irritation with him had vanished like her gown and all the underpinnings beneath. His clever hands had made short work of all her trappings.

Of course, they had. Were he not a businessman, he would have made an excellent lady's maid.

Except, no lady's maid did what her husband was currently doing to her.

His hands were on her thighs now, coaxing her to open for him.

"Decker," she whispered, shyness mingling with excitement and hunger. "What are you doing? You cannot possibly mean to—oh!"

When his mouth found the wildly sensitive bundle of nerves between her legs, she forgot what she had been about to say.

He lifted his head, his bright-blue gaze meeting hers and stealing her breath. "I can. Relax, *bijou*. Let me do penance for being an oaf at the breakfast table."

He *had* been an oaf. She ought to still be aggrieved with him, but maintaining her crossness became impossible when his tongue stroked over her. She gasped, her hips jerking, offering herself up to him, seeking more.

"Mmm," he murmured into her sex as if he were feasting upon the most decadent dessert. "Perfection."

And then, he sucked her into his mouth. And it certainly felt like perfection, what he was doing. Wonderful, wicked man.

A strangled cry escaped her. Sensation blossomed. Pleasure unfurled, beginning there at her center and radiating outward, bringing with it the desperate need for more. She had seen the act, of course, represented in his naughty alphabet pictures at his club. But a hand-tinted lithograph could hardly compare to his skilled lips and tongue.

The desire he wrung from her was intense. She writhed beneath him, moaning when he caught her between his teeth and bit. *Dear. Sweet. Heavens. Above.* His tongue flitted over her in quick, steady pulses, soothing that sting, sending flutters of heat through her.

He licked down her slit next, parting her folds. His tongue sank inside her, thrusting in and out as he had the night before with his manhood. The wet slide, lapping at her core, was electric. And then, his thumb found her already desperately sensitive bud, flicking over her with fast, steady pressure.

Jo lost control. Something deep inside her clenched, and then she felt the same molten rush she had the night before. Her hips swiveled from the bed, and her fingers sank into his hair as she held him there, exactly where she wanted him. The sight of his dark head bent between her legs was so carnal, so thoroughly erotic. It only served to heighten the impact of her spend as it washed over her.

But as the last ripples of bliss subsided, he did not stop. Instead, he buried his tongue deep, as if he were seeking something, lapping up the wetness that seemed to be trickling from her core. He moaned, the sound guttural. A sound of pure, unadulterated pleasure.

He liked this every bit as much as she did, Jo realized. The knowledge only served to heighten each sensation. She sifted her fingers through his wavy, mahogany locks, rocking into his mouth. Now that she had spent once, she was greedy and ravenous. She wanted to spend again. She never wanted his mouth to stop.

She whimpered when he at last withdrew, already at the edge of another climax.

He glanced up her body, his beautiful lips glistening with her dew, and lazily stroked his thumb over her pearl. "I think I want your cream for breakfast every day."

The words had their intended effect. She trembled beneath him, desperate. He swirled over her again, then sank a finger deep inside her channel, working it in and out of her. The wet sounds echoed in the chamber. Her need for him was at once a source of embarrassment and a frantic yearning she could not deny.

"Would you like that?" he asked, adding a second finger, stretching her.

She felt a twinge of discomfort, her body still unaccustomed to such an invasion. But his deliberate thrusts and the slickness of her passage abated that.

"Hmm, Josie?" he asked again, curling his fingers deep inside her. "Would you like to begin every day like this?"

Before she could answer, he dipped his head, delivering a few languid licks to her swollen bud. "Yes."

Oh, yes.

Did he need to ask?

He suckled her again, then stroked her with that clever tongue as his fingers moved. She thrust against him, wanting him deeper. And he gave her what she asked for, reaching a place inside her she had not known existed. As he slid in and out, he used his teeth to abrade her pearl.

That was all the encouragement she needed.

The tangle of need within her tightened into a delicious knot.

Spasms quaked through her. She came so hard, little pinpricks of light burst around the periphery of her vision. And all through it, he stayed with her, bringing her to such impossible heights. He suckled her, then pressed a reverent kiss to her flesh, withdrawing his fingers at last.

As he settled between her legs, she could not help but to glory in the masculine beauty of his body. How different he was from her, all lean planes and sinews, that arrow of dark hair she had detected the day before trailing directly to his engorged cock. He seemed somehow larger, thick and long. The sight of him made the flesh he had awakened between her legs throb in anticipation even as she wondered how he would fit.

That he had yesterday seemed a miracle as she looked upon him now.

He grasped himself, aligning his tip with her entrance. Lowering his head, he sucked her nipple just as he had done to her pearl. Longing arced through her, settling between her thighs in an undeniable ache. She marveled at his strength as her hands settled on his shoulders, caressing over the smooth skin.

He kissed his way to her neck, and then she knew the same burning stretch as she had the night before, the sensation of him entering her. This time, however, there was no twinge of pain, no lingering ache. Her body was ready for his, and after the two climaxes he had just given her, the slide of his cock inside her passage was nothing short of breathtaking.

They sighed as one when he was fully seated. He kissed her throat, her ear.

"Oh Josie, darling," he said, his voice low and decadent. "You feel so damned good, all tight and wet on my cock."

His vulgar words made her want him more. Instinctively, she wrapped her legs around him, moving her hips to get him deeper.

"You feel good inside me, too," she dared to say.

His appreciative groan told her he approved. "Wicked girl." He tongued the hollow behind her ear, making her wild.

And then he began to move in earnest, thrusting in and

out of her slowly at first. Measured and steady. Her body lifted from the bed to meet his. She rubbed her cheek against the fine scrape of his freshly shaved whiskers. Her fingernails raked over his flesh.

His strokes became faster, more frenzied, more furious. He was losing control, his implacable grip on his restraint weakening. All because of her. And she loved it. She was perilously close to the edge, to losing herself yet again.

"Come on me," he urged into her ear. "Spend for me, *bijou*. Bring me there with you."

How could she deny him?

Her body convulsed as wave after wave of intense pleasure washed over her. On a guttural growl, he grew more rushed, each powerful pump of his cock sending her sliding up the bed into the soft mound of pillows. She clung to him, crying out her helpless pleasure as he slammed into her again and again.

Finally, he stiffened and withdrew. Her channel pulsed, mourning the loss. Gripping himself as he had the night before, he came, a torrent of seed jetting from his cock and splattering on her belly and breasts. She was covered in him, sated, mindless, and boneless on his bed.

Groaning, he flopped to his back at her side, his breathing every bit as ragged as hers. For a moment, she lay there in the aftermath of her crisis, attempting to catch her breath, her heart hammering in her chest. He had rocked her so utterly, he had robbed her of the capacity of thought. Speech was beyond her.

"A fine way to spend each morning," he said at last. "Much better than *The Times*, darling. Thank you for showing me the error of my ways."

And then he rolled from the bed to stalk across the chamber, naked as the day he had been born. Utterly shameless.

Not a hint of embarrassment. Though, as well formed as he was, she could hardly fault him for his confidence.

Still unable to move, Jo watched him go, admiring the tight curves of his bottom and the long lines of his legs. Every part of him was lovely—that broad back, the dimple above his buttocks, the muscled calves and thighs.

She sighed. If he saw fit to begin every day thus, she was never going to eat breakfast again.

Chapter Thirteen

Ways to be Wicked

1. ~~Kiss a man until you are breathless.~~

2. *Arrange for an assignation. Perhaps with* ~~Lord Q?~~ *your husband? Strike that,* **bijou**. <u>*Definitely*</u> *with your husband.*

3. ~~Get caught in the rain with a gentleman. (This will necessitate the removal of wet garments. Choose said gentleman wisely.)~~

4. ~~Sneak into a gentleman's bedchamber in the midst of the night.~~

5. ~~Go to a gentleman's private apartments.~~

6. ~~Spend a night in a gentleman's bed.~~

7. *Make love in the outdoors.*

8. *Ask*

One whole week.

Decker gritted his teeth and scrubbed a hand over his jaw.

He had been married to Jo for an entire seven wonderful, frustrating, tiring days, and he still had not had his fill of her. They had crossed off two more items on her wicked list. He had made love to her every morning before they breakfasted together. Sometimes, he returned in the afternoon to take her again, the endless wait until night too much to bear.

Half past one, and he was beginning to fear this would

prove one of those days. Reports from the piano factory lay untouched before him, along with the ledgers of his publishing company. To say nothing of the rough proofs of his erotic serials, corrected for press.

Macfie rapped on his office door.

"Enter," he called, sounding as irritated as he felt.

He had every right to be peeved, he told himself. He had been happy with his life as a bachelor, and now it had been upended by his wife. His wife for whom his obsession grew with each tick of the bloody minute hand on his pocket watch.

"The carriage is awaiting ye as ye asked," Macfie announced. "Along with the cream ice from Claremont's as ye requested fer Mrs. Decker."

"Very good, Macfie." He rose from his desk. No use settling in to work when he could not concentrate on anything but *her*. "Is the cream ice well packed in ice? It is a rather warm day today, and I do not fancy taking a bucket of milk soup home to Mrs. Decker."

Macfie inclined his head. "Extra ice, sir. I know how much ye hate tae disappoint yer lady."

That gave him pause. "How so, Macfie?"

"On Monday, ye asked me tae arrange for five crates of books tae be delivered tae yer house containing all Mrs. Decker's favorite authors and poets," Macfie began. "On Tuesday, ye asked for the cream ice from Claremont's, being that it is Mrs. Decker's new favorite, and ye were right put out when it turned tae soup on yer way home on account of the ice being puir. On Wednesday, ye asked me tae call upon Mercier and Sons with yer request for the diamond bangle ye wanted made in her honor. On Thursday—"

"Macfie?" he interrupted, more vexed now than he had been before.

"Yes, sir?" asked his stalwart *aide-de-camp*.

"Shut up," he said succinctly, for he had heard quite enough. He hardly needed an accounting of all the manners in which he had proven himself hopelessly enamored of his new wife.

Was it her cunny?

Yes, surely that was it.

She possessed a magical cunny. It had cast a spell upon him.

"Mrs. Decker is a lovely woman," Macfie ventured. "I cannae blame ye, sir."

Having his most-trusted man describe Jo as lovely yet again did nothing to improve Decker's mood.

He glared at the man. "Macfie, you do recall the conversation we had concerning your eyebrows, do you not?"

Macfie's expression went grim. "Ye promised ye wouldnae threaten them again."

"Let that be fair warning to you, Macfie. I cannot be trusted to uphold my promises. Not when they concern my wife and your eyebrows." Decker was silent for a moment as he realized how that had sounded. Then, he cleared his throat. "Not that I mean to say my wife has anything to do with your eyebrows, or that she has designs upon your eyebrows…"

He trailed off, realizing he was only digging his own verbal grave deeper by the moment.

"Mr. Decker?" Macfie raised both bushy red brows in question.

"Yes?" it was his turn to snap, his ears going hot.

"I think it is a verra wonderful thing, tae be smitten with yer lady," the brawny Scotsman told him.

Bloody hell. Now, his cheeks were hot, too. "I am not smitten with Mrs. Decker."

Right. Who was he trying to fool? He was *completely* smitten with his wife.

And her magical cunny.

And her ravishing lips.

And her beautiful bubbies, so pale and smooth.

Not to mention her laughter, her smile, her clever sense of humor, those exquisitely responsive nipples of hers…

Glaring at Macfie, he stalked from his office.

"I will not be returning today, Macfie," he called over his shoulder. "Do not expect me."

His *aide-de-camp*'s laughter followed him as he made a hasty exit from his offices.

In the carriage, he found the cream ice as promised—strawberry—and the ice packed tightly around it in reasonably good shape despite the warmth in the carriage. As his driver delivered him back to his townhome on Grosvenor Square—an address so chosen to disturb the peers who looked down their noses at him—Decker told himself he had not spent each of the days since marrying Jo caught up in her.

And then he depleted another few minutes arguing with himself that he needed to find other means of distraction. His club, for instance, which he had abandoned following his nuptials. Yes, he ought to go there. Some time away from Jo would be revitalizing. Restorative. The means by which he could end this unfortunate hold she had upon him.

But by the time his carriage arrived at his home, he found himself clutching the pail of cream ice like a loyal servant about to make a delivery to his mistress. And he found himself imagining where he would find her. The music room? The library? The salon she favored as her sitting room?

He leapt to the pavements before the carriage had reached a complete stop, so eager was he to meet her. Decker did his best not to jog up the walk. He was greeted at the door by his redoubtable butler.

"Where is Mrs. Decker?" he asked without preamble.

Yes, he had lost all his pride. Swallowed it down. He told himself it was his cock doing the talking, this incessant need for her that was driving him to distraction.

"She is not at home, sir," Rhees told him, utterly devoid of expression.

Not at home?

What the hell?

"Right you are, Rhees," he bluffed brightly, as if his soul were not dying a slow and hideous death inside. "I had forgotten Mrs. Decker had plans today."

Plans? She had plans? Where and with whom? She had spoken not a word of it this morning, not after he had made love to her in his bed, not when they had breakfasted, and not before their customary farewell—a lengthy kiss—prior to his departure.

It was not that he did not trust her. Of course he trusted her. And it was not that he did not want her to pursue her own amusements during her day. Of course he did. But it was that…he had expected her to be awaiting him.

And she was not here. Quite the blow, that.

Disappointment suffused him, along with further vexation that he had become so caught up in his wife. Had he learned nothing from his past?

Stupid damned fool.

Grimly, he stalked past his butler, clutching the cream ice like spoils of war.

He was going to eat all the bloody stuff himself.

"YOU LOOK UTTERLY miserable, darling," Callie observed, rather unkindly.

"As if you just watched a carriage run over a puppy," added Lady Helena.

Jo frowned at both of them. "*Et tu, Brute*? The two of you are supposed to be my friends."

Callie, Lady Helena, and Jo had gathered for tea at Callie's home, a long-overdue social gathering in the wake of Jo's nuptials.

"It is because we are your friends that we are telling you that you look as if you are about to attend a funeral," Callie said.

"Or as if someone has just drowned your favorite kitten," Lady Helena chimed in.

"What a grim lot you are," Jo grumbled. "Cease with your bleak similes, if you please."

"You ought to be on your honeymoon," Callie observed. "And yet, you are here in London. Is that the reason?"

Her honeymoon with Decker was something of a bitter subject for Jo. Or rather, the postponement of it was. Their initial plan to attend a yachting regatta in Dover to watch his cutter *Athena* race had been abandoned when an unexpected collision had occurred with three other yachts. The *Athena* had been towed back to port and was currently in repairs.

"Of course that is not the reason," she said. Though it was, perhaps, part of it.

In truth, the opportunity to have Decker all to herself and to escape from London for a week would have been most welcome. In the time since they had wed, they had settled into a routine. And whilst his lovemaking was nothing short of rapturous, it had not failed to escape her notice that her new husband freely gave her the physical connection she sought and yet, the emotional remained decidedly elusive.

"Then what is the reason?" Callie asked, frowning. "Is anyone else famished? I am going to ring for a tray of cakes and biscuits. Is it wrong to suddenly be beset by the urge to eat quail eggs at this time of day? Do not answer that. Tell us what has you so distressed, dearest."

"I could eat quail eggs at any time of day," Lady Helena offered as Callie went to the bell pull.

"I am in love with him," Jo blurted.

Callie turned back to her. "I knew it!"

Was she that obvious? *Good heavens*, what if Decker guessed at her feelings as well?

"How did you know?" she demanded, her stomach churning at the thought of him realizing the depth of emotions she felt for him.

She was not ready to face that yet. Not ready to confront the possibility he would not return the sentiment. Not now, perhaps not ever.

"You made it quite apparent the day I suggested Helena use Decker to cause a scandal," Callie said gently, returning to her seat. "That is wonderful, dearest! I know this marriage was a bit rushed, but I am relieved to hear the two of you are in love."

"Not the two of us," Jo said. "I fear I am alone in my feelings."

"But the way he looks at you," Lady Helena argued, "I would be willing to wager you are wrong."

"I fear not." She sighed heavily. "He has never hinted at the slightest bit of feelings, and for a man of his reputation…"

"Decker *does* have a reputation," Callie agreed, frowning. "However, there is good reason for it, from what little Sin has told me of Decker's past. Apparently, he had his heart broken quite thoroughly in his youth."

Ah, there it was. The confirmation of her fears. That another woman had been responsible for his cynicism. And with it came the burning agony of jealousy, so much stronger now that he was her husband. Now that he had found his way into her heart.

"Do you know what happened?" she asked, almost hesitant to hear the answer.

However, if it would enable her to better understand the enigmatic man she had wed, it would be worth the cost to her pride.

"It was all a frightfully long time ago," Callie said. "There was a lady to whom he had formed a romantic attachment. She hailed from a noble family—the daughter of a baron, I believe. From what I gathered, her father did not approve of Decker, and she eloped with another man. Decker was devastated over it."

The revelation did nothing to quell the misery swirling within her, along with the uncertainties and doubts.

"I see," she managed. "That makes perfect sense, of course."

She knew all too well the bitterness Decker felt toward his noble father. Now, it was clear that the Earl of Graham was not the only source of his demons. She could hardly blame him for feeling as he did, knowing he had spent his life being judged for something that was beyond his control.

"Do not worry," Lady Helena said softly. "That woman is in his past. You are his present, his future, his wife. Her memory cannot haunt him forever."

But what if it could? What if the woman he had loved, the lady he had wanted to marry, would forever be the only woman who owned his heart?

"Jo, stop your restless mind," Callie ordered her knowingly. "Do not, I pray, overthink this. Your marriage is new. Give yourselves time to grow together. Sin was also desperately hurt in his past. The heart can heal and move forward. Indeed, I will be first to attest that scarred hearts love the best."

She wanted to believe her friend, truly she did. But the doubts remained. And now that she knew about this mysterious lady in Decker's past, the one he had loved… Jo swallowed, knowing she did not dare continue in this vein of thought lest she turn into a watering pot and ruin the afternoon with her friends.

Instead, she turned to Lady Helena. "Enough about me, if you please. I am certain it shall all untangle itself as it ought. How is your campaign against the odious Lord Hamish going, my dear?"

A mysterious flush crept over Lady Helena's cheeks. "I do believe I may have convinced someone to aid me in my quest to be ruined after all."

Suddenly, the flush was not so mysterious.

"Tell us everything," Callie demanded.

A knock at the door heralded the arrival of a maid.

"After I arrange for my biscuits, cakes, and quail eggs, of course," she amended, grinning.

EATING CREAM ICE without his wife was, Decker discovered, absolute rubbish.

Actually, everything without her was rubbish.

He was rubbish, too.

What sort of businessman abandoned his offices in the midst of the day, closeted himself in his study, and then mulishly spooned melting strawberry goo down his throat? The pathetic sort.

The rubbish sort.

How many times had he just thought the word *rubbish* within the last minute?

Too many.

"Rubbish," he muttered, taking another spoon of Claremont's cream ice. He did rather think his chef could do better, but Jo had heard about it and had been determined to give the place a try. "Rubbish, rubbish, rubbish."

"What is rubbish?"

Jo's soft voice, coming from the threshold, gave him such a start that he flung a spoonful of cream ice on his own waistcoat. Cursing, he extracted his handkerchief just in time to watch the pink blob fall to his trousers, landing directly on his now-rigid cock.

Thank you for coming to attention the moment she appeared, old chap.

How mortifying.

He stood, clasping his handkerchief over the cream ice-covered fall of his trousers.

Well, if this was not bloody ballocks, he did not know what was.

Her giggle had him raising his head. Her laughter was, as always, infectious. He found himself grinning at her, his levity joining in with hers. She closed the door behind her and moved toward him, infallibly elegant. She wore a gold silk gown embellished with embroidered scarlet leaves and lace sleeves. The line of abalone buttons running from her neckline to her hem was particularly inviting.

He wanted to pluck them open, one by one.

"Were you eating cream ice without me?" she asked as she approached, bringing with her the luscious scent of orange blossom and jasmine.

"Yes," he admitted.

Her smile did nothing to make his rampant erection abate. Her hands settled on his shoulders. "How could you?"

Before he could answer, her lips were on his. Lush, full, tender. Kissing him. He opened beneath the tentative thrust of her tongue. *Damnation,* she had learned a great deal since that first kiss they had shared in his carriage. He ought to know a surge of pride at having been the only man to tutor her. Instead, he resented himself. For he had been the architect of his own demise.

Falling deeper beneath her spell. Venturing into hazardous territory indeed. The sort from which there was no return.

But it was a hell of a thing to stand in his study, kissing his wife, whilst clutching a sticky, cream ice-laden handkerchief over the cockstand tenting his trousers. He cupped her face with his free hand, his mouth responding to hers, scarcely able to stifle his groan of raw need.

Would he ever get enough of her?

Unlikely.

She was the first to break the kiss, tipping her head back, her honey-brown gaze searching his. "Strawberry from Claremont's?"

Her question wrung another surprised laugh from him. "You could taste it?"

"I could." Her lips twitched. "But also, Rhees told me I would find you here, and that you had a bucket from Claremont's accompanying you."

To the devil with the butler for tattling on him. He ought to give him the sack. Decker would if he did not like him so damned much.

"I am afraid I made a mess of myself," he said wryly. "Eating cream ice without you is not the same, *bijou.*"

"You did indeed make a mess," she agreed, her gaze lowering to his besmirched trousers and the handkerchief covering the stain. "Let me see the damage, if you please."

He swallowed. Now was not the time for his wife to see the effect she had upon him at all times of the day. There was something about his cockstand hiding behind a strawberry cream ice stain that felt ridiculously puerile.

"There is no need for that," he reassured her. "I will go and have a change of trousers. I have already decided I shan't be returning to my offices today. There is hardly any sense in strutting about in my businessman's weeds, is there?"

But his minx of a wife had knelt on the carpets before him, her gaze scorching him as if it were a touch. "I insist, Decker. Do not be silly. What will the servants think if you are to go strutting about the household with a stain in such a place? At least allow me to help you blot it dry."

Hell. She could not possibly know what the sight of her on her knees before him did to him. Nor how badly he wanted her to tend to first his trousers and then his aching prick. How much he wanted to slide between her supple lips, to watch his cock disappear in her dainty mouth.

He was a filthy, bawdy man.

But his wife did not appear to mind. She was preoccupied with taking up his handkerchief and shooing away his hand.

"Josie," he protested, prompted by the faintest stirrings of whatever shreds of honor he possessed.

For there was no disguising what had been going on beneath that cursed scrap of linen. Her eyes darkened, her sooty lashes lowering. Her lips parted. Above the modest neckline of her gown, he saw her swallow.

"Oh dear," she said, her voice a low, throaty rasp. "You are dreadfully messy, are you not, sir?"

How was it that the mere act of her calling him *sir* was enough to make his ballocks draw tight? He would have spoken, answered her. Mayhap, he would have heeded his honor and stepped away. But she began moving the ruined handkerchief over his equally ruined trousers.

And as she did so, she massaged his cock.

Just the way she knew he liked.

He inhaled. "What do you think you are doing?"

"Cleaning you, of course," she said, slanting him a deceptively innocent glance from beneath her lowered lashes. "I fear the cream ice soaked through. I must make certain you are not all sticky."

Her fingers made short work of the fastening on his trousers, opening the fall. And then she took his cock in her hand, stroking. The sight of her small, elegant fingers curled around his thick, ruddy rod made him nearly wild with lust. His mettle was already seeping from the slit at the tip. He was so damned ready for her, wild with need, all from her appearing before him and then touching his cock through the barrier of his garments.

Yes, he was pathetic.

She stroked him from root to tip.

He wanted to stop her. Coming in his wife's hand in the midst of the afternoon after he had been wallowing in cream ice and self-pity was hardly ideal. But her grip on him tightened, her thumb swirling over his cockhead, slicking his own moisture over him.

All that emerged from him was a groan of surrender.

"You are fortunate I arrived when I did," she told him, voice low, her lips so near to him that her hot breath feathered over his tip.

Yes, he was. He agreed with her. Completely.

But she could not possibly be thinking of doing what he thought she was.

There was no way his prim wife was about to take him—

Her lips closed over his cock. Just the tip. So softly, as if she feared she would break him. Her tongue swirled over him tentatively.

The day was getting better by the moment.

"Darling," he ground out, still feeling it his gentlemanly

duty to protest. She was his wife, after all, not a woman of experience. "You do not need to do this."

"Mmm," she hummed, the gentle vibration sending a shock of exquisite sensation through him as she released him, then slid her tongue along his length. "And what if I *want* to do this?"

Could she? He would not lie—he had imagined her lips wrapped around his cock more times than he could count. He had wondered what it would be like, how she would react. However, she was new to intimacy, a novice to lovemaking, and his wife as well. With other lovers, he had known how to read a woman's acquiescence, her need for him, to determine whether a bed partner would prefer dominance or submission, powerful passion or tender seduction.

With Jo, he was adrift. Everything he had learned about other women paled. Because she was not any other woman. She was herself. And that made her so very different. So very special.

Once upon a time, *wife* had been a word he had revered. A title he had intended to bestow upon one woman. It shocked him to realize now that what he felt for Jo was far more potent, detailed, complex—*necessary*—than what he had ever felt for Nora.

Jo took him in her mouth once more, sucking, obliterating his ability to think. All there was in that moment was Jo's lips closed around his shaft, her tongue flicking over him, the warm wetness of her mouth engulfing him.

"Damn it, Josie," he bit out, his fingers sifting into her hair.

The gentleman in him dissolved. He was now a beast. Desire took up the reins. Hair pins fell to the Axminster as she laved his rigid flesh, keeping her fingers wrapped tight around the base of him as she lavished attention on his length and cockhead.

She made a carnal noise that sounded like a purr. "Do you like this, Decker? I have been wanting to make you as wild as you make me. I was not sure it would be the same for you."

Oh, it was the bloody same. Indeed, he would venture to say it was better. There was something so damned glorious about her inexperienced attempts to bring him pleasure that heightened his desire. That made him more desperate for her than he had already been before she had gone on her knees. And that, it went without saying, was a tremendous feat in itself.

Good God, he would spill cream ice in his lap every day if he received this sort of attention as a result.

He clenched his jaw and counted to ten, trying to keep himself from ramming his cock down her throat. That was what he wanted, what he craved—her taking all of him, sucking him until he spent and then he could watch as she swallowed his seed.

"I like it," he forced out, knowing she needed the validation.

She could hardly know what she did to him. How badly she made him want her. How effortlessly she brought him to his knees, even whilst she was the one who knelt before him.

"Tell me what I should do," she murmured.

He grasped a handful of her unbound hair, gently guiding her, showing her what he wanted. "Take me in your mouth, darling. Just as you did before. As much of me as you can."

And she did. His cock glided past her lips, straight into the back of her throat. She made a low hum of approval. It required the exertion of all Decker's inner restraint to keep from coming then and there. He bit his lip, forced himself to remain still and allow her complete control over him.

She moved tentatively at first, up and down his shaft.

When a groan escaped him as she ran her tongue over the slit on his cock, she slanted a coquette's glance up at him. The realization she was enjoying giving every bit as much as he enjoyed receiving her attentions made him harder.

He sifted his fingers through the luxurious waves of her dark hair, watching his cock go in and out of her pretty lips. He owned hundreds of erotic lithographs, paintings, and sculptures. He had read the most depraved accounts of sexual congress printed in the English language. And yet, the sight of Jo sucking him was the most carnal, beautiful thing he had ever seen.

She licked the underside of his cock, grasping him at the base and squeezing. "How am I doing, sir?"

There it was again, *sir*.

He had only just introduced her to amorous role playing, but she was a quick learner.

"Wonderfully," he gritted. "Too wonderful. If you continue much longer, I will spend in your mouth."

Her gaze met his once more. "I want you to."

She took him in her mouth again, sucking. He could not keep himself from pumping his hips. He reached the back of her throat once more. *Paradise.* Fire shot down his spine. His ballocks tightened. He was close to the edge.

"I am going to, Josie," he warned. "If you do not stop…"

But the minx did not stop. Instead, she took him deeper. The frayed thread of his control snapped. He was powerless. Mindless. His orgasm was fast and furious, his ballocks clenching as pleasure so intense it was almost violent rocked through him. He pumped again, bucking against her as he came down her throat.

She swallowed, draining him, taking every drop of his spend.

Panting, his heart pounding, he staggered when she disengaged from him, her lips slick with saliva and his mettle. He had never experienced such a rush, such a potent pinnacle, from a woman's mouth.

His breath still ragged, he tucked himself back into his trousers and refastened them before taking her hands in his and helping her to her feet. Her cheeks were flushed, her mouth swollen, and her hair was deliciously wild around her beautiful face. He kissed her forehead reverently, a new tenderness for her bursting open inside his chest.

"Thank you, darling," he managed to say. "That was…there are no words."

He hauled her into his arms, embracing her, wondering if he could keep her here thus, forever. Wondering if they ever had to leave this room. He felt quite sure he could be content for eternity with her in his arms. Mayhap a servant to deliver food occasionally…

She embraced him in return. "Decker?"

He kissed her crown. "Yes, *bijou*?

Her arms tightened. "I love you."

Chapter Fourteen

SILENCE REIGNED IN Decker's study following Jo's ill-timed confession. He had stiffened in her arms.

Excellent, Jo. Perfect way to ruin the moment.

"That is to say, I love that you brought me cream ice in the midst of your day," she added stupidly as she released him and stepped away. She flashed him a smile she hoped was bright and cheerful, not at all forced. Just as she hoped her heated cheeks were not flushed a furious shade of red. "That was so very thoughtful of you."

The words had slipped from her. After learning about the woman in his past who had jilted him, and then returning to find him awaiting her with cream ice, she had been moved to do something to show him the depth of her feeling for him. Decker was a wonderful man. Tender, considerate, kind, and witty. Hard-working, intelligent, compassionate. He made her laugh, he charmed her, he brought her to the heights of passion again and again. He made her feel worshiped.

And she had wanted him to feel the same. She had not, however, meant to tell him she loved him. Not now. Not yet. Mayhap not ever. At least, not until she could be more certain he felt the same way. Her feelings were too new, her heart too afraid of being shattered. If he did not love her back—indeed, if his heart would forever belong to the woman who had come before her—Jo was not certain how she would cope.

"If this is the response I get when I bring you cream ice, I shall do it every day," he teased then, dragging her from the heaviness of her thoughts.

Wonderful man. She bit her lip. "You were pleased?"

He kissed her swiftly. "Could you not tell, darling? I was extraordinarily well-pleased."

Had she saved herself from abject humiliation? The tension had seemingly fled from him. Perhaps they could pretend she had not made such an embarrassing blunder.

She kissed him back, their tongues tangling. She wondered if he could taste the tang of himself the way she still did, mingling with sweet strawberry. He groaned, deepening the kiss, his lips moving over hers with greater demand. If he did notice, he did not mind.

His hands slid to her waist, anchoring her to him.

Without ending the kiss, he began moving them as one. Slowly, intently. He guided her backward, and she went willingly, following his lead. She was his to command. His always, body and heart, everything she was.

Something firm pressed into the backs of her knees through her gown and underpinnings. He broke the kiss and gave her a gentle nudge.

"Sit, darling."

"Why?" she asked.

"No questions." He kissed her again. "Sit."

She did as he asked, lowering herself to the upholstered cushion with as much elegance as she could muster with her hair unbound and her body, mind, and heart at sixes and sevens. Her heart gave a queer little thump, almost as if it stumbled over itself.

"Decker," she protested.

"No objections, either." He towered over her, all dark, brooding handsomeness. "It is my turn."

His turn for what?

But then, he lowered himself to his knees, and she had her answer without ever posing the question. The smile he sent her was doused in sin. He clutched the hem of her gown and lifted it to her waist. The heavy, embroidered silk pooled in her lap, along with her petticoats and chemise.

Her intent, however, had been to shower him with affection. To show him, without words—and later, with words—that the circumstance of his birth did not matter one whit to her. All that mattered was him. Guilt pricked at her at the notion of him feeling as if he must reciprocate, for that had never been her intention.

"You do not need to—"

"Hush," he interrupted, his grin deepening. "Hold your skirts for me, darling. On this, we are in disagreement, I am afraid, for I *do* need to make you come. It is only fair."

Well, when he phrased it thus, who was she to argue?

Jo's sex was already throbbing with need after having brought him to release. Having him at her mercy had only made her want him more rather than sating her. And now, here, she had the most delicious offer of him making her spend in return.

She grabbed fistfuls of fabric, watching him as he caressed his way up her stocking-clad calves. His fingers dipped into the hollows behind her knees, stroking. She felt a rush of wetness at her core and clamped her thighs together to stave off a bolt of longing.

But Decker was having none of that, of course. His knowing touch moved higher, to her thighs, gliding over her with such reverence, she ached. His head dipped, and he pressed a series of open-mouthed kisses up each of her shin bones, all the way to her knees. His hands moved to her inner thighs, parting them, exposing her most intimate flesh to him.

And though he had seen her before and the act was not unfamiliar, she nevertheless knew a trill of forbidden excitement as air kissed her there. And then, his eyes, bright as the summer sky and so deliciously knowing, were upon her as well. He looked at her as if she were the most beautiful sight he had ever beheld. Whenever he looked at her, she felt as if she were.

"You have the prettiest cunny, Josie," he murmured. "Perfect for me."

She could not stifle the whimper of yearning that escaped her as he caressed higher still, bowing his head like a supplicant to deliver a stinging trail of kisses along her inner thighs. Just when she thought she could bear no more of his teasing, he spread her open, parting her lips. His hot breath fanned over her flesh.

"So pink and glistening and beautiful," he said. "And all mine."

"Yes." The lone word hissed from her, all she could manage. It said enough—she wanted him to do what he would to her. To lick her, suck her, bite her, bring her to the same glorious heights of pleasure he had before. She was frantic, bursting with need.

This time, he did not lavish attention upon her pearl first. Instead, he sank his tongue deep inside her in one unexpected thrust. The invasion had her writhing on the chair, seeking to bring herself closer. She thought she could spend from his tongue inside her alone, just like this. Already, she had been so perilously near to coming undone.

"You are so wet, Josie." He licked into her again. "Did you like sucking my cock?"

She was breathless from both his tongue and his question. "Yes."

"Naughty wife," he murmured against her. "I approve

wholeheartedly."

It was the first time in their marriage that he had referred to her as his wife directly. She could not contain the warmth that suffused her at the word. But when his tongue flicked over her pearl, everything else was dashed. He teased her entrance with the tip of his forefinger. So light—the pulses of his tongue, the shallow thrust inside her. It all heightened her desperation. She had learned that her husband was a master of drawing out pleasure. Indeed, he was a master of pleasure. Full stop.

Each time he touched her—each time they made love—was more decadent than the last.

His tongue flicked quickly, inciting ripples of delicious pleasure. His finger dipped into her channel. "I liked watching you take my cock into your mouth, darling." More licks, a deeper thrust. "I loved watching you swallow, take all of me." He sucked her bud then, hard and long. His digit sank inside her.

"*Oh,*" was all she could say. And then, as he curled his finger within her, reaching that fantastic, deliriously sensitive place, "yes."

For a time, she was nothing but a writhing heap of sensation. Every part of her was attuned to him, as if she were an instrument ready to be played. The scent of his study—leather, oiled wood, paper and ink—mingled with the musky scent of her own desire and the potent scent of his cologne. The wet sounds his tongue made as he laved her flesh, licking up and down her seam, as he added a second finger to join the first, filled the room.

She gave herself up to the moment, to the man. Surrendered to passion. When he nibbled on her clitoris—one of the many names he had taught her for that delightfully sensitive part of her body—she lost control. Perhaps it was the rawness of her emotion, the combination of having revealed her love to him, only to retract it, along with the potent, powerful act of making him spend and bringing him to his knees, literally, that made it happen.

Or mayhap it was merely Decker's tongue, which was nothing short of magical as it played over her. Or it was his touch, deep inside her. Or the wicked words he said, the praise, the commands.

When he told her to come, how could she not, with his tongue precisely where she wanted it?

"That's it, *bijou*," he cajoled in that smooth-as-velvet baritone. "Spend on my tongue. I want to lick up your cream."

All that sinfulness combined made her explode. Her climax raged through her, making dark stars pepper her vision. Making her heart beat like the hooves of a horse about to win a race. Faster, faster. Her breaths were ragged and harsh. Wave after wave of bliss crashed over her, imbuing her entire body with a rare, powerful…glow.

That was how she could describe it best.

She was glowing, humming, burning, from the inside out. But she was also whimpering, noisy, embarrassing herself. He had three fingers inside her now, stretching her, filling her, his mouth latched upon her pearl, sucking hard. One orgasm from her was not enough for him. Greedy, beautiful man.

He would wreck her, Elijah Decker, this man she loved.

She saw it in a flash as fresh ripples of pleasure washed over her. As she surrendered to his sensual torture. She was a carriage, out of control, about to topple on her side and roll down a cliff, to crash into a thousand splintered shards in the boulders below.

But that was one of the devils of life, was it not? Recognizing one's fate did not necessarily render it any easier to resist.

In this instance, it just made her want him that much more.

Was there something wrong with her?

She would fret over that later. Just as she would worry over those troubling words she had uttered in damning succession.

For now, Decker was on his feet. She had spent twice, beneath the delicious force of his tongue. But his starkly sensual visage said he wanted more.

"I want my cock inside you," he rasped, holding his hands out to her.

She released her skirts and took them. He pulled her into a standing position, and she went willingly, her knees a bit wobbly. She felt akin to a newborn foal, testing out her legs for the first time.

"Do you want me, Josie?" he asked when she was on her feet, their bodies almost pressed together, chest to hip.

Her skirts billowed forth, crushing into him. She could not help but to notice that his lips were slick and dark, glistening. Her mark upon him, subtle as it was, sent a new sense of possession careening over her.

"Of course I want you. I have always wanted you, I think," she admitted, realizing the truth for herself as the words fled her. "And I want you so much more now that I know the manner of man you are."

His gaze searched hers. "The manner of man I am?"

"Yes, the man you are, Elijah Decker. You are good. Kind. Honorable." She squeezed his fingers. "Sweet. Handsome. Shall I go on?"

He treated her to one of his rarer smiles, the sort that made his bright eyes sparkle and somehow rendered him more devastatingly handsome. "You may go on, darling, but I have a pressing need to finish what we have begun."

As did she.

"Then finish it, sir," she told him boldly, knowing he liked the way she had called him *sir* earlier.

"With pleasure." He pulled her toward his desk, laying her hands flat on the polished edge. "Stay like this, darling."

He was behind her, kissing her neck, her ear, tonguing the whorl, making her knees go weaker still. And then, her skirts were lifting once more. Although the summer day was warm and the air in the study was correspondingly stifling, the air on her bare thighs felt somehow cool. She shivered.

Decker guided her legs apart. And then his long fingers were upon her, finding the slit in her drawers yet again. He dipped into her cunny, then slicked her wetness up her seam all the way to her pearl. Painting that endlessly hungry and all-too-sensitive bud with her dew. She jerked against him, moaning.

He kissed her throat in response. "Tell me what you want, *bijou*."

She struggled to find words. To find her tongue. To remember the dratted English language. "I want you inside me."

There.

She had managed it.

He sank a finger deep, and from behind, the angle was exquisite. She was so incredibly sensitive from her two climaxes that she could have spent again from his finger alone. But she bit her lip, staving off such an unwanted reaction.

"Like this?" he asked, wickedness incarnate.

He slid in and out of her, her eagerness lubricating his path with shameful ease.

"Yes," she gasped when he plunged inside her again, fast and swift. "But I want your cock."

Today seemed to be the day of crossing boundaries. What was one more? He had shown her there was no shame in the pleasure they shared. And he had awakened her to desires she had never known existed. Speaking plainly about her body and what she wanted, felt freeing. Owning the desires that had plagued her but had made her feel filthy and guilty—likely a legacy of younger years spent with her rigid Aunt Lydia—was a wondrous feeling.

"If my lady wants this cock, then it is my duty to give it to her," Decker said then, his finger withdrawing.

In the next breath, he had positioned the blunt head of his rod at her entrance.

"Give it to me," she ordered him.

He hummed his approval as he plunged into her. One swift thrust, and he was seated to the hilt. Each time they had made love thus far had been within one of their chambers. This angle, this position, was new.

She liked it.

There was something about being pleasured in her husband's study, utterly at his mercy, whilst their servants went about their days beyond the closed door, that made her wild.

His big body surrounded hers, his lips on her neck, her ear, her jaw, as he began a rhythm, sliding in and out of her. Slowly and tenderly at first, thrusts that made her sigh at the delicate manner in which he played with her body. But when she tightened on him and arched her back, needing more, everything changed.

On a guttural groan, he clasped her waist, slamming into her. Fast and deep and hard. She splayed her fingers wide on the sleek burled walnut surface to keep from sliding.

"I'm going to spend," he said low in her ear.

His announcement hastened her own crisis. Her inner muscles spasmed, and another wall of pure bliss hit her. In two more pumps, he slid from her, and she felt the hot spurt of his seed on her flesh. He collapsed against her back, his breathing harsh and ragged, and kissed the nape of her neck.

Jo closed her eyes against the force of her own climax, still rippling through her, and tried not to think about her husband's mysterious past or the reason why he had yet to spend inside her. They had time, after all.

Chapter Fifteen

T HE LETTER WAS unassuming from the outside. Plain and nondescript, not a seal or a flourish, no portent of what was to come. Until Decker flipped it over and took note of the scrawl. It was his name, his direction, written in a hand he had not seen in ten years.

But it was still the same.

And he would recognize it anywhere.

Nora.

"Is something amiss, Decker?" Jo asked calmly, unaware of the mutiny festering inside him. "You are looking suddenly Friday-faced."

He glanced up from his stack of correspondence, which he had—for reasons that now eluded him—requested be brought to him while he breakfasted with his wife that morning. For a moment, he was at a loss for words, his stomach churning until he felt sick. He ought to take the letter and throw it into the dustbin. Or, better yet, rip it into a thousand shreds, then set it on fire.

Tell her, said his conscience. *Tell Jo who sent you the letter, and then consign it to the ether.*

He cleared his throat. "Everything is fine. I was merely thinking of the *Athena*. Such a travesty, four yachts crashing into each other at once. I hope to hear how the repairs are faring soon so we can commence our honeymoon."

Liar.

He soothed his guilt by reminding himself nothing he had said was a lie. It had merely not been the heavy news weighing upon his mind in the moment Jo had asked.

"I do not need a honeymoon," said his sweet wife. "You know that, Decker."

He tore his gaze from the letter which felt as if it were burning his hands, taking in the sight of the woman he had married. This morning, she was wearing a navy-blue silk that complemented her dark hair and creamy skin to perfection. His obsession for her had not dimmed. If anything, it had continued to spark and burn. They had made love again last night after sharing a bath, and then again this morning as the sun rose.

"Your patience is admirable, my dear," he forced himself to say. "But just as soon as the repairs are made, we will escape London, I promise."

Her confession yesterday returned to him then.

I love you.

Only one other woman had spoken those words to him in his life, and she had written the letter that was still clutched desperately in his hand. His knuckles ached, and he was wrinkling the paper.

What a devil he was. He had not wanted to hear those words. Had not been ready for them. And he had stiffened, frozen in her embrace. She had hastened to correct herself, but he was not fooled. Jo fancied herself in love with him. They had not spoken of it again, and he was happier that way. It was for the best. He did not believe in love. He had been disabused of that fantastical emotion's existence ten years ago, when he had been little more than a lad in leading strings.

Jo sent him a small smile. "I like it here well enough. There is no need to escape on my behalf."

He had hurt her, he thought, with his reaction. She deserved better than him. But he was not convinced he could offer her anything more than pleasure. Ever. *Hell*, he could not tell her what was in his hands, coward that he was. Or banish it from his life as he ought. No, he was going to read the dratted thing.

He wanted to know what Nora had to say, and yet he did not.

"I am glad you are content here, my dear," he told Jo, before turning his attention back to the letter. "But I insist you deserve a honeymoon. A trip to Dover will be just the thing."

His heart pounded and his hands shook as he opened it.

Dearest Eli,

Undoubtedly, you will not welcome word from me. I expect you ought to detest me for the manner in which we last parted. I cannot blame either sentiment, as both are equally well-deserved. However, I am writing to you in the hope you will read this letter rather than sending it directly to the rubbish heap.

I would like to beg your forgiveness for my defection. My actions were those of a petulant child, a girl who feared her father's wrath and who was not strong enough to withstand his threat of severing all familial connections with me were I to wed a man who was not of his choosing. Please know there has not been one day, in all the days between now and the day I last saw you, that I did not think of you.

I am writing you now as a widow. You may not know that my husband, Lord Tinley, has unfortunately met his reward a year ago. Having observed my mourning period, I felt the time was right to contact you and let

*you know how sorry I am for the events of our past. I
hope to see you again, Eli. I never stopped loving you.
I wish I had been strong enough to deserve your love
then.*

*Yours in regret,
Nora, Viscountess Tinley*

Decker felt as if the breath had been robbed from his
lungs. They burned. His stomach clenched. His reaction to
the words, swirling before him, was visceral. An acute
combination of rage, resentment, anguish, and outrage filled
him.

How dare she contact him, after all this time, and now,
when he had a wife, in such a manner?

How dare she tell him she had never stopped loving him?

Fury won the battle for supremacy within. He crushed the
letter in his fist and rose from his chair with such abrupt haste,
the chair tumbled backward. Decker did not give a damn. He
was going to burn this piece of tripe. And then he was going
to piss on the ashes when it was nothing but a smoldering
heap, just as she had left him.

Viscountess Tinley.

May you rot.

He had not been good enough for her ten years ago, but
now that she had her title and her freedom from Lord Tinley
and her papa, she thought to contact him?

"Decker?" Jo's soft, concerned voice tore him from the
bowels of his past.

He blinked, focusing upon his wife. Her countenance was
strained, a furrow marring her brow. *Bloody hell*, the past had
come rushing back to him with such unrestrained warning
that he had forgotten for a moment that he was not alone. He

had been so consumed with the need to purge this hated letter from his life.

Tell her, his conscience urged.

But he stood there, numb, his tongue refusing to cooperate. What was he to say to the wife who had told him she loved him and had been greeted with silence? *The woman I once believed myself in love with is now a widow who wrote me a letter to tell me she never stopped loving me?*

What did the letter mean? Did Nora want to resume a relationship with him? The very thought made him ill. More than likely, she did not know he was married. News traveled slowly to the country, and Lord knew he was not a subject of proper gossip.

"I have just recalled an urgent meeting this morning with Mr. Levi Storm concerning his electric company," he lied to his wife. "Do finish your breakfast, my dear. I will be home at half past four, as always."

Without awaiting her response, he turned on his heel and strode from the dining room, leaving Jo and his half-eaten breakfast behind. It was not until he was stalking down the hall that he realized he was still clutching the letter.

He made his way to the nearest room with a fireplace—the library, as it happened. Last night had been unusually cool for summer, and he and Jo had settled together before a fire after dinner. The coals were still glowing red. He tossed the letter atop the embers, watching the edges catch flame and slowly curl together, Nora's words disappearing one letter at a time.

He should have cut the ties binding him to his past long ago. He owed as much to Jo, to himself. He wanted to be the sort of man who could be worthy of her love. Forgetting Nora was the first step in what would surely prove an arduous and painful journey.

But for the woman he had married, he would do, he realized, absolutely anything.

JO TOLD HERSELF not to fret over her husband's strange behavior at the breakfast table.

She told herself that as she finished dining alone, with no companion save the footman hovering about lest she need anything. But as she poked at the eggs on her plate, which had long since gone cold in her inability to summon the enthusiasm it would take to consume them, she could not keep her mind from wandering.

And wondering.

Surely his cool, almost angry mien at breakfast was not the result of her humiliating confession the evening before? He had said nothing of her words after she had corrected herself. And afterward, they had not only made love but enjoyed dinner together and then read in the library before a cheerful, crackling fire. They had bathed and then made love again.

In his bed this morning, he had been the same attentive lover she had come to know so well.

What, then, had happened this morning?

His correspondence—that was the only answer. He had been systematically going through a pile at his side rather than his customary newspaper ironed and laid out. And then there had been the letter he had crumpled before recalling he had a prior engagement.

The letter had been long. She would be lying if she said she had not been curious about its contents. His reaction had been quite unlike anything she had ever witnessed in him, now that she thought upon it. And he had left his correspondence by his plate, most of it untouched.

Misgiving unfurled within her. There would be no more breakfast; her hunger had been effectively banished. She rose and circled the table, taking up the neat stack of his untouched correspondence. And that was when she noticed the envelope he had discarded.

The handwriting was undeniably feminine.

Viscountess Tinley.

Her heart sank to the soles of her shoes. The name was unfamiliar to Jo, but that was to be expected. She had only just come out this year, and she had only studied her *Debrett's* as well as had been possible without falling asleep from sheer boredom. It stood to reason she was not familiar with every lord and lady in the realm.

It was not her lack of familiarity with the name that disturbed Jo, however. It was the fact that a woman had written Decker the letter he had run off with. Who was Lady Tinley to him, and why had he been so disturbed by whatever that missive contained?

So many questions.

And no solid answers because Decker was nowhere to be found.

She was sick as she fled from the dining room. Part of her felt as if it had been wrong of her to pry in his affairs. Part of her told her he had left her with no choice after the manner in which he had suddenly taken his leave. The husband who had retreated from breakfast was decidedly not the Decker she had come to know.

Jo tried to calm her madly racing mind as she took his correspondence to his study and laid it upon his desk, along with the envelope. The familiar scents of his study ought to have calmed her. But without her husband in the room, it somehow lost its vibrancy. Not even the naughty engravings on the walls interested her.

Indeed, the absence of her husband only served to haunt.

To mock her.

She had told him she loved him, and he had not returned the words. He was a notorious rake. What was wrong with her, losing her heart to such a man? Why, he had never promised her fidelity. Nor had he told her about the woman he had loved—she had learned that unpalatable truth secondhand. His past, aside from his estranged relationship with his father and his mother, was a mystery.

Was Viscountess Tinley his lover? More importantly—and terrifyingly—was she the lady who had broken his heart?

Jo supposed she had only one place to turn for answers: Decker himself.

Why had she allowed him to simply run off in such haste earlier? She should have been firmer, should have pressed the matter. Being a wife was not as easy a situation as she had imagined it would be.

Jo sighed, thinking it fortunate indeed that she had more business with the Lady's Suffrage Society to attend to today. The distraction would be necessary and much-appreciated.

DECKER ARRIVED AT his offices, still at sixes and sevens, and happier than he ordinarily was to see Macfie awaiting him in the vestibule, as had become their custom over the past several years. If his *aide-de-camp* took note that Decker was fifteen and one half minutes late, he wisely kept mum.

"Just the man I was looking for," Decker said, heading to his inner sanctum. "Do come with me, Macfie, and make haste. I have not the time for tarrying."

That was yet another lie today in what was fast becoming

a vast sea of falsehoods. *Bloody hell*, one would think him no better than his self-righteous prig of a sire. In truth, Decker had finished his rough proofs. He had no meeting with Mr. Levi Storm—at least, not a pressing morning one—and he had nothing to do save review some ledgers from the piano factory, along with a leasehold investment in Belgravia he was not particularly keen on.

He made his way through the busy swirl of the men—and women—in his employ, going about their day. Some lady typewriters had been newly hired and were serving well. Decker nodded as he went, doing his utmost not to appear as agitated as he felt. He had learned long ago that one never showed a weak underbelly in business matters.

Not even with one's own staff.

Macfie, however, was a different matter altogether. Decker trusted the man nearly as much as he trusted Sin.

Decker realized belatedly that he was still wearing his hat and coat as he entered his private office. He had been too damned preoccupied to remove them upon his arrival. He spun about as Macfie crossed the threshold and closed the door at his back.

"Devil take it, man," Decker snapped, scowling, "why did you not say something?"

Macfie's bushy red brows rose. "About what, sir? Yer hat and coat? I thought mayhap ye were a wee bit cold this morning."

He raised a brow, doffing his hat and coat and throwing them into a nearby chair with complete disregard for whether or not they ended up rumpled and crushed. "Why should I be cold, Macfie? We have nearly reached the month of July."

Macfie blinked. "I cannae say, sir. Why would ye walk about in yer outerwear if not to ward off a chill? In Scotland, July can be as cold as a winter's privy."

He sighed, knowing his man was testing him. It was an old game between them. "This is London, Macfie."

"Aye, and London can also be cold as a winter's privy, cannae she?" Macfie returned.

"I concede the point. However, today is not one of those days, as you undoubtedly are already aware," he said. "But enough of all this nattering. You must realize I have a reason for calling you in here at this time of the morning."

"Aye." Macfie flashed an unrepentant grin. "Since ye ordinarily spend all morning scowling at yer desk and hollering for more coffee, with the occasional threat tae my puir eyebrows, I had a suspicion ye needed tae speak with me."

Decker bit back the urge to laugh, much-needed though it was today. "Am I that terrible, Macfie?"

His *aide-de-camp* blinked. "Need I answer ye, sir?"

He gritted his teeth. "Not if you wish to keep your position."

Macfie made an exaggerated effort of rolling his lips inward, as if they were now pasted together. He furthered the comical display by holding his breath. Decker wanted to be irritated with him, but he could not deny the man was hilarious. Furthering the effect, Macfie's face was turning red.

"Are you holding your breath?" he asked needlessly.

Macfie nodded his head in assent, looking as if he were about to burst.

Cheeky arsehole.

"You are fortunate you excel at your position, Macfie," he said somberly, the same old threat. "You may exhale. I wish to have a serious conversation with you."

Macfie released his breath in a noisy display. "Thank ye, sir. What was it ye wanted tae discuss that is serious? The last time I had a serious conversation with anyone, it was after I went for a wee swim in the loch and emerged with leeches feasting on my doodle."

This time, Decker could not help himself. He laughed because he bloody well *had* to. "Dare I ask what manner of conversation such an event precipitated?"

"It swelled up something horrible, tae where I could scarcely even take a piss, and I had tae see a physician over it." Macfie nodded, his countenance earnest. "Never again will I go swimming in a loch. 'Tis a solemn vow. The sea or nothing for me. Now what was it ye wished tae discuss?"

How to follow up leeches on a doodle? Decker was reasonably certain he was the only man in England currently facing such a quandary. But Macfie was all he had for the moment. He needed advice, and he could not very well ask Sin. Happily married men who fancied themselves deliriously in love with their wives could not offer trustworthy guidance.

Decker busied himself with rounding his desk. "Have a seat, Macfie. This may take some time."

His desk here was simple and unadorned. Not nearly as elegant or ornate as the desk in his study and yet, somehow, this desk suited him far better. He was a wealthy man—now in his own right, and to the devil with the Earl of Graham's leavings—and yet simplicity still appealed to him most of all.

Decker seated himself in the familiar comfort of his chair and watched as Macfie folded his massive body into one of the chairs on the opposite side of the desk. The man scarcely fit.

"Out with it then, sir," Macfie invited when Decker hesitated. "I just told ye about the leeches on my doodle, after all."

"Right." He paused, searching his thoughts. "Have you ever been in love, Macfie?"

The Scotsman's expression sobered instantly. "Aye, of course I have."

"What happened, if I am not being so bold?" he dared to ask. "There is no Mrs. Macfie, unless I am mistaken."

Macfie shook his head. "There isnae. The lass I would have had as my bride wanted tae stay where she was, live the life she had always known. I wanted something more. I left, and she remained. That is all."

"Do you have bitter feelings toward her?" Decker asked. "If this female in question were to send you a letter, telling you she still loved you and that she was free to pursue you now, what would you do?"

He had not forgotten about Nora's letter, it was true. Though he had burned it, and though he had vowed to be a man worthy of Jo's love, more emotions had pummeled him on the carriage ride here. He did not want Nora—quite the contrary. No part of him longed to pursue the invitation she had given. But he was…confused. Unsettled. He needed to speak with someone, and Macfie seemed his best option at the moment.

Macfie flashed him a wry smile. "Rose would never tell me that, but if she were tae, I would tell her we are different souls. I am not the man I was when she knew me, and neither is she the lassie."

"And if you had a Mrs. Macfie at home, and you received a letter from your Rose, what would you do then?" Decker asked.

Macfie eyed him for a moment, before breaking his silence at last. "If I had a Mrs. Macfie that I loved the way ye love Mrs. Decker, I would tell Rose tae go and have a swim in the loch, and I would hope the leeches would find her cu—"

"That is quite sufficient," Decker interrupted. "I am sure I can gather the rest. Thank you, Macfie. However, as much as I admire Mrs. Decker, I would not say I am hopelessly besotted just yet."

Did Macfie truly think Decker loved Jo? He had hinted as much before, but still, Macfie ought to know him better. Surely he understood Decker was incapable of such an emotion? Was he not?

Decker looked inside himself, and all he saw was murk.

"I was going tae say her *curmudgeonly arse*," Macfie said, his tone as innocent as his expression. "And I would also argue ye *are* hopelessly besotted, but ye can lie tae yerself all ye like. Now, would ye care tae tell me the whole story, or are ye wanting tae keep feeding me bits, like a fish ye are attempting tae catch on yer hook?"

Decker sighed, and then he confided in Macfie—an abbreviated version of his past with Nora and the letter he had received. When he had finished, Macfie whistled.

"Does Mrs. Decker know of this Lady Tingly?" Macfie queried.

"Tinley," Decker corrected, not that it mattered. Indeed, he was reasonably certain his man was getting the name wrong intentionally. "And no, to answer your question, she does not. I have never shared this part of my past with her as I did not consider it imperative."

The shame he had felt at keeping the letter a secret from Jo returned, burning as hotly as Nora's words had.

"If she learns of it on her own and ye havenae told her, it will go badly for ye," Macfie advised, quite sagely. "Ye love her. This Lady Stringy of yers, she is part of yer past, aye? She broke yer puir heart, but she likely paid ye a favor. Ye wouldnae want to shackle yerself to a lady who wasnae certain ye were the one for her, a lady who wasnae willing tae fight and do whatever she must tae claim yer heart forever."

This time, Decker did not bother to correct Macfie's confusion of Nora's title. "As always, you are right, Macfie. I should tell Mrs. Decker everything. And you know? When I read that letter today, I was furious with Nora all the pain and resentment of the past returned, but I did not, for a second, feel as if I wanted her to be mine. Or that I regretted what happened, the way my life has turned out. I am content with Mrs. Decker and pleased to have her as my wife."

As he spoke the words aloud, he realized just how true they were. The murk cleared, and suddenly there it was: clarity. Astonishing in its brilliance. The talons of the past no longer clawed at him. He felt, for the first time in years, free.

Was it Nora's letter which had opened him to such profundity, was it Macfie's cheeky wisdom, or was it his fierce, passionate wife?

"Of course ye ought tae be content with a fine lady such as Mrs. Decker as yer wife," Macfie said then. "If ye werenae, I would think ye an arsehole."

Decker snorted. "In truth, I *am* an arsehole. I am merely a discerning one."

He thought again of Jo's embrace yesterday in his study, of her soft declaration of love. Of his inability to return it. He had to do better, to be a better man. For her.

"Och, ye arenae an arsehole, sir," Macfie told him quietly, his ordinarily mischievous mien serious. "Ye are a good man. Didnae think I failed tae notice all yer time spent sending coin and pianos and books tae the orphanages. Tae say nothing of the hospitals ye fund."

Decker had arranged for all those acts of charity himself. The notion of carrying on with the Earl of Graham's wealth had seemed anathema to him, but he had hardly wanted anyone to believe him good and selfless. His gifts were often *selfish*—made in a need to cleanse himself of guilt, or to spite his dead sire. Still, even as intelligent and thorough as Macfie was, Decker had not supposed the man would take note and dig deeper when he saw lines labeled as *miscellaneous* on the ledgers.

He flashed his man a smile. "I have to make amends for my sins somehow, Macfie."

"Donae forget to make amends with yer lassie," the Scotsman reminded him pointedly. "Only a fool would fail tae appreciate a wife with such a perfect set of—"

"Macfie," he growled, "do not forget about my threats to your 'puir' eyebrows."

Macfie raised the eyebrows in question. "What? I was going tae say *teeth*, sir."

Jo was surrounded by a flurry of women in the Duchess of Bainbridge's drawing room, the appointed location for this meeting of the Lady's Suffrage Society. The buzz in the room, rather akin to a hive of honeybees, was comforting, keeping her thoughts from wandering too far.

"How many signatures do we have on the petition for the second reading of the bill in favor of suffrage?" the duchess asked Jo's sister-in-law Clara.

One would never look upon Clara and know she had so recently become a mother. She had thrown herself back into the Society's work with aplomb, for time was of the essence.

"Two hundred and four," Clara reported.

"I do believe I can gain two more signatures tomorrow," said the Duchess of Longleigh, a new addition to the society and a recent mother herself.

Like Clara, she was a flaxen-haired beauty, but she was far quieter and more reserved. There was a sadness about her eyes which could not be denied. Jo had heard whispers that her husband, the Duke of Longleigh, was an unkind man.

"The Countess of Corley has promised me she will sign,"

added Callie.

"Viscountess Portsmouth has also indicated her support," chimed in Helena.

"That will bring us to two hundred and eight signatures!" The Duchess of Bainsbridge exclaimed, beaming with excitement. "We will address it to each member in the House of Lords, reminding them this measure of fairness has been brought before Parliament for nearly twenty years. It is time they voted in favor of change."

Her enthusiasm was catching. Soon, the entire room was a flurry of chattering and swirling skirts as the gathered members of the Lady's Suffrage Society celebrated the success of their efforts.

But while Jo was pleased at the number of signatures they had gathered and hopeful the House of Lords would see reason at last, her mind traveled back to her husband's expression that morning at the breakfast table. To the elegant scrawl on the envelope.

Viscountess Tinley.

As the other ladies spoke, Jo took the opportunity to join Callie, who had wandered from a chat with the Duchess of Longleigh at just the right moment. Jo moved toward her.

"My dear!" Callie said, smiling. "I was just en route to your side. Forgive me for taking so long. How are you?"

Jo was silent, considering how she ought to answer such a difficult question. "Do you know the Viscountess Tinley?"

She had not meant to ask the question, but there it was, no way to retract it now.

Callie's smile vanished. "Why do you ask?"

Jo swallowed, made certain none of the other ladies were near enough to overhear the conversation. "Decker received a letter from her this morning. He grew quite distressed upon reading it and left. I discovered the envelope with her name upon it after he had gone."

Her friend frowned. "Did he speak of what the letter said to so disturb him?"

Here was the part that hurt the most.

"No," she admitted. "Indeed, he did not mention the letter at all. Instead, he sprang up and left, claiming he had just recalled a meeting of some import."

Callie bit her lip in a telltale gesture that bespoke her own discomfort. "Oh, my darling."

"What is it?" Jo asked, fear curling around her heart. "Is Lady Tinley the woman you spoke of yesterday?"

"She is," Callie acknowledged quietly.

Jo felt as if she had been dealt a physical blow. The pain was crushing.

"That is…" She trailed off, then tried to gather her whirling thoughts and failed. "I feared as much."

"I never should have told you about her," Callie fretted. "I thought it would help you to understand Decker better if you knew. Had I any inkling he would receive a letter from her, I would not have spoken out of turn."

"No." Jo shook her head slowly, digesting this new information. "You were right to tell me, Callie. My husband ought to have told me himself."

He ought to have told her about the letter this morning as well.

It would seem he had some secrets to which he was insistent upon clinging. Or, rather, a woman.

"You must speak to Decker about this, Jo," Callie said then. "Do not be too hasty to rush to conclusions. I am sure there is an explanation. Decker is a very private man, but he is a good man."

Yes, Jo knew those facets of her husband. He was the man who had wooed her with cream ice, who had given a piano to orphans, who had danced with her in the rain. But he was also the enigma who kept a part of himself from her, who could never quite complete the intimacy between them no matter how many times they made love.

He was also the man who had turned rigid as a statue in her arms when she had foolishly confessed her love to him.

"You are correct," she agreed with her friend, *sotto voce*. "I must speak with my husband."

The sooner, the better.

Chapter Sixteen

*J*O RETURNED FROM the Lady's Suffrage Society meeting later than she had intended. She had scarcely handed off her trappings to Rhees when Decker strode into the hall, his expression grim. Her heart clenched instantly at the sight of him, so handsome. The hurt came rushing back to her, along with all her misgivings.

What if he could never return her love?

What if he was still in love with Viscountess Tinley?

What had been in that dratted letter?

"Good evening," he clipped, offering her an abbreviated bow before turning his attention to the butler. "See that the carriage is readied. I need to get to Hertfordshire as quickly as possible."

"Of course, Mr. Decker," said Rhees, before going off to do as he was bid.

He was leaving? What was in Hertfordshire? Or, dare she ask, *who*?

The icy fingers of dread which had held her heart in their grasp all day squeezed harder. "Decker, what is going on? Why are you rushing off to Hertfordshire?"

"My mother is ill," he said, turning to her once more, all the color leaching from his face. "The situation is grave. I must go to her at once. You shall remain here in London, of course. I will send word to you as soon as I am able."

He meant to travel to see his ailing mother without her? Even as renewed hurt swept over her, Jo's heart ached for him. She knew he and his mother had not had a close relationship in recent years. But his countenance said far more than his words did. He looked as somber as she had ever seen him.

"I will go with you, of course," she decided instantly.

"You cannot," he denied, scrubbing a hand over his jaw. "You must not."

"Yes," she countered. "I *must*. My place is at your side, and there is nowhere I would rather be."

She meant those words, oh how she meant them, even if he did not want her there. Even, much to her shame, if he did not want *her*. How could he believe she would allow him to go anywhere without her when he was in such a state? When he would need her?

"That is generous of you, Josie, but I insist." He frowned. "You have only just returned, and you have not eaten dinner. What manner of husband would I be if I were to drag you away to Hertfordshire to a mother whom I have scarcely spoken with in seven years, and who is perhaps on her deathbed?"

The sort of husband who was not too afraid to want his wife at his side.

She did not say that, however.

Instead, she took his hands in hers. "And what of you? Have *you* eaten dinner?"

His gaze was distant, his jaw rigid, but he did not withdraw from her touch. "No, of course not. I was awaiting you when the telegram arrived from Hertfordshire. Now there is no time. My valet is packing a case as we speak. From what I understand, she is…fading."

"Oh, Decker." Although she longed to throw her arms around him and embrace him, she was not certain if it would be welcome just now. Things between them this morning had been awkward at best. And he seemed more distant this evening, if understandably so. "I am so very sorry."

"There is nothing for which you ought to be sorry. 'Tis the way of life, is it not?" he asked. But while he was doing his utmost to remain stoic, there was an undercurrent of deep emotion in his voice.

Although her mother had died just after her birth, Jo had felt her mother's absence keenly all through her life. As a child, she had pretended her dolly was her mama. She had gone to sleep, staring into the darkness of the nursery, fancying her mother could hear her speak. She understood Decker's pain, even if it was not the same breed as her own.

"I am not allowing you to go without me," she told him firmly. "I will see to it that a hamper is packed with food for the carriage ride, and I will have my lady's maid collect a valise for me as well. We will go together, Decker. I am your wife now. It is only right."

She thought he would argue, but he was silent for a moment, his mien becoming tired. "You are determined?"

As determined as she had ever been.

"Very much so," she told him.

Heavens, if he tried to leave without her, she would see a horse saddled and gallop after him.

"Then I shan't argue the matter," he relented, weariness lacing his baritone as well. "We will be taking the carriage the entirety of the journey. It will be far more efficient than waiting on the next train, securing passage, and then procuring a ride to take us to my mother's home. I will see you back here in one quarter hour."

One quarter hour was scarcely any time at all, but she knew his time to see his mother before she died was rapidly dwindling. She would make do.

She nodded and relinquished her grasp on him with the greatest reluctance. "Of course. I will make all haste."

"Josie?" he called after her when she turned and began bustling toward the kitchens.

She glanced back at him, her heart giving a pang at how lonely he looked. How desolate.

"Thank you," he said.

She wanted to tell him he did not need to offer his gratitude. After all, it was his love she wanted. His heart. All of him.

"You are most welcome, Decker," she said instead.

And then she fled to the kitchens, trying to drive all thoughts of a certain viscountess and that troubling letter from her mind. Nothing was as important as helping Decker to get to his mother's side before it was too late, or being there for him through the difficult days ahead.

Death, like life, was never easy.

Jo had learned that painful lesson a long time ago.

THE CARRIAGE RATTLED over roads, swaying.

Reminding Decker why he preferred the civility of traveling by rail to the drudgery of hooves and wheels. But the necessity of reaching his mother as quickly as possible had proven impossible to ignore.

The sun had settled over the countryside not long after they had reached the periphery of London. They had eaten their impromptu dinner whilst fighting the traffic out of Town, and he had been heartily glad his wife had possessed the forethought to see a meal brought along. Although he had little desire to eat, occupying himself had aided in distracting him from the dread threatening to swallow him whole.

By the glow of the carriage lamp, he was drawn, once more, to the sight of her, sitting opposite him, still dressed in the same afternoon gown she had been wearing when she had returned from her Lady's Suffrage Society meeting. Other women would have balked at flying from London without notice. Others would have been content to allow him to go alone, as he had intended, and to remain in the comfort of Town.

What awaited them would not be pleasant. The telegram had been succinct but clear: his mother had suffered a stroke, and she was drastically weakened. Her doctor feared she had not much longer to live. There was a possibility he would not reach her before she passed.

And although they had scarcely spoken since their fierce row some seven years ago concerning his inheritance from the Earl of Graham—aside from brief letters apprising him of his younger sister Lila's welfare—he loved his mother. He regretted now, as the carriage slowly brought him closer to her deathbed, the years and the anger and the pride which he had allowed to intervene.

Because now? It was too late.

"Decker?" Jo's soft, concerned voice cut through his thoughts. "Talk to me, please."

She was a good woman. Too good. And he was a bad man, a selfish man, a foolish man. If she truly did love him, he hardly deserved that love. *Lord*, he did not deserve her compassion and kindness here and now. What had he ever done to deserve her? Find a list? Coerce her into ruining herself with him until she had been left with no choice but to become his wife?

What a monster he was.

He despised himself in that moment.

All the same, he sighed, unable to give voice to the tumult

swirling within. "What would you have me say, *bijou*?"

"Will you tell me why you have such a strained relationship with your mother?" her query was tentative, still slicing into him. "It is apparent to me how very much you love her."

He raked his fingers through his hair, exhaling slowly. "I do love her. She is a good woman who made the wrong choices. She always loved him more than she loved any of her children, however, and that is her greatest fault. He never loved her enough. Indeed, I question whether he loved her at all."

The admission was torn from him. It felt far too personal, as if he were holding up a magnifying glass for Jo to inspect the ugliest parts of him.

"Him," Jo repeated gently. "Do you mean your father?"

"The Earl of Graham," he bit out, for he refused to think of that selfish bastard as his father. A father was a man who was a part of his children's lives, and Graham had certainly never been that, either for Decker or for Lila.

Especially not for Lila. As a daughter born on the wrong side of the blanket, she did not suit Graham's urge for vengeance. The man already had seven daughters. Decker alone had been the unfortunate beneficiary of the earl's dubious generosity, and only inasmuch as it suited Graham's purposes.

"Your mother was in love with him, and you did not deem him worthy of that love," Jo said.

"Damned right he was not," Decker confirmed. "The Earl of Graham loved himself, his money, and his pleasure, and not necessarily always in that order. He wanted his wealth to carry on in his own bloodline. But not just any bloodline. Only the male bloodline. He had eight daughters and one son. Me."

"That is the source of your quarrel with your mother, is it

not?" Jo ventured. "You told me you love her, that you would do anything for her, but that you are estranged. It was the inheritance which caused your rift."

Once again, she was probing. Prodding him. Examining parts of himself Decker did not like to think about or to acknowledge. And yet, uncomfortable as it was, he also found her tender persistence oddly reassuring. None of the women in his past had ever deigned to see the man beneath all his rakish, devil-may-care trappings.

His Josie did.

My Josie, my wife, my love.

The thoughts emerged from nowhere, but he did not dare speak them aloud.

Instead, he swallowed down a rising lump in his throat, that same, old unwanted knot of emotion, and answered her question. "It was. I did not want to accept a penny of Graham's wealth. I was set to deny it all. My mother told me I had to accept it for my sister Lila's sake. You see, Lila is, like me, a bastard. But, unlike me, a daughter. Do you know what he left her, a sweet girl of five years when he died, whom he had only deigned to meet once in all her life? He left her one hundred pounds. He left more for the care of his bloody hunting dogs than he left for his own flesh and blood."

Decker's rage, the fury he had done his best to abate over the years with whatever distraction at hand in the moment, returned. This time, he had no faceless woman to bed, no depraved party, no bottle, no way to disappear, to forget.

This time, he was a man sitting in a carriage with his wife, on his way to see his dying mother for the last time. A man who regretted the way he had treated both of those women. His hands were balled into fists in his lap, trembling.

Jo slid onto the Moroccan leather bench at his side in a whisper of sound. She brought her sweet scent, her strength, her warmth. His need for her was so intense, it was crippling. He sat there, utterly humbled, as she embraced him. He had never felt so comforted. So cared for. Not since he had been a lad in the arms of his mother.

But this was different. Not at all the same. This was the touch of a woman, his wife. The woman who, just yesterday, had told him she loved him. He believed her. Hell, he *needed* to believe her. Without a modicum of pride, he wrapped his arms around her, clinging to her, holding her so tightly he feared he was hurting her and forced himself to relax his hold.

"I am so sorry, Decker," she whispered softly. "You all deserved better, every one of you."

"Yes, we did." It was, he thought, the first time he had ever acknowledged it. The first time the pain of this particular part of his past had been unearthed to someone other than his mother. "But I damn well know one thing. I do not deserve *you*."

Her hand stroked up and down his spine in a steady, reassuring rhythm. Calming and soothing him as her other arm remained banded around his waist, holding him tight. "I am nothing extraordinary. I am merely your wife, and I care for you. I hurt when you hurt."

She was killing him, his Josie. This sweet, passionate, young, intelligent, funny, compassionate, loving woman he had married. He definitely did not deserve her, despite whatever delusions she insisted upon accepting. It was merely her nature. She was Persephone to his Hades, bringing life into his darkness when he had not known he needed it.

He lowered his face to her throat, inhaling the familiar, beloved scent of orange blossom. He could not resist pressing his mouth to her velvet-soft skin. Her heart strummed steadily beneath his kiss, a reassurance he needed in this uncertain journey.

"I never want you to hurt, Josie," he murmured against her skin, kissing her again because now that he had begun, he could not seem to stop. "You are too sweet, too kind, too good. Too good for me, it is certain."

He thought, for the first time since receiving the telegram earlier, about Nora's letter. About his intention to reveal everything to Jo. He wanted to, and he would, but his emotions were already a maelstrom. He could not bear to add one more struggle to the moment. For now, he was going to be greedy and simply accept his wife's comfort and concern as she offered it to him.

Later, he promised himself, after his mother was well, he would tell Jo about the letter. Or later, after his mother was gone.

The latter plunged him back into the depths of despair and regret. How he wished he had spared his mother some time in the last seven years, an audience, at least. Could he have forgiven her? Should he have forgiven her?

What mattered when death was likely waiting at the other end of this carriage ride?

"You must not hold on to your regrets," Jo told him then, as if she could read his troubled musings. As if she heard them spoken aloud. "There must have been a reason for you to remain estranged from your mother, all these years. Did she force you to accept the inheritance?"

A shudder wracked him. He inhaled deeply of the scent of her neck. She was more potent than a drug to him. He was like an opium eater, needing her to soothe a deep and abiding ache within him. "She threatened me. I told her I would not accept Graham's blood money. She told me if I refused, I would no longer be permitted to have any contact with my sister, Lila. She was adamant. She said she had sacrificed for me, for Lila, that she would not allow me to squander her efforts in favor of my pride." He paused, collecting himself, before continuing. "Part of me knows she was right. Part of me never forgave her for what she did, for what she forced me to do."

"My love." She kissed the top of his head. "You were both trying to do what was right. Pray, do not punish yourself any more than you already have."

My love.

Those words affected him. How could they not? They stole their way into his heart and settled there, refusing to leave. Because they fit there. They *belonged*. Just as she belonged in his arms, his life, at his side.

What would he have done, receiving that telegram today, if he did not have Jo? A dash through the countryside, no food, no one to cling to, no one to accept him as he was. No one to love him. The prospect loomed, horrible as a death.

"Thank you," he whispered, kissing her cheek. It was the closest he could come to a declaration. His emotions were too turbulent, too confused. He did not want to tell Jo he loved her out of gratitude.

He wanted to tell her unencumbered by grief and necessity.

Because he *did* love her. Decker realized it then as the carriage continued to sway over the road and his wife held him in her arms. He clung to her as if she were his last chance at surviving the lashing waves of a sea that threatened to drown him.

He was in love with Lady Josephine Decker.

His wife.

His *heart.*

"You do not need to thank me," she told him, still tenderly stroking up and down his back.

She made him feel cherished. Made him feel as if there

could be light in the darkest moments.

He buried his face in her fragrant hair. Even the clean scent of her shampoo was precious to him. "You are wrong. I have much to thank you for."

Everything, in fact.

The words were there, stuck in his throat, mired in emotion.

To think he had despaired of Sin for finding himself besotted with his countess. Decker had come to understand just how quickly the love of a remarkable woman could change a man. Could make a man whole. Fill in all the pieces of himself he had never known were missing.

"Thank you for sharing these parts of yourself with me," she said then, startling him when she kissed his cheek. Her golden-brown gaze met his, searching through the low light of the carriage lamp. "I did not know you had a sister. Will you tell me about her?"

It occurred to him then just how much he had shielded himself from her. How little of himself he had revealed to her. He had much to atone for, that was certain. And he would begin here and now.

He kissed the upturned tip of Jo's nose. "Lila is a hellion like me. I think you will like her. If...my mother should die, I will become her legal guardian. She will have to live with us. Would you be amenable to that?"

Hell, that had not occurred to him until this moment. His mother's family had disowned her, and the dowager Countess of Graham would not be welcoming a by-blow into her brood of seven daughters. Lila would be his responsibility.

"Of course I would be amenable," Jo said. "If she is anything like you, I shall love her. We will make her as comfortable as possible and welcome her with open arms. You need not fear where she is concerned."

Could she be any more perfect, this woman he had wed?

He kissed her lips softly, slowly, reverently, telling her with his mouth what he could not yet form into words.

The carriage rattled on, delivering them to their destination and whatever lay ahead.

Chapter Seventeen

*H*IS MOTHER HAD aged in the seven years since he had seen her last. The ebony hair which had been her crowning glory had turned entirely silver. The healthy glow had fled her cheeks. She had lost weight, her high cheek bones shockingly angular, her hand in his light as a bird.

Her physician had informed him this was not his mother's first stroke. Why she had never written him of her ailments, he did not know. Her letters had always been impersonal, containing accounts of Lila's studies and the scrapes in which she found herself. There had been nothing of herself. No indication she had grown infirm.

Decker bowed his head, clutching her unresponsive fingers. Dr. Thompson had said she'd had moments of lucidity throughout the day, but the lucidity had waned. This attack had been worse than those which had come before. It had rendered the left half of her body incapable of movement. She had been given laudanum just prior to Decker and Jo's late-night arrival, to ease her pain and unrest. But the situation was dire, the outcome clear.

His mother did not have long to live. He was at once grateful for this moment alone with her and terrified it would prove the last he would ever have.

"Mama," he whispered. "I am sorry."

Simple words. But true. He meant them with everything

he had.

As he stared at her still form, the counterpane tucked around her as if she were merely asleep and not dying, he could not fathom why he had held on to his anger and pride for seven years. Had his self-righteous rage been worth the time he could have spent with his mother?

No.

Tears blurred his vision, but he blinked them away, determined not to weep. Not yet, at least. Not until she was truly gone. For now, she yet breathed. For now, she could hear him. At least, he hoped she could.

Even if she could not, he had this chance to unburden himself, and he was going to take it.

"I know you were doing what you thought best," he murmured, stroking the tracery of blue veins rising in relief from her bony hands. "You did your utmost to protect your children. I understand that now. Would that I had then. But I was young and proud, and I did not want to accept Graham's blood money. I understand why you made the choices you did, and although I may disagree with them, I should have found forgiveness within me."

He paused, studying her face for any signs of life. Her chest yet rose and fell, but her face was still as a plaster death mask. Part of him wanted to rail at her, to cry out, to demand she wake so he could have this last dialogue with her, this chance to free himself of the burden of his pride.

"I forgive you for forcing me into accepting Graham's funds," he added. "I have done a great deal of good with his money, and I will continue to do so. Originally, it was to spite him. To throw away his coin on commoners. But it evolved into something more. I enjoy helping people, Mama. I think that is a trait I inherited from you. You were forever taking care of someone or some creature because it gave you pleasure to do so. Whether it was a son who must have been a terrible duty to you at times, or a stray cat in need of a filled belly, or a man who never acknowledged you in public, or even a toad which had gotten itself trapped in a garden pot, you were a caretaker. None of us deserved you. Right, mayhap the cat. The toad probably would have found his own way out, eventually."

He tried to smile, but his eyes had welled with tears once more. He swallowed hard. "I suppose what I am trying to say in my own selfish way, Mama, is that I should have forgiven you a long time ago. I hope you can forgive me for holding on to my pride and anger when I should have let go. I hope you forgive me for staying away for seven years when I should have held you close, and for not appreciating you until it may be too late."

He inhaled, his body shaking involuntarily as he struggled to contain his sobs. The tears were running freely down his cheeks now. "I also hope you shake free of this. That you open your eyes and rail at me for being such an arse."

Decker paused, praying for that miracle, hoping his mother's eyes would flutter open to reveal that sky-blue gaze so like his own. But she remained virtually motionless, her breathing shallow.

"I am married now, Mama," he continued. "I should have written you. You and Lila ought to have been there at the wedding ceremony. You would love Josie. She has the same endless heart you do. My wife is…incredible. There is no other way to describe her. And I do not deserve her, that much is certain. But because I am a selfish cad, I am not about to let her go. Not ever. I do not want to let you go either, Mama."

He clutched her hand tighter, willing her to wake. For her condition to improve.

"Give me a sign you can hear this, Mama," he begged, swiping at the wetness on his cheeks with the back of his hand. "Please tell me you know how much I love you and how sorry I am. And that I will see to Lila's every need."

He waited, stared. Her eyelashes trembled, fluttering faintly before going still again.

Decker pressed a reverent kiss to his mother's hand, and then, for the first time in as long as he could remember, he prayed.

"MY LOVE, YOU must get some rest," Jo told her husband softly.

The sun had risen, and it was half past six in the morning.

"I cannot," he said, wearier than she had ever heard him.

He had spent the entire night holding a vigil at his mother's bedside. His sister Lila—a pensive young lady who shared Decker's dark hair and bright-blue eyes—had remained until nearly three o'clock in the morning, when she had fallen asleep. Jo had finally convinced the poor, exhausted girl to seek a few hours of sleep in her own chamber. Decker, however, had proven far more stubborn. He had refused to leave or sleep. And so Jo had done the same, remaining in a chair at his side the entire night. Every hour or so, he attempted to browbeat her into seeking some slumber of her own.

She was ashamed to admit she must have dozed off at some point. She woke when the first stirrings of dawn were painting the sky, to find Decker still stroking his mother's hand, watching over her. Jo's heart ached for him. Although the physician had said Decker's mother had been lucid the previous day, there had been no sign to suggest she would reawaken since their arrival.

"I will remain here with your mother," she urged. "I promise you that if there is any change, I will have you fetched immediately. You need to sleep."

He shook his head, his handsome countenance grim. "*You* need to sleep, darling. Leave me here. I shall be fine. Go on."

"I was able to sleep for a few hours," Jo countered. "You have not slept at all. Just an hour or two, Decker. You will make yourself ill if you do not."

His jaw tightened. "I will not leave her. I turned my back upon her for seven years. The least I can do is remain here with her now until…"

He did not finish his sentence. There was no need to, for they both understood what he had been about to say. The desolation on her husband's face broke her heart.

Jo bit her lip against the sting of tears. "You did not turn your back upon her, my love. You did what you thought was right."

"But I was wrong," he ground out, his tone bitter as he raked his fingers through his hair, leaving it tousled. "I was selfish and stupid and filled with my damnable pride. Each letter I received from her, I waited for her to apologize, to tell me she had been wrong, to ask for my forgiveness. And in seven years, she never did."

"Two stubborn hearts," she said. "Please, Decker, get some rest, I beg you."

"I cannot go," he said bleakly. Earnestly. "But I want you to get some sleep, Josie. Go to bed."

"I will not leave your side," she told him firmly, meaning it.

He studied her, his sensual lips tightening. "It would seem we are at an impasse."

She belonged with him. Always. It was as simple and

uncomplicated as that. But it was also her duty to look after him. To urge him to sleep when he had dark crescents shading the skin beneath his eyes. To hold his hand and sit with him if he would not.

"We are," she agreed.

His countenance turned mulish. "I want you to get some rest, *bijou*."

She brushed a stray forelock of hair from his forehead. "Later, my love."

Two more interminable hours passed.

Jo saw a breakfast tray sent up. Decker's mother's house was not nearly as large as his townhome in London, but it bore the mark of gentry, despite her status as an earl's former mistress. She had half a dozen servants and a cook.

Decker scarcely touched the food.

Dr. Thompson would be calling again soon, as promised, to check upon the progress of his patient. Jo very much feared the prognosis would be hopeless. Lila returned to the vigil, settling herself in a chair on the opposite side of the bed.

"Did you sleep at all, my dear?" Jo asked her, taking note of the exhaustion on the girl's face.

"I tried," she said, her tearful gaze going to the form of her mother, still and silent as a grave.

Jo fought against another wave of her own sobs, perpetually threatening to break free. "Have you breakfasted?"

"I am not hungry," the girl said, a tear rolling down her cheek.

Jo understood.

"You ought to eat something, Lila," Decker added. "Mama would not want you to starve yourself."

"And what do you know of what Mama would want?" Lila demanded, her voice shrill with pent-up emotion. "You have been absent from our lives for seven years, Eli."

It was the first time Jo had ever heard someone refer to her husband by his given name, aside from during the recitation of their wedding vows. But that was not what shocked Jo the most. Rather, what took her by surprise was the suppressed anger in the girl's voice.

Decker inclined his head. "I have been absent. I acknowledge that. It was wrong, and I acknowledge that as well. I regret the rift between our mother and myself more than you can know, Lila. However, you must know that Mama sent me regular letters apprising me of your life at my request. Pictures as well."

That appeared to give his sister pause. "She said nothing of that to me. Not in all these years. Whenever I asked her about you, she said you wanted nothing to do with us."

"I suppose it must have seemed that way," Decker acknowledged, "and perhaps it was easier for her to view what happened in those terms. Rest assured, however, I may have been gone, but I never stopped loving either of you."

Lila gave him a hard stare that told Jo there would be many rocky moments ahead in Decker's relationship with his younger sister. In the midst of the night, Lila had been too engulfed in tears to offer many words. It seemed time and some slumber—however abbreviated—had loosened her tongue.

"Lila," Jo said then, seeking to ease the tension, "I will ring for a tray to be brought up for you. When you are peckish, you may help yourself to whatever you would like."

"If you insist upon ringing for a tray, I shan't stop you," Lila grumbled.

Jo did just that and settled in to wait once more.

Silence reigned. The tray arrived, and Lila reluctantly stole some bits here and there, eating no more than a sparrow would, it seemed to Jo. However, it was something. Meanwhile, Decker and Lila's mother remained unresponsive.

At long last, Dr. Thompson arrived.

Decker stiffened at Jo's side, his countenance sharpened to blunt, hard edges as the doctor performed a cursory examination. The doctor's expression was sympathetic but firm as he turned to address Decker.

"I do not expect a recovery, Mr. Decker."

The grim pronouncement tore a gasp from Lila. Jo absorbed the news, which, whilst expected, was a heavy blow to Decker. He had wanted very much to speak with his mother. To have a final chance at erasing some of the old pains between them. To make amends for their rift.

Now, he would not have that opportunity.

She bit her lip as she turned her gaze toward her husband, whose dark head was bowed over the hands clasped in his lap. "It is as I feared, then. How may we…make her more comfortable, Dr. Thompson?"

"I will administer more laudanum," the physician said. "In hours such as these, it is often a matter of easing the patient's distress. Nearness of one's family is immeasurable. You are doing everything you can, sir."

Decker's head raised, and he nodded. "Thank you, Dr. Thompson."

Jo did not miss the sparkle of tears in her husband's sky-blue eyes. Nor did she hesitate to reach for his hands, settling hers soothingly atop his. The gesture said everything that mere words could not.

She was not going anywhere.

HIS MOTHER WAS gone.

Decker held his sister in his arms, her small body wracked

by uncontrollable sobs, weeping along with her. Warring with the sadness was a confusing sense of relief, accompanied by the swelling tide of regret.

Regret that he had waited seven years to forgive his mother, and when he had finally done so, it had nearly been too late. Regret he had not swallowed his pride and tried to make peace with her before she had been lying on her deathbed. Relief that he had been able to tell her what he needed to. He wanted to believe she had heard him, that the brief flutter of her lashes had been her way of acknowledging.

Perhaps forgiving him, too.

When at last their tears waned, Jo was there, ushering them calmly from the room, taking them to a sitting room where tea and sandwiches awaited them. She fussed over Decker and Lila in equal measure, and he found himself being stuffed into a chair, a cup of tea thrust into his hands.

He was thirsty.

Weary.

Not hungry, he did not think. In truth, his guts were churning, and he thought he might vomit. The room seemed to swirl around him. He was a man grown, but he had not been prepared to contend with his mother's death. From the moment he had received that troubling telegram the day before until the moment she had breathed her last, he had been desperate to believe she would recover. She was too young. Too vital. He had too much he wanted to say to her.

He wanted her to meet Jo.

To continue being a mother to Lila.

To cradle her grandchild in her arms.

Hell, did he want a child? What was he thinking? He had vowed to himself he would never saddle himself with heirs. The Earl of Graham's legacy would die with him. It was just the wildness of his emotions, the tumult of the last few days, the lack of sleep, playing tricks upon his mind.

Yes, that was it.

"Decker?"

There was his wife's voice, sounding as if it arrived to him from the other end of a tunnel. So far away. There was a rushing in his ears. *Damn it*, he could not pass out. Not now. He inhaled slowly, trying to still his rapidly pounding heart, trying to regain control over himself.

"Look at me, my love."

The insistence in her tone reached him, grasping him and hauling him out of the fog infecting his mind. He blinked, settling his gaze upon her. Love for her surged inside him, stronger than the grief. Bigger than the pain. He should tell her, he thought for at least the hundredth time.

But the words would not come.

Instead, he allowed his eyes to drift over her face. She had spent the entire night at his side. Little ringlets had come free of her chignon, curling around her face. She looked weary but beautiful as always, concern pinching the fullness of her lips into a firm line. He wanted to kiss her mouth back to lushness again, but he could not seem to move.

Gratitude slammed into him, stealing his breath.

"Drink the tea, Decker," she urged softly.

He did, because she asked him to. It was sweet on his tongue, prepared just as he liked it. Of course it was. His Josie took note of everything. She *cared*.

"I need you to eat something. Just a bit," she was saying. "It is nearly dinnertime, and you've had nothing since breakfast. I am going to speak with the servants, take care of a few matters. You stay here with Lila. I do not want either of you to worry about a thing. Let me take care of you. Will you do that for me?"

He wanted to argue. To tell her he must be the one to

arrange for mourning drapery in the household, a funeral, his mother, everything. Instead, he nodded. Jo wanted to take care of him, of his sister. And he was going to let her.

"I will do that," he rasped.

"Good," she said, some of the tension easing from her countenance.

Perhaps she had supposed he would argue? His bloody mind had turned to porridge. He had not the capacity for thought at the moment. He was entrusting himself to his wife. His wife who loved him.

She turned to go. He caught her hand, moving with such haste, he splashed tea into his lap. But he did not give a damn.

"Josie?"

"Yes, my love?" The tenderness in her expression made him ache.

Tell her you love her.

Three simple words, you dolt.

"Thank you," he said instead.

She nodded, and then she bustled from the room.

Decker turned to Lila. "You had better eat something, my dear. You did not eat enough for a bird earlier."

His sister's lips trembled. "I miss her already, Eli."

No one called him Eli. No one but Mama and Lila and, a long time ago, Nora.

"I do too, Lila," he said sincerely.

And he knew then that he always would.

Chapter Eighteen

*D*ECKER SANK INTO the chair in his study, both relieved to be back in London and weary to the bone. Mourning was a draining practice. The last few days had been an endless sea of protocols being observed. His mother's house had been draped in black, the glasses hung with mourning shrouds. A procession of somber callers had come and gone, including many of the local gentry, none of whom had known his mother's true identity. She had led a quiet, unassuming life in Hertfordshire for the last seven years as the widowed Mrs. Decker, and none had pried into her past.

Undoubtedly most of those who had called to offer their sympathies would never have lowered themselves had they known the truth about his mother. That she had never married but was, in truth, Miss Decker. And, worse, that she had been the Earl of Graham's mistress.

Yet, as Decker had spoken to them, a clear picture of the life she had created for herself there had begun to form. To those who had come to know her since her move to Hertfordshire following Graham's death, she was not a ruined woman. Not a secret, not a source of shame, not a mistress, not a woman who ought to be scorned and shunned.

Rather, she had been a woman of modest means, a kind friend, a dedicated member of the local parish, and a mother who loved her daughter and the son who never came up from

London to visit her. Decker was grateful his mother had possessed the opportunity, unlike so many women in her position, to start anew and to be remembered as the woman she was rather than the decisions she had made.

But the process had also been bittersweet, because he had been forced to face the reality that he had been nothing more than words on a page to her for the last seven years. He could not undo what had already been done. Could not rearrange the past into a more suiting picture.

All he could do was do his best, from this moment on. His best for his wife, for his sister, and for himself, as well. He sighed as he thought of Jo, who had been a comforting source of strength at his side. She had been strong when he had been weak. When his mind had been too shattered with grief to comprehend what must be done, she had seen to every detail. She had become a confidante to his sister as well in the days since his mother had died.

But the nature of their stay at his mother's home had not lent itself to private time alone. Lila had been so distraught over their mother's death that Jo had bedded down in her room each evening, to help her sleep through the night. Although Decker had missed Jo's comforting presence in his own bed, he had been willing to relinquish her for the sake of his sister. Lila was so very young to lose her mother, and the shock and sleeplessness of the initial few days of their stay in Hertfordshire had left him falling asleep the moment his head had hit the bloody pillow.

Now, he, Jo, and Lila had all returned to his townhome.

Jo had decided to personally see Lila settled in her new room and get her personal effects sorted. Which left Decker once more alone, staring down a veritable mountain of correspondence upon his desk, with the distinct, uncomfortable need to explain himself to his wife burning in his gut.

However, he would not put himself before Lila. His sister was an impressionable, terrified twelve years old.

He was a man fully grown.

He could share his beloved wife with his sister for another few hours, until everything was sorted for Lila. Already, Jo had arranged for interviews with prospective governesses in the coming days. Further proof she was a far better woman than he deserved.

He had to tell her about the letter, about Nora, his past. He had to tell Jo he loved her and wanted to start a family of their own. The feelings that had assailed him when he had been at his mother's deathbed had not faded or left him. Indeed, they had only grown stronger.

He loved his wife. The next time he made love to her, he intended to plant his seed in her womb. He would speak with her soon, he promised himself, seeking distraction by the sorting of piles of correspondence. Mayhap tonight. Or when she finished with Lila. Thus far, the moment had never seemed the proper one in which to begin. They had scarcely had a minute alone together since arriving in Hertfordshire.

Decker began with a pile of reports which had been assembled by Macfie, who was proving his mettle and settling matters with aplomb, as expected, in his absence. He had singlehandedly corrected a design flaw in the newest piano, arranged for a second printing of their wildly successful book *Confessions of a Sinful Countess*, and balanced the ledgers for the Black Souls Club. He had also suggested a new lease consideration, along with providing the finalized documents from Mr. Levi Storm's North Atlantic Electric Company.

He was going to have to give Macfie an increase in pay, Decker decided.

A subtle knock on his door interrupted his solitude at last.

Grateful for the diversion, and hoping it was his wife on

the other side of the portal, Decker bid the intruder to enter.

The door opened to reveal his butler, Rhees. "Mr. Decker, there is a Lady Tinley calling for you. I have explained the family is in mourning and you are not at home, but she is being quite adamant in her desire to see you."

Fuck.

One word. A violent, inward curse.

That was all Decker could think. It was as if his mind, already overwhelmed by the loss of his mother and the vast changes that had befallen him in the last few days, abandoned him. His capacity for speech briefly fled.

"Shall I have her discreetly removed, sir?" Rhees pressed. "She claims an old acquaintance, or I would not have disturbed you with such a nuisance."

An old acquaintance.

Yes, they certainly had that.

But that was *all* they had.

He stared at Rhees, struggling to form his response. Part of him felt he ought to refuse her outright, to never see Nora again. But another part of him longed for the end of that once-painful chapter in his life. That part of Decker needed to sever the ties between them, finally and eternally. To let her know he was a happily married man, deliriously besotted with his wife. If he sent her away, she would only return. He had no wish for her to continue haunting him.

"You may see her to the salon," he decided, for it was the only room in his townhome that had been decorated with visitors in mind. The pictures on the wall were pastoral. Unassuming.

Bloody hell, now that he thought upon it, he was going to have to remove his erotic collections from any room Lila may enter. It would hardly do for his innocent sister to wander into the library and observe an engraving of a man with his hand up a lady's skirts.

Damn.

What was that old phrase, turning over a new leaf? That was what he was doing, in all ways. Becoming a version of himself he had never known existed.

Rhees bowed. "I will see her ladyship placed in the salon, sir."

When his butler was gone, Decker stood, taking a second to collect himself. Grief still held him in its greedy grasp. He little desired further upset or discord, but he also felt that this unwanted meeting was something he must endure. If not for himself, then for Jo. He needed Nora to know there was no future for them. Not now, not ever.

He rose from his desk and made his way to the salon. Nora was already ensconced within. Her back was to him when he entered, but he still recognized her silhouette, even ten years on. Not much had changed and yet, for him, everything had. Her brilliant red hair was piled on her crown in a simple style, and her gown was outmoded in shape— quite frumpy, no *tournure*—and clearly of inferior construction.

It was…*shabby*, hardly the dress one would expect a viscountess to wear. But then, Tinley was not a lord with whom Decker was familiar. He had likely been a country fellow, perhaps lean in the purse. And Nora was a widow now, he reminded himself, which would also explain her modest dress. Her portion must be relatively small.

Was that her reason for seeking him out then, he wondered, after all this time? She was out of her mourning period and in need of coin?

When she did not seem to hear his arrival, he cleared his throat.

She spun about, facing him at last. Her face, too, was the

same. Rounder now, and less girlish than she had been ten years before when they had both been eighteen. But still, the same. It struck him now, as he looked upon her, that he had once imagined her the most glorious creature he had ever beheld and yet, her beauty was a pale imitation of Jo's. From the inside, out.

"Eli," she said, rushing toward him as if she expected him to take her in his arms.

He held up a staying hand lest she rush too near. "Lady Tinley," he acknowledged with a mocking bow. "Why have you come?"

She faltered, stopping just short of him, her countenance pinching with confusion. "I have come to see you, of course, Eli. Do you not remember me? I—why, I sent you a letter a bit ago, before I returned to Town."

"I received your letter," he told her, "but it was unwelcome. As is your visit now."

She paled, reaching out for him, her hand falling upon his coat sleeve. "Eli, please. I know you are angry with me, and I cannot blame you. It has been ten years, after all. Ten long, lonely years. Please believe me when I tell you not a day passed when I did not long for you."

He jerked his arm from her touch. "You are out of bounds, madam, and I must ask you to go. I am a married man, and I cannot think my wife would take kindly to the nature of this visit. Nor do I, for that matter. You have no place here or in my life."

"I love you," she said, desperation ringing in her voice. "I loved you ten years ago when I agreed to be your wife, and I have never stopped. I regret listening to my father. I should have gone against his wishes and married you instead of Lord Tinley. Eli, if you knew how terribly I suffered these last nine years...I was shackled to a monster. But he is gone now. It is not too late for us. I had to see you, to tell you. Surely you understand. I had no choice then, but I have a choice now."

Decker stared at the woman he had thought he had loved.

Hell, he had been a lad of eighteen. What had he known then of life, of the world, of anything at all? *Bloody nothing.* That was what he had known. Nora's defection and betrayal ten years ago had shaped his life. He had believed himself incapable of love because of her actions.

Yet, as she stood before him now, an astonishing sense of clarity overcame him.

He had never loved her. He had never felt an inkling of what he felt for Jo.

"You had a choice then, Nora," he said calmly, clearly. "You could have married me. I had asked for your hand and you accepted. But when your father decided I was not worthy of his darling, being an earl's by-blow rather than a viscount, you severed all connections with me. And yet now, you return, ten years later, claiming to love me?"

She touched his coat sleeve again, clinging to him. "I know how you must feel, Eli. I do not blame you for your anger toward me. I am angry with myself. The last ten years have been penance. I have been waiting to contact you, terrified you would revile me."

"You think too much of yourself." He looked at her, truly looked at her, the woman who had left him jaded and broken in his youth, and he felt nothing. A curious absence of…anything. Neither anger nor hatred nor love. Only disinterest. "I hardly revile you. Indeed, I do not feel anything for you. But I must thank you for the choices you made. I understand now, even if I did not in my youth, that you did me a grand favor in crying off. I would never have known happiness and true love if not for you."

What he meant, when he said those words, was that he

was wholeheartedly grateful Nora had deemed him unsuitable. Grateful she had deferred to her father's judgment. Because he could see quite clearly now that she was not the woman who was meant for him. And he could also see that her defection had settled him upon the path that had led him to the woman he loved.

To Lady Josephine Danvers.

To Jo.

To Josie.

Mine.

"Oh, my darling Eli," Nora gushed, completely misunderstanding what he had attempted to convey. "You are my happiness and true love also."

"No," he said, shaking his head, holding up his hands to keep her from advancing any farther. The very notion of her touch repulsed him now. And not just because part of him was convinced she was seeking him out because she knew he possessed untold wealth and she appeared to be pockets to let, existing on a strained widow's portion.

But because there was only one woman whose touch could move him. One woman he loved. One woman he wanted, now and forever. And her name was most assuredly not Nora, Lady Tinley.

"I do not love you," he told Nora. "I love my wife."

JO'S FEET ACHED. Her back ached. Her heart ached.

Every part of her was weary.

The last few days had been exhausting, both physically and mentally. She had spent far too much time contorted in chairs and carriages, not enough time sleeping, too much time crying. She was drained, emotionally exhausted. She missed her husband, his comforting embrace, his kiss. She missed sharing his bed. Missed...

Well, selfish wretch that she was, she missed the way their life had been, before the tumult. Not because she regretted Lila's entrance into their life—quite the opposite—for her new sister-in-law was a tenderhearted delight. But because she could not help but to feel a chasm between herself and Decker, a distance which had not been present before their frantic rush to Hertfordshire and his mother's death.

Poor Lila had just fallen into her bed for a nap, a tear-stained mess once again, and Jo had stayed with her, reading to her until the young girl's breathing had finally become rhythmic and even. Sleep—much-needed—had claimed her at last.

And now, as she emerged from Lila's room, the housekeeper Mrs. Crisply informed her there was an unexpected guest who had been seen into the public salon where they entertained visitors.

"A guest?" Jo repeated, frowning. "We have only just returned to Town."

Mrs. Crisply shook her head, her displeasure evident. "I do believe the lady in question was asking for the master of the house in particular, Mrs. Decker. I thought to let you know."

The *lady* in question? Misgiving filtered through Jo at once.

The housekeeper's subtle disapproval was not lost upon her. Although Mrs. Crisply had been running Decker's house well before he had married her, Jo had nevertheless connected with the efficient, kindly housekeeper from the moment she had become the mistress of Decker's townhome. And she heartily appreciated Mrs. Crisply's warning. After all, though the woman was circumspect and would never carry tales, Jo suspected she must have seen some things which would give her cause for concern during her tenure and whilst Decker had carried on as a bachelor.

"Thank you, Mrs. Crisply," Jo told her. "I will see to this unexpected visitor."

Even if it was the very last thing she felt like doing. Still, a question prodded her, undeniable. Why would this woman, whomever she was, seek an audience with Decker in particular?

Jo made her way to the salon in automaton fashion. But as she approached the room, the familiar sound of Decker's baritone reached her, mingling with a distinctly feminine voice. Puzzled, she stopped just short of the open door, where she had a perfect view of Decker standing far too near to a lovely woman she had never seen before. There was something undeniably familiar about their mannerisms toward each other.

Jo paused, understanding that somehow this woman was no stranger to Decker. That they knew each other. The fiery-haired beauty was saying something in a low, entreating tone.

He said something in return. Jo thought she heard a name. But surely not. No, it could not be…

"Nora," Jo heard him say.

He would hardly be addressing this unexpected caller by her Christian name. Would he?

"I know how you must feel, Eli," the woman said, speaking in such a low tone, Jo could only discern portions of what she was saying. "I do not blame you… I am angry with myself. The last ten years have been penance. I have been waiting…" Awful, ugly suspicion intruded upon Jo's thoughts. This was no ordinary caller, was it?

Dear, merciful heavens.

Her mind spun with denial. *No, no, no.*

Jo looked upon the woman, the familiarity in her manner,

and she simply *knew*. She knew it was Viscountess Tinley, the woman Decker had loved long ago, the woman who had jilted him and broken his heart, left him jaded and guarded. She knew it was the same woman whose letter had distressed him so much that he had fled the breakfast room looking pallid, with a thin excuse.

The letter he had continued to keep a secret from Jo.

His mother's illness and death had taken precedence over Jo's feelings. She had tamped down all the hurt, all thoughts of the letter, all the feelings of inadequacy and doubt that letter's arrival and her husband's subsequent reaction to it had caused. Wounded feelings could mend, after all. Life and death were far more important.

But now, it all returned in a frenzied rush.

And Decker was not railing at the woman or ordering her to leave. He had not stormed from the room. He had not taken note of his own wife standing near the threshold, gazing upon the vignette before her with dawning horror.

Because he was too caught up in the woman.

Here was the personification of all Jo's fears.

The man she loved did not love her. Her husband did not love her. He was keeping secrets from her. And now, his past had returned in vivid, beautiful form to haunt her. To tear him away from her forever.

She had a choice to make. She could either intrude upon this cozy scene, or she could walk away. Her heart thundered. Her mouth went dry. She wrestled with the decision, more uncertain of anything than she had ever been in her life.

"I hardly revile you," Decker was saying, but some of his words were too impossible to hear. "…I must thank you for the choices you made…you did me a grand…I would never have known happiness and true love if not for you."

"Oh, my darling Eli," Lady Tinley said, rushing toward

him. "You are my happiness and true love also."

Jo felt as if a massive fist had grabbed her heart and squeezed it mercilessly. Something seized her, rendering her incapable of moving. She wanted to run, to never hear another word that was being spoken between Decker and this woman. And yet, she could not go.

But then, Decker's voice rang out.

"No," he said, shaking his head, staving off Lady Tinley's advance toward him. "I do not love you. I love my wife."

He *loved* her.

Quietly, Jo backed away from the open salon door. She had eavesdropped enough. And she had heard the only words she needed to hear.

BY THE TIME Decker had seen Nora to the door, he felt lighter and happier than he had since before his mother's death. Finally, he was free of the past.

Forever.

Which meant that it was time to focus instead upon the future and where it would lead him. He sought out Rhees instantly, wondering where his wife was. The time had come to tell her he loved her. He only hoped he was not too late.

Rhees, ever a step ahead of him, it seemed, handed Decker a missive. "From Mrs. Decker, sir."

He thanked his butler and tore open the note.

D.,

It seems to me that there remain items on my list which have yet to be completed. Will you assist me with number two and meet me in your chamber?

Yours,

J.

He did not require the list before him to know what number two had been. Her ways to be wicked were emblazoned upon his brain: *Arrange for an assignation.* Decker's feet were already moving, taking the stairs two at a time. He could not get to her fast enough.

Chapter Nineteen

Ways to be Wicked

1. ~~Kiss a man until you are breathless.~~
2. ~~Arrange for an assignation. Perhaps with Lord Q?~~ ~~your husband? Strike that,~~ **bijou**. ~~Definitely with your~~ ~~husband.~~
3. ~~Get caught in the rain with a gentleman. (This will~~ ~~necessitate the removal of wet garments. Choose said~~ ~~gentleman wisely.)~~
4. ~~Sneak into a gentleman's bedchamber in the midst of~~ ~~the night.~~
5. ~~Go to a gentleman's private apartments.~~
6. ~~Spend a night in a gentleman's bed.~~
7. *Make love in the outdoors.*
8. *Ask your husband to help you disrobe.*

Jo crossed off number two on her list while she waited for Decker to come to her in his chamber. Then she filled in the rest of number eight. She hoped she would be able to strike through that number as well before the afternoon was done.

Satisfied with her progress, she waited for him, heart bursting with love.

At long last, the door opened, and her husband came prowling into his chamber, closing the door at his back with more force than necessary. The action was rather reminiscent of that first day when she had gone to his offices in search of her list and Mactie had slammed the door when he had left.

Jo gave Decker a teasing smile. "It would seem you do not know your own strength."

He paused just short of her, his sky-blue gaze searing hers. "There is a hell of a lot I do not know, *bijou*. Principal amongst them, how to tell my wife I am in love with her."

It required all Jo's restraint to keep from throwing herself into his arms. "Have you tried using your lips and tongue?"

Her cheeks went hot as she realized the implications of her words.

He flashed her a sinner's unrepentant grin. "I have indeed used my lips and tongue upon her many times. Though I fear not nearly enough."

Jo's smile grew at Decker's teasing. After so much heaviness, grief, and pain, it felt good to embrace some lightness. "You know very well I was referring to using your lips and tongue to speak."

"I do," he agreed. "But when your cheeks turn pink, you are even more impossible to resist than you ordinarily are."

They stared at each other for a moment, nothing but silence and two steps between them. She wanted to be brave, to be the one to say the words first. She also needed to hear his confession. She wanted him to tell her everything.

"Did you get my note from Rhees?" she asked, a foolish question, for of course he had.

Why else would he be in his chamber, just as she had requested?

"I did," he said. "I am here, happy to offer you my assistance in the completion of the second objective on your list."

Her heart beat faster, and though an ache blossomed into life between her thighs, she also knew a pang of disappointment. Perhaps she was asking too much of him, too quickly.

Mayhap he was not ready yet.

"But I am also here," he continued, moving closer to her at last, "to tell you I love you."

She swallowed down a lump rising in her throat. It was time for honesty from the both of them. "Decker, I saw you in the salon earlier today with Lady Tinley. I know about the letter you received from her before your mother's death. Her name was on the envelope you left behind. Callie told me about your past with her."

His jaw hardened. "I want nothing to do with her, and I told her as much. I am sorry I did not tell you sooner, or that I did not write to her myself making it clear she was not welcome in my life. But she will never again call upon me, I can assure you of it."

"I know," Jo told him, "because I overheard some of your conversation with her. I am ashamed to admit I was eavesdropping. I did not intend to, but I was afraid, Decker."

"Afraid?" He frowned now, his gaze searching hers. "Of what, *bijou*?"

"I was afraid you were still in love with her," she admitted.

"Ah, Josie." He reached out to her then, taking her in his arms. "I am so sorry for making you wonder and worry. My mother's death forced me to make a great deal of realizations, and one of them is how much you mean to me." He buried his face in her hair, inhaling. "I have been an arse. Can you forgive me?"

She clutched him tightly to her. "There is nothing to forgive, my love."

"Am I?" He raised his head, searching her gaze with his. "Your love?"

"Of course you are." She cupped his beloved face in her hands. "My heart is yours, Decker. It always has been and it always will be. I love you."

"I love you," he said again, before his mouth swooped down on hers.

Jo kissed him back with all the love bursting inside her, all the need, the relief, and the passion, too. It felt as if forever had passed since she had last known the sweetness of his lips on hers. She opened for him, their tongues tangling. He tasted like forgiveness and love and tea and everything she wanted for the rest of her life.

He tasted like *hers*.

She broke the kiss with reluctance, her breaths coming in ragged gasps. "I finally completed number eight on the list. I was wondering if you might aid me with that one now."

"That depends." His flirtatious manner had returned, along with his devilish charm. "What does number eight say?"

"It was meant to have said *ask a gentleman to help you disrobe*," she told him. "But I have made some realizations myself since I first wrote the list, and the most important one is that there is only one man with whom I want to complete it. *You*. No one else will do."

"When you phrase it thus, Mrs. Decker, how can I resist?" He kissed her again lingeringly, slowly, masterfully.

It was a kiss of love and worship and reverence.

A kiss of promise and forever.

She never wanted it to end, and she kissed him back with every bit as much veneration. Lips moved in tender, seductive rhythm. Tongues glided together. Her fingers slid into his hair, sifting through the thick, luxurious strands.

A lingering, nagging question reared its head then. Or rather, two of them. She ended the kiss, trying to gather her thoughts. If this was the moment in which they were both embracing complete honesty, then these questions could not wait, regardless of how badly her body longed for Decker's.

He traced her brow with a gentle swipe of his forefinger, the caress casual and yet at once so caring that it made her heart ache. "Something is bothering you, my love. What is it?"

She inhaled, exhaled. Locked her gaze on his. This was the man she loved. Her husband. She could tell him anything. Ask him any question.

"When you were attempting to convince my brother to give you my hand," she began, "you told him I could be carrying your child when there was no possibility of that."

His sensual lips compressed. "I did. In truth, I was desperate to make you mine and fearful your brother would disapprove of the match. I could not bear the notion of you marrying another, and so I set out to make certain he would have no choice but to accept my suit. I would apologize for my actions, but in truth, I am not sorry, Josie. I wanted you—*needed* you—and now you are mine."

She could hardly argue with that logic. But there was another part of that question she had yet to ask. Her cheeks went hot as she searched for the words. "That does not explain…do you not want children, Decker? You said you had no need of heirs, but…"

He swallowed, his Adam's apple bobbing. She could not help but to notice that even his throat was handsome—every part of him attracted her notice. She wanted to press her lips there, to inhale his scent, to kiss and lick and nip him.

But answers first.

"Ah, Josie." He exhaled, his warm breath fanning over her lips as he pressed his forehead to hers for a moment before straightening again. "That is another realization my mother's death has left me with: I do want children. Your children. I was so caught up in my hatred and anger toward Graham that I vowed never to carry on his legacy. Instead, I was determined to give it to everyone else—to spend it wisely, yes, for not even I could bring myself to profligacy just to spite him However, everything I did—every penny I spent—was to defy him in some way. I gave to orphans and hospitals, I used it to buy erotic art and fund erotic literature. And I will be honest with you. I have yet to find a compromise for myself. But neither will I deny us the chance to have a family because of the bitterness I carry toward the man who sired me. It is time to cut free the shackles of the past in every way."

Her heart hurt for him by the time he finished his earnest explanation. He was such a strong, intelligent, good man. And so much of his life had been defined by his inability to be accepted for who he was. No longer, she vowed.

"Oh, Decker, my love," she said, caressing his jaw. He was so beloved to her, so vital. She wanted to wrap herself around him and never let him go. "We will find a way, together."

"Love is more important than hatred." He kissed her cheek, her nose. "I understand that now. You make me whole. You make me want to be a better man for you. A man who deserves you."

"My darling man, you have *always* deserved me." She caught his face in her hands and dragged his lips back to hers for another lengthy kiss before tearing her mouth away. "My heart has always known yours. I feel it. Here."

Jo took his hand and pressed it over that madly thumping organ.

"I feel the same way," he breathed, his gaze so profound, tears unexpectedly stung her eyes.

"Good," she said, needing to break the heaviness of the moment. "Now help me to disrobe before I die of longing."

He laughed into their kiss, and she had never heard a better sound. She laughed with him, their smiling mouths melding together in sinuous unison. They kissed and kissed until the laughter was gone, and in its place was only a deep, burning hunger.

Longing skittered through her as he kissed to her throat. Open-mouthed kisses made her shiver as his fingers made short work of the buttons bisecting her polonaise bodice. The smooth black cotton slid from her shoulders and arms in a decadent whisper over her flesh. He rubbed the dark shadow of his whiskers on her throat. Her knees felt as if they may give out.

He filled her senses—his scent, his touch, his breaths.

"Let me be your servant," he whispered in her ear, before taking the fleshy lobe in his teeth and tugging.

"Yes," was all she could manage, her nipples throbbing behind her corset, her sex pulsing between her thighs.

She was wet for him already, and he had scarcely touched her.

He seemed to know how desperate she was. Or mayhap he felt the same way. His fingers moved faster, his mouth playing over her skin with greater intensity. Her layers were falling away, slipping to the floor with all her inhibitions. Silk and satin pooled in a heap around her. Laces were loosened. Her corset hit the Axminster as his mouth found her nape.

The slide of his tongue over her skin was electric.

"You are the most beautiful, bewitching, glorious creature I have ever met," he murmured against the side of her neck.

With all her underpinnings gone save her chemise, stockings, and drawers, when he pressed his big body against hers, she felt the rigid outline of his straining cock. She wanted him inside her, filling her. She rubbed her bottom against him, seeking whatever contact she could get.

Her reward was his low groan, a tongue dipping into the hollow behind her ear. His hands were on her hips now, hauling her more snugly to him. Heat licked through her, her core clenching. Every part of her felt heavy, weighed down by desire.

"You want my cock in you, don't you, Josie?" he growled into her ear.

Feeling bold, she reached behind her, finding his length through his trousers. She squeezed him, rubbing her thumb over the tip. His breath was hot and ragged at her ear as she explored him. When her grip on him tightened, his hips pumped forward. His hands slid from her hips, moving upward.

He found her pebbled nipples through the thin layer of her chemise and plucked at them while his tongue traced over the whorl of her ear. She was so wet, she was soaking her drawers. So needy. But he took his time, grinding into her hand, pulling on her nipples, then taking her breasts in his hands and gently massaging them. His forefingers flicked over her painfully sensitive flesh.

She thought she could spend like this, from nothing more than his touch and his body fused to hers, his mouth knowing all the ways to make her wild. She wondered if he could, too. But when she stroked him harder, he made a low sound in his throat and spun her around.

He was impeccably dressed, down to his waistcoat and crisp white shirt. He was so handsome, his bright eyes burning with desire and something else, something more profound.

Love.

"I am going to make you come on my tongue," he told her, his voice low.

Her heart pounded. So did her sex.

What could she say to that? Nothing. She was trembling with desire. Words were impossible.

"Raise your arms, *bijou*," he ordered.

She obeyed. He lifted her chemise slowly, making certain the soft fabric dragged over her hungry nipples as he went.

The teasing was delicious. Her breaths were coming in short, uneven bursts by the time her chemise was finally gone.

He lowered his head and sucked first one nipple into his hot, wet mouth. Then the other. Decker laved one with his tongue and then rolled the other between his thumb and forefinger. Slow, steady licks. The abrasion of his teeth. He rubbed his jaw over the curve, his short whiskers rasping over her flesh. It felt like heaven and torture, bliss and pain, all at once. She was going to demand he forego shaving every other day, just for this sensation.

His mouth was on the peak of her breast once more, sucking hard. He cupped her mound through the barrier of her drawers. Nothing more—just that possessive cradle—so tantalizing, so tempting. She could not stifle the moan he wrung from her.

"Whatever can be the matter, my lady?" he murmured against her breast, slanting her a look laden with sinful intentions. "You sound as if you need release."

"I do," she whispered.

He suckled her again, then blew on her nipple, which stood at lusty attention, elongated and tight. She wanted more. This teasing was not enough. Her fingers had found their way into his thick, wavy hair. She tugged on it, trying to urge him on, arching her back so that her breasts were presented to him like offerings.

"Let me help you." His mouth was on her breast again, stealing another moan as his fingers worked on the placket at her waistband. Her drawers slid down her hips in a whisper of sound.

He released her nipple and then took her wrists, pulling her hands from his hair. "Come."

She was wearing nothing but silk stockings and black satin boots. Jo allowed him to tug her to a chair positioned by the fireplace at the opposite end of the room. He sank to his knees before her, then released her hands and tenderly caressed her ankle. He guided her booted foot to the cushion of the chair, opening her to his brilliant gaze.

"There you are, my lady," he said, his eyes darkening as they settled upon her most intimate flesh. "So pretty and pink and wet. I know what you need."

And then, he filled his hands with her rump, drawing her sex to his mouth. He sucked on her pearl just as he had done to her nipples, groaning in appreciation. The vibration sent a spike of pleasure through her. She was dizzied, perched on her Louis heels, helpless to do anything other than give herself up to him.

She was surrendering, in every way.

But surrender had never felt so good. Nor so right.

DECKER SUCKED ON Jo's swollen, slick pearl, doing his utmost to keep from coming in his trousers. She tasted so good—musky, spicy, feminine and floral, everything that was her. Everything that was good. Love. She tasted like that, too.

There was no denying the sight of her in nothing but her stockings and boots, spread and open for him, had been the most deliciously carnal sight he had ever beheld. No erotic picture could hold a candle to her. For a moment, he had been on his knees before her, desire slamming into him with ballocks-clenching force as he took in the perfection of her glistening lips and that tempting bud demanding his attention. He had mustered all the control he possessed to keep from cupping his rigid cock and stroking himself into oblivion with his face buried in her cunny. Because when he spent this time, it was going to be inside her.

Not into the counterpane. Not onto her belly or thigh. He was going to bury his cock deep in her and he was not going to withdraw until he had filled her with his seed. Just the thought made his cock ache.

He flicked his tongue over her the way he knew she liked, catching the delicate underside where she was most sensitive, and then could not resist licking lower. Down her seam. He delved between her lips, where she was so soaked for him, the evidence of her desire sending another arrow of need straight to his cockstand. He was rigid against the placket of his trousers, aching to free himself as he sank his tongue deep inside her cunny.

Gripping the soft globes of her arse in his hands, he held her firmly, feasting on her, fucking her fast and hard. Her thighs quivered and the most erotic mewls hatched from her throat. More wetness coated his tongue. He lapped it up, savoring her cream, pointing his tongue to thrust deeper. As deep as he could go.

She was close. On the precipice.

He latched on her pearl again, sucking while he released her rump and slid two fingers deep into her drenched channel. She tightened on him instantly, the hot clench of her inner muscles making him groan and bite her clitoris until she came in a gushing spend, her juices dripping down his fingers, his hand. Pleasure pulsed through him as he ran his tongue back to her cunny. He licked up her spend, every drop, greedy bastard that he was.

He was not done with her yet. He wanted her helpless and limp. He wanted to make her come so many times, she could not bear one more lashing of his tongue. He moved back to her pearl, which was more swollen than before, plump and delicious. Alternating between sucking and licking, nibbling and running circles around her with his tongue, he slid a finger back inside her. Then another. He curled them, finding that magic spot within her.

She cried out, her knees buckling.

Decker caught her to him, holding her steady as he added a third finger, fucking her faster and harder. The wet sound of his fingers moving inside her mingled with her panting breaths, her sweet cries of pleasure.

Yes, my love.

I want to ruin you.

Come on my face.

Cream on my tongue.

Coat me with your dew.

Fuck my fingers and my mouth.

Decker was out of his mind with need. He was not certain which of these things he said aloud and which were litanies in his mind. It hardly mattered. Her hips were pumping in wild thrusts. He was sucking her pearl and stroking in and out of her body. This time when she came, she gasped his name and a fresh torrent of her juices leaked from her core. He was right there to lick up every drop again.

In a haze of need and want, he removed her boots and stockings.

She was naked and he was fully dressed, on his knees before her. She towered over him like a goddess, breasts full, eyes dark and drunk with desire, her nipples tipped with hard points, her cheeks flushed. She was all creamy curves and delicious woman.

All his.

He forgot about the little game he had been playing, acting the part of her servant. Everything in him roared to have her now. He rose to his feet.

"Josie," he rasped, tearing at his coat and waistcoat, clawing at his necktie. "I need you."

"I need you too, my love," she said, her hands on him, helping him.

In a frenzied rush, they divested him of every stitch. Naked, kissing, they fell upon the bed together. Jo took his rigid prick in her hand. He was leaking from the tip, and she slicked his mettle over him, rubbing her thumb over the slit in his cockhead in a way that had him groaning, hips swiveling.

"I want inside you," he said, frustration and desire blending to an acute pinnacle.

"Not yet." She kissed down his jaw, down his throat, stroking him as she went.

He forced himself to remain still and allow his wife to have her way with him. Her lips left a trail of fire blazing in their wake as they slowly traveled over his abdomen. Then lower. His cock was standing at attention, thick and protruding and begging to be inside her sweet berry-pink lips.

He realized that in his haste to undress her and have her, he had left her coiffure untouched. His fingers rectified that travesty immediately, sifting through the dark, silken strands, plucking hair pins as he went. When the velvety suction of her mouth engulfed his cockhead, he forgot to care about anything else.

Decker grasped a handful of her hair, wrapping the strands around his fist, and watched as his desperate cock disappeared between her lips. She cupped his ballocks, which were painfully full after so many days and nights without her and taut with the need to spend. And then she took him deep.

Down her throat.

His hips jumped off the bed. He lost control, surging into her. She squeezed his sacs, massaging them, and he nearly lost himself then and there.

"Fuck, Josie," he groaned.

She released him slowly, leaving his cock glistening with

the combination of her saliva and his own mettle. Gripping him in her small fist, she laved her tongue over his tip. When she flicked over the slit, pressing there, and licking up another drop that seeped from him, he knew he could not bear any more torture.

He hauled her up his body. "Sit on my face," he ordered, intending to make her good and slick before he impaled her. He wanted her as wet as the ocean.

"Like in the picture, the naughty letters?" she asked.

She had remembered, his beloved wife.

Decker suppressed another groan. "Precisely like that."

She shifted with his help. He planted his hands on her waist and guided her so that her knees were on either side of his head and his waiting mouth was perfectly aligned with her cunny. He buried his tongue deep, then licked his way to her pearl.

"Oh, Decker." Her throaty moan was all the reward he needed, but he would take the cream she gave him too.

She rode his face with a wild abandon, rocking into him again and again while he filled her and licked her. She came again while he fucked her cunny with his tongue and rubbed her pearl. She moaned, her body stiffening as her climax overtook her, and then he had her where he wanted her.

He rolled her to her back and settled himself between her legs. Grasping his cock, he rubbed himself up and down her slit, until he was wet with her juices and nearly out of his mind with need.

They both sighed as he sank inside her to the hilt. One thrust, and she was gripping him in her tight, welcoming heat. And she was drenched. And perfect. He pinned her to the bed with his cock, giving himself a minute to stay the frantic roaring in his head. She wrapped her legs around his waist, her fingernails raking down his back.

"Go on, Josie," he urged, barely finding his voice, words. "Tell me what you want."

Everything inside him screamed with the need to move.

Her eyes were glossy and dark with desire as they seared into him. "I want you to make love to me, Decker. I want you to spend inside me."

Ah, those words. They were everything he needed to hear.

His ballocks tightened and he started moving, in and out. Though he tried to go slowly, to prolong their mutual pleasure, Jo was thrusting with him, their bodies moving in a frantic rush, seeking relief. He kissed her throat, losing control. Faster and faster he went, thrusting deep and then withdrawing, his strokes harder. He fucked her all the way up the bed until her head was smacking into the ornately carved headboard. And then he cradled her in his hands to blunt the thumps and fucked her some more, until she tightened on him like a vise, bathing his cock in another torrent of sweet release.

He came too, so hard little black stars appeared before him. And he emptied himself inside her, filling his wife with his seed. He felt as if he came more than he ever had. She milked him, draining his ballocks, caressing his back, his shoulders, kissing his collarbone, his neck.

When it was over, he collapsed against her, breathing heavy, inhaling the scent of her unbound hair, savoring the softness of her beneath him, the pulsing heat of her cunny stretched around him.

"I love you," he whispered again.

And he knew then that the bonds of the past had finally been severed.

He was whole again.

Chapter Twenty

$\mathcal{J}$O AND LILA had just returned from a visit to the orphanage, during which Lila played piano and sang for the children and Jo read them stories, when Rhees announced Jo had a caller.

Or to be more precise, three callers.

The sight of her brother, sister-in-law, and nephew in the salon surprised a happy squeal out of Jo.

"Julian, Clara, and little Arthur!" She could not contain her excitement as she rushed forward.

Julian caught her in a brotherly embrace, whilst Clara gave her a half embrace as she cradled little Arthur in her arms. Jo's heart surged as she gazed down at her nephew's sweet, cherubic face, dropping a kiss upon his smooth, velvet-soft forehead.

"Oh, my sweet baby nephew," she crooned to him, before glancing up at Clara. "May I hold him?"

"I was hoping you would," Clara drawled in her thick American accent, smiling warmly. "The little darling was putting my arm to sleep. He is such a large baby already. I can scarcely countenance how much he has grown."

"Nor can I." Jo took her nephew in her arms and gazed down at his adorable, round face. "He is lovely, Clara. I do believe he has your nose now. At first, I thought he had Julian's, but yours is ever so much better."

She slanted a glance in her brother's direction. He was watching her with a bemused expression. She had missed him, she realized. He was a good brother, one who was protective and caring and all the things a brother ought to be. Even if he had been an utter bear over her being ruined by Decker.

Jo could see now that it had been because he loved her and because he wore the heavy weight of responsibility upon his shoulders.

"I thought I had failed you," Julian told her, as if reading her thoughts. "But you look happy, Jo. I do not think I have ever seen you so pleased. Your husband is behaving himself, I trust?"

Jo tempered her smile at her brother's protective question. "He is behaving admirably. And I could not be happier."

In the fortnight since their return to London, she, Decker, and Lila had settled into a comfortable routine. Lila's nightmares were growing more infrequent. Decker had moved all his erotic art to his club, where Lila would never see it. And Jo? She had found her place as Decker's wife, the keeper of his heart, and the wicked wife in his bed. Or study. Or music room. Or carriage. Office. Library…

She forced her mind to more prudent thoughts as her cheeks flared with heat. She was hopelessly in love with her husband and more content than she had ever imagined possible. That was all.

Actually, that was *everything*.

Lila appeared in the salon then, offering a shy curtsy for Julian and Clara. She had gone off for a snack upon their return—cream ice was a favorite of hers, and Chef always kept some on hand for her.

"May I hold the babe?" she asked tentatively.

"Of course you may," Jo said. "Have you ever held a baby before, my dear?"

Lila shook her head, eyes wide with wonder as she gazed down at the little lord in Jo's arms.

"Come and have a seat in this chair and then hold out your arms," Jo instructed. "You must take care with his head and neck. Be very gentle. I will place him in your lap."

Her nephew gurgled happily as he was settled in Lila's arms.

"Oh, what a darling he is." Lila smiled down at him. "He is so small!"

"He is, isn't he?" Jo gazed down at her nephew, wondering what it would be like to have her own child one day with Decker.

A little boy with his bright-blue eyes. Or a girl with his soft, wavy hair. He was no longer holding any part of himself back from her, and she was heartily glad. Thankful, too, for how far they had come.

Jo tore herself away from her nephew, a new eagerness for a child of her own fluttering to life inside her, and seated herself. They settled into a comfortable chat, Lila cooing over Arthur, and Julian and Clara politely inquiring after Jo, Decker, and Lila.

"How do you care for London, Miss Decker?" Clara asked Lila.

"I like it far better than I expected to," the girl said, smiling at Jo. "I am fortunate indeed to have a new sister to help me find my footing here."

"And I consider myself fortunate as well," Jo told her with a wink. "It was dreadfully boring here with no one to keep me company save your brother."

"Our Jo is one of the very best sorts," Julian said, giving Jo a tender, brotherly smile.

Jo smiled right back at him, yet another weight removed from her shoulders now that he seemed to have finally accepted her marriage to Decker. "I learned from one of the best himself."

"Do I know the fellow?" Julian asked with his signature wit, his smile turning into a grin.

"I would like to offer my opinion on the matter." Decker strode into the room abruptly, handsome as ever. His gaze met Jo's as he crossed the Axminster, and she felt an answering tug low in her belly. "I think our Josie *is* the best."

Jo's heart gave a pang at the sight of her husband, his expression filled with so much love, she felt her cheeks heat anew. She rather thought he was, too.

"You are home early again," she observed, pleased.

His work days no longer began so early nor ended as late as they once had. It was yet another of the changes which had been slowly wrought over the last few weeks.

He raised a dark brow at her. "Are you displeased, Mrs. Decker?"

"On the contrary." She could hardly contain her contentment. She was fairly certain she glowed. "I could not be more pleased."

"Ah, young love," Julian drawled wryly.

Jo's cheeks flushed deeper, she was sure of it. But she could not take her eyes from the man she loved. Her husband, her heart, her other half. To think, all she had needed to do to find him was pen a wicked list and unintentionally deliver it to him.

Decker seated himself at her side. "You look happy, darling wife," he murmured to her, *sotto voce.*

"That is because I am," she said.

Clara sighed.

Julian snorted.

Lila continued to coo at baby Arthur.

At her side, her husband's hand found hers hidden in the

voluminous fall of her skirts. Their fingers tangled and held.

"MRS. DECKER IS here tae see ye, sir," Macfie announced, waggling his brows in a fashion that made them appear extra bushy this afternoon. "And she has yer sister with her again. May I say, sir, she is a wee adorable thing, Miss Lila. I cannae see any resemblance at all tae ye. Probably best, considering yer one of the—"

"That is quite enough, Macfie," Decker interrupted his impudent *aide-de-camp* before he finished insulting Decker's appearance.

Macfie raised a meaty hand to his heart, affecting an indignant pose that was rendered all the more hilarious by the fact that he was as massive as an old oak tree. "Always with the interruptions, sir. I was going tae say considering yer one of the most handsome men in all London. Wee Miss Decker cannae be looking *handsome* now, can she?"

"You had better stop lest I think you fancy me yourself." Decker suppressed his smile. "And whilst I could not blame you in the slightest, I am already a picked apple, as they say. See them in, Macfie."

"And a happily picked apple at that, sir." Macfie grinned. "I am happy tae see ye so contented, Mr. Decker. And if I may say so, it is about damned time. All it took was a lady with a pair of—"

"Bloody hell, man, send my wife and sister in," he bellowed.

"I was going tae say a pair of hands strong enough fer the task of bringing ye tae heel." Rolling his eyes heavenward as if in supplication, Macfie turned to leave his office.

"I am not a hound," Decker muttered, scowling at his

infernal man's broad back.

He was reasonably sure he and Macfie would spend the rest of their days bickering like a pair of dowagers, and he would not have it any other way.

The door slammed shut, and he did not flinch.

When it opened again, all thoughts of Macfie were swept easily aside at his wife entering his office, Lila at her side. Decker drank in the sight of Jo, from her upsweep of dark hair to her perfect mouth to her thoroughly feminine form, draped in black. She made mourning weeds look glorious.

Right, of course she did.

Decker stood at their entrance, bowing to both of them before skirting his desk and moving toward them. "My darling Josie, my sweet Miss Lila. You are one quarter hour early."

"Mr. Macfie advised us to arrive at this time," his wife told him, smiling in that way she had that made him long to take her in his arms and kiss her senseless. "He suggested the traffic would be too thick otherwise, and judging from the snarl of carriages out there already, I should think he was right."

There Macfie went again, thinking of everything. How the devil did the man do it?

"Mayhap I will give the Scottish oaf an increase in pay," he said, grinning.

"Mr. Macfie is hardly an oaf," Jo said. "I have become rather fond of him."

"He gives me peppermint candies whenever I visit," Lila added. "I have three in my reticule now. I have been saving them."

"Peppermint candies, hmm?" Decker repeated. Well, at least he now knew the way to his sister's heart. The way to his wife's was paved with cream ice.

"We should be on our way," Jo added. "The ceremony

will be starting soon enough, and we dare not miss it."

No, they dare not indeed. The Children's Hospital he had already endowed before his mother's death—before, even, his marriage to Jo—was opening this afternoon. There was to be a grand ceremony. Not the sort of thing Decker ordinarily troubled himself with, as he abhorred taking a bow for his philanthropic endeavors. But in this instance, the ceremony was special.

As was the dedication of a memorial cot in his mother's name.

Seraphina Decker would never be forgotten. Her legacy would live on, and on, and hopefully over time, the children's hospital would give thousands of children a second chance at life.

"Let us go then," he told the two most important ladies in his life, offering each an arm.

Together, they left his offices, making their way to the waiting carriage.

It was the sort of day when he needed them at his side.

Right. When was it *not* that sort of day?

JO WAS BRUSHING out her hair, seated at her looking glass, when Decker came to her. He was clad in a dark-maroon banyan of fine silk, his feet bare, his hair tousled so that the same rakish lock she loved fell over his brow. She did not rise, merely watched him approach her in the mirror. Their gazes met and held.

A frisson of awareness jolted through her, as always.

"Good evening, Mr. Decker," she said softly, stroking the brush through her hair again because she knew how the act never failed to inspire an answering surge of desire in him.

She was still learning him. Each day, she discovered more, and each day, he showed her how much he loved her just as she strove to do the same for him. He was becoming better at keeping his walls lowered. And for her part, Jo fell in love with the man she had married a bit more, it seemed, with every passing moment.

"Good evening, Mrs. Decker." He reached her, settled his hands on her shoulder, and then pressed a kiss to the side of her throat. "You smell good enough to devour, woman."

She could not suppress her smile. Decker loved the scent of her perfume on her throat. The moment she had made that particular discovery, she had made certain to add a bit of scent behind each of her ears, and then another drop at the hollow where her pulse pounded.

"Mmm," she hummed her approval. "Perhaps you ought to devour me then, my love."

"In time," he agreed, kissing her throat, her ear, nibbling the sensitive place where her neck joined her shoulder. "May I?"

She relinquished her brush to him, sitting still as he worked the bristles through her hair in slow, gentle strokes. "If you ever decide to cease being a businessman, you would have excellent work as a lady's maid."

Jo could not help teasing him. But she loved the attention he lavished upon her.

"Only yours, my love," he said, kissing her crown. "Only ever yours."

She studied his countenance then, taking in the stark angles and planes, the tense manner in which he held his jaw. Today had been an emotional one for him, even if he did not often wear his heart upon his sleeve. The ceremony at the children's hospital he had endowed had been lovely. Of course, the most emotional moment had been the dedication of the cot in his mother's name. Both Decker and Lila had been overwhelmed, Lila's nose going red in her effort to quell her tears.

"Your mother would have been proud of you and Lila today, Decker." She sought his gaze in the glass. "The Children's Hospital is a wonderful and worthy endeavor, and to have her name forever upon it…"

A surge of emotion prevented her from finishing her sentence. The day had been filled with tears enough. She had no wish to once more descend into sobs and sadness.

"She would have been pleased, I think," he said, still brushing her hair. "She always loved children."

"Is that why you patronize so many orphanages?" she asked. "Why you endowed the Children's Hospital?"

"In part." He ran the bristles through her locks once more. "I also feel for those who find themselves in situations that were not of their own making. For the littlest ones. The urchins, the beggars, the helpless. If I can aid them some-how…make them feel less helpless, I will."

Of course he would, as the bastard son of an earl, who was ineligible to claim his title or his lands. Yet another way he proved he was a man worthy of her admiration, her loyalty, her love.

"I was proud of you today too," she murmured. "Proud to stand at your side. Proud to be your wife."

He stilled, his gaze searching hers, his expression pained. "I will never have a title, Josie. I can never make you a countess."

"That is not what I want." She shook her head. "You know that, Decker. All I have ever wanted is you, from the moment I truly learned what sort of man you are."

"And what sort of man is that?" He swept her hair over her left shoulder, baring her skin before nuzzling her nape.

"Hmm? Tell me."

"The best sort." She reached behind her, sinking her fingers into his thick, wavy hair. "The sort who is honorable and handsome and thoughtful and kind and witty and wonderful."

He kissed the side of her throat, and she felt his smile on her skin. "I like the sound of that. It is fitting, then, that all I have ever wanted is you, my love. The sort of woman who is also honorable and beautiful and compassionate and intelligent and fierce and just a little bit wicked and altogether wonderful, too. A goddess, in fact."

"*Oh.*" Her gasp of pleasure turned into a moan as he sucked on her flesh. She raked his scalp with her nails. "I like the sound of that, too."

"Good." He nibbled on her neck some more, kneading her shoulders with his big hands as he did so, working out all the tension she had not realized she carried in her muscles. "I received word today that the Athena is finally repaired and ready to sail again. What do you think of you, myself, and Lila all taking a trip to Dover? It is not the honeymoon I wanted, but I hesitate to leave her here alone."

He was such a good brother. Such a good husband. A good man.

Was it any wonder she loved him desperately?

"Of course Lila must come," she said. "And I should so love to see Dover. I have heard a great deal about the white cliffs, but I have never witnessed them firsthand. Nor have I been to a regatta."

"Truly?" He nipped her ear with his teeth, continuing to massage her. "Never?"

"I spent my formative years moldering in the country with my aunt Lydia because my brother did not have the funds or the reputation to support two younger, unattached females," she reminded him.

"Much to my great fortune." He kissed her cheek. "Imagine if you had not moldered. I hardly think you would have penned your list, and then how would I have known you were destined to be my wife?"

"I think the fates would have intervened in another way," she said. "If not the list."

But she was still heartily glad she had written it. And even more grateful he had found it.

"I think so too, my love." He removed his magical hands from her shoulders and straightened then. "I have a gift for you, Josie. It is…I had intended to give it to you some time ago, but then so much happened. And then, I knew there was something I needed to add to it before it could truly be yours."

"A gift?" She rose to her feet and faced him at last. "But I have none for you."

He smiled. "You are my gift, *bijou*. I think it every day."

And then, he reached into a pocket concealed in his flowing banyan and extracted a velvet box. Decker extended it toward her, his expression suddenly earnest and expectant. Young, too. Almost boyish.

With trembling hands, she accepted the box from him. She flipped it open. Nestled inside was a gold bangle accented with channels of rich, glittering diamonds. At its center was a pearl surrounded by a cluster of diamonds. Golden roses flanked either side of the centerpiece. It must have cost him a staggering sum.

"Oh, Decker." She ran a finger over the filigree and the fine work of the roses. "It is beautiful."

"Do you like it, my love?" He sounded hesitant.

Did the man not realize he could gift her a rock and it would still be her most prized possession?

"It is astoundingly beautiful," she assured him, "and far too dear, I am sure. You ought not to have gone to such an expense."

That was when she turned the sleek gold band over in her hand and discovered the inscription, written neatly on the underside of the bangle.

My heart has always known yours.

It was what she had said to him that night, when they had come together and confessed their love for each other. It was the same words she felt with every beat of her heart. And she knew without having to ask he felt them too.

"You remembered," she whispered.

"I remember everything you say to me," he told her, his gaze bright on hers, shimmering with—unless she was mistaken—the sheen of tears.

She blinked at the sting in her own eyes, making itself known. "I love you so much."

"Allow me?" He took the bangle from her without waiting for her response, then settled it neatly upon her wrist.

The fit was unsurprisingly perfect.

She moved her hand in the light, watching as the diamonds sparkled. "I love this gift, too. I love the thought you put into it, the words etched upon it. How did I ever become so fortunate?"

Her husband gave her a wicked grin. "You gave me a list."

Epilogue

Ways to be Wicked

1. ~~Kiss a man until you are breathless.~~

2. ~~Arrange for an assignation. Perhaps with Lord Q?~~ ~~your husband? Strike that,~~ **bijou**. ~~Definitely with your~~ ~~husband.~~

3. ~~Get caught in the rain with a gentleman. (This will~~ ~~necessitate the removal of wet garments. Choose said~~ ~~gentleman wisely.)~~

4. ~~Sneak into a gentleman's bedchamber in the midst of~~ ~~the night.~~

5. ~~Go to a gentleman's private apartments.~~

6. ~~Spend a night in a gentleman's bed.~~

7. *Make love in the outdoors.*

8. ~~Ask your husband to help you disrobe.~~

There was something about a country house party.

And a list of ways to be wicked, one of which had yet to be completed.

And a picnic hamper.

And a most accommodating counterpane spread over the grass beneath the shade of a tremendous old oak.

And the very best wife a man could ever hope to call his own, seated at his side, looking as if she needed to be thoroughly ravished.

Yes indeed, there was something about all those things that made Decker settle upon the perfect way of spending his afternoon with Jo.

"There is one more item on your list, my love," he told her as they finished the last of their luncheon. They had stolen away from the group at the Duke and Duchess of Westmorland's country house weekend at last, and they were blessedly alone.

The time had never been more perfect.

She cast a minx's smile in his direction. "Is there one more item? I must admit, I had quite forgotten all about the list."

"Liar," he accused without heat, dipping his head to kiss her luscious lips in a quick, thorough peck. "I am afraid you cannot graduate to true wickedness until you complete them all. As your husband, it is my solemn duty to make certain you excel at your studies."

She kissed him again, her mouth opening for his questing tongue before she tipped her head back to gaze at him, her honey-brown eyes twinkling. "Hoping to debauch me, are you, Mr. Decker?"

"Yes, Mrs. Decker. I am." He kissed her again. "Number seven is happening."

"Number seven?" Her eyes went wide. "Happening here? Now? But anyone could happen upon us."

"Here," he repeated. "Now."

And if anyone *did* happen upon them…well, he did not give a damn. They were amongst friends. The sun was high, the day was warm, he was happier than any man had a right to be, and he had every intention of burying his cock in his wife.

Forthwith.

At the notion, his prick twitched to life, hard and ready.

Slow down, old chap. We have to woo her first.

"Are you certain?" she asked.

"Utterly." He kissed her again, sucking on the fullness of her lower lip. "Damn, you are sweeter than strawberries."

Her arms wound around his neck. "I could say the same of you."

Their mouths connected. The air hung heavy all around them, redolent with the perfume of grass and blooming flora. His tongue slid past her lips. She tasted like summer and seduction. Sweet, ripe fruit.

His cockstand rebelled against his trousers, straining to break free.

Yes, he had learned his lesson. No matter how many times he made love to his wife, he still kept wanting her more. He loved her more, desired her more, needed her more. That was the way of it between them.

And he did not just accept it, he embraced it.

Never breaking their kiss, he lowered them both to the counterpane. Plates clinked. The bottle of wine they had brought for their picnic tipped over and spilled into the nearby grass with a rush. At least, he thought that was the source of the sound. The picnic hamper clattered to its side as he thrust it out of the way with an indelicate kick of his left leg.

Admittedly, he ought to have been a gentleman and removed all the remnants of their luncheon from the blanket before seducing his wife. But when had he ever claimed to be a gentleman?

Never, that was when.

And so, he kissed her thoroughly to the musical accompaniment of crashing crockery and tumbling wicker and clinking cutlery. At some point, he realized she was trembling beneath him.

Quite violently.

And then, he lifted his head to find her grinning at him,

her eyes dancing with mirth. She had been laughing, the minx.

"What is so bloody humorous?" he demanded.

Surely not his kisses?

"I think there is a jar of jam beneath my back," she said, giggling, her lips swollen and red and so damned kissable, his cock throbbed just to look at them.

Right. There was a decidedly unwanted jar of jam somewhere beneath her. Supposedly.

He slid a hand beneath her corseted back, sweeping the blanket, and discovered the jar in question. He plucked it from beneath her, tossing it over his shoulder. The sound of cracking glass met his unapologetic ears.

"Decker!" his wife gasped, sounding scandalized. "You have broken the jam."

"To hell with the jam." Decker rolled atop her and straddled her voluminous skirts. "Undoubtedly, the Duke and Duchess of Westmorland have hundreds more just like it. I want to make love to my wife."

She pouted, her honey-brown gaze turning mischievous. "It was good jam."

"I will give you *good*, madam," he growled, lowering his head to take her lips again. "I will give you much, much better than good, in fact."

Her hands settled on his shoulders, clutching him. "A man of confidence. I like that. Give me *better than good*, if you please. I am aching for it."

She knew just what to say to make him crazed with lust. A wild thrill soared through him, landing in his ballocks. He was more than ready for her. He leveraged himself on an elbow and grabbed a fistful of fabric, intending to give her what she wanted.

Belatedly, he realized she was wearing a gown with a

cumbersome tier of skirts and two dozen tiny pearl buttons running down the front.

"Why the devil are you wearing something so deuced difficult to get you out of?" he grumbled.

"It seemed an excellent idea at the time," she said. "I am regretting the choice more and more by the moment. But how was I to know you intended to ravish me on a picnic luncheon in the midst of a country house weekend?"

Fair enough.

Still…

"When have I ever shied away from the opportunity to ravish you, *bijou*?" he asked, raising a brow. "Surely you ought to know me better than that by now."

"I will remember it next time," she promised, lips parted.

Oh, he liked the way her mouth opened, as if in invitation. He would accept that invitation, but he had promised her *better than good*, had he not? And he had every intention of delivering.

He worked his way down her body, fighting with her skirts. What the devil was with all these asinine flounces, anyway? The whole affair was far too elaborate. He wrestled them to her waist, instructing her to hold the hems in place. The picture that greeted him was worth the fuss.

Neat satin boots, laced up. Curved calves encased in silken stockings. Frilled drawers. Lush hips. As he watched, she inched her legs apart, revealing herself to him. The slit in her drawers was an alternate gate into heaven, parting to show him sleek, pink flesh, her plump pearl peeking from between her folds.

On a groan, he buried his face there, in the apex of her thighs. He sucked her until she came, and then he sank his tongue deep inside her cunny, licking up all her spend. When she was soaked and thrashing, he rose over her, releasing himself from his trousers and sinking into her in one long thrust.

He was deep inside her, planted to the hilt.

She was so tight, so hot, clutching him, dragging him to the abyss where only she could take him.

He lowered himself over her, planting his elbows on either side of her beautiful face on the counterpane. She smelled like orange blossom and sun-drenched skin. He wanted to stay in this moment forever. But her cunny was clenching, urging him on. And desire pounded through him, spurring him to finish what he had begun.

He found a way to swivel his hips into hers that made his groin brush against her pearl with each thrust. She moaned, her hands everywhere on him, her lips landing feverish kisses anywhere they could reach. His Adam's apple, his ear, his jaw, his lips.

Another series of strokes, and she was coming undone for him again, the tremors rushing through her making her cunny spasm around his cock, holding him, draining him. She found her release, throwing back her head on the counterpane and crying out to the underbellies of the leaves rustling overhead and the endless blue of the country sky beyond.

He emptied himself inside her on a groan, his seed spurting into her depths. No matter how many times he and Jo made love, this beautiful communion—their bodies joining, him losing himself inside her—each experience was new. Like a little renaissance between them. Her every movement, breath, look, excited him.

He lived for her.

There was no other way to describe the manner in which she consumed him.

Holding her close, his cock still lodged within her, he rolled them to their sides. He caressed her beautiful face and kissed her long and slow, showing her the way he felt, all the emotions tangled up within him. Sometimes, deeds were better than words.

The wetness of her tears startled him, kissing his fingertips.

He jerked his mouth from hers, searching her gaze. "What is it, Josie? What is the matter?"

"Nothing." She gave him a tremulous smile. "It is only that I am so very happy, so complete."

His heart was thundering in his chest as if he had just run the perimeter of the park. "I am happy and complete too, my love. You make me that way."

He cupped her cheek, an exquisite feeling of tenderness for her washing over him.

"Do you think…" She hesitated, chewing her lower lip before continuing. "Do you think we could be…*more* complete, Decker?"

He searched her eyes, trying to understand her question. "Do you feel unhappy, my love? Is there something missing? Something I can change, something I can give you?"

She shook her head slowly, and then, the tears were welling again, filling her expressive eyes, trailing down her cheeks, bathing his fingers. "I am not unhappy at all. And as for something missing…I am not sure if he or she was missing before."

Everything within him froze. He stilled. Hope rose in his chest, buoyant as an ascension balloon. "Josie?"

She placed her hand over his, pressing his palm to her cheek. "We are going to have a baby, Decker."

The news hit him in the gut. *Hell*, he was still inside her. He had just made love to her on the *ground*.

He stiffened. "Why did you not say anything sooner? My God, I just…took you in the dirt. I was not careful. Josie. A baby? Truly? Do you mean it? How do you know?"

He realized he was rattling off a mad list of questions. That he was scarcely making sense. His mind and his heart were a jumble of thoughts, exuberance, love. So much love. Excitement. Fear, too. But the excitement was first. It was stronger. A child of their own. *Ye gods.* The prospect was thrilling.

He was happy. So damned happy.

Decker blinked against a sudden rush of his own tears. "Josie? Say something."

"I mean it, Decker," she said softly. "We are going to have a child. I missed my courses, and, well, with the way of things…"

She did not need to continue. They made love like animals. He knew it. They both loved it. He took her every chance he had, everywhere he could. And she did the same. Their love and their passion were healthy and strong, burning brighter and hotter than any flame.

He kissed her swiftly. "How do you feel, darling? I did not hurt you just now, did I?"

"You could never hurt me, my love." She smiled then. "I am with child, but that does not mean I have suddenly turned to porcelain."

Their lips met again, this kiss longer and deeper than the last.

"How do *you* feel?" she asked him when their mouths parted. "Are you…is this what you want?"

There had been a time when a child, a family, a wife, love, had been beyond his comprehension. When he had thought he would sooner perish than welcome any one of them into his life. But he had learned his lesson.

"I feel happy," he told his wife. "I feel astonishingly, blissfully happy. You and this babe and however many we should be blessed with after—you are all I want. Now and forever."

Another tear rolled down her cheek. "Do you mean it, Decker?"

He kissed that tear away. "Of course I do, my love. Now and forever. My heart has always known yours."

Their mouths met, one in love and need and hunger. He rolled them so that he was on his back and she was atop him, and they made love again, slowly and deliciously, beneath the warmth of the sun.

THE END.

Author's Note

Dear Reader,

Thank you for reading Jo and Decker's story! I hope you enjoyed this second book in my Notorious Ladies of London series and that you fell in love with Decker and Jo as much as I did along the way.

Please consider leaving an honest review of *Lady Wallflower*. Reviews are greatly appreciated! If you'd like to keep up to date with my latest releases and series news, sign up for my newsletter or follow me on Amazon or BookBub. Join my reader's group on Facebook for bonus content, early excerpts, giveaways, and more.

If you'd like a preview of *Lady Reckless*, Book Three in the Notorious Ladies of London series, featuring Lady Helena Davenport and her brother's proper, already betrothed best friend the Earl of Huntingdon, do read on. I've also included a bonus sneak peek at *Her Virtuous Viscount*, Book Six in my Wicked Husbands series, so don't miss it.

P.S. If you're looking for the Duke and Duchess of Westmorland's love story, you can find it in *Fearless Duke*. You'll find Sin and Callie's happily ever after in *Lady Ruthless* and Julian and Clara's in *Restless Rake*.

Until next time,

Scarlett

Author's Note on Historical Accuracy

In June of 1885, a petition signed by 208 women—including doctors, countesses, and viscountesses amongst them—was addressed to each member of the House of Lords to support the bill then before the Upper House, which would have extended the right to vote in Parliamentary elections to women. I've used that real historical event as the model for the Lady's Suffrage Society petition drafted by Jo and the other ladies in this book. It would take many more years of petitioning, bills being presented, campaigning, fighting, and raging against the status quo for women to finally win the right to vote in the twentieth century.

The Victorian era tends to have a modern reputation of being a conservative period ruled by prudish mores. However, that simply isn't the full picture. During the Victorian era, erotic and pornographic art, photography, and literature flourished. In many cases, because of existing decency laws, erotic art and literature were privately produced rather than publicly mass-produced. Specifically in the case of erotic literature, many books or story collections were published in limited runs and distributed only to club or subscription members. I have done my best to accurately portray Decker's erotic collections based on similar collections of the time period, including the set of naughty alphabet lithographs.

Finally, although I often mention language in my author's notes, I feel it is worth mentioning again here that all the sexual acts in this book and the language—including curses—were actively in use in 1885 and well before that. That's right, even the word *fuck*. And all the other fun stuff, too. Now, do read on for those excerpts I promised!

Lady Reckless

Notorious Ladies of London Book Three

BY
SCARLETT SCOTT

Lady Helena Davenport is desperate to avoid the odious betrothal her father is forcing upon her. The only way out is to orchestrate her own ruination. Everything is unfolding according to plan, her escape finally within her grasp. But there is just one problem when the moment of scandal arrives: the rake she selected for an assignation is nowhere to be found. In his place? The man she secretly loves.

Gabriel, the notoriously proper Earl of Huntingdon, is outraged when he discovers his best friend's innocent sister, Lady Helena, has decided to give herself to a scoundrel. His impeccable sense of honor will not allow such a travesty to occur. When Gabe confronts her, the last thing he expects is to find himself tempted to commit wickedness.

Fortunately, Gabe is strong enough to resist. After all, he already has a betrothed of his own. However, he is now tasked with the unhappy duty of following about Lady Helena to keep her from committing further folly. And the more time he spends with the infuriating minx, the more impossible it is to resist her.

Helena is running out of time to save herself from an unhappy marriage. With the Earl of Huntingdon haunting her every move to keep her from ruining herself, her hope is dwindling. Until she settles upon the one certain means of securing her freedom, even if it means she risks making Huntingdon hate her forever…

Chapter One

1885

S HE WAS NOT going to go through with it. Huntingdon checked his pocket watch for at least the tenth time since his arrival, relief sliding through him. One quarter hour late for the appointed assignation. Lady Helena must have seen the error of her reckless decision.

Thank merciful heavens.

His heart, which had been pounding with pained expectation ever since his arrival at the nondescript rooms where she had arranged to meet—and lose her virtue—to Lord Algernon Forsyte, eased to a normal rhythm at last. The notion of the innocent sister of his best friend so sullying herself had been appalling. Horrifying, in fact. He had scarcely been able to believe it when Lord Algernon had revealed the plan to him the night before.

Over a game of cards.

The swine had been *laughing*.

And then he had dared to include Lady Helena's maidenhead in his wager. As if she were a trollop so accustomed to being ill-used that anyone's prick would do. Huntingdon had been disgusted and outraged. He had also made certain he had won the game and that Lord Algernon would never again bandy about Lady Helena's name without fear of losing his teeth.

Huntingdon's sense of honor had prevented him from going directly to Lady Helena's father. The Marquess of Northampton was an unforgiving, draconian clod, and the repercussions for Lady Helena would have been drastic, he had no doubt. It had been his cursed compassion, along with his decade-long friendship with Lady Helena's brother, which had brought him here this morning to save her from ruin himself.

Huntingdon paced the stained carpets, trying to tamp down his impatience. He would wait for a full half hour just to make certain she had not been somehow waylaid. As distasteful as he found it to be cloistered in Lord Algernon's appallingly unkempt rooms, he had only—he checked his timepiece once more—ten minutes remaining until he could flee and forget all about this dreadful imposition upon his day.

A sudden noise drew him to a halt.

Surely it was not a knock?

He listened, and there it was again. A hesitant report. Once, twice, thrice.

His heart began to pound once more and the heavy weight of dread sank in his gut.

She had come after all.

He stalked to the door and hauled it open. There, on the threshold, stood a lady, her face obscured by a veil. There could be no doubt as to her identity. Huntingdon grasped her forearm and pulled her into the room before anyone happened upon them. The fewer witnesses to her folly, the better.

She gasped at the suddenness of his actions, stumbling forward and tripping over the hem of her skirts. There was nowhere for her to go but into his arms. Huntingdon was scarcely able to throw the door closed at her back before he had warm, feminine curves pressed against him.

The scent of bergamot and lemon oil, undeniably welcome in these shabby rooms badly in wont of cleaning and dusting, washed over him. Her hat fell from her head as she was jostled into him, revealing her face. He found himself looking down into the astonished emerald eyes of Lady Helena Davenport.

He had a moment to note her breasts were ample and full, crushed again his chest, and her lips were wider than he remembered. She had the most entrancing dusting of freckles on the bridge of her nose, her pale-blonde hair coming free of her coiffure in silken wisps.

She looked like a Renaissance Madonna.

But she had come to this cesspit to be thoroughly ruined.

The part of him which could never be entirely governed by reason, propriety, and honor suddenly rose to rude prominence in his trousers. He was seized by a crushing urge to taste her lips. To slam his mouth on hers and give her a punishing kiss.

Would she kiss him back?

Would she be scandalized?

He inhaled sharply, shocked at himself, at the cursed weakness for the flesh he could never seem to overcome no matter how hard he tried. *This is wrong.* He exhaled. *Think of Lady Beatrice.* Inhaled again. A mistake, as it turned out. All he could smell was *her*.

She clutched at his shoulders as if he were a lifeline. "Huntingdon! What are you doing here?"

He settled her on her feet and released her, stepping back, recalling his outrage. This was his friend's sister. Shelbourne would be devastated if he knew what she was about. And as Shelbourne's friend, he was duty-bound to act as another brother to her.

"I am saving you from the greatest mistake of your life, my lady," he told her grimly, trying to forget the way her body had molded to his. "What in heaven's name were you thinking, arranging an assignation with a disgusting scoundrel like Lord Algernon Forsyte?"

"I was thinking I would be ruined," she snapped, irritation edging her voice now that she had regained her balance.

She was angry with him, he realized, astounded. She ought to have been awash in gratitude, thanking him for his generosity of spirit. Instead, her lips had thinned, and her jaw was clenched. Her brilliant green eyes glittered with irritation.

He blinked. "You *wanted* to be ruined?"

Surely he could not have heard her correctly. He had expected her to say Lord Algernon had wooed her with pretty words of love and coerced her into meeting him here. He had imagined she would tearfully thank him and then promise to never again do anything so rash and dangerous.

"Of course. Why else do you suppose I would have arranged to meet him at his private rooms?" she asked.

What the devil?

Huntingdon struggled to make sense of this bloody mire. "You do not fancy yourself in love with him, then."

"No."

"You know a man such as he will never marry you," he pressed.

"I would not marry him either."

He frowned at her. "Then I fail to understand the meaning of this horrible folly, Lady Helena."

"The meaning is freedom," Lady Helena said, tipping her chin up in defiance. "Mine."

Want more *Lady Reckless*? Get it now!

Her Virtuous Viscount
Wicked Husbands Book Six

BY
SCARLETT SCOTT

Jilted by the woman he loved, Tom, Viscount Sidmouth, has decided he will happily remain a bachelor for the rest of his life. He wants nothing to do with affairs of the heart. And he most certainly wants nothing to do with the wild widow next door.

After spending years trapped in a loveless marriage, Hyacinth has returned to London on a mission to experience everything she missed. Balls, parties, flirtations, and assignations—she wants it all. She isn't about to allow her disapproving neighbor to spoil her fun. She's living her life one raucous celebration at a time.

Until she inadvertently winds up in the viscount's garden late one night and he kisses her senseless. There's something about the handsome, forbidding lord that makes her want to abandon her rules.

And Tom? He's beginning to think that perhaps the only way to forget about his broken heart is to lose himself in a fling. Why not with the wicked woman who drives him to distraction? It's not as if he is going to fall in love…

Chapter One

London, 1879

*H*YACINTH WAS ON her second bottle of champagne. At least, she thought she was, when she realized her beloved puppy was no longer at her side.

"Has anyone seen Adelaide?" she asked the drawing room at large.

No one seemed to notice she had spoken.

Lady Esterly was kissing a…footman? Lord Villiers had dipped his head to Lady Covington's throat. Someone—she could not make out the gentleman's face—was playing a violin, and quite beautifully, too. Had she hired musicians this evening?

Dear me, I do not recall.

Her vision was beginning to get fuzzy about the edges. She probably required spectacles even when she had not indulged herself to the point of Bacchanalian bliss. Now that she was thoroughly in her cups, the latent deficiency was proving more pronounced. However, the room was also beginning to swirl, which was a clear indicator she had overindulged.

Southwick had never allowed her to consume even a drop of wine with her dinner. Spirits—like everything she had thrown herself into following her arrival in London—were new to Hyacinth. A joy and a curse, in the true way of life.

Freedom. Why would it be any different than captivity had been?

But none of her ponderous musings helped her to locate her beloved pug. Adelaide was the one pleasure Southwick had allowed her, and her sole comfort in five years of misery.

"Adelaide," she called above the din of the violin and Lady Downe chortling over a sally Mr. Buchanan had told her. "Lady?"

There was no answering scamper of paws. No big brown eyes staring up at her from an adorably rounded face, no tongue lolling. Guilt struck her, for Adelaide was notorious for wandering. Indeed, it had been one of Hyacinth's primary concerns in moving to London from the country. So many servants, so many doors, a busy road filled with carriages, parties laden with revelers—all of them, opportunities for Adelaide to fancy herself going on an adventure and wind up forever lost.

But Adelaide could not be lost!

Adelaide—Lady—was all Hyacinth had left, aside from her friendships with Alice and Charlotte. And even those had been strained by necessity from the time she had spent shackled to Southwick. Neither woman had been the sort with whom Hyacinth had been permitted to convene. The result was a stilted friendship, even if Alice had obligingly introduced Hyacinth to most of the men and women in attendance this evening.

There was no telling where her friend had disappeared to now, or with whom. Alice was a widow just like Hyacinth, and her set was rather…wild. As was Alice. Hyacinth's old bosom bow had changed quite a bit since the days of their mutual comeout.

But none of these thoughts solved the mystery of where Lady was.

"Adelaide," she called again, attempting to drown out the dratted violin. "Lady! Had anyone seen my pug?"

No one answered her. No one so much as glanced in her direction. At least, she thought none of them did.

Spectacles. Or less champagne. One of the two…

Hyacinth left the drawing room. Down the main hall she went, passing a couple in a desperately passionate embrace that left her feeling flushed and envious all at once. Ah, to experience such tenderness—a man who did not take pleasure in cruelty and control.

Not yet, she reminded herself. Her wounds were still too fresh, even with Southwick gone. For now, she was living her life as she wished, directly flouting every one of his edicts.

Still lonely as ever.

She spied the housekeeper as she neared the end of the hall, the small salon which exited to the gardens, adjacent to the servants' stair.

"Mrs. Combes," she said, relieved, for the woman seemed to always have the answer just as surely as she carried the keys rattling about her august personage. "Have you seen Adelaide? I cannot seem to find her."

"I am sorry, Lady Southwick," Mrs. Combes said, "but I have not seen her since I last noted her trotting toward the rear of the house. It is possible one of the chamber maids thought she needed to take a turn in the gardens."

Hyacinth tempered the urge to embrace Mrs. Combes, who had followed her from the country—another one of her few comforts. Mrs. Combes knew how to run a household. And she also knew Hyacinth quite well. Perhaps too well.

"Thank you, Mrs. Combes," she said. "I shall have a look about in the gardens."

A sudden onset of weariness hit her then. Perhaps it was because she had stopped consuming champagne. Perhaps it was because she was so aggrieved with herself for becoming so sotted, she failed to notice what had happened to her beloved Lady. Whatever the reason, Hyacinth found herself dearly longing for quiet. For no more revelers.

She paused. "Mrs. Combes, do you think you could convey to my guests that I have sought my private chambers for the evening and that they ought to move their revelries elsewhere?"

The housekeeper nodded. "Of course, my lady. I would be pleased to tell your guests as much."

Hyacinth had no doubt she would. Mrs. Combes disapproved of the fast set with whom Hyacinth rubbed elbows since her arrival in London. But the dear woman would never utter a word to suggest as much.

"Thank you, Mrs. Combes," she said. "I am off to the gardens to find Lady."

Still feeling somewhat dizzy—fine, inebriated—Hyacinth made her way to the gardens. Part of her still expected Southwick to appear from some darkened corner, demanding to know where she was going. Icy, iron fingers, disapproving frown, inescapable rage. But she shook herself free of those memories.

He could not haunt her from the grave.

She refused to allow it.

She was *free*.

Or something like it.

Her fingers fumbled with the handle on the doors leading to the garden, within a small, cozy chamber she had turned into her private salon from its former, robustly masculine study. It had been all bleak mahogany and the carpets smelled of tobacco smoke. Likely down to the previous occupant, but it had reminded her so dreadfully of Southwick that she had ordered the rugs replaced on her first day here.

After she finally had the latch undone, she found herself enrobed in inky summer darkness. London at night was not nearly as noisy as London during the height of the day was. Excepting the cacophony emerging from her own open windows, that was. A wonder the neighbors did not loathe her.

Then again, perhaps they did?

She had spied a glimpse of the lord next door—a golden Goliath who had hastily disappeared behind a shiny black door with its lion's head brass knocker. But that was all she knew of her neighbors thus far. How strange it all seemed. After so many years of rustication, Hyacinth was still growing accustomed to the peculiarities of Town life.

Still the quiet and darkness of the gardens this evening pleased her. A cool breeze bathed her cheeks as she slipped down the gravel path. Odd, that. She had not realized she had been overheated until now.

"Lady," she called, expecting her darling to come rushing to her. "Adelaide! Come to Mama, you naughty little puss. Where are you?"

What Hyacinth was decidedly *not* expecting was the disapproving masculine drawl which emerged from the murkiness at her left.

"If you are searching for the pup that was abandoned to suffer a dreadful fate in the rosebushes, you may cease your caterwauling, madam."

She jumped, pressing a hand to her thumping heart. And she swore she would not have been more shocked if the devil himself had appeared in the gardens of her leased London townhome.

Hyacinth's eyes frantically searched through the darkness, attempting to discern the speaker. Where was he? *Who* was he?

More importantly, why was he holding Adelaide hostage?

"What in heaven's name are you doing in my gardens, sirrah?" she demanded.

Though her eyes had grown accustomed to the moonlight, she could still only find the vaguest shape of a man near the colossal rosebushes which were attempting to overtake the gardens. The silver light of the moon glinted off what appeared to be golden hair.

The neighbor next door, then? The disappearing Goliath?

"Believe me, madam," he said crisply, in a voice that was low and rich and deep, "*your gardens* are the last place in which I would hope to find myself at such a time. Indeed, I had hoped to be long asleep by this hour. However, the pitiful sounds of your creature in terrible pain lured me from the comfort of my bed."

Adelaide in pain? Her heart leapt anew at the suggestion. "Where is she?"

"Is the mongrel a female, then? I ought to have known." There was a grimness in his voice now, a harder edge to his words. "Nothing but trouble, the fairer sex. Even in canine form."

She moved nearer, captivated by the smooth baritone. By the man. Even in his cool agitation, there was something about that voice. And if he had heard Lady in distress and had rescued her? Why, Hyacinth could scarcely countenance the notion of such a man. A man who *cared*.

"Lady is indeed female," she said, her eyes searching the details of his face now that she was close enough to detect him.

Adelaide was in his arms.

Being cuddled, the traitorous little minx. Had he just dropped a kiss upon her head?

Not that Hyacinth could blame Adelaide, of course. That broad chest looked an inviting place to nestle. Indeed,

Hyacinth entertained a brief, foolish vision of herself held to that chest. Of those strong, masculine arms embracing her rather than hurting her as she had grown so accustomed from a man.

Mayhap she *was* a harlot, just as Southwick had always told her she was. Perhaps her constitution was lacking, her conviction absent, her morals corrupted. Did she deserve what Southwick had done to her?

Yes, said that awful voice inside her.

The one that inevitably made her pour another glass of spirits.

"She may have some thorns embedded in her paws," the interloper in her garden said then. "She was crying and howling when I came upon her and quite caught up in the rosebushes. I freed her, but in the darkness, I cannot see her injuries properly."

Something inside her shifted. Softened. *Melted.*

This man, whomever he was, had heard a crying dog in the night and had come to her rescue. Surely he could not be all bad? Even if he had somehow found his way into Hyacinth's gardens where he decidedly did not belong. And even now, he was concerned about whatever injuries she may have sustained thanks to those hulking, overgrown rosebushes.

Hyacinth ought to see them removed, truly. But they were so lovely to behold, their fragrance so enchanting.

Not worth Lady getting hurt again, however.

"Injuries," Hyacinth repeated, her tongue feeling thick and unused. "What manner of injuries can she possibly have sustained? She was scarcely in the gardens for a few minutes."

"How do you know how long she was here in the gardens?" the man asked, sounding outraged.

And that was the trouble, was it not? Hyacinth did not. Because she had been too busy consuming champagne and hosting a party. Because she had failed to notice when Adelaide had gone missing.

"It cannot have been long," she lied, hating herself in that moment. "Give her to me, if you please. I shall see to her inside. Nothing can be done for her in the darkness."

"Do you promise to take better care of the poor mutt? I find myself reluctant to relinquish her, now that we are acquainted."

Surely he was jesting.

Hyacinth narrowed her gaze, peering at the man through the darkness. "You are suggesting you will steal my companion?"

"Your companion whom you deserted in the gardens?" he asked pointedly. "Forgive me, my lady, if I question your sincerity. This unfortunate canine was whimpering, crying, and altogether caught up in the rosebushes. I shed a few drops of blood myself, rescuing her from her plight."

Oh, poor Lady. It was not the first time she had been embroiled in the rosebushes. And since her favorite bone had landed deep within the tangle, Hyacinth knew it would not be the last. Lady would attempt to rescue her prized bone, thorns or no.

Something about this man's championing of Adelaide had wound its way around Hyacinth's heart. Or what remained of her heart, anyway—the charred and scarred remnants, more like.

"Thank you, sir," she managed. "Adelaide is beloved to me. I would never want her to be in pain. If you rescued her, I owe you a debt of gratitude."

He was silent for a moment. Hyacinth took advantage of the time to draw nearer, to take in even more details of his face, his form. He was tall. Deliciously handsome. The Goliath next door suddenly had a voice. And she liked it, much to her trepidation.

"A debt of gratitude, you say, madam," he repeated, his long fingers stroking Adelaide's fur.

And fancy that, Hyacinth, envious of her own *dog*!

But oh, to feel such a tender touch upon her skin rather than wrath. To be soothed and stroked instead of punished...

"Yes," she repeated, cursing herself for the breathlessness in her voice. For the catch, the tremble. "A debt of gratitude. How can I repay you?"

What was it about this mysterious intrude in her gardens who had cared enough for Adelaide to find his way to her rescue in the midst of the dark night?

"I can think of any number of ways you might repay me," he said slowly. "But the first one to come to my mind cannot be shaken, regardless of how much common sense, intellect, and reason would like to disperse it."

That sounded promising. Now that Lady was found and in good health, cuddling with this man who had Hyacinth at sixes and sevens, all was well in her world again.

She ran her tongue over her suddenly dry lips. "What do you want from me, sir? Ask, and it shall be yours."

Within reason, she ought to add.

But something about this man—perhaps his rush to attend a wounded dog, perhaps his mannerisms, or perhaps both—made her think she could trust him. Made her think he was good. Trustworthy, even.

"A kiss," he said. "That is what I want from you."

Want more? Get it now!

Don't miss Scarlett's other romances!

(Listed by Series)

Complete Book List
scarlettscottauthor.com/books

HISTORICAL ROMANCE

Heart's Temptation
A Mad Passion (Book One)
Rebel Love (Book Two)
Reckless Need (Book Three)
Sweet Scandal (Book Four)
Restless Rake (Book Five)
Darling Duke (Book Six)
The Night Before Scandal (Book Seven)

Wicked Husbands
Her Errant Earl (Book One)
Her Lovestruck Lord (Book Two)
Her Reformed Rake (Book Three)
Her Deceptive Duke (Book Four)
Her Missing Marquess (Book Five)
Her Virtuous Viscount (Book Six)

League of Dukes
Nobody's Duke (Book One)
Heartless Duke (Book Two)
Dangerous Duke (Book Three)
Shameless Duke (Book Four)
Scandalous Duke (Book Five)
Fearless Duke (Book Six)

Notorious Ladies of London
Lady Ruthless (Book One)
Lady Wallflower (Book Two)
Lady Reckless (Book Three)

Sins and Scoundrels
Duke of Depravity (Book One)
Prince of Persuasion (Book Two)
Marquess of Mayhem (Book Three)
Earl of Every Sin (Book Four)
Duke of Debauchery (Book Five)

The Wicked Winters
Wicked in Winter (Book One)
Wedded in Winter (Book Two)
Wanton in Winter (Book Three)
Willful in Winter (Book Four)
Wagered in Winter (Book Five)
Wild in Winter (Book Six)
Wishes in Winter (Book 3.5)
Wooed in Winter (Book Seven)

Stand-alone Novella
Lord of Pirates

CONTEMPORARY ROMANCE

Love's Second Chance
Reprieve (Book One)
Perfect Persuasion (Book Two)
Win My Love (Book Three)

Coastal Heat
Loved Up (Book One)

About the Author

USA Today and Amazon bestselling author Scarlett Scott writes steamy Victorian and Regency romance with strong, intelligent heroines and sexy alpha heroes. She lives in Pennsylvania with her Canadian husband, adorable identical twins, and one TV-loving dog.

A self-professed literary junkie and nerd, she loves reading anything, but especially romance novels, poetry, and Middle English verse. Catch up with her on her website www.scarlettscottauthor.com. Hearing from readers never fails to make her day.

Scarlett's complete book list and information about upcoming releases can be found at www.scarlettscottauthor.com.

Connect with Scarlett! You can find her here:
Join Scarlett Scott's reader's group on Facebook for early excerpts, giveaways, and a whole lot of fun!
Sign up for her newsletter here.
scarlettscottauthor.com/contact
Follow Scarlett on Amazon
Follow Scarlett on BookBub
www.instagram.com/scarlettscottauthor
www.twitter.com/scarscoromance
www.pinterest.com/scarlettscott
www.facebook.com/AuthorScarlettScott
Join the Historical Harlots on Facebook

Printed in Great Britain
by Amazon